"I don't want to have to spell it out,"

he said, and she wished his face was a little less grim. "I think you are already well aware of the importance of winning, and although your track record in London speaks for itself, I want you to remember that you're in New York now, where standards are high, and those that don't rise to them go. We can't afford to lose this one and it would be as well for you if we didn't."

She looked into his face, dark and serious, watching her with his eyebrows half raised, almost as if he had asked her a question. She understood exactly what he was saying, and hated him for it. "I think you've made yourself perfectly clear, Conrad."

His eyes were piercing as he looked back at her. "Yes, I hope I have," and he picked up the telephone.

"Is that all?"

"For now."

She turned to go.

"Oh, one thing," he said, as she was opening the door. "I'll pick you up at seven tonight."

A CLASS APART

SUSAN LEWIS

HarperPaperbacks
A Division of HarperCollinsPublishers

This is a work of fiction. The characters, incidents, and dialogues are products of the author's imagination and are not to be construed as real. Any resemblance to actual events or persons, living or dead, is entirely coincidental.

HarperPaperbacks   *A Division of* HarperCollins*Publishers*
10 East 53rd Street, New York, N.Y. 10022

This book was first published in Great Britian by Fontana Paperbacks.

Cover photography by Anthony Loew

First printing: November 1990

Printed in the United States of America

HarperPaperbacks and colophon are trademarks of HarperCollins*Publishers*

10 9 8 7 6 5 4 3 2 1

Acknowledgments

My thanks to all my friends who have
helped me in more ways than they will know.
Especially to Melanie, for the title.
My thanks also to the staff of Cliveden House.
And a very special thank you to Toby, my agent,
and to Laura, my editor,
without whom I could never have managed it.

" . . . AND EARLIER TODAY, A POLICE SPOKESMAN confirmed that a full scale hunt for the killer is now underway. So far there has been no evidence to suggest a motive for the killing, and police are asking anyone who was in the vicinity who might have seen or heard anything suspicious to come forward . . ." The sound of the newsreader's voice was coming through an open door in the block.

She squeezed her eyes shut tightly in an effort not to listen. She didn't want to think about the murder. Not now.

Using the bannister as a steadying guide she continued up the stairs, trying to ignore the fear that had crept its way into her heart.

Finally she reached the door at the top. She hesitated a moment not knowing what to do. She looked around the empty hallway—it offered no encouragement. The telephone began to ring inside the flat making her jump. She listened as it continued to ring, but no one answered. The door downstairs slammed and as abruptly the ringing stopped.

Silence.

Slowly, she lifted her hand and knocked. The dull sound echoed along the hallway.

She looked around again. She was quite alone. Fumbling in her bag, she pulled out a key. As she slid

1

it into the lock, her heart began to pound. All she wanted to do was run away.

The door clicked open and she stepped through. The flat was in darkness despite the bright sunlight outside. All the curtains were pulled.

She called out, loudly, but there was no reply.

Edging her way down the hall she came to a halt outside the bedroom door. She pushed her hand against it, then realizing that her deliberate movements were making her more nervous, she pushed it sharply and stepped inside. The room was empty.

She swallowed hard, and looked around. The curtains were closed in here too.

She turned back into the hall. A few more steps and she was in the kitchen. She called out again, but still there was no reply.

The window was open and a cat suddenly leapt from the sill and landed on the floor in front of her.

Catching her breath and trying to ignore the violent beating of her heart, she stooped to stroke it.

Suddenly the phone began to ring again, and putting the cat onto a chair, she walked to the sitting room to answer it. Unafraid now, the telephone giving her the sense of another presence in the flat, she pushed open the door.

And then she screamed—and screamed and screamed. And the phone rang—and rang and rang.

ONE

"**K**ATHERINE CALLOWAY! SAY THAT AGAIN!" ELLAMARIE shrieked.

"I couldn't bear to, you heard me the first time," Kate answered. She was laughing, but the look in her eyes betrayed her lack of certainty.

Ellamarie turned to Jenneen as if she expected her to repeat it, but Jenneen only grinned and shrugged her shoulders.

"You're not kidding me, Kate, are you?" Ellamarie said, eyeing her suspiciously.

Kate shook her head and poured them more wine.

"Didn't he . . . ? Well . . . I can't believe it. This is Stephen French we're talking about. *The* Stephen French."

"I know."

"But Kate, he's gorgeous."

Smiling, Kate sat back in her chair and studied her fingernails. "Mmm, yes, he thought so too."

Ellamarie looked at Jenneen again. "This woman has not had sex for over a year, and now she turns down no less a person than Stephen French. Don't just sit there, speak to her. Say something."

"Like what?" said Jenneen.

"I don't know. Anything. Look, what I don't get," Ellamarie continued, turning back to Kate, "is why? I mean all this time. Apart from anything else, you've

3

just got to be dying for it. I dread to think how many batteries you must have been through by now."

Kate gave a shriek of laughter and Ellamarie shuddered. "How can you laugh about it?"

"I don't. At least I do, but I'm not exactly putting the flags out."

"Myself," said Jenneen, leaning forward and helping herself to a stuffed olive, "I think it's something to be proud of. Do you think there's any chance you might, well, you know, heal over after a certain time? You could be a virgin on your wedding night you know, Kate. A virgin who's had all the fun. Now wouldn't that be an achievement?"

"Jenneen! Will you try and take this seriously? We've got to find her a man. And quick. Shit, if she carries on like this much longer she might start fancying the dog."

"Don't be vulgar, Ellamarie," Kate laughed. "Besides, I haven't got a dog."

"They're easier to get hold of than men though," Jenneen looked thoughtful. "And easier to train."

"Stop it! All I said was that I didn't have sex with Stephen French, and now you're trying to pair me off with a poodle or something."

"I was thinking more along the lines of a Great Dane," said Jenneen, grinning.

"Oh shut up. I wish I'd never told you now."

"How does it feel?" said Ellamarie. "I mean, you know, to turn someone like him down? Shit! What I wouldn't give to have seen his face."

"What do you mean, how does it feel? There's nothing *to* feel."

"No, I suppose not. But come on, Kate, don't you just yearn for an erection sometimes?"

Kate threw a cushion at her. "I said stop it."

"Hey!" Jenneen suddenly yelled. "I've got it."

"It doesn't show." Ellamarie looked in the general area of Jenneen's crotch.

"No, someone with an erection."

"Permanently?" said Kate.

"I don't know about that, but he sure had one at lunch today. I was going to save him for myself. But, now that I know your need is greater than mine, well . . . Never let it be said I'm not generous when it comes to my friends."

"Who is it?" said Ellamarie. "Or should I say, how big is it?"

They collapsed into laughter again, until Jenneen finally managed to tell them about Joel Martin who was, by the happiest of coincidences, as Kate was writing a novel, one of London's top literary agents. Jenneen had interviewed him on her weekly television show, together with the author Diana Kelsey, as part of the running series of interviews she was doing with agents and their clients.

"So I see my adoring public missed my show again this afternoon," she finished.

"It's the time," Kate complained. "I'm nearly always out during the . . . hey, hang on! What am I talking about? I recorded it. Now, how's that for loyalty? Satisfied?" She ran across to the video. "Now we'll just have to hope I got the right channel. It'll be a first if I have."

She pushed the button to rewind the tape, then sat back on the floor. "I want you to know that I am only watching this to see the erection. Nothing else. Forget blind dates."

"But it won't be blind, will it?" said Jenneen. "I mean, you will have seen him."

There was a knock on the door and Kate looked at her watch. "That'll either be Mrs. Adams from upstairs wanting to borrow something else, or it'll be Ashley."

"I don't know how you put up with that old lady," Jenneen said, as Ellamarie got up to answer the door. "Does she ever do anything for herself?"

"Not much," Kate admitted, "but she's not a bad old stick really."

Opening the door, Ellamarie was relieved to see it was Ashley standing outside, her dark hair plastered to her head and her collar pulled high round her face. "Is it raining?" Ellamarie inquired.

Ashley pulled a face, then shook out her umbrella and handed it to her.

"How did it go?"

"Don't ask me." Ashley peeled off her wet coat. "I couldn't keep my mind on anything long enough."

"Julian there?"

"No, he's in Paris. Giles Creddesley chaired the meeting. And picked his nose. God, he's revolting!"

"But have you got an answer yet?" Ellamarie asked.

"From Newslink? Tomorrow."

"What did Giles think of the presentation?"

"I think he liked it, but you know him. Anything that's not his idea is never quite up to the mark. Anyway, I don't much care. I'm more worried about what Julian will say if we lose the account."

"You won't!" said Ellamarie, confidently. "Now come along inside, we're about to watch a blue movie."

"A what!"

"A man with an erection. For Kate."

"Not for me." Kate looked up as they came into the room. "Hi, Ash, how did it go?"

"Right now I'm more interested in a glass of wine and a blue movie," she answered. "But all right, I think."

"OK, everyone!" Jenneen cried. "Get ready, here comes the future Mr. Calloway."

They watched in silence for a while, until Ashley burst out laughing.

"What's the matter?" said Jenneen.

"He talks in quotes."

"A sign of a well-read mind. Well," Jenneen

turned to Kate, "what do you think? As I said, I was going to have him for myself, but under the circumstances I think you might get better use."

"What circumstances?" said Ashley.

Jenneen filled her in on the details of Kate's date with the infamous Stephen French.

"But I thought the book you were writing was all about the adventures of an oversexed journalist," Ashley said, looking at Kate.

"I've got an imagination, haven't I?"

"But what are you feeding it on?" Ellamarie wanted to know.

"It hasn't been hungry, until now." Kate swiveled round to face Jenneen. "I think he's absolutely gorgeous. What's his name again?"

"Joel. Joel Martin."

"And is he a good agent?"

"Who cares? Oh, of course, you do. Well, yes, or at least so he tells me. And the writer there with him, she couldn't sing his praises highly enough."

"How soon can you get him here?" Kate grinned.

"Oh well, if you're not that keen, then we'll just forget it."

"Jenneen! Sometimes . . ."

"OK. Just leave it to me."

"Are we going out anywhere?" Ashley was looking at her watch. "I'm starving."

"Food coming up," said Kate. "It's such a ghastly night I thought I'd cook, save us going out."

She went off to the kitchen and the others fell into the easy and idle chatter that was an integral part of the evenings they spent together. The Barnes Conference was what they called these evenings, owing to the fact that, in their early twenties, they had shared a house in Barnes. Now, in their early thirties, and nearing the top of their chosen careers, their friendship was every bit as strong. They were, as Jenneen put it whenever she was feeling philosophical, four women pursuing their lives in a London of the 1980s, all of them successful and capable of loving no more nor less than their mothers and grandmothers before them, but who had to contend with the social pressures that promiscuity, equality and the sixties had thrust upon them. And the prejudices too.

Kate opened the door of the microwave and, putting the dish on the work surface, caught a glimpse of herself in the mirror. She shook her head, allowing her new curls to fall around her face. Shame Stephen French had been such a bore, the idea of a good Yuppie stockbroker had rather appealed to her.

Hearing Ellamarie's burst of laughter, she popped her head through the serving hatch demanding to know what all the noise was about.

"It's Jenneen," Ellamarie gasped, wiping the tears from her face. "She's being disgusting again."

"Me?" Jenneen cried.

"Perish the thought," Ashley said.

Leaving the doors open, Kate started to dish up. "Oh hey, I've just remembered, any chance of two extra tickets for opening night, Ellamarie?"

"I'll find out. But I thought you were all coming on the second night?"

"That's what I meant," said Kate, bringing the food in on a tray. "Daddy says he'd like to come. Mummy's coming home for the week and he thought it would be a treat for her. If she'll agree." Kate's mother had been in what they all referred to as a convalescent home ever since Kate's brother had died in an accident three years before. Mrs. Calloway had been unable to accept the death, and in the end it had been necessary to send her somewhere where she could be looked after properly.

"How are rehearsals going, Ellamarie?" Ashley asked.

"Not bad. Very slow though."

"And Bob?"

"Is loving every minute of it."

"Where is he tonight?" Jenneen asked.

"Where he always is on a Friday night. Home with wifey."

Ashley looked sympathetic. "I don't know how you stand it, Ellamarie."

"Neither do I, but what the hell. I have him four nights a week, sometimes five if I'm lucky. He gave me this tonight." She held out her arm to show them the tiny gold bracelet Bob had slipped onto her wrist before they left the rehearsal rooms. Her pale face shone, highlighting the freckles that bridged her rather aristocratic nose, as the others made all the right noises. "Isn't he just the most wonderful man?" she sighed. "He said it was because I had remembered all my lines. Which, I can tell you, is more than can be said for Maureen Woodley."

"Isn't she playing Viola?" Kate asked, taking a mouthful of lasagne.

Ellamarie nodded. "And do you want to know why? Because she's shaped like one."

"Oh, Ellamarie!" Ashley choked.

"Well, she is. She's got to be at least a hundred round the hips, and her neck, Jesus, have you seen that neck? Even a giraffe would find it difficult to compete."

"God, you can be a bitch at times," Jenneen laughed.

"Which is no more than she is. I could kill Bob for giving her the part. She just keeps ramming it down my throat."

"Well, you know why he didn't give it to you," said Kate.

"I know, I know. But it doesn't make it any easier." She started to mimic Bob. " 'Slowly, slowly does it. One step at a time. Don't rush. You'll get there in the end.' And any other variation you can think of on that. I've heard them all. But hell, Maria isn't so bad a part,

I suppose," she added grudgingly. "Now, enough about me, what about you, Ashley Mayne?"

"Me?"

"Don't come the innocent. Are you going to tell the great Julian Arbrey-Nelmes about the grand passion that burns in your heart, and if so, when?"

Ashley flushed, and her insides began to draw into a knot. "I think so," she said.

"Think so! You've got to."

"It's all very easy for you to say, you're not the one who has to do it."

"And if you had done it before, then it wouldn't be so difficult now. Besides, I don't know what you're worried about, the man's simply crazy about you."

Ashley grinned. "That's what I like to hear."

"From him. Get him to tell you, not me."

"When's Blanche coming back?" asked Jenneen.

"Wednesday," Ashley answered, the smile disappearing from her face.

Ellamarie waved her fork in the air. "Don't worry about her. If Julian really intended to marry her he would have done it by now. It's you he wants, but you keep playing hard to get."

"I'd hardly call spending five nights a week together hard to get," Kate remarked.

"Well, you know what I mean," said Ellamarie. "And look at it this way," she went on, helping herself to more wine, "how old is Alex now? Seven? Yes, seven. It's time you were adding to your family before he gets too old." She was referring to Ashley's son, the only good or worthwhile product of an early marriage that hadn't worked.

"Or before I get too old," said Ashley.

"And Julian adores him, so what's the problem?"

"Blanche."

"Rubbish. She's been away for over two years, if he loved her then he wouldn't have put up with it. And he's only put up with it because he's had you. Who he wants, not her. Now, pick your moment. You're seeing him tomorrow night, aren't you?"

Ashley nodded.

"Tell him then. It'll be the best Christmas present he's ever had, I promise you."

"And then next will come the wedding," said Kate, looking dewy-eyed. "God, it's simply ages since I went to a wedding. When do you think it will be, Ash?"

"I thought Easter." Ashley allowed herself to get caught up in the mood for a moment.

"Oh dear, why wait?"

"Valentine's Day?" Jenneen suggested.

"No, definitely Easter. We'll stand a better chance of good weather."

"How many bridesmaids?" said Ellamarie.

"Oh, isn't it bliss!" Kate sighed. "What will you wear?"

"Oh stop it," said Ashley, pulling herself together. "If he could hear us now he'd probably run a mile."

Ellamarie's eyes could speak volumes without her uttering a word, and Ashley got the message. Get off that negative road, they were saying, and Ashley wished she could. She had been having an affair with Julian Arbrey-Nelmes, the Chairman of Frazier, Nelmes Advertising Agency where she was an Account Director, for well over a year now, but in that time neither one of them had admitted to their feelings. Ashley was sure that he cared for her, probably more than cared for her, but he had never shown any inclination to break off his long-standing relationship with Blanche Wetherburn. Ashley did not want to admit to the fear that Julian's ambition would dictate the direction of his heart, but in the end she knew there was every chance it would. As far as Julian Arbrey-Nelmes was concerned, Blanche met all the requisites. The right background, connections, breeding, everything that would be important to a man in his position. She was even related to Conrad Frazier, Julian's American partner. Furthermore, Blanche was a gentile. But Ashley refused to believe that Julian would put any store by something like that.

By the end of the evening, the others had talked her into doing what she knew she would have done anyway. But, secretly, none of them would have wanted to be in her shoes. Telling a man you loved him when he had not broached the subject first, was no easy thing to do. Old-fashioned it might be, but the unwritten rules of the procedure of love were deeply rooted in them all.

"I've decided," Ashley said, as she was leaving, "that if we win the Newslink account tomorrow, then everything will go well. If we don't, then . . ."

"You and your silly superstitions," said Kate. "You have a serendipitous life, I've always said so. You'll win, you wait and see. You'll win them both."

TWO

IT HAD BEEN ONE HELL OF A DAY. IT SEEMED THAT IN THE world of advertising, people had never heard of Saturday. Ashley's telephone had hardly stopped ringing, with everyone wanting everything done not yesterday but last week. Finally she had left the office just after three, telling her creative team to cope as best they could and had rushed down to Surrey to see Alex for an hour.

She only just made it back to London in time—thank God for her father driving her up. Alex would enjoy the trip, he had said. Her mother had stayed behind to fix the evening meal. Keith, Ashley's ex-husband, and his family would be dining with them, as they usually did on Saturdays.

Julian arrived at her flat in Onslow Square just after eight to take her to dinner. Ashley had been a bundle of nerves all day at the thought of what lay ahead, and she felt no better now as the waiter showed them to their table. Julian nodded towards the old man sitting in the corner and Ashley managed to wave. Neither of them actually knew the old man, but he was always there whenever they came, napkin under his chin and his round spectacles slipping down over his nose, with a smiling mouth settled comfortably between.

The waiter pulled out a chair for Ashley to sit down and she was surprised to see a bottle of champagne sitting in a bucket beside it. She looked at Julian and saw that he was smiling. It was his way of saying thank you, and well done. It was one of the things she had come to love most about him, his thoughtfulness, and sense of occasion.

The waiter popped the cork, and Julian waited for the glasses to be filled before looking into her eyes and saying, simply: "To you."

Ashley swallowed the lump that was rising in her throat, surprised that she was so close to tears, and raised her own glass. "How about to us?"

He smiled and reached across the table to take her hand. She looked down at his fingers as they curled round hers, feeling the same thrill that always came over her when he touched her.

When she looked up she found that he was studying her face, and she gazed back at him. There was a long silence as she used her eyes to tell him what she was feeling, and his fingers tightened round hers. A basket of bread was thrust between them, and the moment was broken.

Julian leaned back in his chair. "So," he said, "as I didn't see the final portfolio, perhaps you'd like to fill me in on what it is you are intending for Newslink. I spoke to David Mackay this morning, by the way. He was very impressed. Said there was no way he could turn you down in the end."

"Of course there wasn't," she said. "A lot of work went into that presentation."

He grinned. "And don't I know it."

Ashley picked up her glass of champagne. "Well, while you were flying back and forth across the Atlantic and then living it up in Paris, we workers were continuing with the historical theme I first told you about. You know, taking each one of their magazines and newspapers, and weaving them into a dramatic sketch. Each publication will have a separate commercial, but the overall feel will be the same, giving the company an easily identifiable image, aimed also at illustrating the long history of the paper. You know what I mean, dramatize important events that they have covered over the past two hundred years, add a touch of comedy, with a good slogan at the end. Hilary came up with some, but as far as I know David Mackay is still making up his mind about them."

"Sounds fine," said Julian, sitting forward. He liked listening to her ideas, they were usually good, and sometimes brilliant. He was often surprised by her enthusiasm, but knew that the company, and its success, was almost as important to her as it was to him and his partner.

They were soon engrossed in a lengthy discussion of the Newslink account, batting around ideas, padding them or discarding them, and more often than not making one another laugh. When the food arrived they relaxed again, and decided to drop the subject of work for the rest of the evening.

"You are very beautiful this evening, Ash," he whispered after the waiter had cleared the table.

"Thank you," she said. Then she laughed. "So you like the dress?"

"I do," he answered, "but I like the person inside much more."

Her heart began to beat a little faster. There had been a teasing note in his voice, but his eyes remained serious. Maybe now was the time to tell him. But there had been so many moments like this between them, when he had seemed to want to say more, but never had. She watched him as he poured the last of the champagne, trying to find the words she longed to say. But they wouldn't come, and she wondered if she had the courage.

"Where did you get the tree?" he asked, leaning back in his chair.

She looked baffled for a moment, then realized that he was talking about the Christmas tree in her flat. "Actually, I bought it in Harrods," she said, knowing it would amuse him.

"Harrods!" he cried. "You go to Harrods for your Christmas trees?"

"Tree," she corrected. "And why not?"

"I don't know," he laughed. "Tell me, is it called a 'top people's tree?' "

"Naturally. A 'top people's tree' for two top people."

"Me and you?" he said.

"Yes, me and you."

"Then who, might I ask, are all the presents for?"

"You."

"Me! They were all for me?"

She nodded.

"But there were at least six there."

She nodded again, smiling at the look on his face. "Well, cheer up," she said, "you should be grateful. I've been rushing around all day trying to get things organized. I didn't get away from the office until gone three."

"You have bought me six presents?"

"Seven actually."

"But why?"

"Because I wanted to."

"But, Ashley, why?"

"Well, aren't you just a typical man," she said, feigning exasperation. "Can't accept a gift without wanting to know why."

"But so many?"

"I couldn't make up my mind."

Julian grinned. "Well, aren't you just a typical woman."

"Actually," she paused while the waiter poured their coffee, "I bought them, I suppose, because I wanted to think of us being together on Christmas Day. You know, opening our gifts together."

It was very quick, but she didn't miss the cloud that momentarily dropped over his eyes. Then he broke into a smile again. "That sounds wonderful," he said.

She felt suddenly shy, and desperately wanted him to mean it. "Do you really think so?"

"Yes," he answered. "Yes, really I do."

She started to laugh, a dawning euphoria making her dizzy. "Do you know what else I thought? I thought you might wake me on Christmas morning with bucks fizz and smoked salmon, isn't that the way you said you liked Christmas? We could have it in bed, and then we could open our presents before you cook lunch."

"Me cook lunch?"

"Yes, you. The liberated man. You have equality now, don't forget."

"Oh yes. I must admit it does slip my mind from time to time. Anyway, go on." He was enjoying the game, and loved the way her dark eyes were shining.

"Well, I thought we could invite one another to lunch, you know, to make up the party, and have lots to eat and drink, then go back to bed in the afternoon to sleep it off, before we go visiting in the evening."

"I like it so far, but tell me more about the afternoon," he said. "You know, the bit before we go visiting."

She looked thoughtful for a moment. "Well, I haven't quite decided what we will dream about yet. If that's what you were meaning?"

"No, I want to know what I'm going to do before I go to sleep."

"Oh, you mean you're offering to do the washing up?"

He gave a shout of laughter. "You're adorable."

There was a short silence. "I'm serious," she said. "We could have a wonderful Christmas together, you know."

"Yes, we could."

She looked into his eyes waiting for him to go on, but he signaled for the waiter to bring the bill. She looked at her watch. "It's early."

His eyes were dancing. "I know, but I thought we might go home and rehearse what comes between the washing up and the dreams, you know, ready for Christmas Day."

As they walked from the restaurant, his arm about her shoulders, the words were buzzing around in her head. I love you, I love you, I love you. But not now, she would wait until they were home, sitting beside their "top people's tree" and then she would tell him. And he would take her in his arms, and tell her how long he had been waiting for her to say those words.

Driving back in the car they held hands, but didn't speak. From time to time Julian turned to look at her, but his face was inscrutable. He was thinking about the picture she had painted of the fantasy Christmas, and how much he wished it could come true. But it had been a game, nothing more than a game, they both knew that it could never be. He was grateful to her for never having told him how she felt about him. It was a silent agreement between them that they shouldn't speak of their feelings, and not once had she broken the rules. For that, but not for that alone, he loved her. It would make it easier in the end. It had always been Blanche, and though he didn't care for Blanche in the way that he cared for Ashley, he did love his fiancée, and he would marry her. In the end, his need for success would dictate his life. And with Blanche it would all be possible.

The lights on the tree were still burning as they walked through the door, and while Ashley went to make some coffee Julian poured them a nightcap.

When she came into the room, he was standing beside the tree in the colorful semi-darkness, his hands in his pockets, staring thoughtfully down at the beautifully wrapped gifts. Quietly she put the tray on the table and went to join him. She would tell him now. The time felt right. She would make the fantasy Christmas a reality.

He smiled down at her and slipped his arm round her shoulders. Why did she have to look so beautiful tonight? But then, to him, she looked beautiful every night. It would have been no easier, no matter when he decided to tell her.

"Are you thinking what I'm thinking?" she whispered, fiddling with a light on the tree.

"I don't know," he said.

"I was thinking how nice it would be if we really could spend Christmas together."

"Mmmm," he said, and tightened his hold on her. "But it's all a dream, only a dream."

"But it needn't be." Her voice was so soft he could hardly hear her.

She turned in his arms to face him. "I said it needn't be." He looked down at her, his hands resting on her shoulders. "Don't you understand, Julian? Don't you know what I'm trying to say?"

For a fleeting moment his eyes darkened in anger but he continued to look at her, knowing and unable to stop her.

"I love you, Julian," she whispered, "I love you."

He pulled her into his arms and crushed her against him. Dear God, why, oh why was she doing this to herself? To them both?

She could feel his heart beating, hear him breathing, and she waited for him to speak.

As the silence lengthened and still he didn't answer, she pulled away.

He looked down at the tree again, hating himself for what he was doing to her.

Ashley sat down on the settee. She was surprised to find that, for the moment, she was calm. Staring into the fire, she realized that he must have built it up while she was making the coffee. Coffee! It was still standing on the table, where she had put it. The brandy was beside it, untouched. Perhaps by reaching out for these tokens, she could regain her dream.

"You haven't drunk your brandy."

"Ashley . . ."

They spoke at the same time.

He came to sit beside her and tried to take her hand, but she reached out for the coffee and began to pour.

"Black or white?" she said.

"Black, please."

"Yes, of course."

She handed him a cup, and turned back to pick up a brandy. Julian caught her hand and, turning her to face him, put his coffee back on the table. She tried to turn away.

"Ashley, please, listen to me."

"Don't you want your coffee?"

"Ash, darling, please. Look at me."

She bowed her head. "I can't."

He pulled her into his arms. "Darling. I'm sorry.

I'm so sorry. What can I say?" He felt her stiffen. "I thought you knew. I thought you had always accepted that one day it would be . . ." he stopped.

"Over? Is that what you were going to say?" There was no trace of bitterness in her voice, only sadness. "Of course I did." She was struggling to hold back the tears. "And, Julian, I'm sorry for what I said, I take it all back. Please, forget it."

"I never meant to hurt you, Ash."

"I know you didn't."

Suddenly she could feel the panic beginning to bite. It had come from nowhere, shouting to her, telling her that this was the end. They had had their last dinner. Never again would she see him smile into her eyes in that way that had seemed to tell her he loved her. No more days together, no more nights, no more laughter. It was over. She had lost him, but then, in truth, had she ever really had him? She felt his hand stroking her hair, and for one terrifying moment she thought she was going to beg him to stay.

"I've been a fool," she said. "It's my fault. You never made any promises, you never said you would leave Blanche. But in my naiveté I wanted to believe that you would."

"No, it's my fault. I should never have let things get this far."

"No, please don't say that. It means you regret that it ever happened."

"To see you so hurt, I do regret it."

She sat up straight, still not looking at him, and tried to laugh. "Oh, but I'll survive," she said, hoping by her words to give herself strength.

"Of course you will," he said. "Soon you will meet someone. Someone who is . . . well, right for you."

A flash of anger sparked in her eyes. "Someone Jewish, is that what you mean?"

"No, that's not what I meant. I'm sorry." He

wanted to tell her how much it hurt him to think of her with another man, any man.

She turned away from him, trying to close herself from his presence. Julian knew that by staying he was only prolonging the pain, but he couldn't bring himself to leave. The moment he walked through that door it would be the end, he could never come back.

His hand was resting on her back, and he felt her shoulders begin to shake. She was crying. Pulling her round into his arms, he tried to hold back his own tears. God knows, he had never felt like this before. It was as if his insides were being crushed. He held her for a long time, and she cried into his shoulder, trying to pour out the pain of losing him. He stroked her hair, and kissed the top of her head, cursing the fate that had led them to this.

Finally she looked up, and this time she looked into his face. He looked back at her, tear-stained and disheveled, and knew that he had never loved her more.

"Kiss me, Julian," she whispered.

As he covered her mouth with his, feeling her lips begin to tremble, he knew that it would be the easiest thing in the world to throw everything to the wind and tell her how he felt. To forget the rest of his life, and stay with her. But his plans had been made, and he must see them through.

"Will you make love to me, Julian?" she breathed. "Just one last time." He looked at her, feeling the need for her rising. But seeing her face so filled with distress, he knew it would be the wrong thing to do. He shook his head, and she fell away from him, sobbing.

"You know it wouldn't be right," he said, taking her hand. "It will only make it worse when I go."

Hearing those words, Ashley wanted to die.

She stood up, straightening her dress and flicking her hair. He heard her swallow before she spoke.

"Would you like me to resign now, or would you like it in writing on Monday?"

He sighed and shook his head.

"I can't continue working for you, Julian. You must see that. I feel so humiliated. God, I've made such a fool of myself."

"Don't! Don't say that. I don't want you to leave."

She ran her fingers nervously through her hair. "I just don't know what to do."

"Would it help if you took some time off? Came back again after Christmas?" He saw her flinch as he said the word and looked away.

"Maybe," she said.

"At least that way we won't have to keep bumping into one another for a while."

"No."

He knew he was being selfish suggesting it, but perhaps it would be for the best. It would be painful for him too, to keep seeing her and wondering what she was doing, how she was coping.

"Right now I feel as though I never want to see you again," she said. "It might be easier that way."

"Why don't you decide in the New Year?"

She nodded and gave him a weak smile. His heart turned over. Perhaps now he should go. Before he gave in.

"Promise me one thing, Julian," she said.

"If I can."

"Never call me. Never write me a letter. Never ask me how I am."

He didn't answer.

"Please, Julian, promise me. Promise me that you will never again try to get in touch with me out of the office. That you will never speak to me again, about us."

"But . . ."

"Please. If you make me this promise then I will know that it is over. That I can never hope. Then I will never sit beside the phone praying that you will call. Never go into the office praying that today you will say something. For me, Julian, please promise."

He rubbed his thumb and forefinger against his eyes, loving her for trying to be so brave. "OK, I promise," he said finally.

He looked at his watch. She saw him look, and turned away as he stood up.

In silence they walked to the door.

"Take care of yourself," he said, stroking her hair from her face.

She nodded but couldn't look at him. "Yes, you too."

When he'd gone she fell back against the wall, fighting against the pain and the panic. She looked around. The place seemed so empty.

Slowly she walked back to the drawing room. The Christmas tree winked at her from the corner, and she walked over to switch off the lights. As she turned away her foot knocked against something. She looked down to see the parcel that he had tried to open earlier when he had arrived. She picked it up and looked at it. What would she do with them all now? But this was only the first hurdle. How was she to face Christmas without him when she had made such plans? And the New Year? How was she going to face life at all now? Did she even want to? The whole world seemed to be closing in upon her, and she knew what was to come. Having to deal with the rejection, the pain, the loneliness. It had happened before when her marriage ended. She had survived. But not this time. She didn't want to have to go through it all again. The way her thoughts would torture her whenever she thought of him with Blanche. The emptiness at the end of each day, with nowhere to go, no one to see. The yearning of her body in the night when she ached for him to hold her close. She knew what was in store, and she knew she couldn't face it.

Walking toward the bathroom, it was as though life had slipped from focus, and the pain that had earlier bitten into her heart with savage teeth now came in slow, relentless waves. She kept seeing his face, serious yet smiling down at her. The love that she thought she saw burning in his eyes. And as if it was a long time ago, she remembered saying the words: "I love you, Julian, I love you." And she remembered, too, how he had said nothing.

The aspirins were in her hand. She looked down at them, surprised. There must have been twenty or thirty, small and white, resting innocently on her palm. She pushed them around with her finger, dropping some on the floor.

She took a glass from the shelf and let the water run until it was spilling over. Looking up to the mirror she hardly recognized the person who stared back, and with wide, frightened eyes she watched her reflection as she placed two pills on the end of her tongue. They slipped down so easily, carried away by the cold, refreshing water. She lowered her eyes and looked at the others, still in her hand.

Suddenly an ambulance siren blasted into the night. It was followed by another, and then another. She waited for the noise to die, then looked back to the mirror.

Her shoulders began to shudder as the sobs tore through her body. She threw her hand violently against the wall and scattered the pills across the floor. "Julian! Oh Julian!" She clutched the sink and fell to her knees. What was she thinking? Was she so weak that she would think of ending her life? He would ring. He would break his promise and ring her. It wasn't over. It couldn't be. He cared too much for her just to walk away and leave her like that. "He will ring," she cried aloud. "Oh God, please, he's got to ring."

THREE

TRYING TO GET INTERVIEWS AROUND ANOTHER FILM SHOOT was always difficult, but even more so when it was raining. Jenneen's crew had already been irritable when they'd arrived late grumbling that the directions to the location had not been good enough, so it was almost no time at all before they had begun to lose patience with the director, who on the best of days seemed incapable of making a decision, but today . . . ! Well, Jenneen should have been warned when he rang her at seven-thirty that morning to ask her what he should wear. Freezing rain and a force nine wind around the wharf, and the man didn't know what to wear!

"Try Bermudas and a bowler," she had snapped, and hung up.

Still, the pop star she had gone to interview had been a nice enough guy. Waiting around the sets of pop videos could be eternally dull business, but he had seemed to keep his cool. Which was more than she could say for that pompous bitch of an agent of his. Jenneen had made a mental note to cut her out of the film altogether, with the exception of the "up the nose" shot she had had no difficulty in persuading the cameraman to do. With that sourpuss edited out Jenneen felt sure it would be a good film. And that was what Jenneen Grey was about—making good films.

When she had first come to London at the raw age

25

of twenty-two, and had thought herself so very grown-up and sophisticated, it had come as a brutal shock to hear her Northern accent being so mercilessly mimicked by the grand researchers and reporters she had worked with then. She had been unable to laugh along with them, knowing that despite their laughter, their cruelty and snobbery was real. In the end, deciding that if you can't beat 'em, join 'em, she had invested part of her then meager salary in elocution lessons. She had been a good student, and within a year had virtually discarded the broad Yorkshire tones. Only when she was angry did she sometimes slip back into them. But not often.

She laughed to herself now, to think of how eager she had been to please everyone in those days. It had seemed so important then. But things looked very different now, standing where she was, so near to the top of the tree. Bill Pruitt, the editor of the afternoon show she presented each week, was determined that she was going to make it to the very top. It was almost nine years ago when he had first asked her what it was that she really wanted.

"The truth?" she had said.

"Mmm," he nodded. "The truth."

"Promise you won't laugh?"

He had smiled. "I promise."

"I want to be famous," she announced, quite calmly, but her eyes were burning.

"Famous?"

"Yes. Famous. But not only famous. I want to have earned my fame for the good, entertaining and necessary programs that I make," and she had blushed at how trite he must have thought she'd sounded.

And now, all these years on, she was almost there.

Bill had warned her about keeping a squeaky clean reputation, telling her that it would be for her own good, as well as the good of the TV station. But that was something she had not handled quite so well. Not that anyone knew about her private life; at least, not yet, but she didn't know how much longer she would be able to keep it out of the press.

Wearily she pushed her feet into her slippers, and went into the kitchen to collect the cocoa she had made. She looked at her watch then picked up the telephone and dialed Ashley's number. No answer.

Jenneen wondered if she should go round there. But Ashley had said something about working late so there was probably nothing to worry about, Ashley would be at the office, burying her pain in paperwork.

Jenneen, Kate and Ellamarie had spent the whole of the previous day with Ashley, trying to make some sense of what had happened. They had all quite genuinely believed that Julian was as crazy about Ashley as she was about him, and now they each blamed themselves for having got it so wrong. Ashley had spent most of the day in a daze, and Jenneen had known that it had been as much from lack of sleep as from losing the man she loved. The most bitter blow of all was that it had happened now—only two weeks before Christmas.

Jenneen leaned back in her chair and, curling her feet under her, let her filming notes fall to the floor as she began to think about Christmas. Wouldn't it be wonderful if this year, just for once, she could meet someone she really liked. A man who was just waiting to meet a woman like her. Petite, blonde, very feminine, so her friends told her, and with a quick tongue that never ceased to surprise even those who knew her. It was laughable at times, to see people's eyes widen in disbelief when they had tried to manipulate her into doing something she disagreed with. Her mild and affable face belied the sharp brain behind, and the quick response of her tongue could send people reeling. But Mr. Right, well, he would love her for her complexity. He would make her feel secure, protected from all those vicious tongues at the studios. He would make her feel loved. Funny though, but try as she might, she just couldn't imagine it—or him either, come to that.

A car door slammed outside, breaking her reverie. Dismissing her romanticism she retrieved her notes from the floor. As she began to read she heard footsteps crunching up the steps outside. Automatically she tensed. "Please God, don't let it be my bell that rings," she breathed.

But she already knew. It was almost as if she could smell him.

The bell rang. "Go away," she hissed, "please God, please, make him go away."

Slowly she got to her feet and walked over to the window. Pulling back the curtains an inch she peered down into the street below. Sure enough, there was the beaten old Audi parked right outside, and oh God, there he was, looking straight up at her. What a fool she had been to look out.

The bell rang again, more insistently this time.

Without speaking on the intercom she pressed the buzzer to release the door downstairs. Pulling open her own front door, she went back into the sitting room to wait.

She could hear his footsteps, taking the stairs two at a time. God, anyone would think he was eager to see her. The bastard! She hated him with such venom that at times it frightened her. She wished she knew what she had to do to get him out of her life, but short of murder, what else was there?

She heard the door close, and could feel the cold air he had brought in with him.

"Hello, Jenneen," he grinned, taking off his coat and going to help himself to a drink. "Ready for bed?" he said, looking at her dressing gown.

She didn't answer. She had nothing to say to him.

"Oh, I see," he said, "bad day was it?"

Her eyes were fixed on the chair opposite so he sat in it. She turned away.

"Oh come on now, Jenn, you're going to have me thinking you aren't pleased to see me."

She looked at him, taking in his short, cropped hair that used to be fair but was now a manky mousy color, and the bloodshot gray eyes that darted about the room before they came to rest on her again. She shuddered as he slurped on the Scotch he had poured himself, then turned to pour himself a refill.

"Just say what you want and get out!" she snapped.

"Now, that is no way to treat an old friend, is it?" He took another large mouthful of whiskey and gasped as it burned his throat. "Good whiskey, Jenn."

"It's cheap, especially for you," she answered.

"Dear oh dear, Jenn, now is that a way to speak to a friend who visits you so often, who cares about you like I do? A friend who so closely guards your little secret?"

No preamble, just straight in for the kill. She stared into the fire.

"Look, I'd be a little happier, Jenneen, if you'd be a touch more hospitable to me. After all, I am doing you a favor, you know, by telling no one."

"No one would believe you, you scum!"

"Ah, but you don't know that for sure, do you?"

"Get out of here. Go on, just get out of here. Get out of my life!"

He ignored her and began to play with the remote control of the TV set. After flicking through the channels he decided there was nothing he wanted to watch, so put it down again.

"I'm hungry, got anything in?"

"No."

"You must have something. And I know you wouldn't like to see me go hungry."

Her lip began to curl. "You filthy, rotten bastard. You come here to blackmail me, and you have the fucking cheek to expect me to feed you."

A dangerous glint flashed in his eyes. "Calm down, Jenneen. You don't want to make me angry, now do you?"

"What the hell have you got to be angry about! You've got a damn nerve coming in here, taking my drink, demanding food, upsetting my life . . ."

"Stop right there." He got to his feet and slowly began to circle her. "Upsetting your life, you say. That's a good one. *I* have upset *your* life. Yet again, I am going to have to remind you just exactly what you did to my life."

"Shut up!" she yelled.

"Oh, you don't want to hear it, eh? You don't want to be reminded of how with one vindictive statement you wiped out my entire career. Destroyed everything I had worked for. Shall I remind you what it was you said? Those words that were all over the papers the next day and annihilated a man and his future?"

"Don't kid yourself, Matthew. You were all washed up long before I said what I did. You just wanted someone to hang the blame on. If it hadn't been me, it would have been someone else."

"I hadn't been having an affair with 'someone else.' No, I had been sleeping with *you*, Jenneen Grey. She who is an expert on men and their prowess in the sack. But of course I'm forgetting, you've had so many. How many was it last week, Jenneen? Five? Six?"

She flinched, and turned to the window.

"More? Well, I don't want to know. You sleep with whoever you like. As many men as you can get. Or women!" he added.

Jenneen closed her eyes. She had known it was coming.

"Lost your tongue?"

She didn't answer.

"Pity you didn't lose it that night you were interviewed on the *Late Night Chat Show.* If you'd lost it then, perhaps neither of us would be in the mess we're in now."

"Look, Matthew," she turned to him, her eyes pleading. "You know as well as I do that you were sacked from the drama series because of your drinking. It was nothing to do with what I said. For God's sake, if someone was destroyed every time a woman aired her dirty linen in public, there wouldn't be many people at the top, would there?"

"You're a liar, Jenneen, and you know it. I threw you over the night before that show. *I* threw *you* over! And your bloody ego just couldn't take it. 'Is he a good lover?' you said. And then you laughed. I'll never forget that laugh, Jenneen. 'Is he a good lover? I'll be truthful with you,' you said. 'He's so pumped full of drugs or alcohol it's like going to bed with a log that has a protruding twig in the right place.' Isn't that what you said?" He was shouting now and advancing across the room toward her. "Isn't that what you . . ."

"Stop it!" she cried, hating the way he worked himself into a frenzy of anger.

"I was the leading man in that drama, Jenneen, I was on the brink of becoming a national heartthrob. OK, it sounds pathetic, but it pays the bills. And you destroyed it all in one night." He stood over her, the smell of whiskey on his breath sickening her.

She clenched her fists. "How much do you want this time?"

Matthew eyed her with hatred, as if he might strike her, but then the anger seemed to subside and he relaxed a little. "That's better," he said. "You pay. That's right, you pay."

"How much do you want? Tell me, how much?"

"I will," he said, "when I'm ready. Now I'm hungry, go and make me something to eat."

Jenneen went into the kitchen and began to pull out the pots and pans. She could hear him in the sitting room, helping himself to another drink. She wanted to cry, but she knew it was no use. For months now she had pleaded with him, begged him, to leave her alone. But he kept coming back. Shouting at her, abusing her with vile language, and sometimes beating her. Every day she lived in terror of the hold he had over her. Dear God, if only she hadn't gone to the party that night. Was it as long ago as two years? It was the night she had first met Matthew.

The irony of it was that she really didn't want to go to the party at all. She had the startings of a cold, and was feeling pretty awful, and the man who was to escort her made her feel about the same. Funny, she couldn't even remember his name now.

As the evening wore on, her escort, sensing her disinterest, became engrossed in someone else, and feeling miserable and lonely, Jenneen sat in a corner, sipping whiskey and biting back the tears of self-pity that often come before an attack of flu.

She couldn't remember now how she had got talking to the woman, or much about their conversation. But whoever she was, the woman seemed kind and friendly, and genuinely interested in whatever Jenneen had to say. They laughed a lot, she remembered that, and they agreed a lot too, but what about, Jenneen couldn't, or didn't want to remember.

It must have been midnight, maybe even later, when Jenneen finally tried to stand up to leave. But she'd drunk more whiskey than she'd realized, and she fell back onto the settee, giggling. The woman laughed softly, and asked if she could help.

Jenneen looked around for her escort, but he had disappeared. "Typical!" she thought to herself, and then suddenly she started to cry. The woman seemed quite startled at first, but placing an arm round Jenneen's waist, she led her from the room. Vaguely Jenneen remembered being led up the stairs, hearing the

woman whispering soothing noises, telling her that she
was far too ill to go home tonight.

She didn't recall protesting, but like a child she allowed the woman to help her out of her clothes. Jenneen didn't know even now, how many times the
woman had kissed her before she became aware of
what was happening. But she didn't stop her. The
woman's lips were soft, her hands cool and gentle, tenderly soothing the loneliness from her body. There
were no rough hands on her breasts, no heavy bulk
pushing against her. Only warmth and comfort, and a
sensual feeling she had never experienced before. And
then she was moving her own hands. Touching, explor-
ing, and wondering at the strange softness of the skin,
the light smell of perfume, the silky hair that fell across
her face.

How much later was it when the door opened?
Hours? Minutes perhaps. She looked up to see a man
standing over the bed, watching them, a smile curling
his lips, and a glass in his hand. She didn't know him
then, but it was Matthew Bordsleigh, an as yet little
known actor. The woman lying beside her seemed
pleased to see him, and not at all embarrassed. She invited him to stay and watch, and he did. Jenneen never
knew what possessed her to go through with such an
"act of perversion," as her family would have called it.
And Matthew Bordsleigh sat on a chair in the corner,
quietly sipping his Scotch, never taking his eyes from
the naked female bodies writhing before him on the
bed.

It was more than a year later when she next saw
him. They recognized one another, but could not immediately recall where they had met. Jenneen had so
determinedly pushed the night of the party to the back
of her mind that she never thought of it any more. She
was too ashamed.

It was Matthew who remembered first. Her reaction was to deny it. It must have been someone else.

Don't be ridiculous, she'd been sleeping with him for the last two months hadn't she? How could she possibly have gone to bed with another woman? Would a lesbian behave in bed with a man like she did with him? But he insisted, until finally Jenneen admitted it. He laughed at her crushing humiliation, telling her not to mind about him, he was a liberated guy, and no, he wouldn't dream of telling anyone.

He kept his promise, but it did not stop him suggesting distasteful threesomes from time to time, and Jenneen grew to hate him for it. But she carried on seeing him, not really knowing why. She should have been warned when she first noticed that his drinking was becoming a problem. The night he threw her over he was more drunk than she had ever seen him before. They argued, and she tried to stop him from having any more, telling him he was making a disgusting spectacle of himself. He laughed at her, saying she was a one to talk about disgusting spectacles. And then he hit her. The first punch didn't hurt much, but the second did, and the third, and the fourth. How many times he hit her she couldn't remember, but the pain she could. Finally, he stormed out, shouting obscenities over his shoulder, and telling her not to expect him back. It was a blessed relief.

The next day she was to appear as a guest on the *Late Night Chat Show*. As the new presenter of the afternoon features program it was important to promote herself, as well as the program. She had to wear dark glasses, and her mouth was badly cut inside. Nevertheless, she was determined to go through with it. It was only when she was in the make-up room before the show began that she realized the full extent of what he had done to her face. The eyes looking back at her from the mirror, normally so calm and blue, were purple and red and swollen—she looked hideous. He had spoiled her first appearance on television. The very thing she had worked so long for. She should have been carried away with a sense of achievement, bubbling over with euphoria to have realized her dream, but he had taken it away from her. She hated him. She hated him with a growing vengeance, and swore that she would get back at him somehow. She didn't realize then how soon that would be, or how much it would cost her.

"You're taking your time out there."

His voice brought her back to the present, and she felt her fingers tighten on the knife she was holding. How she would love to push it into him. To see the look of horror, of disbelief, and then agony. To see him fall dead at . . . She shook herself. She must pull herself together, get a grip. She'd find a way out of this some-how, but that wasn't the answer.

She went into the sitting room and slammed down a plateful of food before going to sit on the settee. He sauntered over to the table and sat down. She could hear him eating, and the sound grated on her nerves. She looked at the bottle of whiskey that was sitting on the floor beside the fire. It had been full when he'd ar-rived, now it was half empty. But she didn't care. Hopefully it would kill him. Yes, she'd give him money if that was what he was going to spend it on.

Eventually she heard his knife and fork go down, and then giving a heavy sigh punctuated by a stomach-curdling burp he leaned back in his chair and picked up his Scotch. For a while he said nothing, only looked at her. Any minute now he would tell her how much he wanted. She would go ʟo her handbag, or maybe her checkbook, hand over whatever he asked for, and then he would go. It was the easiest way.

A smirk twisted his face and she wondered how she could ever have found him attractive. His teeth were stained with tobacco, his face swollen with drink, and the once athletic body was beginning to sag.

"Take off your dressing gown," he said, picking at his teeth.

She ignored him.

"Did you hear me? I said, take off your dressing gown."

"Drop dead!" She got to her feet intending to leave the room. Quick as a flash he was behind her, pinning back her arms. She didn't have time to marvel at how a man as drunk as he was could move so quickly before he had pushed her onto the floor. Towering over her she could see the gleam in his eye.

"Take it off!" he snapped.

Knowing that it would only be the worse for her if she didn't do as he said, she slowly began to undo the buttons. She turned her head to gaze into the fire, trying to disassociate herself from her own body. He waited, looking down at her, until all the buttons were undone. Then, taking her by the arms, he yanked her to her feet.

"That's all!" he said. "If you'd only learn to do as you were told you'd make life a lot easier for yourself, Jenneen. Now, fifty pounds, check or cash. I don't mind which."

Realizing that he was not going to rape her after all, she was so overcome with relief that she almost ran across the room and fumbled in her bag for her checkbook. Her hands were shaking with anger and fear as she wrote the check.

He laughed when she handed it to him, then tucked the near empty bottle of whiskey into his coat pocket and left.

After he had gone she sat in the chair for a long time, staring into the fire. Why had she let that woman take her to bed that night? But was it so bad to have been to bed with another woman? She shuddered. Of course it was. People where she came from thought women who did things like that were disgusting and contemptible. And if her mother ever found out, she would never be able to hold her head up again. And her father, she dreaded to think what it might do to him, or what he might do to her.

And her friends? What would they think? They'd never trust her again. If she greeted them with a kiss they would always be wondering, did she have more than a friendly love for them? She couldn't bear it. She couldn't bear to see everyone she loved turn away from her. To see that look in people's eyes when she went into work. The sniggers and whispers behind her back. No, she had to tolerate Matthew's abuse, it was the only way. She could only thank God that he didn't know the full extent of her debauchery.

FOUR

ELLAMARIE AND BOB HAD KNOWN ONE ANOTHER FOR OVER two years, occasionally working together, and frequently bumping into one another in the close-knit community of London's West End theaters. Ellamarie hadn't known at first, but Bob had fallen in love with her almost the first time he had laid eyes on her.

He had no ready explanation for the strength and immediacy of his feelings. Of course, Ellamarie was a beautiful woman, but as a director he spent a great deal of time with beautiful women. For some reason she held an attraction for him that he had never felt for anyone else. He was as surprised by his feelings as he was mystified, but try as he might, he could not deny them. In all the years of his marriage he had never strayed, had never felt the need or the inclination. He was comfortable with his wife, and happy too, and coupled with the excitement and drive of his work, he had always assumed his life to be fulfilled. But from the moment that Ellamarie Goold had walked into his life, all that had changed.

He was sitting in the old Church Hall where the rehearsals for *Twelfth Night* were entering their second week, watching Ellamarie make her entrance with "Feste."

He had surprised everyone by asking to see this particular part of the scene, but he had done it only to satisfy Ellamarie. He knew she would be angry if she didn't rehearse something that morning.

He watched her with a critical eye. It was her first professional role in Shakespeare, and she had thrown herself into it body and soul—once she had come to terms with not playing Viola. Bob smiled to himself as he watched her prepare for her first exit of the scene, and was impressed by how readily the required blush came to her cheeks.

She lifted her head. "Peace, you rogue, no more o' that. Here comes my lady: make your excuse wisely, you were best," and she swept from the stage.

"Hold it! Hold it there!" Bob called, before she was fully gone. He walked over to them, knowing he was being watched closely by the rest of the cast.

"I think, Ellamarie," he said, as he reached them, "perhaps you could smile a little more as you prepare to leave. No, not with your mouth, just your eyes, a touch flirtatious, you know. And Geoffrey, watch her go, and keep watching her until she has cleared the stage altogether, then clasp your hands together."

Ellamarie was looking at him, but he avoided her eyes.

"I thought," said Geoffrey, unwittingly helping him out, "that as Maria leaves, perhaps I could take a couple of steps after her, wait for her to go, then turn back for my next line."

Bob thought about this. "Try it," he said, "and don't forget, really camp it up. Maybe slope the steps." He gave an illustration of what he wanted, making everyone laugh, then stood back again to watch. "Take it from 'Many a good hanging prevents a bad marriage.' " He was still looking at Geoffrey.

Maria and the Clown rehearsed to the point of Maria's exit again, and this time Bob let her go and allowed the scene to continue up to the point of Maria's re-entry, when he nodded toward the stage manager who, taking her cue perfectly, yelled "Lunch!"

Ellamarie picked up her bag and stormed into the ladies' room. Dammit! Why hadn't Bob given her the chance to go further? Surely he had seen how ready she was to do more. More than anyone else, he knew how important it was for her to prove herself. Not only to the others, but to herself too. The sly glances and whispers of her fellow actors had not passed her by, and she was determined to prove to them that she was right for the part. That there was no question of perks for the director's mistress. She knew she could successfully discard her American accent, and had, but even that had not persuaded Maureen Woodley that Ellamarie Goold should be in the cast. As far as Maureen Woodley was concerned, *no* American should ever touch Shakespeare. It was an insult to the Bard. And coupled with the fact that the American had only got the part because she was getting laid by the director, the whole thing was an outrage.

Stalking past the basins she slammed the door to a cubicle and locked it. She must calm down before she faced him. If they had a fight over lunch everyone would know, and she would not give that bitch Maureen Woodley the pleasure of seeing her upset.

By the time she had counted to ten at least five times she was ready to leave. She turned to pull the chain, then stopped as the outside door opened and she heard someone saying her name.

"Just the very sight of Ellamarie Goold makes my blood boil. She doesn't pick up on the verse lines, she flaunts herself across the stage as if she were the only one on it, then has the cheek to hover on the side while the rest of us are playing. God, she makes me sick!" There was no mistaking the husky tones of Maureen Woodley. "Did you see her actually prompt Richard this morning?"

"Mmm," Ellamarie heard Ann Hillier answer.

"But how dare she prompt Richard Coulthard, of all people!"

"Well, he did forget his lines," Ann pointed out.

"But it's not her job to prompt."

"No, I suppose not. Where shall we go for lunch?"

"And then did you hear her discussing pauses with Nicholas Gough earlier? Anyone would think she was an authority on Shakespeare the way she carries on."

"Maybe she is," said Ann.

Ellamarie's blood had run cold when she first heard Maureen bitching about her, but now she was trying to stop herself from laughing. Shit, Maureen Woodley sure was stupid. Couldn't she see what a bore she was being? Ann Hollier was big news in the theater, what the hell did she care about what Maureen Woodley thought?

"Just let her try prompting me," Maureen continued, her strangled voice indicating that she was applying her orange lipstick, "she'll have a nice treat in store for her if she does."

With that Ellamarie pulled open the cubicle door and stalked out. She had the satisfaction of seeing an orange line snake toward Maureen's nose, before she flung her bag across her shoulders and trilled: "Well, Maureen, I sure do love treats, so my book'll be at the ready," and she started to turn away. "Oh, but I'm forgetting," she stopped and smiled, making sure she caught Maureen's eye in the mirror before she looked pointedly at the script that was lying on the wash basin, "you're not off your book yet, are you? Oh well, some you win. Treats later maybe," and with that she threw the two women a beaming smile, and sailed out of the room, but not before she saw the answering gleam in Ann Hollier's eye.

Everything about London and its turbulent past set Ellamarie's romantic soul into motion, and though Bob laughed as they walked toward the Tower of London, he grudgingly admitted that yes, it affected him too. They were wrapped in woolly hats and scarves to keep out the cold, and once out of sight of the rehearsal rooms, Ellamarie slipped her arm through his. Bob always felt uncomfortable when she did this, afraid that he might see someone he knew, or more importantly someone who knew his wife. It was an unnecessary fear, because he often walked along like this with actresses, but he supposed that his guilt was the reason for his discomfort. He didn't pull away, he knew Ellamarie would be hurt if he did.

"So you see," she was saying, "I'm worried about them all."

"They're grown women, darling," he answered, "I'm sure they can look after themselves."

"Oh sure they can, but it still doesn't stop me from worrying. I saw Ashley yesterday, for lunch. You should have seen her. She looks awful. What beats me is how he could have done it to her?"

Bob shrugged. "I'm sure he had his reasons."

"Don't take his part," Ellamarie objected. "I won't allow it. He's a bastard son-of-a-bitch and that's all there is to it. And someone's got to do something about Kate. I mean, it's not natural to be so long without a man."

"She's out with a different man almost every night, from what I can gather," said Bob.

"But she doesn't sleep with them."

"Not everyone is as insatiable as you, darling."

She laughed. "That's because not everyone has you."

He squeezed her hand. "I thought Jenneen was fixing Kate up with this chap, Joseph?"

"Joel. She is. But who's going to fix someone for Jenneen?"

"Ellamarie, stop it. Next thing I know you'll be running some kind of dating agency."

"Well, I want everyone to be as happy as I am," she said, pulling him to a stop and turning him to face her.

"You, my darling, are having an affair with a married man."

Her smile disappeared. "Don't remind me."

They walked in silence for a while, watching the people passing, and looking up at the ancient City buildings that surrounded them. Ellamarie wished her father could be with them now, he would just love to hear her talk about the Tower, and all she had learned about the people who had lived and died there. She felt sad whenever she thought of him, so far away in Wyoming, still believing that she would go back home to him one day, when she knew she never would.

She shook herself. "Was your weekend good?" she asked Bob.

"OK."

He could feel her eyes on him and grinned. "I missed you," he whispered, turning to look at her. "Did you miss me?"

She seemed to think about this for a minute. "A bit," she admitted.

He raised his eyebrows. "Just a bit?" He sounded more Scots than he usually did.

She nodded.

A fire engine screamed past, and like everyone else they stopped to watch it go by.

"So how did the rehearsals measure up this morning?" she asked him, when they were walking again.

"Good. Yes, good. There's still a great deal of work to do, but I think we're getting there. I've decided that we won't rehearse this afternoon."

"You mean you're giving us the afternoon off, sir?"

He chuckled. "Certainly not! No, I thought this afternoon, as the whole cast plus stand-ins are with us today, we might have a group discussion. Do some analysis."

"Sounds heavy."

"No one ever said Shakespeare was light."

"I was kidding. Tell you what, why don't we start now? Give me, the poor American, a fighting chance."

He looked at her, and though she was laughing at herself, he could see that she was serious. "OK," he said, "I want to take a look at the four different types of love in the play. Orsino, who is in love with love. Olivia who falls in love at first sight. Viola who has a secret love . . ."

"I think it would be truer to say Viola suffers a secret love." Her voice was meaningful.

She saw his eyes flicker toward her, but he made no comment. "And Malvolio . . ." he went on.

". . . is in love with himself," she finished.

"Precisely. And it is those four themes that I want to discuss this afternoon."

"I see." She seemed to go off into a world of her own, and Bob let her be. He needed to think about the interview he was doing later on the BBC, when he would be quizzed about his adaptation of *Twelfth Night*. He hated doing the promotion ritual for his productions. Actors, he felt, were better suited. But he had once made the mistake of being a lively interviewee, and ever since he had been pestered to do more. The BBC had offered to come to the rehearsal rooms, but Bob didn't trust Maureen Woodley. It would be like her to point the interviewer at Ellamarie and whisper something damning in his ear. There was quite enough attention focused upon them as it was, without television taking up the cause.

He felt Ellamarie's eyes upon him and turned to look at her. She smiled, and he lifted his hand to stroke her face.

"Where were you?" She always felt uneasy if he went into deep thought when he was with her. She was scared that he was thinking about their illicit life together, that it was all an error on his part. She needed constant reassurance from him. And Bob knew it.

"Oh, I was on an island somewhere," he grinned. She seemed to relax. "When is it?"

"Desert Island Discs?" He was relieved that she had unwittingly given credence to his story. "Friday next. And you? Where were you?"

"Me. I was somewhere, long, long ago. In a fine dress, and with many riches. Handmaidens and fools fawning at my feet. And a lover at my side, speaking true love with his eyes, and offering his heart to me."

"And did you take it?"

"Yes."

Ellamarie felt her heart turn over as his humorous blue eyes creased at the corners. "But you already have mine."

She reached up and smoothed her fingers over his beard. "No, not all of it, only a part of it. In my dream you offered it all."

He pulled her closer and brushed his lips against her hair. "I know you don't believe it," he whispered, "but here and now, my heart is yours, completely. There is no need of a flight through time to find it."

"I wish I could believe you, Bob. Oh, I wish I could believe you."

He hugged her, then turned with his arm about her, to walk on.

"Are you sure you're not hungry?" he asked.

"Sure."

"How about some coffee somewhere?"

"No thanks. I'm happy just walking."

Tower Bridge was raised, so they stood at the side and watched the ship come through.

"How big was the bit?" he said, turning to face her.

She looked confused.

"The bit that you missed me?" he explained.

A light began to shine in her eyes. "Enormous."

He pulled her into his arms. "Good, I'm glad. I want you to miss me." He squeezed her tightly. "God, you feel so good. Even through all this," and he plucked at her sheepskin coat.

She unbuttoned her coat, inviting him to slide his hands inside, and rested her head on his shoulder.

"What did you do at the weekend?" he asked. "When you were missing me so much."

"Where shall I begin? So many parties, so many people to see, things to do. And the men. Hell, it's difficult being so popular."

"Pretty ordinary sort of weekend then really?"

"Mmm."

Suddenly, before she knew what had happened, Bob had snatched her hat from her head. "Hey!" she cried.

"Who are they? Tell me!" he said, "I'll challenge every one of them!"

"Not until you give me my hat back!"

"Tell, or I shall throw myself in the river!"

They were both laughing by this time, but Ellamarie held firm. "Never!"

At the sight of her face, fresh and clear in the cold air, and her bright blue eyes dancing, he caught her in his arms and pressed his lips to hers. At first she was startled by his sudden embrace, but then she relaxed against him and began to return his kiss. Her hat was dropped to the ground, forgotten, and her red hair was caught by a gust of wind. She clung to him, pushing her body hard against his.

"Oh God, I've missed you so much," he groaned. "I hate being away from you."

She was silent, and he knew what she was thinking. That they need not be apart. That it was him, and only him, that forced their separations. That if only he would allow it, they could be together, always. And in his heart he knew that they could not carry on as they were. It wasn't fair to her. She deserved more than these snatched meetings, the secrecy, the hidden looks, the furtive telephone calls. She was young and beautiful. She should be shouting her love to the world, living life fully with a man who could give her everything. But he could not give her up. He loved her too much.

"Will you stay with me tonight?"

She nodded, and felt the familiar flutterings inside.

"At the house?"

She looked at him. "Why at the house?"

"Linda's going to be ringing me sometime, I'll have to be there."

The mood was broken, and Ellamarie pulled away.

"I'm sorry," he said.

"It's all right." She buttoned her coat and picked up her hat.

"She's ringing to tell me what time to collect my mother from the station on Friday."

"I see."

"My mother is coming to stay with us for Christmas." He wished he would just shut up.

"Oh yes, Christmas," she sighed.

"Have you decided yet what you are going to do?"

She turned to face him. "I'd like to spend it with you."

He gathered her in his arms, not wanting to see the tears that were shining in her eyes. "And I want to spend it with you too. But you know that's not possible."

"I know."

"You won't be alone though, will you? I mean, what about your friends, what are they doing?"

"I don't know," she lied. She wanted him to be guilty. She didn't want him to know that she had already been invited to spend the time with Kate and her family.

"You've been invited to lots of parties, you'll enjoy yourself."

"Oh for Christ's sake, Bob, don't be so goddamned patronizing. Yes, I can take care of myself. But it doesn't change anything. It's still you I want to be with, it's still you I want to wake up to on Christmas morning. Instead I have to think of you with her! Waking up to her, and sharing the day with her, and wondering if you think of me at all."

"Ellamarie, I think about you all the time. Every moment I'm away from you I spend wanting to be with you. You know that." He caught her by the shoulders. "I love you. I love you."

"But there's always your wife."

"I've told you so many times how it is with us. We have no life together, you know that. My life is here with you."

She didn't answer.

He looked at her face, sad, and thoughtful. He hated himself for the lies he told her. "Come on," he said, glancing at his watch, "it's time we were getting back."

As they walked, her hands were so firmly thrust into her pockets that this time he linked arms with her.

Inwardly she mocked herself. Here she was, Ellamarie Goold, who had had her life so carefully mapped out. The success, the recognition, the brilliant performances she would give, on and off the stage. And everything had gone according to plan, until Bob McElfrey had come into her life. Bob McElfrey, who had fought so hard to win her, until finally she had thought, "Oh, what the hell. I've never had an affair with a married man before. It might be fun!" She had never once thought about the consequences. Such a child she had been then. Thinking only of those she knew who had such affairs, and the glamor that seemed to be attached to them. The awe with which they were all treated. Then, was it envy? at the tasting of forbidden fruits, at the excitement of being swept off into the night at a moment's notice. Tales of nights of passion, of love that supression only made deeper. Oh, how wonderful it had all seemed, from the outside.

But now she was facing the truth. The reality of unfulfilled promises. The waiting that turned to misery and pain, which he must never know of. The heart that filled with hope that must never be spoken of. The snatched moments of happiness that were never real, only borrowed. The stolen ecstasy of feeling his body against yours, of hearing him tell you that never before has he felt like this. And you believe him because you want to. Because you have to. Why is it that the passion that burns for this man is stronger than any other? That the love is deeper, the joy greater? Or is it? Is it just the great myth of the Eternal Triangle? The triangle that deceptions, suicides and murders were made of?

She was becoming introspective again.

FIVE

With a sigh, Kate closed the book she had been reading and turned over. Her eyes were misty, but there was the shadow of a smile on her face. Finishing a book always left her with a heart and mind full of conflicting emotions.

She glanced up at the clock. It wasn't even six in the morning yet. She pulled the sheet up around her face and closed her eyes.

Beside her she could hear him breathing quietly, not yet awake. She let her hands fall to her sides, and willed him to wake up.

A few minutes later she wriggled further into the bed as she felt his hand brush over her thighs and up across her belly. She parted her lips, and waited for the warmth of his mouth over hers. And as her nipples began to expand under his touch, she felt his tongue push deep into her mouth. She turned to him, and against the soft mound of her tummy she felt him harden and grow. He took her hand and placed it round his penis, and slowly, very slowly, she began to move her fingers back and forth.

Keeping his mouth firmly on hers he lifted her leg and placed it round his waist. With a brief and gentle push he was inside her. They moved together, gently, pushing closer and closer. He moved his hands under

her, lifted her, and as he gave one final, deeply penetrating thrust, he whispered her name.

Kate lifted her hand to stroke his face. The pillow
was cool beneath her fingers, and she opened her eyes.
The reality of no one there was so awful she closed
them again. It had felt so real. But didn't it always?

As she moved she felt the moistness on her thighs,
and sighed. Her body was on fire, tingling, and achingly
aroused.

She reached out and fumbled in the drawer beside
her bed. Her fingers closed round the cold shaft of the
vibrator and she sneaked it beneath the covers. She
turned on her back and began to tease herself toward
orgasm.

After several minutes she stopped. It was no good.
There was no warmth, no real comfort to be gained
from what she was doing. It wasn't only sex she craved,
it was love too.

She jammed the vibrator back into the drawer and
got out of bed. Turning on the shower she began to
sing, at the top of her voice. Mrs. Adams from upstairs
banged on the ceiling, so she lowered the volume. The
water was lukewarm, the song cheerful. By the time
she got out of the shower she felt better.

At nine o'clock she was ready to leave. Into the car,
along the Fulham Road, cross over to Sloane Square,
where she stopped off at Peter Jones to see if her new
curtains were ready. No. On then to Victoria and *Gracious Living Magazine*.

She had intended to give up journalism altogether
when she'd left the magazine three months before, and
concentrate solely on her novel. However Margaret
Stanley, the formidable features editor at *Gracious Living*,
had continued to call her up on a regular basis and send
her off on assignments. Margaret Stanley was a woman
who did not take no for an answer.

Jillian, the photographer, was waiting when Kate
arrived, so ditching her car in Margaret Stanley's space

in the small car park, the two of them braved the arm-pits of commuters and took the Tube into the West End. They were doing an interview with the cast of *Les Misérables.*

The morning went well, a whole stack of splendid interviews piling into her notebook. Kate was sorry she couldn't join the cast for lunch, but, she whispered to Jillian, she was quite hopelessly broke, so really had to go and meet Daddy. Jillian grinned and winked at her. Kate knew what Jillian was after. Or, more to the point, who Jillian was after.

Her father was pleased to see her, he always was, and they talked over the novel she was writing. She hadn't plucked up the courage yet to tell him about all the sex in it, she'd blame it on the editor later. Providing she got an editor. But her father had influence, he would see to it. He had seen to practically everything else in her life. Not that she didn't have talent, of course. But with the world being the way it was, talent didn't always count for everything.

Back at the theater in the afternoon, Kate noticed that Jillian had made her play for the member of the cast she'd had her eye on all morning. By five-thirty the two of them were ready to start the preliminaries of the sexual encounter that would come later.

Kate grinned and shook her head at Jillian as they parted company. "Don't you ever want more?"

"More what?"

Kate shrugged. "Well, more of him."

"I don't know how big he is yet."

Kate burst out laughing. "Serves me right for ask-ing a silly question. Have fun."

"Be sure of it, darling," Jillian smiled, and headed off in the direction of the wine bar where she had ar-ranged to meet the actor.

Kate was already plotting how she would write about it later.

*   *   *

As she let herself into the flat the phone was ringing.

"Kate? It's Jenn."

"Oh, hi. I've just got in. Where are you?"

"At home, packing. I've got to go to Brighton tonight, we've got an early call there tomorrow, so I just wanted to let you know I won't be able to make it this evening."

"Oh, pity. Well, don't worry. What about Ashley? Have you spoken to her?"

"She's probably on her way. Today's the day, you know."

"Sorry?"

"Blanche. She flies in tonight. Ash is in a pretty bad way. I told her not to go back to work, but she insisted. I don't know how she stands it, seeing him every day like that."

"Me neither. I'll go and crack open a bottle of wine. Give me a ring soon as you get back, OK?"

"Will do."

Ashley arrived ten minutes later.

"You look terrible," said Kate.

"Thanks. I feel it."

"Did you see him today?"

"Of course."

"Speak to him?"

"Yes."

"What did he say?"

"Good morning, Ashley. How are you?"

"And what did you say?"

Ashley smiled. "I said, 'I'm fine thank you, Mr. Arbrey-Nelmes, I hope you are too.' "

"God. And Blanche is arriving tonight?"

"Yep."

"What time?"

"I don't know. She's flying into Gatwick at eight-thirty."

"Is he going to meet her?"

"I don't know. Yes."

"He would be, the rat!"

"He's not really a rat, you know, Kate."

"No, sorry, of course he's not. He's just pretending to be."

Ashley smiled despite herself. "Well, I haven't come here to talk about him, God knows I've done enough of that lately. What have you got to drink?"

"How would a bottle of Châteauneuf-du-Pape suit?"

"Start pouring."

Their conversation was stilted; it was all too obvious that Ashley's mind was elsewhere. But every time Kate tried to broach the subject of Julian, Ashley was firm.

"Talking about it never mended a broken heart," she said.

"But it helps to soothe it," Kate insisted.

"And you've soothed me enough lately. If I talk about him now, tonight, I think I might go mad."

"OK. Then how's Alex?"

Ashley's face softened immediately. "Wonderful. I spoke to him earlier—well, at least I got a quick hello out of him. But Dad was taking him off somewhere so he told me I had to be quick."

"You're so lucky really, you know, Ash." Kate's expression was almost wistful as she spoke. "He's a lovely kid. I hope I have children one of these days."

"You will," said Ashley, "but don't be in too much of a hurry."

"I'm thirty," Kate pointed out. "I wouldn't exactly call that a hurry."

"No. But you've got your career, you're writing a book, and you have perhaps the best social life of the four of us. You'd have to give all that up if you had children."

"But I'd want to give it up. It would be something worth giving it up for."

"Don't be too sure about that."

"Besides, I wouldn't have to give it up. I mean, look at you. You've got your career as well. And you don't do so badly with your social life."

"Don't I?"

"Not from where I'm sitting."

"How often do I do anything at the weekends? When you all go off shooting, or point-to-pointing, or whatever it is you do, I'm never there, in case you hadn't noticed."

"Do you want to be?"

"Yes. Yes I do. But of course I want to be with Alex too. I can't expect my parents to cope with him seven days a week. As it is they already have him for five, which is plenty at their age. And what about holidays? Julian wanted to take me away in the summer, but I couldn't go. Oh I know he said to take Alex too, but it's not the same having a child around, especially when the child isn't his. You've got your freedom, Kate, you should hang on to it as long as you can. If I hadn't got married when I was twenty, life would look a whole lot different for me now."

"I don't see how. And you can't say you don't have freedom; you have a damn sight more than most mothers."

"I know I do. But that's not to say you will. And although it looks as though I've got my freedom, I can promise you, I'm never free of guilt. I know, every night when I go home, that I should be going home to Alex, but I'm selfish and I stay here in London. I wouldn't change it, but I wish the price weren't quite so high."

"Oh, for God's sake, Ashley, the price isn't high at all. OK, I might have the ball gowns, the GTI and the monthly allowance, but just what does any of it actually mean? Until you split with Julian you really did have everything. What more could you have wanted?"

"Julian."

Kate flushed. "I'm sorry," she said, "that was tact-less. But surely you can see what I'm getting at."

The telephone rang and Kate went to pick it up.

Ashley thought over what Kate had said. They had had conversations like this before, and Ashley knew that in a way Kate resented her. But didn't she resent Kate too? And Ellamarie and Jenneen. Ellamarie had said that there should be some kind of melting pot for their friendship so that they could help themselves to the bits of one another's characters they liked best. Jenneen's answer had been poignant: "But isn't that why we have each other?" And how many times these last few days had Ashley thanked God that she did have her friends?

She could see Julian now, waiting at the airport for Blanche. Her heart contracted, and she couldn't stop herself thinking of the lonely nights she'd spent since they'd parted. And the agony of seeing him every day since. It was torture. A failed marriage, and now a failed love affair.

"Daddy," Kate said, as she put the phone down. "Seems I left my diary in the restaurant at lunchtime. He's coming over."

"Well, it's about time I was on my way," said Ashley, getting to her feet.

"Oh no," Kate cried. "He won't be staying long."

"No honestly, I think it's time I was going. An early night will do me no harm."

"Oh Ash, I feel terrible."

"Please don't," said Ashley. "I was on the verge of collapsing into a heap of self-pity anyway, think yourself lucky you escaped."

Kate smiled. "Well, you know you can always come back if you change your mind."

"Thanks," said Ashley. "But I think I know what I'm going to do."

"Oh?"

Ashley tapped her finger against her nose, and smiled.

Inside she was aching. She didn't want to be alone. Not tonight. She knew she couldn't bear it. There was only one place she could go now. She didn't know if it was the right thing to do, but she had to talk to someone.

The taxi drove off into the night leaving Ashley standing outside the restaurant. It was bitterly cold, and she pulled her scarf up round her face to keep out the wind. She was already beginning to wish she hadn't come. Her stomach felt knotted. Sometimes the pain of losing him was almost too much to bear.

The door opened and a woman stepped out into the street. She was laughing, and turned back to look up into the face of the man who followed her. He put his arm round her, and they ran off down the street, eager to be home and away from the cold—together. Ashley watched them until they were out of sight, and thought of Julian. She looked at her watch. The plane was due in about now, and he would be waiting. She thought of his handsome face, expressionless, but smiling if he caught someone looking in his direction. He was like that. Always ready with a smile.

She sighed. It was partly because of that ready smile that she was here now—outside this restaurant. Their restaurant.

The rain started again, so she pushed open the door and went inside. There weren't many people dining, and looking around the room her eyes soon found the person she was looking for. A waiter came to take her coat, but she thanked him and said she didn't know if she was staying. Her heart was beating hard. Somehow, in a strange sort of way, she felt as though she was meeting Julian. She wondered what he would say if he knew she was here, and why.

As she approached the old man's table he was already looking up, his face crinkling into a greeting. He looked towards the door expectantly, then back to her.

"Hello, my dear," he said.

"Hello." She stood beside the table for a moment, feeling awkward, her hands still in her pockets.

"Are you alone?"

She swallowed. "Yes."

"Oh, I see," he said, and she could tell that he did.

"Would you mind . . ." her voice broke. She cleared her throat. "Would you mind if I sat down?"

He gestured toward the chair opposite him and signaled to the waiter. "Would you like a drink?"

She nodded. "A mineral water please."

"Make that a large Scotch," the old man told the waiter, "and my usual."

Ashley smiled. Seeing the old man, and sitting in this restaurant, brought all the memories of the times she had sat here with Julian flooding back, as she had known it would. Times they had laughed, precious moments they had shared. It was a mistake to have come here.

"Miserable weather, don't you think?" said the old man, looking toward the door as some people came in, shaking the rain from their umbrellas.

"Awful."

"Still, it's what one expects at this time of year, so I suppose we shouldn't grumble."

Ashley looked at the lines in his face, and wondered what it was like to be him. To be old and able to look back on life. Would he change anything now? His blue eyes were watching her from behind his spectacles, twinkling and knowing.

"Do you mind if I smoke?" he said, taking out a packet of cigarettes.

"No, no, please," she answered.

"Do you?" he offered her one.

"No," she said, taking one and thanking him.

"Pretty unsociable these days, isn't it?"

"Have you ever tried to give it up?" she asked.

"Not really. For me it's one of life's little pleasures. Even more so now that I know I shouldn't. Makes me feel like a rebel."

"Then let's rebel together," she said, taking the light he was offering.

"Are you going to eat?" he asked. "I can recommend the venison. Unless you're a vegetarian, of course."

"No, I'm not a vegetarian."

"Good."

"Good?"

"Yes, good. People today seem to have so many principles, I'm sure they don't realize they're principlising themselves out of fun. If you can call eating venison fun—which I do."

"But surely you don't mind people's principles?"

"Of course not. But I mind fanatics, the ones who try to impose their beliefs on you. According to someone somewhere, almost everything you do is dangerous. You musn't smoke or drink. Two things that give me great pleasure. Then you mustn't eat the things you like, or breathe the air around you. In the summer it is dangerous to sunbathe, and in the winter the rain is no longer rain, but little drops of acid. I shouldn't wear the shoes I'm wearing, because they're made of leather, nor the hat that keeps me warm, because it's made of fur. Shall I go on?"

She smiled. "I think I get your point."

He sipped his drink, then put it back on the table. His eyes suddenly took on a look that she could only describe as mischievous. "Do you know what I did today?" he said, leaning across the table and looking around to make sure no one else could hear. She shook her head. "Well, today I had tremendous fun. It was very risky, I might tell you, but today I felt brave. To hell with them all, I thought. So, prepared to take the consequences, I lit and smoked a whole cigarette on the

A CLASS APART   59

Tube. Right down to the very last. And I snarled, and
looked mean, and challenged anyone to utter a word.
I didn't care. I like to live dangerously."

"Very dangerous," she agreed. "Did anyone object?"

"No."

"Oh."

He stuck out his bottom lip. "The carriage was
empty."

She burst out laughing, and wanted to hug him.
"Do you often take your life into your hands in this
way?"

"Oh yes. Last week I bought a fur hat and walked
out of the shop with it on. Sadly no one sprayed me
green." He brightened suddenly. "But there's still
hope, I wear it every day."

The waiter arrived, ready to take Ashley's order.
Quickly she picked up the menu and looked it over.
But even to think of food made her stomach churn. She
put the menu down again. "Nothing for me, thank
you," she said. "But can you bring us two more
drinks?"

"I'm afraid, madam, that it is not permitted not to
eat," the waiter said, picking up the menu and handing
it back to her.

Ashley looked confused. She knew she would be
unable to eat anything, but she didn't want to leave.

The old man said: "The lady will have venison,
George, with a selection of vegetables."

"Oh no, no really, I couldn't eat it," Ashley cried,
looking from one to the other.

"But you must!" declared the waiter.

"But I can't," said Ashley. "I'm not hungry."

"I cannot permit that you don't eat," said the
waiter.

"George, I have ordered the lady's meal, she will
have venison with a selection of vegetables."

The waiter hurried off. He wanted no further argument.

"Really, I couldn't eat a thing," Ashley protested.

"No, I dare say you couldn't," said the old man, "but I could."

"But I thought you'd . . ."

The old man held up his hand. "I know, I can eat it again. Besides, he might try to make you leave if you don't order something, and it's not every day I have a beautiful young woman sitting at my table, even if that beautiful young woman is sad, and wishing perhaps that she was with someone else."

Ashley looked at him. His eyes were smiling and she felt a lump rising in her throat. She swallowed hard before she spoke. "I'm sorry. Does it show?"

"A little."

She looked down at her hands, clenched in a ball on the table in front of her.

"Let me guess. It has something to do with your young man. The one I see you with from time to time, in here."

Ashley nodded. "He's going to marry someone else," she said, and caught her breath on the surge of feeling that speaking the words aloud brought. "Of course, I always knew he would. He never lied. But I hoped he wouldn't."

"Does he know?"

"Know what?"

"How much you love him."

Tears were stinging her eyes. "Yes," she said.

The waiter brought more drinks.

"You must think I'm ridiculous, coming here with my heart on my sleeve, torturing myself with memories."

"Why ridiculous?"

"Because I am. I thought that seeing you would . . . well, would . . . I'm pathetic and ridiculous."

"There is nothing ridiculous about the pain you

are feeling," he said. "When your life suddenly loses its purpose, it is confusing, bewildering, and it hurts very much. It can break your heart to lose someone you love, and that is not ridiculous."

"But I can't think about anything else. I go to sleep thinking about him, I wake up thinking about him, and I spend all day talking to him, in my imagination. And I keep wondering why? Why did it have to happen? If God didn't want us to be together, then why did he let us happen at all?" She gulped at her drink.

"Would you rather it hadn't?"

"No. But I didn't want it to end. I thought he loved me, you see, I truly believed he loved me. And now I know he didn't."

"Did he ever tell you he did?"

"Not in so many words."

"But you knew?"

"Yes. At least I thought I did. But I was wrong. Oh God, I was wrong. But I believed, just like in all the books you read, the films you see, that it would all work out in the end. I told him how I felt, believing that it would change things. And that is why I am ridiculous. I've made a fool of myself. You know, feeling like this is the worst thing in the world."

"You may be right. Rejection is never easy to bear. A feeling of unimportance to the person of most importance can tear at your heart like nothing else can. And it brings a feeling of frustration, and anger, and a need to explain to that person that you love them, that you care for them so much that you cannot exist without them. And each hour that passes only heralds the beginning of just such another, and each day becomes a burden, almost too heavy to carry." His eyes had a faraway look, and she guessed that he was remembering something from his own past. He pulled himself back to the present and smiled.

She wanted to reach out and touch his hand, but she was afraid to.

"I was in love with my wife," he said, "and I lost her. She died. Five years ago now. At the time I didn't think it was possible to carry on. Life without her seemed worthless, empty. I hadn't realized, until she was gone, how very much I did love her. That is one of the saddest things about life, that you don't realize how much you love someone until they aren't there any more. And then it is too late. You were wise to tell him how you felt, even though it didn't change things. If you hadn't you would always be wondering. But these things usually happen for a reason, and you are young, you have a whole lifetime ahead of you. There will be someone to share it with, and although it may not seem possible, you will love him whoever he is, and don't be afraid to tell him. You should never be ashamed of the way you feel."

"But for one person to mean so much, to rely on them for your happiness, surely it's not right? Surely it's wrong to center your whole existence round one person?"

"That's what being in love is like."

"But it hurts so much later—when they go. You know, I have actually wished that Julian had died. I thought that if he had died, then my memories would be complete, and that I needn't have lived with the knowledge that he didn't love me. I will never love anyone like that again."

He smiled.

"You don't believe me."

"Yes, I believe you. I don't think you will ever love like that again. We never love in the same way twice. Did it ever occur to you that maybe he does love you?"

"All the time, until he told me he still intended to marry Blanche. That's her name, by the way. And now I know the truth."

"Is it the truth? Did he say he didn't love you?"

"No, but he didn't have to. He's not cruel. At least, not in that way."

"Maybe he is hurting too. It was probably very difficult for him to tell you that it was over. Why don't you speak to him again? Maybe it would help."

"No. I can't speak to him, not about us. His mind is made up, and I must live with it now. I lie awake at night, thinking back over the times we had together, and wondering where I went wrong. What I could have done to prevent this happening. And thinking, if only I'd done this, we would probably still be together. And if only I'd done that, he would probably have fallen in love with me. I long for sleep, but I'm afraid I will dream about him. I'm afraid of waking up, and feeling that everything is all right, only to remember, seconds later, that he's not there any more. It's like living in a nightmare."

"I know. But like all nightmares, it will pass, that I can promise."

She sighed. "If only there was some way of easing the pain now."

"If there was, my dear, you can be sure an American would have bottled it and sold it by now."

She smiled. "It's funny, isn't it, how when you feel like this, you are sure that you are the only person in the world that has ever been hurt. Oh yes, other people have been hurt, but they can never know what *you* are going through. It could never have been as bad for them as it is for you."

"We each have our own ways of feeling pain and loss, and at the time, it is worse for you than for anyone else, no matter who you are." He picked up his glass. "When you are ready you will pull yourself up and fight back. Some days will be good, and you will think that the worst has passed, and then something will happen, and you will feel bad again. And it is on those days, when it is almost impossible, that you must be brave, and fight. In my experience the fighters always win. But you have to be brave. Take life by the horns, and live it. Rebel against the misery that saps your strength, and tell yourself that you have a whole new life in front of you, and accept the challenge. One day you will be old like me, and then you won't have so many opportunities for new beginnings. And think how lucky you are, how exciting it is, to be starting a new phase in your life. It is all ahead of you, and there is no knowing what lies in store. Don't look back."

"You're making it sound an enviable position to be in. I might say, it would be easier if I didn't see him at all. We work together, you see."

"Ah, not easy. However, the bigger the challenge, the greater the victory."

"Real fighting talk."

"From a fighter. And you can do it."

"Do you think so?"

"I know so."

"Then I think I'll start by lighting a cigarette on the Tube tomorrow," she said, and they both laughed. "I'm feeling better now, having talked to you. By the way, what happened to the venison?"

"George gave in. He probably guessed that I would eat it, and knows that I have been warned about eating too much red meat. God save us from people who have our best interests at heart."

She chuckled. "But thank God for them too."

"Indeed."

"I've really unburdened myself tonight. I'm sorry."

"Don't be. Unless you're going to let it pull you under."

"I won't, I know I'll get over it. It's just at the moment I still miss him and I could strangle him for making me feel so childish, and ridiculous."

"Which brings us full circle to where we started this evening."

She frowned. "Yes. I've spent the last four days going round in circles, I'm afraid."

"Mmm. Never seems to get you anywhere, does it?"

"Unless you call back where you started, somewhere."

"I don't."

She sighed heavily.

"I think you'd better buy yourself a fur hat as well tomorrow," he said.

Ashley looked at the kind old face and smiled. "Thank you for listening."

"Thank you," he said, and she knew that in some small way it had meant something to him too. Impulsively she reached across the table and squeezed his hand. His eyes were shining brightly, and she was glad she had come.

 SIX

THE RAIN HADN'T STOPPED ALL THE WAY TO BRIGHTON, AND Jenneen was more than glad to arrive at the small hotel she had booked herself into. Tomorrow night she would stay at the Metropole with the film crew, but that was tomorrow night. Tonight was different.

She peered around the gloomy reception as the girl disappeared to search for a key. Tatty sofas and other uncared-for secondhand furniture were strewn around the place. The windows were uncurtained, and she could see the rain still streaming down outside.

She shivered, and turned back to the desk. The

young girl appeared from a small room at the back with a key. She pushed the book toward Jenneen.

"Thank you, Mrs. Green," said the receptionist, and handed her the key.

"I think I shall be returning rather late tonight." Jenneen stooped to pick up her bag. "Perhaps you have a key that I can take with me. If you want to lock up early."

"Of course," said the girl, "here, take mine. I shan't be going anywhere, not tonight in this weather."

Jenneen took the key and headed toward the stairs with her overnight bag.

"I hope you enjoy your stay," the girl called after her.

Jenneen smiled, but didn't look her full in the face—she didn't want to take any chances. Her hat was pulled well down over her eyes, and her scarf all but covered her mouth. No, there would be little chance of recognition, and the young girl hadn't seemed particularly interested anyway.

Jenneen carried her bag up to the second floor and pushed open the door to room six. It was exactly what she had expected. A large double bed, a small battered closet, no doubt from the local secondhand shop, and the customary bible, sitting on the table between them. She picked it up and slipped it inside the closet. Bibles always made her uncomfortable, particularly on a night like tonight. The window had probably seen many months pass by since it was last open. She guessed that in daylight she could probably see the sea.

Beside the window was a small desk-cum-dressing-table, with a mirror on the wall above it. Dumping her bag on the bed, Jenneen switched on the wall lamp and sat down on the stool.

She listened as she heard someone banging around in the next room, and then, ignoring the noise, turned back to the mirror.

Her hands were shaking. Only slightly, but

enough for her to want a drink. She had prepared for this, and taking the bottle of Bushmills from her brief-case, she went into the bathroom to find a glass. There were two. Another reason for booking into a double room. She poured some whiskey into one of the glasses, took a large gulp, poured some more, then carried it back to the dressing table.

She felt a little steadier now as she looked into the mirror. Her face was still almost covered by the hat and scarf; she took them off and dropped them onto the end of the bed. Then she took off her fur coat and laid it beside them.

Sitting down again she reached for her bag and un-zipped it. The dress she wanted was sitting on the top. Quickly she slipped out of the jeans and sweater she was wearing, stripped off her underwear, then turned, naked, to look into the mirror again. She studied her reflection for a long time. Her face was expressionless, and her neat blonde hair was flattened to her head from wearing the hat. Her eyes roamed across the winter white skin of her shoulders, and small breasts. She touched them gently, watching her movements in the mirror as she moved one hand downward and across her flat tummy. It was there that the mirror stopped. She looked at her face again.

"Jenneen Grey," she whispered to the reflection, then pulling at the corners of her mouth she breathed: "Mrs. Green."

As she turned back to her bag her movements were slow and deliberate. This time she took out her make-up case, and unzipped it. First the brown pencil. Lightly across her fair eyebrows, darkening them, giving her face a heavy, almost mannish look. Then the mascara—black. It evened the look of her eyes, and suited her. Again the pencil. Across the lids, and down, round and under the bottom lashes. She sat back to look and grinned as she jabbed the pencil against her cheekbone. A beauty spot, and why not?

The blusher. Red. She stroked the brush several times across her cheeks, slanting the makeup up round her eyes to her temples, lifting her cheek bones, and giving the impression of a change of shape to her face. Longer now, and thinner.

Next the lipstick. A deep, rich red and highly glossy. This was the most intricate part of the operation. Changing the shape of her mouth would change her whole face. She dipped a thin brush into the pot, coating it with the greasy substance, then carefully traced an outline round her lips. She sat back to study herself. She was definitely getting better at this, although the new mouth looked too large for her face; but that didn't matter, if anything it helped. She coated the rest of her lips in the gloss, then reached for her dress.

Enjoying the feel of silk against her skin, she draped it round her shoulders and watching herself in the mirror all the while, fastened the buttons, one by one, and tied the belt.

She was almost ready. She took out a comb and drew her hair away from her face, then clipped it to the top of her head. The wig she took from the bag was dark and cropped, with a hint of chestnut.

She stood back from the mirror to admire her new identity. How easy it was to become another person. How easy it was to live another life. Her pulses began to race, the excitement and anticipation building up inside. She looked at her watch. Ten o'clock. Almost time to go. Just one more thing to do.

She took the stockings and garter belt from her bag. Her hands were shaking again. Whiskey, more whiskey. She gulped at it and sighed. That was better. Up came the dress, and she fastened the belt about her waist, then slipped the stockings up over her legs. One last mouthful of whiskey, then she picked up her coat, flicked the lights, and left.

The rain had stopped when she got outside, but

it was bitterly cold. She pulled her coat tightly round her. Once or twice she had an eerie feeling that she was being followed, but whenever she stopped to look, no one was there. She told herself that she was imagining things, and hurried on.

She tried not to think what her friends would say if they could see her now. Their looks of horror, reproach, disgust even. And they would ask the question that she knew she could never answer, and hardly dared even ask herself.

Why? Why did she feel compelled to do this?

The risk—the terrible, senseless risk that she took every time she did it. Maybe that was it. Maybe that was what gave her the thrill. The danger of discovery. She wouldn't think about that. She was Mrs. Green now, and Mrs. Green didn't care about such things. Mrs. Green did everything Jenneen Grey couldn't do, but on these unfathomable nights of madness needed to do. Mrs. Green was everything Jenneen wanted to be—tonight.

By the time she arrived at her destination it had started to rain again. She was surprised to see so many people, standing at the bar, or dancing on the two round dance floors, either side of the DJ stand. They looked very young. But of course they were. At least ten years younger than she was. Discotheques like this were for the young.

She crossed the room to the smaller bar at the back, and settled herself on an empty stool. A waiter asked her what she would like to drink and she ordered a large Scotch. She looked around the room again. How innocent the young. Nubile young girls, just waiting to be asked to dance. And the shy, awkward youths, too self-conscious to ask. God, who'd be twenty again?

She sipped her Scotch slowly, and felt her body swaying in time to the music. Would anyone ask her to dance? She hoped so. She loved the feel of a young body, moving next to hers. Lithe and firm, yet still in-experienced.

The time ticked by and she was into her second Scotch and wondering if she was wasting her time when she noticed two youths, neither of them any older than eighteen, standing at the other side of the room, watching her. She swallowed hard, and felt the sweat beginning to rise in her hands. She turned away, back to the bar, and lifted her glass. When she turned back they were still looking at her. They were saying something to one another, and smiling. She smiled back, and they nudged one another and winked. Inwardly she laughed. How predictable.

She waited, but it wasn't a long wait. They started moving toward her, stopping before they reached her. She knew she would have to do something to encourage their final steps. She licked her lips, pouted then turned to face them with an enticing smile. It worked. They smiled back, and covered the rest of the distance.

"Hello," said the tallest, and by far the better looking of the two.

"Hello."

"On your own?"

She nodded.

"I'm Neil," he said, "this is Sean."

"Hello, Sean."

They stood there, looking awkward. "Aren't you going to tell us your name?" Neil asked, eventually.

"Mrs. Green."

"Is that what we have to call you?" he said, surprised.

"If you like."

"Don't you have another name?"

"Jane."

"Mind if we join you?" Sean pulled up a stool and sat down beside her.

"I think you already have," she laughed, and they laughed too.

They glanced at one another, grinning, trying to think of something else to say. "Tell me," said Neil, "what's a good-looking woman like you doing here all by herself?"

Jenneen smiled, and felt her age. Woman, eh? No longer a girl, but the lines never changed. She shrugged. "I was fed up sitting at home alone."

"Do you live in Brighton?" Sean asked.

"Just outside. Do you?"

"Yes, we both do."

"Do you work here?"

"College," Neil answered.

"Oh." She drained her glass.

"Can we get you another drink?" Neil offered.

"Mmm, please."

He summoned the waiter and ordered three Scotches.

Sean suggested that they go and sit on one of the semi-circular settees in the corner booths. Jenneen agreed.

Jenneen smoothed the silk of her dress along her thighs as she settled herself between Neil and Sean. There was another awkward silence while the boys tried to think of something else to say. Jenneen was enjoying herself.

"Do you often sit at home on your own then?" Neil asked.

"Ever since my husband left me." The lies slipped out so easily.

"He must be mad!" Sean declared, looking at her legs.

She smiled. "Thank you."

"Would you like to dance?" said Neil.

"I'd love to."

Sean looked a little put out. Still, plenty of time, the night was young.

As she danced, Jenneen could feel Neil's eyes on her, dropping occasionally to look at her breasts as they moved freely inside her dress. He looked up and seeing that she was watching him, blushed. She laughed aloud.

"What's funny?" he shouted above the music.

"Nothing!"

He laughed too, turned to Sean and winked. Sean did not relish this communication—it looked like Neil was going to walk off with the girl, again.

Jenneen stayed on the dance floor with Neil for the following two dances, then as the music slowed, she left and went to sit down.

"Don't like the slow ones?" Neil asked, flopping down beside her.

"Yes," said Jenneen. "It's just that I'd like to sit down for a while."

They sat in silence, listening to the music, watching the dancers. They all laughed and applauded as the DJ announced the engagement of a shy and very youthful looking couple. He asked them which record they would like, and their choice was very romantic, one that Jenneen liked.

"Fancy another dance?" Neil said, taking her hand.

She allowed him to lead her onto the floor, and felt her blood begin to race as he took her in his arms. The look of hunger in his eyes, in deep contrast to the raw inexperience of his body, and the vulnerability of his youth, were like a magnet to her. Gently she molded her body to his, and followed his inexpert swaying, sadly out of time to the music.

"I think you're beautiful," he whispered in her ear as he ran his hands over her back.

She didn't answer, but smiled at the clumsiness of his approach. She pressed her body closer and felt him hardening against her. Then moving her hands inside his jacket, she stroked her fingers across his lower back. She heard him gasp, and was waiting for him as his mouth came round to find hers.

When the record was over, they went to sit down

again. She was laughing. "French kissing on the dance floor!" she said. "It makes me feel young again."

"But you're not old," Neil objected, casually draping his arm across the back of the seat.

"No, not very," she admitted. The look on Sean's face made her smile. "Would you like to dance?" she said to him.

He needed no second bidding, and eagerly led her back to the floor.

He danced rather well, better than Neil, and despite the ugliness of his blond crew cut, Jenneen decided that he wasn't so bad after all. How was she to choose between them? Well, she wouldn't worry about that. Maybe she'd let them decide.

The record came to an end and it looked as though Jenneen was going to leave the floor. Keeping hold of her hand Sean pulled her back as the next record began and she smiled and put her arms round him again.

"Can I take you home tonight?" he blurted out, and was immediately embarrassed when he saw that he had made her laugh.

"Maybe," she said.

The evening wore on and the three of them talked, and danced, and drank. And the more they drank, the braver they all became. The boys were being outrageous, and openly suggestive.

Jenneen went to the ladies' to retouch her make-up and found that it was far less smeared than she had thought it would be. As she was returning she saw that they were arguing about something, and thought she heard one of them mention something about money. She noticed that her glass had been refilled, and guessed that they must be coming to the bottoms of their pockets. She sat down and picked up her glass.

"Thank you for the drink," she said, taking a sip.

Sean looked uncomfortable, and began to fiddle with his collar. Jenneen watched him, but when he didn't say anything she turned back to watching the dance floor.

He studied her profile a moment, and then took a large gulp of his drink. "We were wondering, are you on the game?"

"Fuck me, Sean! That's a bit strong, isn't it?" Neil choked, but looked at Jenneen all the same, waiting to hear her answer.

She laughed. It was an understandable observation. Funny how Mrs. Green could laugh at something like that. Jenneen Grey would be outraged.

"Why?" she asked.

"Nothing," said Sean. "I'm sorry, I shouldn't have said that."

Neil was watching her, looking her up and down, and he noticed that she had undone another button at the top of her dress. She saw him looking and leaned forward to pick up her drink. He swallowed. Jesus Christ, she was driving him crazy. As she sat back he slipped his arm across her shoulder, and pulled her face round to kiss her. She let him, but didn't move her hands. Finally she pushed him away, and turned to look at Sean, who was studying the dance floor with self-conscious interest. She laughed, and taking Sean's hand placed it over her breast. She waited for him to do something. Embarrassed, he began to scratch his head, but when she let his hand go he didn't pull away. He could feel the nipple straining against the silk and reached up to put his arms round her neck. He opened his mouth wide, too wide, and she pushed her tongue against his, beginning a long and sensual kiss.

Neil had moved round, shielding them from the dance floor, and she felt his hand move along her thigh. Momentarily she tensed, but then she let her legs slip slightly apart. He went no further than the top of her stocking, so she wriggled in her seat toward his fingers. She heard him catch his breath as his fingers touched her, and found her naked. She groaned into Sean's open mouth as Neil moved his fingers, and caught hold of her hand and pressed it to his groin.

She broke away, and looked from one to the other.

"So?" said Neil, grinning all over his face. "Which one of us is to be the lucky one?"

She smiled, and picked up her drink, sipping it slowly. She waited until she had finished, then put the empty glass back onto the table again.

"Well?" asked Sean, his voice thick.

She laughed, and tossed the hair away from her face. "How about both of you?"

They looked at each other first with amazement, and then excitement. Sean nodded first, then Neil broke into a grin. "Why not?" he shrugged. "I'm game."

"Then I'll get my coat," she said, and stood up.

 SEVEN

BOB EASED HIMSELF QUIETLY FROM THE BED, NOT WANTING to disturb Ellamarie who was still sleeping, and padded across the room. He looked at his watch. Ten minutes to three, still plenty of time before he had to be at the station.

Outside he could hear the hustle and bustle of Christmas shoppers coming from the King's Road. He slipped into his robe and went out to the kitchen to make some coffee.

There had been no rehearsals this afternoon. They would rehearse again on Monday, the day before

Christmas Eve, when they would break until 29 December. It was going well, though he could wish that Maureen Woodley was responding a little better. Maybe he should give her some extra time, alone. But how could he find the time himself? His production of *Don Giovanni* was going back to the Colisseum in February, and the Old Vic was practically pleading with him to do *Long Day's Journey Into Night.* And to add to it all, a film offer had come his way which he badly wanted to do. It had been almost two years since he had directed a film; he had won a BAFTA for *Remember Sundays?*

As he set two cups on the work surface he noticed a wallet of photographs which Ellamarie must have left on the table. Waiting for the kettle to boil he picked them up and started to flick through them. His face was smiling as he looked at them. They had taken them just over two years ago now, when they had gone to Scotland for a long weekend together. A honeymoon was what they had called it, and a honeymoon was indeed what it had been. He would never forget how they had made love for the first time, on the side of a mountain in the early evening sun. He could still see her now, her pale skin against the backdrop of green grass and wild flowers, reaching out her arms to him and whispering for him to make love to her. He swallowed the lump that had formed at the back of his throat as he remembered wondering at the time if it was possible to go on loving someone so much; it was, in fact he loved her even more now. And here was a picture of Mr. and Mrs. Duff who ran the small hotel they had stayed in. How Ellamarie had made them laugh. He felt sad as he went through the photographs, knowing that it was her uncertainty about their relationship that had made her steal back into the past. Then he laughed as he came across the miserably out of focus ones that she had taken of him on horseback, riding through a glen, and . . .

Oh Christ! How could he have forgotten? He had to get to Scheiders this afternoon to pick up Linda's new riding boots. And where was the list she had given him for things she wanted him to pick up from Harrods? He must have left it at the theater. Hell, that meant he'd have to go back there. And he'd left her present there too. Damn it! He looked at his watch again. He'd never have time to do it all, it would just have to wait until tomorrow. His mother would have to stay the night in the mews house with him here in London. He wouldn't tell Ellamarie that, of course. He sighed. Life would be so much easier if he could just stay here in London, with Ellamarie. He was going to miss her over Christmas, but there was no use thinking about it, he had to go home and that was that.

The kettle switched itself off, and he spooned the instant coffee into two mugs.

"Out of milk, I'm afraid." He jumped, and looked up to see Ellamarie watching him from the doorway.

"Then we'll have black," he said, but he didn't turn back to the coffee, instead he continued to look at her. Her face was still flushed from sleep, her mane of hair in chaos about her shoulders. She hadn't bothered to cover herself, and standing there in her pale nudity, he was entranced by her lack of self-consciousness.

She gave him a knowing smile and walked across to him, winding her arms about his neck. He ran his hands over her skin as he kissed her on the mouth, reacting to the sensation of her nudity against his robed body. She turned in his arms to present herself to him, and he could feel the desire rising in him once again. She murmured softly as he cupped her breasts in his hands and stooped to kiss them. As his mouth became more urgent, she gripped his shoulders, digging her fingers into his skin. Reluctantly, he moved away. Tomorrow he was returning to his wife, and he was afraid that in the throes of passion Ellamarie might mark him.

He kissed her lightly on the end of her nose. "You're insatiable," he whispered.

"I know," she grinned, and slipped her hand inside his robe. Feeling her take him between her fingers and move gently back and forth, he leaned back, unable now to stem the rising tide. She was smiling, looking into his face and watching the changing expressions. He reached out for her, but she pushed his hands away, and opened his robe. He did nothing to stop her and allowed his robe to fall to the floor. She kissed his neck, his shoulders, and wound her fingers through the thatch of hair on his chest. His breathing became heavier as she stopped to follow her hands with her mouth.

Then she dropped to her knees, kissing his belly, breathing against him. He looked down at her, meeting her eyes, and as she ran her tongue round her lips, he gripped the edge of the work surface, groaning aloud and closing his eyes, waiting for the warmth of her mouth to take him. Gently she began to kiss him, lingering kisses, with her mouth open, around the top of his thighs, across his belly, and around his testicles, taking them one at a time into her mouth, caressing them with her tongue until he thought he was going to explode.

Then with the tip of her tongue she began to trace the outline of his penis, kissing and biting gently along the stem. She lifted it away from his belly, and with her fingers lightly teasing, she held him in her hand, breathing softly onto him, letting him feel the moisture of her breath.

"Oh God, Ellamarie," he groaned, pulling her toward him. "Please, please, *now.*"

As she lifted him toward her mouth, he knew he was only moments away from climaxing. He sobbed as almost violently she covered him, and sucked him, and squeezed him with her tongue. Her hands held him, her mouth held him, and he burst into her, pulling at her hair, pushing her face hard into his groin, gasping as she drew every last drop of juice from his body.

He tried to catch his breath, and clung on to the surface behind him, not trusting his legs to take his full weight. She got quickly to her feet and circled her arms about his neck. His eyes were closed, but he could feel her looking at him, and pulled her head onto his shoulder.

They stood like that for a long time. She listening to the beat of his heart as it finally became steadier, he brushing his fingers over her bare shoulders.

"I love you," he whispered, when he had finally regained his breath. He tilted her face to look at him. "You're something else, you know that, don't you?"

She smiled. "Coffee?" she said, uuraveling herself from his arms.

He nodded and went to stand behind her as she poured. "I've got a surprise for you," he whispered in her ear, pulling her closer.

"You don't mean . . . ?" She turned to him with a seductive gleam in her eye.

He laughed. "No, not that. But if you don't put some clothes on, it could well be," and slapping her on the bottom, he went off into the lounge.

When she came in to join him she was wearing the pink satin robe he had bought for her birthday. He was relieved. Although his mother's train was not due in until six o'clock, time was running out. He looked at his watch, and immediately wished he hadn't. It was stupid of him, and something he tried never to do when he was with Ellamarie. She said nothing, but he didn't miss the look that flitted across her face. She handed him his coffee, and curled up at the other end of the settee where she could look at him but still reach out and touch him.

"You said you had a surprise for me. Am I going to like it?"

"I think so," he said, smiling and casting a sideways look at her. "I hope so."

"Then tell me what it is."

"See if you can guess."

"Hell, I don't know where to start. Give me a clue."

"Well, let me see. I know. Out of all the things in the world, what would you most like to happen?"

She stared at him. Was he . . . ?

He knew he had made a terrible mistake. He thought quickly, desperate to stop her from saying what was in her mind. "Yes, a film!" he declared. "I have been asked to direct *The Famous Tragedy of the Queen of Cornwall.* And I thought you might like to take the part of the Queen."

She turned quickly to hide her disappointment, and picked up her coffee.

"Well, aren't you pleased?" he asked, the levity of his voice sounding forced, even to him.

"Sure," she said. "Sure I'm pleased."

He turned away, furious at himself for the way in which he had broken the news to her. She saw his hand shake as he lifted his cup, and her heart went out to him. She knew that he was sorry, that he was mad at himself for leading her on, and he had only been trying to make her happy.

She lit up her face with a bright smile, and he only just managed to get his cup back onto the table before she threw herself across the settee and into his arms. She kissed him briefly on the mouth. "Did I ever tell you how crazy I am about you? Jeez, I can't believe it. A movie! Me, in a movie! *The Famous Tragedy,"* and she started spinning round the room. "When did it happen?" she asked, stopping a moment to look at him. "Why didn't you mention it before? When do we start shooting?"

He was laughing. "Oh, not for quite some time yet. You know what these things are like."

"But Bob," she cried, squeezing her hands together, "it's just wonderful. Can you believe it? Me, a movie star. Hell, it's what I've always wanted. Shakespeare and movies. Now I'll have done both. Does it mean we will be going to France and Cornwall? Will you go on a field trip first? Can I come too?"

He nodded.

"Oh God, I can't believe it," she shrieked. "For how long? It means I'll have you all to myself."

"Funny, I was thinking I was going to have *you* all to *myself.*"

"I can't wait! Is there a script I can read yet?"

"There will be, right after Christmas I hope."

"How is it?"

"It's going to be good. Very good, in fact. There are a couple of things that I want to discuss with the writer, though. But I think it should be ready for you to see at the beginning of the New Year."

"Oh Bob!" she said. "Just wait till I tell Jenneen, she'll be so thrilled for me. And Ashley. And Kate."

"And me." He pulled her back into his arms.

"And you," she sighed. "Oh, I love you so much, do you know that? I love you so much I could die."

She curled up in his arms, and he stroked her hair. Inwardly he gave a sigh of relief that the awkward moment had passed.

She was happy. It was what she wanted, to be with him, always working with him. And although her hopes had soared for a moment earlier, she knew in her heart that one day it would happen, and they would be together.

"What time do you have to leave?" she said, turning his watch round.

"In about half an hour. I have to go back to the theater first, to pick up some things."

"Oh?" She looked surprised. "I thought you'd brought everything with you?"

"No. I've just remembered, I've left some things there that I need to pick up."

"The script," she said, grinning up at him.

He laughed. "No," and almost immediately wished he had said yes.

"Then what?" She didn't know why she was pushing it. It wasn't important that he had to go back to the theater. But there was something in his manner, something that told her he didn't want her to know what he was going back for.

"Nothing important." He shifted position.

"If it's nothing important, then why are you going back for it?" she said, hating herself, and wishing she could stop interrogating him.

"Because I have to."

"Then what is it?"

He sighed. "All right," he said, "it's a Christmas present."

She sat up. Her heart was beginning to pound. "It's for her isn't it?"

"Yes," he said, and tried to take her hand.

She pulled away. Why couldn't he have lied to her? Jesus, hadn't she tried everything she could these last weeks to stop from thinking too much about Christmas? About him spending it with his wife. About her being alone. Her folks unable to fly out, or not wanting to fly out, and her unable to go back home.

"Ellamarie," he said, his voice was soft and pleading.

She didn't answer.

"I'm sorry. I shouldn't have told you."

"No," she said, shaking her head. "No, it's me. I'm being silly. Of course you've bought a gift for your wife. It wouldn't be right if you hadn't. I'm just being silly."

"I would rather be here, with you," he said, knowing it to be only half true.

"Would you?"

He nodded.

She was silent for a while, and Bob remained still, waiting for her to speak. When she did, she said what he had been dreading she would say.

"Earlier," she said, not looking at him, "earlier, when you said, you know, that you had a surprise for me?"

He tensed, and ran his fingers across his eyes.

"Do you know what I thought you were going to say?"

"Yes."

She turned to look at him. "I thought you were going to say that you were leaving your wife."

"I know. I'm sorry."

"Of all the things in the whole world, that is what would make me the happiest," she said. "That we could be together, always."

He took her hands in his, and looked into her face. "We will be. Soon, we will be."

"But when? Oh Bob, I know I shouldn't ask, but don't you know what it's like for me? Thinking of you with her. Talking to her, eating with her, sleeping with her."

"Just be patient, darling. We will be together, I promise."

"When will you tell her?"

"I don't know. Soon." He was beginning to feel trapped, but could see no way out.

"You've said yourself, she doesn't need you. It's the horses she loves. They're her life. She never comes up to town, never comes to see any of your plays. She has cut herself off from you. Surely she can't expect you to be happy, living like that."

"She doesn't see it like you do."

"Then just how does she see it? From where I'm sitting she doesn't see it at all. She's selfish, Bob. She doesn't think about you, or care about you. You've told me, time over time, that that side of your marriage has been dead for years. Surely she'd be happy if you gave her the house and the stables. She would have what she wants, and you could come to live here, with me. We could be together. Isn't that what you want?"

"Yes," he said, twisting her hair round his fingers, "yes, that is what I want. And I know what you're saying makes sense. But it's not easy to just cut off more than eleven years of your life."

"Well, can't you start by telling her that you have found someone else? You don't have to say that you are leaving. Give her some time to get used to the idea. And then, after a while, when she knows that you are serious, that you really are in love with someone else, she'll let you go. She can't want to make you stay if she knows you're not happy. You're not happy there, are you, Bob? It is me you want, isn't it?"

"Oh my darling, of course it's you that I want."

"Then tell her, Bob. Tell her, please."

"I'll try."

"No. Say you'll do it. Please say that you will tell her."

He was looking past her, his mind racing. What could he say? What could he do? He felt her hand on his cheek and she pulled his face round so that she could see into his eyes.

She looked like a child gazing at him, her eyes round and pleading. How could he deny her? He smiled and nodded. "OK," he said, "if the opportunity arises, I'll tell her," and he felt sick inside.

She threw her arms round him. "Oh, I love you," she cried. "You will never regret it. I promise, you will never regret it."

"I know," he said, but there was no warmth in his voice.

The drone of voices, accompanied by telephones and thundering typewriters, reached them through the closed door of Bill Pruitt's office. Everyone was talking about it. Jenneen Grey had not turned up for the shoot on Thursday morning. Ambitious Jenneen Grey, who lived for her work, had simply just not shown up.

Shaking his head, Bill closed his eyes and sighed. Anyone else would have lost their temper by now. Would have been shouting and raving, even threatening, but not him. He had been the editor of this program since its conception seven years ago, and it had always been a happy ship. He did not believe in the heavy-hand tactics of some of his colleagues. If there was a problem, then he wanted to know about it, and in his own paternal sort of way he would sort it. Having Jenneen Grey on board had never been easy. He was aware of the resentment of the others, particularly Stephen Sommers and Geoff Pentland, two reporters who believed that the kind of reporting done by Jenneen Grey should be left to a man. This series of interviews was practically the first thing that Jenneen had handled that could fit into a "woman's category," as they put it. At last Bill had thought that Steve and Geoff were beginning to settle down and accept her. But now she had blown it. Bill knew what they were saying out there. That Jenneen Grey thought this lightweight stuff was beneath her, that she was too grand to take on something as mundane and straightforward as these agent/client interviews, and had decided to make a stand by refusing to turn up at the location. He had heard Geoff's remark earlier about PMS, and being at home and having babies. Bill loathed that kind of sexist attitude, but on this occasion he had not risen to it. He had to speak to Jenneen first.

But it had got him nowhere. How could he defend her if she wouldn't even tell him where she had been yesterday morning?

He sighed again and turned away from the window. Jenneen was sitting by his desk, her head lowered, and her fingers pulling at a handkerchief in her lap.

"Jenn," he said. He saw her tense so he walked over to stand beside her. "Look at me, Jenn." She lifted her head and he saw that her eyes were red and swollen from all the crying she had done in the past twenty-four hours. "If you won't tell me where you were, then at least tell me something that I can tell Maurice Fellowes. Jesus Christ, make something up if you have to, but don't keep saying you're sorry. It might be good enough for me, but it won't hold with Maurice."

Jenneen shook her head. "I can't, Bill. I just can't."

"Then tell me the truth. If you like I'll promise it won't go any further, and then I'll make something up to tell Maurice. How's that?"

Jenneen bowed her head again. How could she tell him? How could she ever tell anyone? In sane moments even she could not believe in "Mrs. Green." She shuddered inwardly, sick with herself. It was the same feeling she had had the morning she had woken up in that seedy little hotel room in Brighton, and found the two boys, limbs intertwined with hers, asleep in the bed. She gagged as she felt the waves of self-loathing come over her again. But her own self-loathing had been nothing to what she had felt toward the boys.

"Can't you just make something up anyway?" she asked, glancing up at Bill, hardly able to meet his eyes for more than a second. And the look of pleading—and was it pain?—he saw in her eyes forced him to agree.

"I think you'd better go home for the rest of the day," he said. "Whatever has happened, it seems to have left you in some sort of shock, you look drained. Do you think you'll be all right for the studio tomorrow?"

She nodded.

"Have you done your links?"

"They're on my desk," she answered.

"Give them to Christine so she can get them to autocue, and then go home. I'll ring you later to see how you are."

She stood up to leave.

"Jenneen," he said as she reached the door. She turned back. "Nothing can be that bad."

Her eyes were cold, and her smile edged with bitterness. "It can," she whispered. "Oh yes, it can."

Strolling through Harrods was one of Kate's favorite pastimes. She often went, even when there was nothing particular she wanted to buy. It was exciting pushing through the crowds, wondering who she might be rubbing shoulders with. She was supposed to be buying Christmas presents this afternoon, but like every other year, she was buying as much for herself as she was for everyone else—probably more. She was quite laden down, what with the things she'd had to get for Mrs. Adams who lived upstairs as well, and her arms were aching. That alone should have been good enough reason to leave. Her father didn't like her shopping at Harrods so near to Christmas. It had been on the news again only last night that the IRA were planning another Christmas bomb package. Last year they had hit Harrods.

But Kate could not resist it. If she couldn't buy her Christmas presents in Harrods, then where else was she going to get them?

She had no reason to go to the fourth floor, other than it was Christmas and she just simply had to go to the fourth floor. As she stepped out of the lift she could already hear the tinkling of Christmas carols and the excited laughter of children coming from the Kingdom of Toys. She wondered if she would see Santa, and almost laughed out loud at the absurdity of her own excitement. Suddenly a little boy, unable to contain himself a moment longer, broke free of his mother and pushed past her, almost knocking her over.

"Ben!" his mother shouted after him. "I'm so sorry," she said, turning to Kate, and helping to pick up her bags.

"Please don't apologize. I'd be doing the same if I were his age."

"Mummy! Mummy!" yelled the errant Ben, who could not be seen, only heard. "Come and see this! I want one!"

"Oh dear," said the woman, "I knew it was a mistake to come here."

"Good luck," Kate laughed, and watched the woman weave her way toward the shouting voice.

Kate knew where she was heading, and after winding and pushing her way through what could only be described as an infant obstacle course, she found herself among the dolls' houses, the dolls, and all the pretty dresses and accessories to dress them up in. It was like being in Fairyland, and her eyes sparkled like those of a five-year-old. She laughed as she played with them. Some talked, some walked, most cried, a few wet themselves, one danced, and some did nothing at all except look pretty. She wished she could buy them all. She was completely oblivious to the odd looks that people were giving her.

She was giggling to herself at a doll who was telling her it was hungry when she noticed two blue eyes peering up at her from round the side of the counter, watching her with interest. They were the prettiest blue eyes she had ever seen, framed by wisps of white hair and round pink cheeks. She was a dream child, a tiny cherub. Kate looked back at her and smiled. The blue eyes opened a fraction wider.

"Hello," said Kate.

The little girl planted her thumb in her mouth.

"Does that taste nice?"

The child continued to stare.

"My name is Kate. Will you tell me yours?"

The little girl shook her head.

"Oh, I see. It's a secret is it?"

The little girl nodded.

"Then you mustn't tell me. Not if it's a secret."

The little girl took her other hand out of her coat pocket and reached out to touch the doll that Kate was holding. Kate bent down and handed it to her. "Do you like this one?"

Another nod.

"Would you like to hold her?"

The little face brightened, and taking the thumb from her mouth, the child wrapped her tiny, fat arms round the doll.

"I wonder if she speaks?" said Kate.

"No." The little girl's voice was no more than a whisper.

"I think she does," said Kate.

The little girl shook her head.

"She's still just a baby, is she?"

"Mmm."

"Will she be able to speak when she's as old as you?"

"Yes."

"And how old are you?"

"Four. How old are you?"

"Me? I'm thirty."

"My mummy is older than you," the girl announced with pride, suddenly talkative.

"Is she?"

"Yes. My mummy is twenty-six."

Kate laughed. "Oh, very old. Have you got any brothers and sisters?"

"A brother."

"And how old is he?"

"Six."

"Is he nice?"

"Sometimes. But mostly he's horrible! He hits my dolls."

"That isn't very nice, is it?"

"But I knock his soldiers over, and he gets cross with me, and shouts."

Kate had to fight with herself to keep from hugging the little girl. "I had a brother once," she said. "He was just the same. Boys can be awful sometimes, can't they? Tell you what, would you like to look at some more dolls?"

The little girl nodded, and so together, lost in a land of make-believe, they went from one doll to another, pulling strings, combing hair, laughing and giggling, and having a perfectly wonderful time. The child wouldn't be parted from the doll that Kate had first given her, so they were set upon trying to find a sister for it, no brothers allowed, when suddenly they were brought tumbling back to reality.

"Elizabeth! What are you doing?"

Elizabeth spun round, and Kate, on her knees, looked up to see a woman staring down at her, her face red and her eyes brimming with relief.

"Hello," said Kate, standing up. "I'm sorry, I know children shouldn't speak to strangers, but she's so pretty I couldn't help speaking to her. I meant no harm."

The woman smiled. "It's all right. It's just that I thought I'd lost her. Should have known that she would find her way back here, though."

"Mummy, can I have this dolly for Christmas?" Elizabeth held the doll up for her mother to see.

"No, Lizzie. You've got quite enough already."

"Oh please, Mummy. I promise I'll be a good girl."

"That's a promise I've yet to see kept."

Kate laughed. "She looks far too angelic to be naughty."

"That's what everyone thinks," said the woman. "You should see her at home."

"Please, Mummy," Elizabeth begged.

"I said no. Now let go so that I can put it back."

Kate looked down at Elizabeth's face and saw that she was about to cry. "If it's all right with you," she said to the woman, "I'd like to buy it for her." It was out before she could stop herself, and she was almost as surprised by her offer as the woman appeared to be.

"Oh no, no. You couldn't possibly."

"No, please, I'd like to."

"But it's far too expensive."

"Not really. And I'd like to."

Elizabeth was looking up, listening to the exchange going on far above her head. "Please, Mummy."

"But you don't even know us," said the woman, unable to think of any other objection.

"I know, but . . . Please, it would make me very happy."

An assistant appeared, and Kate seized the opportunity. "Could you wrap this doll please," she said. "I'd like to buy it."

The woman beside her seemed unsure of what to do. She waited until the doll was handed back, nicely wrapped in a pink box, then made to offer Kate the money.

"No, please don't," said Kate, and she looked down at Elizabeth and smiled.

"Really, I don't know what to say," said the woman. "It's so kind of you. Say thank you to the lady, Elizabeth," she added as Kate handed the parcel to the little girl.

"Thank you," said Elizabeth, smiling all over her face.

"You're very welcome," said Kate, and suddenly Elizabeth dropped the parcel and threw her arms round Kate's knees.

Kate stooped to hug the tiny figure. "You really are a very special little girl."

"I must say, you are extremely honored," said Elizabeth's mother, smiling. "Even I don't get that sort of treatment. At least, not often."

Kate let the little girl go, picked up the parcel and handed it to her. "I really must be going now."

Elizabeth's mother looked at her watch. "Would you like some coffee?" she asked.

"No thanks," said Kate, picking up her bags. "I'm late already. But thank you for the offer." She was already walking away.

"And thank you for the doll," the woman called after her.

Kate ran down the stairs and out into the cold air, trying to blink back the tears. Holding the child in her arms had made her acutely aware of the emptiness in her life, the loneliness that she tried to pretend wasn't there. She longed to have a child of her own, but she had no idea that the longing could be so overpowering. She told herself that it was Christmas, and people always get over-emotional at Christmas.

But the feel of the tiny body, so fragile, and so trusting in her arms, was to haunt her for some time to come.

EIGHT

JULIAN SAT AT HIS DESK, TAPPING A PEN AGAINST HIS FINGERS, one foot resting on an open drawer. Everyone had gone home, it was past seven o'clock, and though there was always something to do here at the office, today there was nothing that couldn't wait. The last-minute rush for Christmas was well in hand, and he had time now to sit back and reflect on the past week.

Getting the Newslink account was one of the best things that had ever happened to his agency. Conrad had been vociferous in his congratulations when Julian had rung to tell him. And it wasn't often that Conrad could be moved in such a way. Julian knew that he had a good team working for him now, one that could easily compete with Conrad's people in New York. He was able to call upon some of the biggest and best directors to make the TV commercials, as well as some of the most talented art directors. The ideas that Ashley and her team had come up with for Newslink were not far short of brilliant, and after the stress and anguish of the creative review they had just undergone, Julian was in a position now to sit back and feel satisfied, contented.

So why wasn't he?

Blanche had come home on Wednesday, and he had been genuinely delighted to see her. Though she must have been tired and suffering from jet-lag she had insisted that they go out for a late supper, where they could be alone, and talk.

As usual, she had been full of fun, and had made him laugh about the things she had got up to in Sydney. But she said that she was glad to be back and with him again, she really had missed him.

He was quite taken aback when she told him that she had had an affair with someone in Sydney. He couldn't think why he was so surprised, he had suspected it all along. But nevertheless, it was a shock to hear her admit to it. She explained that she wanted no secrets between them, and that though she enjoyed the affair very much, it had only been an affair, and that he, Julian, was the only man that she truly loved.

"Of course, I expect you have had affairs too," she said. "And don't tell me you haven't. I've seen the way women look at you. You'd be more than a saint if you hadn't succumbed. But don't worry, I don't mind. I think it's right, don't you? To sow your wild oats before you marry. That way neither of us will look back and have regrets."

He said he supposed she was right.

"So," she prompted. "What were their names? Or was there only one?"

He dismissed it by laughing and saying that they were too numerous to mention, and that he was glad she was back, so that he no longer had to fight off the hungry masses. He didn't want to tell her about Ashley. It would somehow cheapen what he felt for her if he were to tell Blanche, in an offhand way. So he kept it to himself.

Then they talked about the letter Blanche had written him several weeks before, when she had asked him if he had any objection to announcing their wedding date at a small, intimate party at her father's house on Christmas Eve. He smiled at her, and taking her hand told her that of course he had no objection. And so, over the last couple of days, they had started to make plans for their wedding.

It was partly because of the honeymoon that he was still here at the office. He had intended to get out the atlas in the hope that it would inspire him with a few ideas. But ever since his secretary had gone home he had just sat there, doing nothing. He tried to think of all sorts of things. About the agency, about Christmas, about the wedding, but his mind seemed to reject them all, until he knew that there was no point in denying it any longer: he couldn't think about anything else because all he really wanted to think about was Ashley.

He had seen the look on her face when he had come out of his office unexpectedly today, and had found her talking to his secretary. He had noticed that she had become more friendly with Amanda this last week, and he knew why. He knew the pain she was suffering. Wasn't he feeling it himself? But there was nothing to be done. He had ended it, and that was how it was going to have to stay. He had every intention of marrying Blanche, indeed he wanted to marry Blanche. But he wanted Ashley too.

Seeing her around the place was making it more difficult to bear. He didn't want to ask her to leave. He couldn't do that to her. He hated himself enough as it was. It had taken every ounce of willpower he had, to walk away from her that night. He would never forget the look of confusion and betrayal in her eyes when she realized that he wasn't going to tell her that he loved her too. And the Christmas tree, the bloody Christmas tree. She had done it for him. And the presents, all for him. He was such a bastard! He should never have let things go on so long. In his stupidity he had believed that it would all work out fine in the end. But it hadn't. She was miserable, and he was miserable, and there was nothing he could do about it.

He got up and walked round his desk. Then he walked back again. He walked to the window and looked out. The traffic was in its usual snarl; just how he felt inside. He walked to the door of his office, then back to his desk. He sat down, stood up. Walked to the cabinet and poured himself a drink. He was behaving like an idiot, but his guilt was so great he was finding it difficult to bear.

He missed Ashley. He loved her. Yes, damn it! He loved her! But he also loved Blanche. It was a different kind of love, but he did love Blanche. Besides, everyone expected him to marry Blanche now. He couldn't just back out, and desert her too. But she could handle it much better than Ashley could. Ashley might be tough at work, but when it came to love, and her son, she was vulnerable. And he had hit her where it hurt most.

He thought about Alex. How could he have done it to the child? He couldn't bear to think of Alex hating him. He wanted to make it up to him in some way. But how could he? He had hurt Alex's mother, and Julian knew that Alex could never forgive that. But surely there was something he could do to make it up to the boy. And to Ashley. If he married her, they would all be happy. But what about Blanche?

Dear God, was there nothing he could do to ease this conflict?

He poured himself another drink.

And then he had an idea. He would buy them both, Ashley and Alex, something very special for Christmas. Something that they both really wanted. He thought about it, and the more he thought about it, the better the idea seemed. All he had to do was think of something. And then that came to him too.

He picked up the phone and dialed. It wasn't as easy to fix as he had assumed, but several phone calls and two gin and tonics later, it was done.

He heaved a sigh of relief as he put the phone down for the last time. OK, his conscience was an expensive one, but what else could he do? It was something that would make both Ashley and Alex happy, and, although he didn't want to admit it, would ease his guilt too.

He put on his coat, and turned off the light and left the office.

The days leading up to Christmas were busy ones for all of them. They had hardly been in touch with one another the last week, so by the time they met up in the cocktail bar at the Ritz, the night before Christmas Eve, there was a great deal to catch up on.

Kate was in a great dilemma. Ellamarie had come straight from rehearsals bringing Nicholas Gough, who was playing Sebastian in *Twelfth Night*. Nicholas was someone whom Kate had had her eye on for some time, but until now he had remained elusive. She had just been on the point of saying how pleased she was to see him when Jenneen had arrived with Joel Martin. Kate's mouth fell open, and for several seconds she had been unable to speak.

"Careful, your libido's about to dribble over your chin," Ashley whispered.

"Are you surprised?" said Kate. "I mean, look at him." She leaned over to whisper in Ashley's ear. "I'm going to get laid tonight if it's the last thing I do."

"Ah, here's Bob," Ellamarie interrupted, and threw her arms round him as he came in.

"Merry Christmas, everyone," Bob cried, and lifted the glass Ellamarie pushed into his hand.

The others raised theirs too.

"Can't we sit down?" Ellamarie grumbled. "My feet are killing me."

"I don't know why," Bob said, under his breath, "you've spent the best part of the afternoon on your back."

She choked on her drink and looked around to see if anyone had heard.

From the expression on his face, Joel Martin had.

"Do you have to?" she said to Bob, trying not to laugh.

"No, but you were begging me." Bob took another drink.

"I was not. Besides, I didn't mean that. We're in the Ritz now, try and behave, will you?"

"Over here!" Ashley called, patting a seat next to her.

Treading on Bob's foot, Ellamarie pushed her way through the crowd and went to join the others who had made their way to the corner of the cocktail bar.

"Joel Martin," Joel said, extending his hand to Bob.

"Bob McElfrey. You came with Jenneen, didn't you?"

"In a manner of speaking," Joel answered. "She tells me you do this every year at Christmas."

"What, the Ritz?" said Bob, looking around. "It's a tradition of theirs."

"Tell me, who's that sitting next to Jenneen? I don't think we were introduced."

Bob looked over. "Ashley Mayne," and seeing the look in Joel's eye, he added: "Forget it. Getting over a broken heart at the moment."

Joel nodded, very slowly, and kept his eyes on Ashley. Ashley turned away. She wouldn't have admitted it to Kate, but handsome as he was, she had disliked him on sight.

Bob and Joel strolled over to the table and the others moved round to make room. They were all laughing at something Jenneen had said, and Joel noticed that Ashley was blushing.

"Ah, Bob," said Jenneen, pulling him down between her and Ellamarie, "perhaps you can answer the question."

"What question?" said Bob.

"Jenneen, please," said Ashley.

"No, I want to know," said Jenneen. "Bob, tell us, because you know everything. Why is a blow job called a blow job?"

Bob's mouth dropped open and Ellamarie burst out laughing.

"Well?"

Bob looked to Joel and then to Nick, in the hope they might help him out. They both shook their heads, and Jenneen was still waiting.

"Well, do some women actually blow on it?" she prompted. "And if they do, do they get a tune out of it?" Ashley, Kate and Ellamarie looked at one another and collapsed into laughter.

"That would surely depend on how musical one's ear is," said Joel.

"I beg your pardon?" Ellamarie choked.

"I mean, if one considers cries of ecstasy to be music, then yes, one can indeed get a tune out of it."

Several heads turned as they shrieked with laughter.

"Well, what I want to know now," said Jenneen, "is do you actually enjoy it?"

"Are you kidding?" Bob cried.

"I don't mean you," said Jenneen. "I mean Ellamarie. Or Kate. Or you, Ashley. Do women actually enjoy it? Do you swallow it?"

"Jenneen!" Ashley groaned.

"Yes?" said Jenneen.

"People can hear you."

"So what? I'm intrigued to know, and I'll bet they are too," she said, staring at a woman at the next table. She turned back to Ashley. "Do you swallow it?"

"Me?" said Ashley.

"Well, I wasn't talking to Bob."

"I'm not answering that," said Ashley.

Kate piped up. "Darling, one can swallow anything, provided it is sufficiently seasoned . . ."

Jenneen looked at her.

"Molière," Joel said, by way of explanation. "And I should like you to know I take my condiments everywhere with me. All three of them."

"I think this conversation is getting out of hand," said Ashley. "Shall we change the subject?"

"Orgasms?" Jenneen suggested.

"I'm going to the ladies' room," said Ashley, getting to her feet.

"Some folk like to be more private about their comings and goings than others," Ellamarie explained to Joel.

Ashley tugged her hair and Joel's eyes followed her as she weaved her way across the room and disappeared.

Suddenly remembering the purpose of inviting Joel Martin, Jenneen introduced him to Kate. His expression, as he looked her up and down, was one of lazy calculation. Kate felt her blood begin to race. Jenneen and Ellamarie exchanged knowing glances, and Nick got up and wandered over to talk to someone he knew.

"Holy shit!" Ellamarie suddenly cried.

Bob looked up. "Oh no," he groaned, "that's all we need."

"Who is it?" Joel asked, following their gaze and seeing two extremely distinguished looking men standing at the door.

"Ashley's ex," Bob sighed.

"The dark one or the fair one?"

"The fair one."

"Who's that divine creature with him?" Kate whispered to Jenneen.

"I don't know, but he can have me any time."

Ellamarie nudged Jenneen. "That must be Blanche," she said, as a petite, smiling face emerged from behind Julian. "I think someone had better go and warn Ashley," and she got up to go. Kate and Jenneen followed her.

Blanche was looking around, her face alight with pleasure, heavily engrossed in "celeb-spotting," as she called it. Julian was amused by her excitement. As a waiter showed them to a table, he told her she had been away from London for too long.

A few minutes later Julian caught Bob's eye across the room, and they nodded and smiled to one another. Blanche noticed, and strained to see who it was that Julian had just acknowledged.

"Oh Julian!" she gasped, turning to him and clutching his arm. "Isn't that Bob McElfrey, the director? I didn't know you knew him."

"Yes," said Julian.

"Oh do let's go and say hello to him, darling. I've always wanted to meet him."

Having seen Bob sitting with someone he didn't recognize, Julian assumed that it was safe to go over. He had always liked Bob, and he would enjoy introducing him to Blanche, and Conrad.

Bob saw them coming and guessed immediately that Julian had misread the situation. He looked around wildly. How could he warn him? No solution seemed to offer itself, so Bob just sat back and hoped that Julian and his party would simply say their hellos and depart the table before Ashley decided to return from the ladies' room.

He was out of luck. As he stood up to shake hands with Blanche he caught sight of Ellamarie pushing her way through the crowd toward him. Ashley was right behind her. He turned to shake Conrad by the hand.

"Jesus Christ," Ellamarie muttered, "I didn't think he'd be so stupid."

"What? What's happening?" said Jenneen.

"Look!" Ellamarie hissed, inclining her head toward their table.

"Fucking hell!" said Jenneen, then clapped her hand over her mouth as a passing waiter turned to look at her.

"My sentiments exactly," said Ellamarie.

Kate took hold of Ashley's hand. It was like ice. "What do you want to do?"

Ashley shook her head, and they all looked at one another, neither of them able to think of an answer. Ashley's face was white, her eyes transfixed by the figure of Blanche Wetherburn, laughing and smiling up into Julian's face, totally oblivious to what was happening elsewhere in the room.

"We'll go over," said Ashley. "There's nothing else we can do."

"We could always go back to the ladies', until they've gone," Kate suggested.

"No," said Ashley. "I'll have to meet her sometime. It'll be easier with all of you here."

"Are you sure?" said Kate, still looking very doubtful.

Ashley forced a smile. "Sure," she said. "Come on, we're causing a jam standing here," and she pushed her way ahead of the others.

Bob, seeing Ashley coming toward them, turned

to Julian. Julian was laughing at something Joel was saying, and there was no way Bob could warn him. Then the carol service in the Long Gallery began.

"Blanche," Bob cried, grabbing hold of her arm, "why don't we go and watch the carol singers?" And before a startled Blanche had a chance to answer, he had swept her out of harm's way. Well, it was the best he could think of on the spur of the moment. Ellamarie would be proud of him.

Julian watched them go, and turning back to the table he remarked to Conrad: "She'll be talking about this for . . ."

Conrad looked up to see Julian staring at something in what seemed to be total horror. He turned round to see who, or what, had caused such a sudden transformation in his partner.

"Hello, Julian," Ashley said, her voice little more than a whisper.

"Hello," Julian's voice was no louder.

"Julian," said Ellamarie, through clenched teeth.

"Hello, Ellamarie. Kate, Jenneen."

Kate and Jenneen gave him curt nods, and sat down.

"I had no idea that you would be here tonight," Julian said, turning back to Ashley, and trying to put the sound of polite inquiry into his voice.

"No," said Ashley, "I don't suppose you did."

Julian flushed. Conrad, having read the situation almost immediately, looked on with amused interest.

"How are you, Julian?" said Ellamarie, breaking the embarrassed silence.

"Very well, thank you."

"I trust you are enjoying this," she said, belatedly sweeping her arm to indicate the carol singers.

Julian didn't answer. He looked at Ashley again, but she was watching the concert, and sipping champagne.

Jenneen turned to Kate. "Have we found out yet

who that is with him?" she whispered, flicking her eyes
toward Conrad.

Kate shook her head. "I'll fight you for him,
though. He's beautiful."

Jenneen laughed. "By the look of it there are a few
others you'll have to fight too," and she nodded toward
the next table where the women, with complete disre-
gard for their men, were openly admiring the man with
jet black hair and an expression to match.

Conrad was aware that they were talking about
him, but chose to ignore it. He was used to it. He sipped
the champagne Bob had offered before he'd left, and
out of the corner of his eye watched Julian and Ashley.

"Where's Bob?" said Ellamarie, looking around.

"Watching the carol singers with Blanche," said
Julian, still looking at Ashley. He saw her flinch and
felt pleased. He needed to know that she still cared.

"Blanche who?" said Ellamarie, looking at him
with innocent eyes.

Julian wished himself a thousand miles away.
"Oh," he said, suddenly pulling himself together. "I'm
forgetting my manners. Ladies, this is Conrad Frazier,
Conrad, let me introduce you."

Jenneen, Kate and Ellamarie all gave Conrad their
most attractive smiles, but his only response was one
of polite disinterest.

"And Ashley you've met," Julian added.

Conrad looked Ashley up and down in quick ap-
praisal.

"Actually, we haven't ever met," said Ashley, gritting her teeth. At any other time she would have been
intrigued finally to meet the partner she had heard so
much about, but under these strained circumstances,
and given Conrad Frazier's aloof and arrogant manner,
she was finding it extremely difficult to be polite.

Julian appeared surprised that this was their first
meeting. "Ashley's an Account Director here in London," he explained. "She's a very good one too."

"Patronizing bastard!" Kate hissed to Jenneen.

Ashley looked at Conrad's face and decided she would be very happy for this to be their last meeting too. Remembering just in time that he was her boss, she shook his hand, then turned away before he could treat her in the same offhand manner he had her friends.

"Somehow I don't think Ashley's impressed," Ellamarie muttered to Jenneen.

"Why don't they go?" said Kate.

"Because Blanche is over there with Bob," said Ellamarie. "Jesus, he is so stupid at times, he just doesn't think."

"Here they come now," said Jenneen, and as one the three of them, Kate, Jenneen and Ellamarie, looked up. Loyal to Ashley they might be, but they were all dying to get a good look at Blanche.

"I always imagined her to be dark," said Ellamarie.

"Me too," said Kate.

Jenneen nudged them, and nodded toward Ashley.

"Oh God," Kate whispered, "it must be like living a nightmare."

And indeed it was. Despite all the champagne she had drunk, Ashley was now quite sober. Her stomach was churning, and all she wanted to do was run. It was hard to comprehend that standing there, right in front of her, was the man she loved. And he was treating her like a stranger. That hurt more than anything else. And she now had to endure the humiliation of being introduced to his future wife. She closed her eyes, trying to fight off the rising nausea.

Blanche was upon them and taking Julian's hand. She turned and smiled at Ellamarie.

"I borrowed your husband for a while," she said. "I do hope you don't mind."

"Not a bit," said Ellamarie. What else could she say?

Blanche looked at Julian expectantly.

"Blanche," he said at last, "let me introduce you. This is Ashley, Ellamarie, Jenneen and Kate. Bob and Joel you've already met. Ladies, this is Blanche Wetherburn uh, Conrad's cousin."

Conrad choked and turned away to hide his smile. Bob too couldn't resist a grin.

"Hello," said Blanche. "Now let me see if I can remember your names. Darling, you really are perfectly dreadful at this sort of thing. You," she said, turning to Kate, "are Kate." Kate nodded. "And you," she continued, looking at Jenneen, "are Jenneen." Jenneen smiled a very insincere smile. "And you," Blanche went on, "are Ella Mary . . ."

"Ellamarie," Ellamarie interrupted, smiling sweetly. "Mur, as in murder." Bob avoided Julian's eyes.

"Perhaps we should be going back to our own table now," Julian said.

"And I am Ashley," said Ashley, standing up and holding out her hand. "It's so nice to meet you, Blanche. I've heard a great deal about you." Blanche took Ashley's hand, and looked at her with interest. "I work at Frazier, Nelmes," Ashley explained.

"Oh, I see," said Blanche, and she did. "Very nice to meet you. I expect we'll be seeing a lot more of one another, in the future."

"Really?" said Ashley. "That will be nice."

Julian looked decidedly uncomfortable and was longing to tear Blanche away. But Blanche wasn't finished yet.

"Yes," she was saying, and she turned to Julian. "I don't think there's any harm in telling anyone now, do you darling?" and she reached out for his hand.

Julian closed his eyes.

"You will be the first to know," Blanche went on, turning back to the table. "Julian and I have set the date. We are going to be married at Easter."

NINE

Jenneen dropped Ashley at her flat. She offered to go in with her, but Ashley had insisted that she wanted to be alone. She had a lot to do before she went home tomorrow, she told Jenneen, and there were more reports to be got together so she'd have to go into the office in the morning. And she hadn't wrapped all of Alex's presents yet. If she didn't get a move on she'd never get any sleep tonight.

Jenneen's heart went out to her. Fate had a cruel way sometimes of adding to the agony one already suffered. If only Julian and Blanche hadn't decided on Easter.

She waited for Ashley to go inside, then drove off.

Her heart sank as she pulled up outside her own flat in Argyll Road. Sitting on the steps, his long gray raincoat falling over his knees, head resting in his hands, was Matthew.

"Dear God," she muttered, "they're all crawling out of the bloody woodwork tonight." She was tempted to drive on, but he had seen her, and she knew that he would only wait till she returned.

She opened the car door and got out. "What are you doing here?" she snapped.

He looked up, but made no move to get to his feet. "I wanted to see you, Jenn."

She slammed the door and locked it.

"I think we should talk."

"I don't think we have anything to say to one another, Matthew."

"I do," he answered.

"You want something, don't you? You wouldn't be here if you didn't."

He grinned. "You've got a very suspicious nature, Jenneen Green, uh Grey."

Jenneen froze. Was it a deliberate slip of the tongue?

"Something the matter?" Matthew asked, pulling himself to his feet.

"Yes, you!"

"Don't be like that, Jenn. Look, I promise, I haven't come here tonight for any other reason than to see you. I don't want any money, no favors. I just want to talk."

"Pull the other one, Matthew."

He shrugged. "OK, don't believe me. But you'll see."

Jenneen looked at him suspiciously. It wasn't like him not to be drunk when he came to see her, and she could tell just by looking at him that he wasn't. He smiled and she looked away.

"You're shivering," he said. "Why don't we go inside? I think you'll want to hear what I've got to say." To her surprise she saw that he looked doubtful and unsure of himself. "At least, I hope you will," he added.

Had something happened that she didn't know about? Had he decided that his revenge had gone on long enough? Oh please God, if only that were true.

"Let's go in and have a drink."

"No thanks," she said wearily, "I've had plenty already."

"Then keep me company," he said.

"You mean sit and watch you while you do an impression of a sponge," she replied, nastily. "No thanks."

"I'm on the wagon," he said.

"Oh? I wonder how long you'll be able to keep that up."

"Please, Jenn, I'd like to talk to you."

"Matthew, I've already told you, we have nothing to say to one another."

He thrust his hands in his pockets and turned away. For a moment she thought he was going to leave, but then he turned back. "Look, it's just that I want to tell you how sorry I am, and I can hardly do it here, in the middle of the street, now can I?"

"Matthew, I'm not interested in your apologies. The only thing I am interested in is seeing you disappear from my life, for good!"

"Jenneen, please," he said. "I've got to talk to you. Please! Let me come inside."

A sudden gust of wind made her pull her coat tighter round her, and she wiped the drizzle from her face. She knew she had no choice but to take him in. If she didn't, he'd probably only force his way in.

She led the way up the stairs to her flat. Once inside she took off her coat and followed him into the lounge. He was at her small bar, pouring two drinks. She was surprised to see him with an orange juice. Perhaps he really did intend to become a reformed character.

"So," she said, leaning against the wall. "What do you want to talk about?"

"Us."

"What do you mean 'us'? There isn't any us."

"No," he admitted. "But there used to be."

"That was a long time ago."

"I know, but I haven't forgotten."

Her eyes sparkled with anger. "Forgotten what? The way you beat me up? The orgy of benders you were committed to, and tried to drag me into? Your vile accusations? Is that what you remember, Matthew? Because it's what I remember."

"I suppose it is," he sighed. "And I can't say I blame you. There's no excuse for the way I behaved toward you, except maybe I just couldn't see sense for a while. I ruined my own life, and I tried to hang the blame on you. I've tried to punish you ever since, and now I'm ashamed, Jenn. Truly ashamed. And I want you to know that I don't blame you. I never did, really, but as I said, I suppose it was just that I couldn't make any sense of anything at the time. But I've decided to try and make a go of it again, and I wanted you to be the first to know."

She regarded him closely, suspicion still in her eyes. "You're not seriously expecting me to congratulate you, are you?"

"No. No, that would be too much to expect."

"You're damn right it would."

"Jenn, please. Don't be angry with me. I'll repay the money I took from you, I'll do anything to make it up to you."

"It's too late, Matthew, you'll never be able to do that."

"At least let me try."

She looked at him, his eyes were sad, and she wondered if he really meant it. He was looking better. He had lost some weight, and his pallor was healthier than the last time she had seen him. He was looking into his glass, and she was reminded of a little boy whose mother had walked out and left him. She couldn't help it, but she found herself feeling sorry for him.

"Matthew," she said, her voice much softer now.

He looked up.

"Do you really mean it? Do you really want to make it up to me?"

He nodded. "Yes, Jenn. I do."

"Then leave me alone. Please, just leave me alone."

He sighed. "I want to. Believe me, I want to. But I can't. I know it's going to sound absurd after everything I've done, but I think I'm in love with you."

She stared at him. Had he gone completely mad? "You do remember that it was you who finished it between us?"

"Yes," he said. "I remember."

"Then why?"

"I don't know. I don't understand it myself." He sounded weary and defeated. His shoulders began to shake, and she realized that he was crying.

"Oh my God," she said under her breath. "Matthew, please, pull yourself together."

He looked into her eyes, and for the first time in over a year she was reminded of how handsome he was. She wiped the tears from his cheeks with her fingers, and allowed him to take the glass from her. Then, taking her in his arms, he kissed her. Tenderly, with no building passion, just tenderness and love.

She pushed him away. "Matthew, stop! Please stop! I can't! Not after everything . . . No, stop!" she cried, as he took her in his arms again. This time he pressed himself against her, and buried his tongue in her mouth. "I can't stop, Jenneen," he growled. "I love you, don't you understand?" She felt herself beginning to weaken. Oh God, what was happening to her? Did she have no control over her sexual appetite? This was madness. After all he had put her through, the humiliation, the degradation, still she responded to him.

Kate was lying in bed, her head propped up on one arm, gazing down at Joel, who was still sleeping. After a minute or two she touched the dark hair that was stuck to the side of his face, and ran her thumb across his early-morning beard. His eyelids were so dark they looked shadowed. She leaned over and dropped a kiss onto them.

His long lashes fluttered, and slowly his eyes began to open. Immediately a pain shot through his head. His hangover was worse than he had thought it was going to be, and all he wanted to do was sleep.

Quickly he closed his eyes again, and turned over. Kate snuggled in behind him, molding herself to his body. She was running her fingers across his belly, sending his muscles into spasm. He caught her hand, and pulled it up to his chest. Jesus, there was nothing worse than waking up in someone else's bed when you had a hangover. Especially when that someone was a woman desirous of attention. He turned onto his front, leaving her hand trailing across his back. If she wanted to tickle him somewhere, then let it be there. He liked that, and it would send him off to sleep again.

But Kate had other ideas, and finally Joel had to give in and accept that there was to be no more sleep for him. Not yet anyway. It would be easier if he were like other men, those who awoke with an erection. But he had never been good first thing in the morning.

He sighed, and turned to face her. The look in her eyes confirmed all he had suspected. Some women were never satisfied. But he had to admit that the idea was beginning to grow on him, so to speak.

"Something you want?" he whispered.

She nodded.

"I thought so." Holy shit, the way she was looking at him he could do anything with her. His mouth twisted into a smile. "Just what exactly did you have in mind?"

"This," she said, taking him in her hand, and feeling him begin to grow.

"Oh," he said, looking into her eyes.

She leaned forward and kissed him on the mouth, but his arms remained folded across his chest.

"Is there something in particular that you would like to do with it?" he asked.

"Whatever you would like me to do with it."

He really was beginning to wake up now. He didn't know her well enough yet, but she would soon catch on to what he wanted.

"What about here?" he said, pushing his fingers between her legs.

She gasped, and nodded.

"Then ask me."

She looked confused.

"Ask me to put it there," he said.

"Please will you put it there," she said softly.

"Beg me!" he murmured, closing his eyes.

She couldn't do as he said.

"Beg me!" he said again.

She swallowed, and opened her mouth to speak.

His eyes were gleaming as he looked at her. "You want it, you beg for it."

"I can't," she whispered.

He pushed his fingers into her. "Come on," he said. "Tell me just how much you want it. Let me hear you beg."

He was becoming harder and harder now. This kind of talk, or was it power over women, never failed to turn him on. Especially with a woman like Kate Calloway. So refined and proper.

"Please!" she said.

"Please what?"

"Please will you make love to me?"

"You mean, will I fuck you?"

She nodded, her cheeks were crimson.

"Then say it?"

He heard her swallow.

"Go on," he said, his eyes burning. "Ask me to fuck you."

"Will you fuck me?"

He rolled over on top of her, and pushed into her. "Ask me again!" he cried. "Go on, beg me, beg me to fuck you, hard!"

She said nothing, but clung to him, as he thrust himself against her.

"Tell me how it feels," he said, his voice unsteady.

"It feels good," she sobbed, and began to move with him.

His love-making was fierce, and he rolled her over and over, pushing her and pulling her, squeezing her breasts, bruising her mouth with his kisses. He rolled onto his back and pulled her onto him again.

"Ride me!" he growled.

By now Kate could feel her inhibitions fleeing. His mouth was a thin line of aggression, his eyes blazed with lust. She leaned forward and placing a hand either side of him she rode him with all her might.

"Speak!" he yelled. "Say something to me."

She chose the richest vocabulary she knew, and screamed it into his face. He caught her by the hair, and threw her onto her back. His mouth was almost cruel as he pressed it to hers. She arched her back, and clawed her nails across his buttocks. His fingers dug cruelly into her shoulders and he cried out to God as finally he was spent.

Soaked in his own perspiration, he rolled over onto his back, covering his eyes with his arm, and breathing heavily. She put her arms round him, and looked into his face, but he didn't move.

The spasms inside her body were beginning to ease, and she waited for him to regain his breath before he spoke. "You know," she whispered, "last night. Last night was the first time for me in over a year."

He didn't hide his surprise. "A year?" he said, but he didn't lift his arm from his eyes. "That's a long time for anyone, especially a woman who fucks like you."

She wished he would lift his arm. "I suppose you could say I was saving myself," she said.

This time he raised his arm and looked up into her face. He wasn't smiling; on the contrary, he looked almost angry. "Then all I can say is I hope it was worth waiting for."

She kissed him on the cheek. "Oh, it was."

He looked at his watch. Alarm bells were starting

in his head, and he knew he would do well to get out of here fast. She was serious, she really had been saving herself. Holy shit! Why him?

"Would you like some breakfast?" she said quickly.

"I think it's time I was going."

"So soon?" she said. "After all, it is Christmas Eve."

"What difference does that make?"

"None, I suppose. But do you have to rush off?"

"I've got a lot to do today. Still got presents to buy." He pulled himself up from the bed.

"What about some coffee then?"

"No thanks, haven't got time. Where are my clothes?"

"Where you left them."

He scratched his head.

"In the drawing room."

"Oh yes," and he left the room.

Kate stayed beside the bed and watched him go, furious and humiliated. A few minutes later she heard him whistling in the lounge as he pulled on his clothes. She slipped on her robe and went to stand in the doorway.

"What are you doing for Christmas?" he said, when he saw her watching him.

"I'm going down to my parents, this afternoon."

"Oh." He sat down on the settee to pull on his socks.

"What are you doing?" she asked.

"Going to my brother's in Hampstead."

"How super."

He didn't know if she was being sarcastic or not. People like her often used the strangest and most unsuitable vocabulary. "Where's the nearest Underground?"

"South Kensington. Go to the end of the street into Fulham Road and turn right," she said, deliberately directing him in the opposite direction to the Tube, and she flounced back into the bedroom. Of all the rotten bastards! She had never felt quite so used in her life. How dare he just come here, fuck her and leave? Treat her as though she was some common pick-up. Men! She hated them!

"Let yourself out," she called. "I'm going to have a bath." She slammed the bathroom door, and locked it. Two could play at this game.

She turned on the taps, and sat on the edge of the bath, feeling utterly miserable. She had really liked him. OK, he was a bastard, but that made him more of a challenge. Besides, she had wanted to talk to him about her novel. They could have more in common than sex, if only he would give it a chance. And now she would probably never hear from him again. She felt cheap. Men could put it wherever they pleased, then just pass on to the next one. Didn't they realize that for women it was different?

She heard a tap on the door, and looked up.

"Kate!"

Be thankful for small mercies, she thought, at least he remembers my name. "Yah," she answered, and began to hum.

"Can I come in?"

"What do you want?"

"To say goodbye."

Well, what was the harm? She unlocked the door and opened it a fraction.

"Bye," she said, and started to close it again.

He jammed his foot against it. "Is that all?"

"Is that all what?"

"All that I'm going to get?"

"Exactly what else did you have in mind?"

"Well, I thought perhaps a kiss."

She let go of the door, and turned back to the bath. She knew she was being weak, but she couldn't help herself.

Joel watched her as she leaned over to turn off the taps. He was sorry now for having been so abrupt with her. He turned her to face him. "I think I'll call a taxi," he said. "So how about that coffee before I go?"

"There's a phone beside the bed," she snapped. "I expect you noticed it when you were in it, last night."

"Kate, come on, don't be like that. I thought we had a good thing going here."

"Oh really?"

"Didn't you?"

"I don't know what to think."

"Look, I'll give you a call over Christmas. Arrange to meet up when you get back to London. How's that?"

"How the Almighty doth bestow favors," she mumbled.

"Sorry?"

"Nothing. I'll write my number down for you. When will you ring?" God, did she have no pride?

"Tomorrow, wish you Happy Christmas, eh?"

"Promise?" This was called groveling.

"Promise," he said, and tipped her face up to his. "Do I get a kiss then?"

She smiled, and put her arms round his neck.

"I'll go and call a cab," he said as he let her go.

She followed him into the bedroom, and jotted her parents' number onto a piece of paper.

"Tell you what," he said. "I'll make the coffee."

"A man in the kitchen. What one's always wanted."

He hardly had time to drink it before Mrs. Adams was at the door asking if she could borrow some milk. She forced her way into the flat in her usual inexorable fashion, and looked disapprovingly at Joel as he lifted the entryphone to speak to the taxi driver who had arrived downstairs.

Kate almost pushed Mrs. Adams out of the flat. "Here's your coat," she said to Joel, slipping her telephone number into the pocket.

Joel swallowed the remainder of his coffee and put the cup back on the table. "Thanks for a great time," he said, brushing his mouth against hers.

"Bye," she said. "Don't forget to ring me tomorrow." But he had already gone.

Ellamarie rang Ashley at the office to tell her how Maureen Woodley had shown up at the Ritz after she'd left, in a dress that was two sizes too small, and a slit up to her waist.

"Cellulite, darling, she looked like a Jaffa."

Ashley laughed, but she sensed the misgiving in Ellamarie's voice when she told her that Maureen Woodley had decided after all this time to let it drop that she knew Bob's wife.

"You don't think she'll do anything though, do you?" Ashley asked.

Ellamarie was graphic in her explanation of what she would do to Maureen Woodley if she did, and then changed the subject to Kate who had taken Joel back to her apartment, "desire bursting from every orifice. And I've just called Jenneen, and you'll never guess who's there with her? Matthew. Matthew Bordsleigh."

"But I thought it was all long over between those two."

"Didn't we all? But he's there all right. He answered the phone."

"Well, I'm glad," Ashley sighed. None of them knew how Matthew had been ruthlessly blackmailing Jenneen for the past year.

"Everything OK your end?" said Ellamarie.

"Oh, perfect," said Ashley, knowing she sounded bitter.

"That reminds me, Julian's friend, or partner, whoever he is . . ."

"Blanche's cousin," Ashley interjected.

"Blanche's cousin. Well, he took Maureen Woodley home last night. At least I think he did. He chose the right person of course—if that's what you can call her—Maureen's a helluva good massager of egoes, and with one the size of his they were probably at it all night long."

Their conversation was brief as Ellamarie was in a hurry, but she had wanted to make sure Ashley was all right after her early departure from the Ritz the night before.

Ashley managed to assure her that she was, then when she rung off went back to the media plan she had been studying. Half an hour later she was through and gathered up her things to leave. She looked around the office. It was in this room that Julian had first . . . No! Stop it! Just get out of here before you start again. Quickly she picked up her coat and left the room.

"Merry Christmas!" she called to Amanda, as she passed her office.

"Merry Christmas, Ashley!" Amanda called back. "Have a great time!"

"You too," said Ashley. She turned to walk on, and someone crashed into her, sending her bag and the files she was carrying cascading all over the floor.

"Can't you look where you're going?" she heard a voice growl.

She whipped round. "Well, of all the . . ."

"Of all the what?" said Conrad Frazier, a flicker of amusement in his eyes.

"Nothing," she said, slamming her eyes at him. She stopped to gather her belongings, but not before she had noticed his disheveled appearance and the growth on his chin. So, Ellamarie was right.

To her amazement, he walked right on past her. "Aren't you at least going to help me pick this lot up?" she called after him.

"No," he said.

She was so shocked by his rudeness, she couldn't think of a thing to say. And then suddenly, with no warning whatsoever, she burst into tears.

"What's all the noise out here?" said Julian, coming out of his office. He didn't notice Ashley. "Conrad," she heard him say. And then he chuckled. "Well, by the look of you, old chap, it was quite some night last night."

"I've known worse," Conrad answered.

"Ashley!" Julian suddenly cried. She froze. Please don't come over. Please don't say anything, she begged him silently.

"What are you doing down there?"

"Picking up the things that Mr. Frazier knocked out of my hands," she said, not looking up.

"Let me help you." Julian crossed the room.

"No, no. It's all right. I've got everything now." She stood up, running the back of her hand across her eyes.

Julian saw straightaway that she was crying. He turned to Conrad. "What's happened?"

"She came crashing into me," he said. "Though what she's crying for I can't imagine." And then, for the first time, he got a good look at Ashley's face. "Oh God," he groaned, as he recognized her. "Look, I'm sorry. It was my fault. I wasn't looking where I was going."

"You're damn right you weren't!" said Ashley, tears streaming down her face. "But then, I suppose someone as self-important as you never has to."

"Now hang on a minute," said Conrad, taking a step toward her.

"Don't come near me!"

"The woman's hysterical!" he snorted.

"Look, leave this to me," Julian interrupted, and turned his back on Conrad. "Are you all right, Ash? Are you hurt?"

"What the hell do you think," she shouted, and stormed off.

"Are all the women who work here like that?"

"Leave it, Conrad."

He shrugged. "Sure. I need some coffee," he said to Amanda, whose eyes were fixed on him with an expression of slavish devotion, and he disappeared into Julian's office.

Julian stared down the corridor again, but Ashley had gone. What a bloody mess everything was turning out to be. Damn her! And damn Blanche too!

TEN

ASHLEY ARRIVED HOME AROUND SEVEN. ALEX WAS WAITING, hardly able to contain his excitement, but nevertheless he insisted on going to bed almost immediately, believing the sooner he did the sooner Christmas Day would arrive. Ashley tucked him in, and had to swallow hard against the lump in her throat as he threw his arms around her neck and smacked a wet kiss onto the corner of her mouth.

When she went downstairs again she found her mother in the kitchen preparing the turkey and her father sitting at the table. They were laughing about something as Ashley walked in, but stopped when they saw her. She noticed their quick exchange of looks before her mother asked her if everything was all right. Ashley smiled, perhaps a little too brightly, and said yes, of course it was, then picked up an apron. She had just slipped it over her dress when there was a knock at the door. Her father went to answer it. When he came back it was to tell her that there was a Mr. Caffin at the door, asking for her. Ashley looked at her mother, but her mother only shrugged her shoulders.

Ashley listened to Mr. Caffin for several minutes before what he was saying actually began to sink in, but even then she was too stunned to speak. It seemed that the gleaming white Mercedes sports car that was parked in the driveway beside her father's Rover, was hers. She walked over to it, and to her further amazement there was a tiny Labrador puppy sitting in a box on the front seat. The puppy, she discovered, when she read the note from Julian, was for Alex.

That night Ashley cried as if her heart would break. The gifts had told her, more than anything he had said or done before, that Julian was never coming back to her. He had paid for her love, and now they were even. In the early hours of Christmas morning, she crept into bed with Alex, and held her son until morning.

A few miles away, in another part of Surrey, Kate and Ellamarie drank too much red wine with Kate's father, while Kate's mother busied herself in the kitchen, preparing lunch for five. She would keep Jonathan's warm, she had said, as he was sure to be late. Kate and her father no longer tried to persuade her that Jonathan was never coming back, they just let her go ahead and do things for him as if they too believed that he would come. Every time the phone rang, both Ellamarie and Kate held their breath, silently praying that it would be for them. But Christmas Day passed with neither Bob nor Joel calling.

Then on Boxing Day, when they returned from the hunt, Joel arrived. Kate couldn't believe her eyes. He hadn't rung to say he was coming, he had just turned up. It never occurred to her to be cross with him for taking her for granted, she was too happy to see him.

Ellamarie stayed at home with Mr. Calloway while Joel and Kate took a stroll around Frensham Ponds. They were gone a long time and Ellamarie was beginning to be embarrassed, able to read the thoughts that were going through Mr. Calloway's head, when they finally turned up again. Kate's cheeks were flushed; it was confirmation enough of what they had been doing.

Joel stayed for dinner, then returned to London.

Ellamarie tried to fend off the waves of longing and fear that swept over her. Hour after hour passed, and she willed Bob to call her. He didn't. Unable to stop herself, she picked up the phone and rang him. His wife answered; hurriedly Ellamarie replaced the receiver. After that she kept torturing herself with images of him at home with his wife. The Christmas tree, the gifts, the togetherness. It was easier when she drank, so she kept her glass full, and longed for the time when she could go back to London. He would have told his wife everything by then. He had promised.

Matthew had begged Jenneen to let him stay at her flat. Not knowing what else to do, and so confused and horrified by what she had already done in letting him stay even one night, Jenneen had tried to refuse. Matthew was persistent, and in the end she had given in and left for Yorkshire. She would deal with him when she got back. Right now she just needed to get away.

Her parents were welcoming, and she was pleased, and sad, to see them. She loved their simplicity and warmth. The steamy kitchen, cluttered and clouded with the mouthwatering aromas of chicken and roast potatoes. The coal fire burning in the grate was flanked by two old armchairs that had been there ever since she could remember. One of them was always offered to her when she was at home. It was like being in another world, and hard to imagine that it was only a couple of hundred miles from London. Jenneen felt out of place in her parents' home. She didn't like the feeling, but neither did she regret it. Her life was different now.

"More gravy, dear?" her mother asked. It was Boxing Day night, and the aunts and uncles had gathered round the table in Jenneen's mother's best room, the room that was only ever used on birthdays, weddings or at Christmas—and, now that her brothers were getting older, when a young lass was brought home for tea.

Jenneen nodded and watched her mother's veined and roughened hand as she poured the gravy over her dinner. She caught her eye, and as her mother smiled and Jenneen saw the pride in that smile, the dams around her heart broke, and she allowed the love, the same love she had felt as a child, to flood in. No matter how much her life changed, no matter what the future might hold, her mother would always be the most important person in the world for her.

Later, when their meal was finished, they took a stroll down to the working man's club at the end of the road. Jenneen's father was especially pleased that she had agreed to come, he liked nothing better than to show off his famous daughter. Jenneen began to relax and enjoy herself. Soon she found herself dancing with Jim Woodruff, her childhood sweetheart and now the manager of the local supermarket. He had married Jenneen's old school friend Lindsey. She was at home looking after the children, Jim told her, but he knew she would love to see Jenneen if she could find the time to drop round before she went back to London.

It was during their third dance together that Jenneen whispered something in his ear then, without a word to anyone else, left the club and returned home. Once there she took out her makeup and painted her face. Then she stripped, put on her fur coat and boots, and went back to the club where Jim was waiting in the shadows. She drove him out onto the moors. When she took off her coat and presented her naked body to him she could see that he was shocked, but she didn't care. Mrs. Green craved satisfaction, anyone and anywhere would do. It was cramped in the back of the car, but Jenneen sat astride the bemused Jim Woodruff and rocked him to orgasm.

The bitter shame that followed was the worst she had known. Her mother's face, kind and sad, kept forcing its way to the front of her mind's eye. Her father, brusque and awkward, yet so trusting of his daughter and proud of her success, made her cry scalding, merciless tears of remorse and shame. What would it do to them if they knew? She shuddered and looked at herself in the mirror. Dear God, what vile spirit lurked in the shadowy recesses of her soul?

It was almost ten o'clock on Boxing Night when Ashley pulled up outside her parents' house. She recognized Keith's car immediately. Even after all this time her heart still leapt to think of seeing her ex-husband.

It wasn't that she cared for him still. She had got over that a long time ago. Her feelings for Keith now were proof indeed that time did heal. No, it wasn't because she still loved Keith that her heart beat faster at the thought of seeing him, it was because he still loved her. They had had so many awkward scenes over the past year, when he had all but begged her to go back to him. If not for their sakes, then at least for Alex's. He had offered her so many promises, so many ideals, but she knew she could never have gone back to him. She had loved Julian, and Keith was part of her past.

As she carried a sleepy Alex in through the door, she wondered if her mother had told Keith about Julian. She hoped she hadn't, but Keith would have been bound to ask, and her mother wouldn't lie to him. Ashley felt annoyed with Keith for coming early. He wasn't expected until the next day, when, following the usual routine, he and his family would come for Saturday dinner. If he had kept to their plans, she would have been here to meet him.

"Is that you, dear?" her father called, coming out into the hall and turning on the light.

"Yes, it's me. Keith here, is he?"

"In there with Mother. I'll take him on up to bed, shall I?" he said, taking Alex from her arms.

She handed over her son then looked around for the puppy. "Think I'll go and put the kettle on before I go in. Come on, Caesar."

Caesar looked torn for a moment. Alex was going one way, and he was being beckoned another. But Ashley caught him by the collar, and his decision was made for him.

She filled the kettle, and stretched lazily. She would just like to go on up to bed, but she had better say hello to Keith.

"Hi, Ash." He was coming into the kitchen.

She turned round. "Oh, hello."

"Belated Merry Christmas," he said. "I've brought a present for you. It's under the tree."

She smiled. "Thanks, but you shouldn't have."

"I wanted to. Did Alex like his?"

"He loved them. The train set is rigged up in his room, you'll be able to see it tomorrow. Dad's just taken him up to bed now. He's dead beat."

"Where have you been?"

"Over to Kate's. Ellamarie's staying there too."

"Oh." His annoyance showed. Her friends were part of her new life, one that he didn't belong to, and he resented them.

"Did you have a nice Christmas?" she asked.

"Yes, not bad. Mum's a bit under the weather, but Dad's as fit as ever."

"What's the matter with your mother?"

"Touch of flu, I think, nothing serious. And what about you? How are you?"

"Oh I'm fine, just a bit tired."

"Your mum told me about Julian," he said, after a minute or two. "I'm sorry."

Ashley looked at him, and wondered if he was; his face was serious, and there was a look of genuine sympathy in his eyes. "Oh, well," she shrugged, "I'll get over it, I suppose."

"Yes, I suppose you will," he said. "It just takes time."

There goes that phrase again, she thought. The kettle boiled, and Ashley turned away to pour the water into the pot. "Where were you planning to take Alex tomorrow?"

"I thought I'd take him to the cinema. There's a Stephen Spielberg showing in Esher, *The Goonies*. Apparently it's got a pirate in it, One-Eyed Willie."

Ashley laughed. "Sounds just up his street. He's got a new friend though, did Mum tell you?"

"You mean him?" said Keith, pointing at a weary Caesar, curled up in a makeshift box in the corner.

"Yes, him."

"From Julian, I hear."

"That's right."

"And a Mercedes for you?"

"I'm afraid so."

"Very generous of him, considering."

"Very," said Ashley. "Would you carry the tray in? I'll get out some biscuits."

Ashley waited for him to go, then bolted up the stairs to give Alex a goodnight kiss. She hadn't wanted Keith to come with her. The scene of doting parents standing over a sleeping child made her uncomfortable with Keith. They had made that mistake once before and Keith had ended up in tears, and his raging and pleading had woken Alex. She didn't want a repeat of that. If Alex knew that Keith wanted them back so desperately, and with Julian no longer in their lives, he might just take his father's part in trying to persuade her into a reconciliation. And right now, feeling as she did, she just wasn't up to fighting them.

When she went downstairs again, Keith was sitting on the settee, watching television with her parents. She went to sit beside him, careful not to get too close.

Her mother was dabbing her eyes as the final scenes of *La Traviata* were played out on the screen.

Finally the opera came to an end. Mrs. Lakeman sighed, and picked up her tea. "Did you have a nice time at Kate's, dear?"

"Yes," said Ashley. "She sends her love. So does Ellamarie."

"How's Kate's mother?"

"Not too good, I'm afraid. She was calling Alex Jonathan all day, which didn't go down too well."

"Oh dear," said her mother. "He didn't misbehave, did he?"

"Not really."

"How could he? He's his father's son," said Keith, and immediately wished he hadn't.

"Well, I'm for bed," said Mr. Lakeman. "What about you, Rachel?"

"Well, there's a Gene Kelly film on at eleven. Thought I might . . ." She caught her husband's eye. "No, you're quite right, I am a bit tired. Besides, I've had enough telly for one day."

Ashley made to follow her mother, but Keith grabbed her hand.

"Goodnight then, you two," said Mr. Lakeman.

"Night, Dad," said Ashley.

"Goodnight," said Keith.

Keith pressed the button on the remote control to turn off the television.

"Think I'll go on up myself," said Ashley.

"Don't go yet. Why don't we have a nightcap? Just the two of us."

Ashley didn't want to be rude, but neither did she relish the idea of "just the two of us."

"Come on," he said, going over to the drinks trolley. "It's not often we're on our own and able to talk."

She sighed. "I'll have a Cointreau."

Seeing his pleasure made Ashley feel sad. It was

a strange world that created this mysterious chain of love.

"I was wondering," he said, coming back with their drinks, "will you be here for New Year's Eve?"

"I haven't really thought about it."

"It would be nice if you could be. For Alex, I mean."

"Oh, I don't know. He doesn't really understand about New Year's Eve yet. He'll be asleep by ten o'clock."

Keith laughed. "I guess you're right. Nothing going on in London then, I take it?"

"Nothing that I know of, yet. How about you? What will you be doing?"

"Haven't actually planned anything," he answered. "Play it by ear, I suppose."

She nodded and sipped her drink. She couldn't help wondering how things might have turned out had they stayed together. It was at moments like this, when she was feeling lonely and vulnerable, that she remembered all the good times. All the times when they had sat together, just like they were doing now, and talked into the night. There was no doubt she had loved him once, but that seemed such a long time ago now. So much had happened since.

It was dark in the room, only the glow from the fire and a distant lamp lit up their faces, and she thought how romantic this could be. She looked at Keith and found him watching her. She smiled. She would always have a fondness for him, even after all that had happened.

"What would you say to coming out for dinner with me on New Year's Eve?" he said, quietly.

She turned away and immediately felt guilty for it.

"I'm sorry," he said, "I shouldn't have said that. It's too soon, of course."

"No," she said. "Please don't be sorry. I'd love to

have dinner with you on New Year's Eve. Thank you for asking me."

"Do you mean it?"

She smiled and nodded.

"I'll come up to London if you like."

"No, let's go somewhere local."

"OK. I'll book somewhere. How about the Grange?"

It was the restaurant where he had proposed to her. "OK, let's go to the Grange."

He raised his glass to her as if sealing their arrangement. "I was going to ask you anyway. It's not just because of Julian."

She smiled.

"You still love him?"

Ashley stiffened.

"Sorry," he said, "I . . ."

"It doesn't matter. The answer is yes. Yes, I do still love him."

"Would you take him back, if he asked?"

She nodded. "Yes. Yes, I would."

"I thought you'd say that." He hesitated, fiddling with his glass. "But you won't come back to me?"

"Oh, Keith, please," she said, putting her hand on his arm, "don't let's go all through that again."

"I'm sorry," he said. "I can't help it. I love you so much, and I miss Alex. It's terrible seeing him like this you know, only on the occasional weekend and sometimes during the week. I want to help him with his schoolwork and share in his sports days, as his real father, not just a visiting father. And I should have been the one to buy him a dog, and I should have been with him on Christmas Day. I'm afraid of him growing up without me. Afraid that things are happening so quickly that I shall be left behind and I won't even know him any more, my own son."

He looked down at the wedding ring that she still wore, despite the fact that they had been divorced for over two years. "Things are different now, you know," he said. "I hardly drink any more, or gamble. I haven't looked at another woman in ages. It's only you that I want, Ash. You and Alex, my own family."

Ashley pulled her hand away and sat forward.

"I'll wait, Ash," he said. "I don't care how long it takes, I'll wait. I'll always be here if you need me. I'll always care. And I'll never let you down again, I swear it."

"Oh, Keith," she said. "I believe you really do mean it."

"I do, Ashley. I've never stopped thinking of you as my wife. And all that business three years ago . . ." he looked away unable to carry on. Ashley reached out for his hand. She knew how painful it was for him to talk about the way he had threatened to kill himself if she didn't go back to him. And then the threats to take Alex away to a place she would never find them.

He gripped her hand tightly. "Just tell me that maybe one day there is a chance you will be my wife again."

"I can't say it. You know I can't." She leaned back and rested her head against the settee. Life would be so much simpler if she could love him again. They could be a family again, a real family. And Alex would have his father and she would have the love and security she wanted. She would always want to work, she knew that; she also knew that Keith would take her back on any terms, just so that he could be with Alex again. And she wouldn't have to dread going into the office every day. She could join an agency nearer to home. If she were to return to Keith, then everything would be all right. It would all work out.

She felt his arm go round her shoulders and allowed him to take the glass from her hand. Turning back to her he took her in his arms and kissed her gently. Feeling confused and lonely, she let him go on kissing her.

ELEVEN

THE REVIEWS FOR BOB MCELFREY'S PRODUCTION OF
Twelfth Night were, in the main, exceptional. Even Bob
himself had not dared to hope for such a reception.
Modestly he put it down to the modern interpretations
of Shakespeare's plays that had plagued the theater in
recent years, and the critics seemed to agree with him.

"If we didn't know it before, we certainly know
it now," wrote one, "we want our classical Shakespeare. And we want our lighter Shakespeare too.
Thank you to Bob McElfrey for giving it." "It is a piece
of theater, unsurpassed in recent years," wrote another.
"A delicate, and romantic story, told with all the feeling
and humor we have come to expect from one of our
finest directors." There were also those who wrote jubi-
lantly, of how the timing and delivery had them
"laughing in the aisles," and "crying out for more." But
one critic had been cruel in her write-up on the performance given by Maureen Woodley: "She was better
cast as Viola disguised as a man, it was only then that
she approached belief."

Bob thought that was a bit strong, but he had to
admit that for some reason Maureen had not got to
grips with her character. And what was worse, she
didn't seem to care. Bob had been so angry with her
he had hardly spoken to her when they had all joined
up for the first-night party afterward. He didn't want

to risk a showdown, not when everyone else was basking in their triumph. But no one had been surprised when he had called for rehearsals again the following day.

The stage manager had booked the rehearsal room for the day. Bob felt it might be better for Maureen to be away from the theater until they played again tonight. He had called the whole cast for the afternoon; Maureen's wasn't the only performance that needed sharpening, despite what the critics had said.

Ellamarie was sitting at the side of the room with Nicholas Gough. They were watching Maureen rehearse with David Flood, who was playing Orsino. Every now and again she caught Bob's eye, and her heart turned over. Eventually Bob grinned and turned his script table away from her, deciding that he really must concentrate harder on the task in hand.

Ellamarie smiled, able to read his mind, and felt a surge of joy that Christmas was finally over and they were back together again. She returned her attention to Maureen Woodley. Despite her feelings toward Maureen, she had to admit that she was a gifted actress—at least this morning she was. Ellamarie shook her head, and wondered what had happened to Maureen the night before.

Bob hardly interrupted Maureen's performance at all, there was no need, but whenever he did, Maureen responded perfectly. And she smiled at him, and laughed when he delivered the lines himself. Then, with the scene over, she turned to him for his approval, and got it.

The next scene did not include either Maureen or Ellamarie, so they both watched as the others rehearsed. At least Maureen did, but Ellamarie was still, from the corner of her eye, watching Maureen. Maureen barely took her eyes from Bob.

As the morning wore on Ellamarie's expression turned from interest to incredulity. Maureen Woodley had a crush on Bob! Ellamarie was shocked. She'd no idea that Maureen harbored feelings of that kind for him. She'd certainly never noticed them before. When had this started?

Ellamarie became so engrossed by Maureen's double-edged performance that she hardly noticed when Bob called out for the others to come and join the discussion. He turned to look at her, and Maureen's face contorted with anger. Ellamarie flinched to see such venom.

"I want you all to listen to this," Bob was saying, as the others crowded round. "We're talking about options for pauses." Everyone laughed and groaned. "Yes," he said, holding up his hand, "that old one." He turned to David and Maureen. "Right," he said, "run that last bit again."

"Where shall we take it from?" said David.

"Take it from 'My life upon't,' " Bob answered, and stood back to watch with the audience of other actors.

"My life upon't, young though thou art, thine eye Hath stayed upon some favor that it loves; Hath it not, boy?"

"A little, by your favor."

"What kind of woman is't?"

"Of your complexion."

Bob held up his hand. "Maureen, why not pick up the cue for 'Of your complexion' immediately, but then hold for the rest of the line. Do you see what I mean? 'Of . . . your complexion.' I think you've been caught a bit on the hop there, maybe you shouldn't be so slick with an answer. Try it."

Maureen smiled at him, and turned to face David. "Of . . . your complexion," she repeated. "Oh yes!" she shrieked, turning back to Bob. "That's exactly right. It feels absolutely perfect. Thank you."

Bob nodded to her, then looked round as he felt

the stage manager tugging at his sleeve. She was pointing to her watch.

"OK, everyone," he shouted. "Get some tea, and back in ten minutes. I'm not going to run the whole thing through, but I do want you all here, so no running off."

He went back to his table and took the libretto for *Don Giovanni* from his case. He'd have to spend the day at Lilian Bayliss House tomorrow rehearsing, so he might as well take the opportunity of this break to go over the opera again. He opened it, groaned inwardly, and decided a cup of tea might help.

Pushing open the door of the small kitchen at the end of the room, he stopped at the sound of Maureen's high-pitched voice. Nobody had seen him come in, and he was just in time to hear Maureen, with an affected American accent, drawl toward Ellamarie's back: "O Romeo, Romeo! wherefore art thou, Romeo?" She lowered her voice and mimicked Bob's mildly Scottish tone. "At home with my wife, dearest."

"Maureen!" She spun round as Bob snapped her name. "A word, please."

Maureen followed him out into the hall. He motioned for her to close the kitchen door, then waited beside his table. There was no one else around, they couldn't be overheard.

"Maureen," he said, the smooth tone of his voice belying the anger in his eyes, "you know there are still things that need perfecting in your performance. Perhaps if you concentrated a little harder on that, and less on other members of the cast, we might get somewhere."

Maureen's face turned puce, but she didn't quite have the courage to say what was on her mind.

"Now go and get your tea and work over your lines with David. By ridiculing Ellamarie you are also ridiculing me, and I will not stand for it, do you hear me? You are *not* irreplaceable."

To his dismay, she looked on the brink of tears. He hadn't expected her to cry. Shout, and stamp her feet, yes. But not tears.

"Look," he said, his voice conciliatory, "I'm sorry that I've had to speak to you like this. We won't mention it again, OK?"

Still without speaking, she turned quickly and went back into the kitchen. He watched her go. He didn't trust her. She was an actress, and a damned good one. And again, not for the first time, he remembered that she had said she knew his wife. He would have to watch her. Or perhaps more to the point, he would have to watch himself.

"Feel like some food?" Ellamarie asked.

"Mmm, yes, I do."

"Shall we go out? We can always go somewhere in the King's Road. Have a pizza or something?"

Bob thought about it. "I'd rather stay here. Why don't I go out and get a takeaway?"

"Sure. What do you fancy?"

"Chinese?"

She nodded. "Shall I come with you?"

He shook his head. "No need." It was a good opportunity to get to a phone and ring his wife. Something he had been meaning to do all day, but the afternoon rehearsal hadn't ended until five and he hadn't had the opportunity, with Ellamarie being so close at hand.

He picked up his keys from the bureau and, stooping to kiss her, left.

Ellamarie was particularly excited about tonight's performance. All her friends were going to be there, and they were going on for dinner after, at the Villa Dei Cesari. She was sad, though, that her father couldn't be there too. He would adore the play, she just knew it. She would mail him copies of the reviews.

One critic had gone so far as to say that Ellamarie

Goold was someone to look out for in the future, "I'm sure," he had written, "that we will be seeing a lot more of this gifted and beautiful young actress." She wished she could be there to see his face when her father read that. He would be real proud. Her mother probably would be too, but her mother hardly ever showed any emotion. Poppa had thought to call her at the theater before she went on last night, and it had meant so much to her. It had been so long since she had last seen him.

She undressed and went to fill the tub.

She was longing to know what Bob had said to Maureen earlier, but knew she couldn't ask. He didn't like to discuss what went on between him and other members of the company. This was as much for her sake as for theirs.

She had played with the idea of telling him that Maureen had a fad for him, but she hadn't. Hell, what was the point anyway, Maureen would get over it. A pity Blanche's cousin, whatever his name was, had gone back to the States so soon.

The phone began to ring, so she pulled a wrap round her and went to answer it.

It was Kate calling to wish her good luck, and to tell her that her mother and father wouldn't be able to make it after all.

"Is Joel still coming?" Ellamarie asked.

"You bet he is. He's picking me up at seven-thirty. Does that leave us enough time to get there?"

"Plenty. It doesn't start till eight-thirty. By the way, Nicholas Gough was asking about you today."

"Oh God!" said Kate. "What was he saying?"

"Just asked if you were coming tonight."

"What did you say?"

"I said you were. I didn't tell him Joel was coming as well, though."

"He doesn't expect . . ."

"Uh-uh," said Ellamarie. "At least, I don't think so."

"He wasn't too terribly cross about me going off with Joel when we were at the Ritz, was he?"

"He didn't say he was. But I think he was a bit put out. After all, it was you who asked me to fix you up all those months ago."

"Well, he certainly took his time getting interested," Kate complained.

"He was seeing someone else."

"Oh well, too bad. He's missed the boat now, I'm afraid."

"He's a nice guy, Kate."

"Oh don't, you're making me feel guilty. Have you spoken to any of the others today? I'm supposed to be meeting them in the bar."

"Jenneen called earlier. She's bringing Matthew. And wait for it, Ashley is bringing a friend."

"No! Who?"

"Search me. Someone she met in a restaurant, I think she said."

"But who is he?"

"No idea. But she says we'll just love him."

"I can't wait," said Kate. "Did she tell you what happened last Saturday, at the office?"

"No."

"It was so *awful*. It was Julian. He got hold of her, apparently, and tried to kiss her. Told her that he was sorry, and could he see her again."

"Jesus Christ! What did she do?"

"Well, apparently Conrad Thingummy broke them up. Just as well, by the sound of it, as Blanche was on her way up the stairs. Seems as soon as Julian heard Blanche's name mentioned he turned white and disappeared, leaving poor Ash to contend with that philistine from New York."

"What did Conrad say?"

"Plenty, all of it insulting. They had quite the most furious row. But then little Alex walked in on them, and Ashley said that Conrad's manner suddenly changed, became something approaching human when Alex appeared. But what do you make of Julian, though? I mean, can you believe it? But at least even Ashley got mad this time."

"He's a selfish, egotistical bastard," Ellamarie snapped, surprising Kate with her vehemence. There was a short pause.

"I was going to ask," said Kate, a little less animated now, "but, well, has Bob said anything to his wife yet?"

Ellamarie sighed. "Well, if he has, he sure hasn't told me. So I figure we can take it that he hasn't."

"Oh, Ellamarie. Are you cross?"

"As hell. But what can I say? And now is not the time. Not with the play just opening and all."

"Where is he now?"

"Just coming in through the door. He's been to get a takeaway."

"You mean you can eat?" Kate cried. "Aren't you terribly nervous?"

"Nothing stops me from eating," said Ellamarie. "Anyway, I'd better go, he's banging around in the kitchen to let me know he's back, like a spoiled child. Needs constant attention, does Bob."

"Like all men," Kate laughed.

Ellamarie hung up and went into the kitchen to find Bob picking at the food.

"Can't you wait?" she said.

"I'm starving. I haven't eaten all day."

"Well, let's at least get it onto plates," and she whisked the cartons from his hands.

He stood watching her while she banged the drawers open and closed, took out knives and forks, and salt and pepper, and all but slammed them on the table.

"Are you angry about something?" he asked.

"No."

"Who was that on the phone?"

"Kate."

"Is she coming tonight?"

"Yes. With Joel."

"Oh, she's still seeing him, is she?"

"Yes. Why not? You sound surprised?"

Bob looked at her. "Something's eating you, Ellamarie. What is it?"

"Nothing's eating me. I already told you."

She reached the plates down from the cupboard, and dished out the meal. Then she turned on the oven, and put hers inside.

"What are you doing?" he said.

"Keeping mine warm. I'm going to bathe first."

"And there was me thinking you'd got undressed for me."

She didn't laugh.

He shrugged and sat down at the table with his food.

When she came out of the bathroom, he was sitting in front of the TV, watching Ann Hollier and David Flood being interviewed by Terry Wogan.

"I'd forgotten they were on," she said. "Have I missed much?"

"It's almost over."

"Then why didn't you call me?"

He looked at her, blankly.

"Why didn't you call me?"

"I'm sorry," he said, "I didn't think."

"I guess you never do," she remarked.

"Ellamarie, will you stop this. If I've done something to upset you, why don't you just spit it out?"

She looked away, and dug her fork into the food that she had brought in with her. But her appetite had vanished. She pushed the plate away.

"Something the matter?"

"Why don't you quit asking me if something is the matter?"

"For God's sake," he said. "Suddenly I can't say anything right."

"People who don't say anything at all, usually don't."

"And what is that supposed to mean?"

"Exactly what it said."

"Then forgive me for being stupid, but I don't understand."

"That's just it, isn't it, Bob. You don't understand!"

"If I knew what it was that I was supposed to be understanding, then perhaps I could try."

"Try understanding that you made me a promise before Christmas, one that you appear to have conveniently forgotten."

"What promise?"

"Oh, that's rich!" she cried. "What promise? You know what promise. The promise that you would tell your wife about us. The promise you made to me that we would be together. The promise . . ."

Bob stood up and switched off the TV. "Why have you suddenly brought this up now?" He turned round to face her, but she was staring out of the window. He walked over and pulled the curtains.

"Because I hardly ever think about anything else."

"But now, before a performance?"

"Yes, even now, before a performance. There are other things in my life, Bob, besides acting. And you happen to be one of them. At least, I thought you were."

"You're getting worked up about nothing, Ellamarie."

"Don't patronize me," she shouted. "It might be nothing to you, but it's not to me. And that's it, isn't it? It's nothing to you. This whole goddamned thing, it means nothing to you. I don't matter. You didn't even call me over Christmas. You must have known what I would be going through. Joel came round to see Kate on Boxing Day, and do you know, when he knocked on the door I was actually stupid enough to think that it was you who had arrived. I was fool enough to think that you had kept your promise, that you had told her, and that you were coming to tell me everything was all right. How goddamned stupid can anyone get? But I should have known better. Jesus Christ, I should have known better. You're weak, Bob McElfrey. You're weak, and spineless. You thought you could keep me hanging on, dangling around like some brainless puppet. Well, I've got feelings too! I hurt too, you know. But then, why should you care? You've got her and her goddamned horses, and you've got me, and the theater. Why should you want to lose any of it? You've got everything, you bastard! And don't walk away when I'm talking to you!"

"I'm walking away," he said, "because you are being irrational. You don't know what you're saying, and I don't want a row before the performance; neither do you. We'll discuss this later."

"Like hell we will!" she yelled. He stopped in the doorway, but didn't turn round. "There won't be a later," she went on. "There is no later for me and you, Bob, do you hear me? No later! No more! I'm sick of it, and I'm sick of you!"

He turned back and she saw that his face had paled. "I think you should stop now, Ellamarie, before you say something you will regret."

"I'm saying we're through. Finished. Over! Do you understand? We're through. Now there's the door."

"I'm driving you to the theater."

"I can drive myself. Now get out! Go!"

She saw his jaw tighten, and she knew that he was barely managing to control his own temper. "Go and get dressed. I'll wait until you're ready. Then I'll take you to the theater."

"The theater, sure, where the rest of your fan club is waiting. Maureen Woodley now, isn't it?"

"What the hell are you talking about?"

"Don't kid me. I've seen the way she looks at you,

and don't tell me you haven't. How much encouragement have you given her, Bob? Is she next in line? Get rid of Ellamarie Goold, bring on Maureen Woodley. You're like one of them goddamned horses your wife keeps. You're a stud! Well, this is one mare that doesn't need servicing any more."

Bob glared at her. "You're disgusting, Ellamarie. And if that's the way you feel, then perhaps you're right, we'd better say goodbye now. See you get to the theater on time," and picking up his coat, he slammed out of the flat.

That night Ellamarie Goold gave the best performance of her life. Not that anyone noticed particularly; only she knew how she was feeling inside.

After Bob had left, she had thrown herself onto the couch and cried and cried. She knew she had gone too far. She had said so many things she didn't mean. Something inside her had snapped, and she had lost control. She was terrified that he wouldn't forgive her. That she had spoiled everything, and that he would never come back to her.

When she arrived at the theater he was in his office and his secretary had told her that he didn't want to be disturbed, so she went back downstairs and shut herself in her dressing room, and locked the door. She didn't want to see anyone, not till curtain up. Oh yes, she would go on. After attacking him with her cruel and suspicious mind, she couldn't let him down again.

Making up to go on, she looked at herself in the mirror, but could only see his face, hurt and confused, looking at her, not knowing why she was saying what she was saying. How could she have done it to him? Bob, who had only loved her, cherished her even, and would never deliberately do anything to hurt her.

There were three curtain calls, interminable, and prolonging her agony. She had to get off. She must get away, before she broke down again.

She ran back to her dressing room, and again locked the door. Somebody knocked, several times, but she didn't answer. She knew it wouldn't be him. He would have no more to say to her.

She lit a cigarette. It wasn't often she smoked these days, Bob didn't like it, so she had tried to give it up. But she needed something now, to calm her nerves.

She thought back over the past two years, and all the times they had spent together. But hadn't she always known in her heart that one day this hour would arrive? When it would be all over. Married men never leave their wives, she had always told herself that, even though she had never wanted to believe it. Not men like Bob. He was loyal, and honest, and she had never considered what it cost him to cheat on his wife, even if he didn't love her any more. Yes, she knew that this day would come sooner or later. And sometimes, in bleak moments, usually at the weekend, she had imagined how it would be. A tender, heartrending parting, with both of them doing the sensible thing. Not like this. They had never had a real fight before—and it was all her doing.

There was another knock on the door, but she ignored it. She didn't want to see anyone. She knew her friends would be waiting for her out front, but she couldn't face even them right now. If only she could see her father.

She knew she was fooling herself. Her father would be horrified to think that she had been committing a sin of the bible with a married man.

She buried her face in her hands and sobbed.

Again there was a knock at the door. "Ellamarie! Ellamarie! Can I come in?"

It was Ashley. Poor Ashley, who had suffered, like she was suffering now. Who had tried to put a brave face on things, like she had done tonight.

"Ellamarie! Are you in there?"

At last she got to her feet, and unlocked the door.

She turned away, and let Ashley open it herself. But it wasn't only Ashley who came through the door. There were bundles and bundles of flowers as well, with Ashley tucked in behind them.

"What were you doing?" said Ashley. "I was beginning to think you weren't here."

"Just taking my makeup off."

Ashley dumped the flowers on the tiny couch in the corner, and went to sit beside Ellamarie at the mirror. "The others are in the bar getting a drink. They'll meet us out there. Thought I'd come and give you a hand, and tell you how marvelous . . ." She stopped as she saw Ellamarie's red eyes. "What's the matter, Ellamarie? Have you been crying?"

"No. Just got cream in my eyes."

"Oh." There was a brief silence before Ashley spoke again. "He's waiting outside, you know. He wants to know if it's all right to come in."

Ellamarie looked at her, hardly daring to believe her.

"Well, what do you say?"

Ellamarie looked toward the door. Then her hands flew to her cheeks and she turned back to the mirror.

"Here," said Ashley, passing her a tissue. "Blow your nose, and wipe the makeup from under your eyes. I'll go and tell him the coast is clear."

Ellamarie stared at her reflection in the glass, doing nothing to cleanse her eyes. She wondered what he was going to say. He would have calmed down by now, Bob never stayed mad for long. But did he want to see her just to finalize everything? To make things more civilized, so that they could continue to work together? Maybe he was going to ask her to quit the production. Her understudy could take the part until they found someone else. Oh God, not that. Please not that.

She turned round in her chair and saw that he was standing in the doorway. She looked at him, tall and dark, with fine gray lines through his beard and around his temples. His face was inscrutable, but she noticed that his jaw was set and his knuckles showed white on the handle of the door. He looked back at her across the room, and she knew she had never loved him more.

She looked down to her hands, and found that she had pulled the tissue into tiny pieces. "I know I can't expect you to forgive me," she whispered, "but I am sorry for all those things I said. I wish I'd never said them. You must hate me now ... and I can't blame you, but I'm sorry, oh Bob, I'm sorry," she sobbed.

"I love you, Ellamarie."

She looked up. "What did you say?"

"I said, I love you, Ellamarie."

In a moment she was in his arms. "Oh Bob!" she cried. "I love you too. I'm sorry for everything I said. I didn't mean any of it. I don't know what made me say it. Oh Bob! Don't ever leave me, I'm sorry."

He held her tightly, and let her cry on his shoulder while he stroked her hair. "Sssh, now, don't cry, hen."

She looked up into his face, and he smiled. "You look terrible," he said, tracing the little white valleys that her tears had made through the makeup on her cheeks. Taking her by the hand he led her back to the mirror, and dipping the tissues in the cold cream, he wiped her face, sometimes kissing her, and sometimes laughing at her as she pulled faces at him, or cried. Then he pulled her to her feet, and undressed her.

"Did you bring something to wear for dinner?"

She nodded, and pointed to the dress hanging on the back of the door.

He took it from the hanger, and slipped it over her head. Then he turned her round, and zipped her up.

"Shoes?"

"Over there."

He pushed her back into the chair, and replaced Maria's shoes with Ellamarie's.

She was looking down at him, and reached out her hand to stroke his face. "I don't deserve you."

"It is I who don't deserve you," he said. "It was my fault, Ellamarie. It was all my fault. I should have realized. Things haven't been easy for you lately, and I have been selfish, and uncaring. It's a lot for you to put up with, what with the play opening, Christmas, and not seeing your parents. And me. It has all been too much of a strain on you, and I'm sorry. I'm sorry for not seeing it sooner. And I'm sorry that I haven't said anything to my wife. But I will, my darling, I promise you, I will."

"Oh, you don't have to, Bob," she said, throwing her arms round him. "As long as we're together, at least some of the time, it's enough. I shouldn't have tried to push you. I tried to make you do something that I know is against your nature. I understand now. You don't want to hurt your wife, I can see that now. And I love you for it."

He kissed her, tenderly, tracing her lips with his, and his heart was full of love.

"Are you ready for dinner?"

She nodded. "Do I look OK?"

"You look beautiful."

"You're biased."

"Of course."

As he led her out of the dressing room, he leaned back inside the door to turn off the light. He didn't see Maureen Woodley slip back into her dressing room. And he missed the look she gave Ellamarie.

TWELVE

KATE BRACED HERSELF AND WAITED FOR THE NEXT BLOW. IT came. Followed by another. And then another. She cried out, then stifled her scream with her hand, biting into her flesh until she could taste blood. And then she felt his lips on her skin, and his fingers, gentle and soothing, as he stroked her buttocks. She turned over and looked up into Joel's eyes. They were bright and excited. He pushed his hips forward, and grabbing hold of her hand he rubbed it against his penis. It was hard, like rock almost.

He turned her over onto her face again.

"No," she whimpered, "please. No more."

She felt his weight sink down on the bed beside her, and then over her. Using his knees he parted her legs, then moving his hands round to her belly, he lifted her from the bed and with one quick move he had entered her. Thank God, the sadistic pantomime was over.

Later, lying together in the darkness, Kate rested her head on his shoulder and listened to his breathing. She tried to stop the tears spilling over onto his chest. He would be cross if he knew she was crying.

She had no explanation to offer, not even to herself. He had asked her if he could beat her, and she had agreed. But when he had asked he had seemed timid, embarrassed almost, at even suggesting it. And she had put her arms round him and told him that she would do simply anything he wanted her to. Anything to please him.

She had had no idea then that he would use such violence. Sometimes, when he had finished with her, she found it difficult to walk the following day. She wished that she had the courage to tell him to stop, that she couldn't take any more. But she was afraid she would lose him if she did.

Finally, she fell asleep, the crescents of angry weals dealt by the cane he had used on her burning into her flesh.

The telephone woke them the following morning and before she could stop him Joel had reached out to answer it. To Kate's relief it was Margaret Stanley from *Gracious Living*. She shuddered to think what he might have said had it been her father.

As she listened to Margaret's voice at the other end of the phone she felt Joel reach out round her body to fondle her breasts. Her nipples were sore, and she twisted away from him.

"Are you listening to me, Kate?" Margaret said.

"Yes, yes," Kate answered. "What angle were you looking for exactly?"

"Come into the office first, we'll talk it over. You don't have to be there until three-thirty. I've made all the arrangements. And Kate, I'm sure there's no need to remind you, but this is royalty you're going to be speaking to. Best behavior and all that, eh?"

"Royalty?" said Kate.

"Haven't you been listening to anything I've said?" Margaret bleated. "Have you got someone there with you? No, don't answer that, it's none of my business. But get him out of your bed and get your ass over here. This is a biggy," and she slammed the phone down.

Kate stared at the receiver. Who exactly had Margaret been talking about? She had mentioned royalty. But who? Suddenly she sat bolt upright.

"Holy shit! The Queen!"

Joel reached out and pulled her back. She shrugged him off and ran out of the bedroom.

"What the hell's going on?" he grumbled, following her into the kitchen.

"The Queen. I'm going to interview the Queen."

"In China?"

She looked at him blankly.

"The Queen is in China."

"Then the Prince of Wales. Princess Diana. I don't know. This afternoon. I must ring my father and tell him. He just won't believe it." She rushed for the phone.

Joel strolled into the bathroom and turned on the shower.

"Didn't you hear what I said?" Kate shouted after him. "I'm actually doing an interview with someone from the royal family."

"I'm impressed," he called back, then closed the shower door behind him.

Linda McElfrey got up early that morning, as she did every morning. She took Moonlight down to the gallops at six-thirty, then pointed him toward the open countryside where she gave him his head and allowed the drizzle to wash across her face, and the wind to tear at her hair. It was her favorite time of day. The stable lads would just be taking the other horses down to the gallops now. She wanted some time alone. Time to think.

Bob had been distracted lately, not quite himself. If she asked him what was on his mind, he would only laugh, and say that she was imagining things, and that nothing was on his mind. But she knew him too well. She knew when things weren't right. And she also knew when it was a production that was getting him down. He didn't always talk about it, he was a private person really, didn't like people trying to delve too closely into his thoughts. But it was that inner person, the drive that was powered by solving things for himself, that had made him what he was today. Linda knew that, and she never interfered.

This time it was different. All over Christmas he hadn't been irritable exactly, but neither had he been relaxed. By the time he left to return to London, Linda felt that somehow they had grown apart. He returned, as promised, for New Year's Eve and they had a quiet evening at home with his mother, just the three of them. They talked and laughed, and toasted one another at midnight. But whatever had been on Bob's mind over Christmas obviously hadn't gone away. And it was still there, all these weeks into the New Year.

Linda was a strong woman, in both mind and body. She prided herself on her well-run stables, and her equally well-run marriage. They had been together for eleven years now, eight of those years married. They had shared a closeness from the very beginning, their different interests keeping them together, rather than pulling them apart.

Now, for the first time, Linda wondered whether she was doing the right thing. Perhaps she should take more of an interest in his work, and in him. Perhaps they had led separate lives for too long. She knew that Bob wanted a family, but she had always resisted. She was thirty-eight now, and maybe she should stop resisting.

It was past eight-thirty when she returned to the stables, and she was famished. Her mother-in-law, who was staying until the end of the month, was waiting for her at the kitchen door, peering out through the misty rain.

Moonlight trotted into the stable yard, steaming and wet through. He flicked his back hooves, his way of saying he had enjoyed the morning's exercise. Linda stroked his neck.

"Time for breakfast now, eh?"

Her mother-in-law waved to her. "I've got the kettle boiling," she called.

"Be right there."

Barry, the stable lad, ran over to take Moonlight, and after asking about the other horses, Linda went inside to have her breakfast. The kitchen was warm and cozy, and the smell of sizzling bacon and eggs was mouthwateringly welcoming.

"There's a towel warming by the fire," said her mother-in-law, "go and dry yourself off, and I'll dish up."

Linda picked up the towel and began to rub her hair.

"There's a piece in the local paper about Bob," said Violet McElfrey. "I've left it there on the table for you to read."

"Thanks." Linda brushed her tangled hair. "What does it say?"

"Oh, the usual," said her mother-in-law. "Local celebrity, rave reviews, another masterpiece; you know, the same as they always write."

Linda laughed. "So much for the proud mother. Still, you're right. Sometimes I wonder if they just have a format piece on him, and whenever he does something they just change the name of the play, and the names of the actors."

"Precisely," said Violet. "But I'll put it in the scrapbook anyway. Two rashers or three?"

"Make it three, I'm starving. Is Barry coming in?"

"No. He had his an hour ago."

"You were up early this morning."

"How can anyone be expected to sleep with all that clattering of hooves going on outside," Violet complained.

"I've told you, take the room at the front of the house, you won't be disturbed then."

"No. I don't mind really. Besides, it gives me something to do, cooking breakfast for you lot."

"And don't think we aren't grateful," said Linda, sitting down at the table. "Especially me. I hate cooking breakfast. I keep meaning to draw up a roster, so that we can take it in turns to cook. But I daresay most of those half-wits don't know one end of a frying pan from the other, so I don't suppose there's much point."

Violet put a plate in front of her daughter-in-law, and turned back to the stove. "Think I'll have three slices too," she said, raking the bacon out of the pan. "Tea?"

"Mmm," Linda nodded, her mouth full.

Violet poured two cups, and put them on the table. The phone began to ring. "Oh no. Who on earth can that be?" She went to answer it. "Shall I tell them to ring back after breakfast?"

"Yes," said Linda. "Unless it's Bob."

Violet picked up the phone. "Hello. Yes. Yes, it is. She's having her breakfast, can you call her back in about half an hour? Oh, I see, well, I'll see what she says. Hang on a minute." She turned to Linda. "It's urgent they speak to you, apparently."

Linda's stomach tightened. Some sixth sense was telling her that this wasn't going to be good news. "Who is it?"

"She didn't say. Will you take it?"

Linda nodded, and slowly got up from the chair. Her hair was still damp, and her boots felt heavy on her feet as she walked across the flagstoned floor to the telephone. At the last minute she stopped. "I'll take it in the drawing room," she said.

Her mother-in-law looked surprised, but she waited until she heard Linda pick up the phone in the other room, and then she put the receiver down in the kitchen. She had sensed Linda's unease, and wasn't one to pry.

"Hello," said Linda. "Linda McElfrey here. Can I help you?"

"Mrs. McElfrey," said the voice at the other end. "It's Maureen Woodley here. I don't know if you remember me, we met at Badminton last year."

"I don't think I do remember," said Linda, "but I know who you are. Is there something I can do for you?"

There was a short silence.

"Hello? Are you still there?"

"Yes," said Maureen. "I'm still here."

"Has something happened to Bob?" Linda's voice was perfectly controlled.

"No," said Maureen. "No, it's nothing like that."

"Then what can I do for you?"

"Well, it is about Bob. It's just that I thought you ought to know."

Linda already knew what she was going to say. "Know what?"

"That your husband is having an affair with one of the cast from *Twelfth Night*, and has been for some time. I'm only telling you because I thought you should know. It's awful when a man is cheating on his wife, and everyone knows but her. So I thought I should tell you."

"I see," said Linda, trying to keep her voice steady.

"And . . ." Maureen paused, sounding uncertain. "I just thought you would like to know. But I'm sure that it's nothing too serious. It's you that Bob loves, everyone knows that."

Linda felt a flash of anger. "I take it Bob has confided all this to you," she said.

"Uh, well, no." Linda waited for her to go on. "They are together most nights, when he's in London."

"Who is she?"

"As I said, one of the cast."

"Is it you, Maureen?"

"No, no, it's not me." Maureen sounded surprised.

"No," said Linda, "of course, it wouldn't be. Bob would never be so stupid as to pick someone who is capable of doing what you're doing now."

"I beg your pardon?"

"I think you heard me."

"Really, I'm only trying to help. I'm telling you this for your own good."

"And tell me, Maureen, what possible good do you think it will do, telling me?"

"So that you can fight to keep him."

"So that I can fight to keep him?"

"Yes."

Linda hesitated before she spoke. "Let me tell you this, Maureen Woodley. Even if what you are saying is true, and I doubt it, I don't need any interfering little busybodies who get pleasure from sticking their noses in other people's business ringing me up to tell me. Now, I suggest you put the phone down, and go and tell Bob what you have done. I will let him deal with you. As far as I am concerned I never want you to ring this number again, or to attempt to make contact with me in any way. You must be a particularly sick person to do what you have just done. Goodbye." And Linda slammed the phone down.

She hadn't raised her voice but she was shaking, and she kept her hand pressed on the phone. She gazed toward the window, trying to steady her nerves, but she was overcome by fear and the growing knowledge that the very roots of her life were giving way beneath her. She should have known, of course. All the signs had been there. Maybe she had known, but hadn't wanted to admit it. But now that bitch of an actress had faced her with it.

Her first instinct was to ring Bob. But if Maureen Woodley had been telling the truth, he wouldn't be at the mews house. Nevertheless, she dialed the number. There was no reply.

She could go up to London. Go to the theater, and find him. But his mistress, whoever she was, would be there. Linda didn't like scenes any more than Bob did.

But she must do something. She loved her husband, and she didn't want to lose him. And in her heart she knew that he still loved her. At the moment he might think that he didn't, but she knew that he did. They could work this out.

She walked back into the kitchen, still reeling from the telephone call.

"Come on," said Violet, "your breakfast is getting cold."

Linda looked at it. "I'm not hungry."

Violet put down her tea and stared at her daughter-in-law. Linda was gazing into the fire, her hands in the pockets of her jacket, her hair falling across her face.

"Who was that on the phone?"

"No one important."

Violet started to clear the table. Linda would talk when she was ready. The telephone call had been something to do with Bob, Violet was sure of that. But it was something about Bob that didn't concern his mother. Not yet, at any rate. She wasn't blind. She had noticed that things had been strained lately. If Linda and Bob were having problems, well, it was for them to sort them out. They both knew that they could rely on her, but it must be for them to come to her, she wasn't going to interfere.

She turned on the tap and began to fill the washing-up bowl with dishes. Linda was still standing in front of the fire, deep in thought.

"I'll make some fresh tea," said Violet, "your other one's turned cold."

Linda looked up, then glanced at the table. "No need. I'll drink that one."

Violet pulled a face and shrugged.

Linda picked up the cup, and drank the cold tea. Then she walked over to her mother-in-law and slipped an arm round her shoulders.

"Violet," she said. "How would you feel about becoming a grandmother?"

". . . yes, and I've actually got a letter here from Kensington Palace saying thank you very much. Can you believe it?" Kate grinned across the room to Ashley, then turned back to the phone.

"Oh, absolutely," she said. "Of course I'll get it framed . . . Oh honestly, Daddy, surely one's enough? . . . OK . . . Yes, see you at the weekend . . . No, no, I promise I will come this weekend . . . OK, see you then." She put the phone down, and immediately Ashley saw her face fall.

"Something the matter?"

"Yes, everything, if you must know. Ellamarie's not speaking to me because I stood up Nicholas Gough the other night. Jenneen keeps shouting at me for moping around, and now my father is complaining because I haven't been to see him. And as for my book, forget it, I can't do it. Is that enough to be going on with?"

"Sounds plenty to me," said Ashley. "Why did you stand up Nick?"

"Because Joel was coming round."

"Joel rang after Nick, I presume."

"You presume correct."

"Ellamarie fixed that date up to try and help you out, you know."

"I know." Kate pushed at her hair irritably. "Everyone's trying to do everything to help me out. Well, I just wish everyone would leave me alone. I can run my own life, thank you very much. And don't you start having a go at me as well. We can't all manage our lives as well as you, we're not all *that* fortunate."

"Steady on now," said Ashley.

"No, just you steady on. You're about to start pon-tificating to me about what I should and shouldn't do, just like everyone else. Well don't! Take a look at your life, Ashley, and then take a look at mine. You reek of good luck and privilege. You've got that wonderful old man you're always going to visit, so you can talk about Julian any time you like." Ashley's eyes flashed, but Kate went on. "You've got your ex-husband sniffing around, who just can't wait to have you back. You're doing so bloody well at that damned agency I suppose you're going to be promoted any day now—another something to alleviate Julian's conscience, to add to the gleaming white Mercedes sports car that you drive your perfect son around in at the weekend. You make me sick, Ashley. All of you make me sick," and with that she burst into tears.

Ashley went to sit beside her and put her arms round her. She let her cry, then when Kate was calm again she said: "I take it you still haven't heard from him?"

Kate shook her head.

"When did he say he would call?"

"Last week some time."

"Have you tried calling him?"

"Oh, just a few thousand times," Kate answered, bitterly. "He's not there. Either that, or he won't speak to me. The trouble is it's been like this for weeks. I don't hear from him for days on end, then suddenly he just turns up out of the blue, or drops a note through my front door to tell me what time to be ready. He al-ways assumes that I will be waiting, and available, and—damn and bloody blast it!—I always am."

She turned to look at Ashley. "I haven't told any-one else this," she whispered, her face red and swollen from crying, "I've been too ashamed to tell anyone. But sometimes, some nights, I walk to his flat and stand outside. I'm too afraid to go in, so I just stand there, in the hope that he might come out. Can you believe it? God, how can I humiliate myself like this?"

Ashley smiled and reached out to touch Kate's hair. "I've done it too," she said. "So many nights I've driven round to Julian's, parked and just sat there in the car. I've never known why. After all, I see him every day. I suppose it's some bizarre need to torture ourselves."

Kate hugged Ashley. They could give one another the understanding and support that only women who were made to suffer by a man could give.

"I can't write either," Kate said, as she pulled away. She tried to laugh. "I haven't been able to write for weeks. Oh, I can write for the magazine, I can do that standing on my head. But my book, it's over. I know I'm not going to be able to do it."

"You will," Ashley assured her. "Not now maybe, but you will."

Kate got up and started to pace the room. "Ash, I'm sorry for all those things I said to you just now. I'm jealous, you see. I'm so jealous of you that I hate you sometimes. I want to be like you. I want to be able to throw myself into my work, the way you do. How much new business have you won these past two months for Julian Arbrey-Nelmes?" She spat out his name, then held up her hand. "No, don't tell me, I don't think I could bear it. It's in the millions anyway, isn't it?"

Ashley didn't answer. Kate was right. She was right too about the promotion. Julian had only hinted at it, but she knew it would be coming her way soon. If her instincts were right, it would happen at Easter. His apology for marrying someone else.

There was a knock at the door.

"And that'll be Ellamarie. She's been with Bob today, all day, talking over the *Queen of Cornwall.* She's got her first feature film, and she's got Bob. And Jenneen—she should be here too to rub my nose in her success. If she wasn't filming somewhere in the Highlands, no doubt she would be."

Ashley got to her feet. "Right, you can cut the self-pity now, Kate. I'll answer the door."

Ellamarie came bursting in with the news that Nicholas Gough was to play Tristram, and wasn't it just marvelous that the three of them, her, Nick and Bob, would be working together again? "The world is just perfect," she sighed, helping herself to wine.

Kate burst into tears and ran out of the room.

Ellamarie was astonished. "What did I say?"

Ashley told her.

Ellamarie groaned. "Oh shit! I should have known. I got carried away with myself and didn't stop to think. But hell, Ash, what does she see in him? He's an out and out bastard."

"Try convincing her of that." Ashley looked at her watch. "Look, I've got to run. We're doing a night shoot tonight and I'm supposed to be there at eight, and I told Keith I'd meet him for a drink before I left. Can you stay with Kate for a bit?"

"Sure," said Ellamarie. "How are things with you and Keith?"

Ashley shrugged. "I'll let myself out. Good luck."

Ellamarie gave a grim smile and went to find Kate in the bedroom. She was lying on the bed, so Ellamarie walked over and pulled the curtains.

"How are you feeling now?"

Kate looked up. "Furious! Absolutely bloody furious."

"Can't say I blame you. He's a bastard."

"Oh, not with him," said Kate. "With myself. For putting myself in the position where he can treat me like this."

"Well, how were you to know?"

"I just should have." She shuddered. "God, I can hardly bear to think about the way I'm behaving."

"Then don't." Ellamarie walked over and sat on the bed. "He's not worth it, you know."

"I know that. But sometimes I worry, Ellamarie. Sometimes I worry that I will never meet anyone. I'm thirty now. The years are just whizzing past, and what have I got to show for them?"

"I would have said quite a lot, but then it depends on what you want to show for them."

Kate shrugged. "Oh, I don't know. I want my career, I suppose, very badly in fact—but is it enough? How did you feel when you were thirty?"

Ellamarie thought for a moment. "The same. There is a kind of stigma, fear maybe, attached to being thirty. And a feeling inside that something has changed, and maybe a small part of you has died. No, that's too morbid. Maybe it's that the childish part of you finally grows up. And it's the end of a decade, arguably the most important decade of your life. I sure was unhappy about it at the time. But I think, no, I know, that I'm much happier now. I suppose I've had some time to get used to it, though. Maybe you should look at it as one of life's full stops. Now you have the chance to begin a new paragraph."

"Or the end of a paragraph and the beginning of a new chapter."

"Either way, you should look forward, and think of what you are going to put into your new chapter. After all, you're the one who's writing the novel."

"Yes," said Kate, perhaps a little too quickly. "Yes, I've always got the book. But that's not really what I'm getting at. You see, what I need, really, is, well, I need somebody."

Ellamarie reached out and took her hand. "Sure you do," she said. "You wouldn't be human if you didn't. You're not the first one to have doubts, you know. I was past thirty before I met Bob."

"But that's half the trouble. I don't want to be past thirty. Past thirty is too late."

"Too late for what?"

"Well, not too late perhaps. Just late." Kate looked into Ellamarie's face. "Do you ever think about children, Ellamarie?"

"Having them, you mean? Children of my own?"

"Yes."

Ellamarie looked thoughtful. "I guess I do. Sometimes. But I've a long way to go before anything like that can happen."

"But don't you want any now?"

"It's not that I don't want any now, it's that I can't have any now."

"But why?"

"Oh, Kate. Bob is still married. And I've got my career. There are so many things I want to do first. Don't you?"

"Yes. But I want something else. Something tangible in my life. Creating a character in a book is the strangest thing. It's like giving life to your fantasy man. Your ideal man. Sometimes I long to meet him, and it's sad to think that I'm yearning after someone who only exists in my mind, or on the pages of a book."

"That's only because you haven't met anyone. The two will take completely separate identities once you do."

"That's just it," Kate said. "Meeting Joel was like meeting that character. He was just how I described Alan Young. And now I feel as though my own book is rejecting me. I know it sounds stupid, insane even, but it's how I feel."

"No, I don't think it sounds insane," said Ellamarie. "Odd maybe, to anyone else. But I have had a similar experience with characters I have played. Not quite the same, I know. But I understand how something that doesn't really exist can take over your life."

"Romantic nonsense. That's all it is. And how's this for nonsense? I just long to have a baby, Ellamarie. A little girl of my own. Sometimes I want it so badly

I can't think about anything else. I know you'll think I'm mad, but I've even considered stopping taking the pill, but then common sense prevails. And I suppose it prevails because I also want someone to love, and to love me too. And the thing that makes me the saddest is that now it is already too late to be what I always wanted to be. A young mother. And the man I marry, if I ever do get married, will never know me in my twenties, and by the time my little girl is ten, it's very likely that I will be forty, forty-five even. Somehow life is passing me by."

Ellamarie laughed. "Well, if you put it like that, it's charging by."

"Sorry," Kate said, "I'm being morose. But that's how it feels to be Katherine Calloway and thirty."

Ellamarie smiled. Darkness had overtaken the room completely and she reached out to switch on the lamp. As she did, the telephone rang, and Kate jumped, violently.

"I'll answer it," Ellamarie said. She lifted the receiver.

"Hello."

She looked at Kate, then looked away again. "No, I'm sorry," she said, "she's just gone down to the car. We're already late. Can I get her to call you? Sorry, could you repeat that? Yes, thank you, I'll tell her. Goodbye."

"It was him, wasn't it?"

Ellamarie nodded, and saw a look of anguish cross her friend's face. She knew what Kate was feeling only too well.

"I know it's difficult, honey, but I promise you, it's for the best. He's no good, and in your heart you know it."

Kate turned away and buried her face in the pillow. Ellamarie sat with her, holding her hand until finally Kate sat up again. "Please," she said, in a small, quiet voice, "don't ever mention any of this to my father. Not about the way I've been behaving. Not about wanting a baby. None of it. He would be so upset. He really wants me to write this book. Since my brother was killed he has set all the ambition he ever had for both of us on my shoulders, and I just couldn't bear to let him down. I'm not going to let him down."

"Of course I won't say anything to him," said Ellamarie. "But remember, Kate, it's your life. You must do what you want to do. You can't be a substitute for your brother, you know, and no more should you."

"I know," said Kate, and she laughed suddenly. Ellamarie watched her face, and what she saw there made her uneasy.

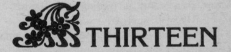

THIRTEEN

CRADLING THE PHONE WITH HER SHOULDER, ELLAMARIE stood at the buffet pouring herself a drink ". . . hell, I go back home for ten days, and when I get back everyone's disappeared. Where have y'all been? I've been trying to call you for days."

"Oh really, Ellamarie, you'll just have to try and keep up," Ashley teased her. "I've been at the bottom of a gravel pit with the crabbiest director I've ever worked with. Jenneen, when I last heard from her, was in Rome, and Kate is in Monte Carlo with—wait for it—Joel."

"Joel!"

"Yes, Joel."

"I don't know what to say," said Ellamarie, which

made Ashley laugh. It wasn't often Ellamarie was lost for words.

Jenneen, Ashley, went on to tell her, was filming the playgrounds of the rich and famous, and Kate had been suddenly swept off to the south of France by Joel Martin.

"But when I left she was seeing Nicholas Gough. At least she'd been out to dinner with him once or twice," said Ellamarie.

But ever since Joel had spoken to Ellamarie on the telephone he had been pestering Kate night and day. Eventually Kate had given in and seen him—lunch only, she had insisted. And over that lunch Joel had been so charming, and attentive, that she had fallen right back into bed with him.

"So you see, your strategy worked," said Ashley.

"It wasn't meant to work—not like that. Joel Martin is a creep as well as a bastard."

"How is Bob?" said Ashley.

"Fantastic! He's right here preparing to go off and be interviewed by someone from *The Times.*"

"Well, I am impr . . ." Ashley looked up as the door of her office opened. It was Julian. She flushed, and her voice faltered as she told Ellamarie that she would have to ring off.

"No need," said Julian, "I only popped in to make sure that you were going to be at the awards ceremony tomorrow night."

Ashley put her hand over the receiver. "Of course," she said. "Shouldn't the winners always attend?"

"I like your confidence," he chuckled, and closed the door behind him.

"Was that who I think it was?"

"None other," Ashley answered. "What on earth is going on over there?" she asked as she heard Ellamarie shriek.

"Let's just say that I think Mr. McElfrey missed

me while I was away." Bob moved his mouth further up and bit her on the shoulder. "I think I'd better go before this turns into a dirty phone call."

"Some people have all the luck," Ashley laughed, and they hung up.

Monte Carlo meant several things to Kate; one of them was dancing at Jimmy'z, another was trying, and failing, to make her fortune in the Salles Privées. It was the last night of their stay, and Joel and the author they had come to see, Royston Robberts, had dined alone on Royston Robberts' yacht, while Kate, together with Maggie Robberts, had dined at the Hotel de Paris. Later they met up with the men at Jimmy'z, then went on to try their luck, one last time, at the gaming tables.

It was not quite the season yet for Monte Carlo, though with the Easter holiday not far away it was beginning to get busy. The casino was crowded, and as Kate walked in on Joel's arm her face suddenly lit up. Walking across the room, talking animatedly to a corpulent yet obviously affluent Arab, was Jenneen. Kate called out, but Jenneen didn't look up.

"Jenneen!" Kate called again, trying to push her way toward her. Suddenly Kate stopped. It wasn't Jenneen who turned round to look at her at all. "I'm sorry," Kate mumbled, and moved away again.

The look the woman had given her had unsettled her, though Kate couldn't think why. Once or twice during the remainder of the evening Kate strained her neck to see if the woman was still in the bar, but there was no sign of her.

Joel had laughed at her, and told her to stop being nosy. There were plenty more interesting things to do in Monte than search a casino for somebody she didn't even know, he teased her, and from the gleam in his eye Kate knew what at least one of those things was. In his quest for sexual gratification he had taken to making love to her in public places, and in order to please him Kate had not worn underwear since they'd arrived. Now he pulled her onto his lap and pushed his hand beneath the ruffles of her dress. Kate gasped as she felt his fingers enter her and looked around to see if anyone was watching them. They were in the darkest corner of the casino and Royston Robberts had taken his wife off to the chemin de fer table. After several minutes of caressing her almost to the point of orgasm Joel pushed her from his lap and told her to stand in front of him, holding her skirt up while he unzipped his fly. His penis leapt from his trousers, and turning her round he pulled her back onto his lap and pushed it deep inside her. A few minutes later he summoned a passing waiter and ordered champagne. As the waiter walked away again Kate flinched as Joel gripped her by the shoulders and buried his face in her neck in an effort to drown his voice as the semen burst from his body.

The following morning they took Royston Robberts' helicopter to Nice airport, and from there they flew back to London. Kate had had an absolutely marvelous time and was more in love with Joel than ever, she told Ellamarie when she got back. Ellamarie made no comment.

Matthew was waiting at the door as Jenneen dragged her suitcase up over the stairs. He rushed down to help her, dropping a light kiss on her cheek and giving her a big smile. He seemed pleased that she was back, and Jenneen couldn't help but be touched by it.

The filming had gone on longer than anyone had anticipated, and she had been away for almost three weeks. She didn't tell Matthew that when she had returned to Heathrow, two days earlier, she had caught the train to Yorkshire to spend some time with her parents.

"So how was it?" he said as he put her suitcase inside the door and turned back to put an arm round her.

"Much like I told you on the phone," she said.

He laughed a little uneasily. "Come on. I'll make some coffee, and we can talk."

She sighed, and took off her coat. More than anything else, she would have liked to come back to an empty flat. Now wasn't that ironic? All those times when she had come back to no one, when she had felt sorry for herself and there had been no milk in the fridge, the bread was stale, and the flat was freezing cold. And now here she was, walking into a warm flat, with coffee being made for her and no doubt fresh bread in the cupboard, loving arms to hold her, and all she wanted was to be alone. What in the world did it take to satisfy Jenneen Grey?

"What are you doing?" Matthew called from the kitchen.

Jenneen collected her thoughts. "Coming."

She wandered into the lounge, and she smiled to see everything so spick and span. She smelled the polish as soon as she walked in, and the carpets were still lined from the back and forth of the Hoover. The windows gleamed, and everything looked so fresh. There was even a vase of flowers on the table. Dear Matthew, he really was trying hard.

She sat down, and put her feet up on the coffee table. Come what may, it was good to be home.

Matthew came in with the coffee, and set it down in front of her.

"Where did the flowers come from?"

"A flower shop."

She smiled. "They're beautiful, thank you."

"I wanted everything to be nice for you when you got back," he said. "I've really missed you, you know."

She picked up her coffee, and began to drink it. "Did you manage to get everything I asked you to get?"

"It's all in the kitchen. Ellamarie rang earlier. She and Bob will be arriving at the same time as everyone else. She doesn't have a performance tonight."

"Oh, that's good," said Jenneen. "What about the others? Are they all coming?"

"As far as I know. No one's rung to say otherwise."

Jenneen yawned. "I could do with some sleep before everyone arrives. What time is it?"

"Half past four."

"I think I could manage an hour."

"Good idea. I can be getting on with things for you, if you tell me what has to be done."

"You don't know how to cook, Matthew," she laughed.

"I can always learn. Anyway, I wasn't offering to cook, exactly. More like cleaning vegetables, or cracking eggs."

"Don't worry. We can do it together, when I get up."

"I'll go to the off-license and get the wine then," he said.

She picked up a magazine from the pile sitting beside her, and started to flick through. "What's this?"

"I got them this morning, from the travel agents."

"What for?"

"What do you mean, what for? For a holiday."

"Where are you thinking of going?"

"Well, as the brochure might suggest, skiing."

She nodded, and continued to flick through. She wasn't really looking at the pages, she was too tired to think much.

"Well, what do you say?"

She looked at him.

"How about it? You've been working so hard lately, I thought you could do with a break. We both could."

Still she didn't answer.

"Don't you think it would be good to get away, just the two of us? The sun, the snow, all that fresh air and exercise. And the après-ski of course." He didn't mention anything about the group of people he had met at a pub while she was away who had invited him to join their party. He knew he wouldn't be able to go without Jenneen; she would be paying.

"I don't think I can, Matthew. Not right now."

"I didn't mean right away. In a couple of weeks, before the snow disappears. What do you say?"

"I don't like skiing."

"How do you know? You've never been."

"It just doesn't appeal."

"You'll love it, once you're there."

"I won't. I'll probably break my leg or something worse. No, Matthew, I don't want to go skiing. But why don't you go?" She deliberately didn't make any reference to the fact that she knew he had no money.

"I don't want to go without you. The whole point of a holiday is so that we can spend some time together."

"It's a nice thought, Matthew, but honestly, I just don't fancy the idea."

"It might grow on you."

"I don't know," she said. "Look, why don't we talk about it later. I'm so tired now, I can hardly think straight."

"Are you sure you should be holding this dinner party this evening? I mean, if you're so tired. Why don't I ring everyone and put them off. We can have a nice quiet evening, on our own."

"No," she said. "No. I haven't seen anyone for three weeks, and it's too late to put them off now anyway. If I get some sleep, I'll be fine." She had to face Kate again sooner or later. Please God, that she hadn't really recognized her that night in the Casino.

He shrugged. "If you say so." He went to sit beside her. "Do I get a kiss, before you disappear again?"

She closed her eyes, and smiled. When she opened them again, he was studying her, waiting for her to answer.

"You've hardly come near me since you came in."

"I'm sorry." She put her arms round him and he held her close, running his hand over her hair, gently kissing her face.

"It's so good to have you back, Jenn," he whispered, and he moved his mouth to find hers.

"OK," he said as she pulled away, "off you go then, and get some sleep. I'll go fetch the wine." He pulled her to her feet. "What time do you want me to call you?"

"About six."

"I'll have a bath waiting for you."

She was in the bedroom, slipping out of her clothes, when she heard a ring on the doorbell. Vaguely she wondered who it could be, but people often rang the wrong bell; it was probably for someone else in the block.

She pulled back the bedcovers, and slipped inside. The sheets were freshly laundered and she could have almost felt tender toward Matthew if she hadn't known that he had done it with an ulterior motive in mind. She hadn't been fooled for one minute about the skiing holiday.

There was a knock on the door, and Matthew poked his head round. "All right?"

"Mmm, wonderful."

"There's someone out here," he said, "says she knows you and you're expecting her."

Jenneen frowned. "Who?" She hadn't invited anyone round this afternoon.

"Her name's Maggie. Maggie Dewar."

Jenneen groaned, remembering. She sat up. "Where is she?"

"In the lounge."

"Come in, close the door," she whispered.

Matthew looked confused. "Who is she?" he said as he crossed over to the bed.

Jenneen swung her legs out. "She's the daughter of a friend of my mother's."

"But what's she doing here?"

"She's come down for some interview at a hairdresser's in the West End."

"That still doesn't explain what she's doing here."

"I told her, in a rash moment, that she could stay here when she came down. I'd completely forgotten. My mother must have given her my address. I didn't realize she was planning to come so soon."

"What are you going to do with her?"

"What *can* I do with her? She'll have to stay, I suppose. Oh damn it! What a bloody nuisance. Have you told her I'm here?"

Matthew nodded.

"Then I'll have to get dressed again. Damn! Bloody damn!"

"No, don't get up," he said. "I told her you were having a nap so get back into bed, I'll see to her. I'll make up the bed in the spare room for her, shall I?"

"Yes," said Jenneen. "Do you think we've got enough food for an extra one tonight?"

"Definitely. I went mad at Sainsbury's."

"I can imagine," said Jenneen, raising an eyebrow. "Do you mind seeing to her?"

"Not at all. She seems quite a sweet kid. Go on now, get back into bed. I'll call you at six."

Jenneen did as she was told, and Matthew tucked her in and kissed her. Why, oh why did she make rash promises that she had no desire to keep?

As he had promised, Matthew called Jenneen at six and ran her a bath. She didn't want to get out of bed, she had been fast asleep and was still tired.

She was surprised to hear voices as she came out of the bedroom, until she remembered that Maggie Dewar had arrived. She'd better go and say hello.

As she walked into the lounge, Jenneen noticed, with a flicker of annoyance, that Maggie and Matthew were already through the best part of a bottle of wine.

That was all she needed, a drunken teenager at her dinner party; and she was none too pleased with the way Matthew was drinking again lately. Still, that was his problem, and Maggie just better not be sick, that's all.

Hiding her irritation she greeted Maggie warmly enough, and made her feel as welcome as she could. She needn't have bothered. Maggie was obviously already quite well settled in, and seemed to have hit it off rather well with Matthew. But of course, she would remember Matthew from the drama series he had been in a couple of years ago, and no doubt from the few commercials he had done since. It took Jenneen no time at all to see that Maggie had done wonders for his ego.

Matthew went to get another glass. "Like some wine, Jenn?"

"No, not yet. I'll go and have a bath first."

"Anything I can do in the kitchen?"

"Yes, you could start the soup."

"What are we having?"

"Cream of Brussels sprouts."

"Ugh!" said Maggie, pulling a face. "Sprout soup!"

Jenneen looked at her, her annoyance thinly disguised.

"Just wait till you taste it," said Matthew. "It's delicious."

Maggie looked unconvinced.

"What do I have to do?" Matthew said quickly, sensing the rich retort Jenneen was on the point of delivering.

She looked at him; obviously he wanted that holiday more than she had realized. "Make the stock first. There's a recipe book in the kitchen, the big *Reader's Digest* one. You'll find the instructions in there."

"OK." He turned to Maggie. "Want to help?"

She shrugged, clearly the idea held no appeal.

Jenneen went off to the bathroom. She could tell already that this girl was going to be a trial to have around. Why did she have to come today? She was too young to be at one of their dinner parties, she would spoil it. Jenneen toyed with the idea of sending her to a hotel, but she knew Matthew would hear none of it, and she didn't want an argument. Oh well, Maggie could be his responsibility. He could put her to bed when she crashed over, drunk.

She bathed and dressed quickly, wanting to get into the kitchen before too much damage was done.

Matthew seemed relieved when she came to take over, but hovered around, trying to help. He was hell bent on being nice to her, and it was beginning to get on her nerves.

"Look," she said finally, when he had asked for the fifth time if there was anything else he could do. "Why don't you take Maggie down to the wine bar? I'll get on much better on my own."

"I was only trying to help."

"I know, and you're wonderful. But I promise you, I'd rather be left alone. Too many cooks and all that."

"I'd like to go to the wine bar," Maggie piped up. "I've never been to a London wine bar."

"They're no different from anywhere else," said Jenneen irritably.

"Come on then," said Matthew, realizing he could only save the situation by doing as Jenneen wanted.

Maggie went to get her coat. "Make sure she only has orange juice," Jenneen hissed.

Matthew nodded. "See you in about an hour, eh?"

"Make it an hour and a half. Everything should be well underway by then."

An hour later, with the fish pie in the oven, the soup simmering nicely and the sorbets chilling in the fridge, Jenneen poured herself a large glass of wine, and sat down to relax for five minutes.

She needed to think about what she would say if Kate mentioned the night she had seen her. Of course, she would deny that she had been in Monte Carlo at that time, but it was difficult to lie to Kate, or to any of her friends, come to that. How foolish she had been not to have put on Mrs. Green's wig that night. She had been careless, but she had never dreamt that there might be anyone she knew at the casino. Thank God Mrs. Green had insisted on the makeup; she was a tart, and wanted to look like one. Funny, though, how she would never accept money. The Arab had been more than extravagant in the sum he had offered, but Mrs. Green had refused. But she hadn't refused when the Arab had suggested she spend the night on his yacht. And neither had she refused when she had found out what he had in store for her there.

Jenneen shivered, and tried to push the images of that night of debauched concupiscence from her mind. She picked up the newspaper she had brought in with her and tried to concentrate on the article about Bob. A few minutes later the doorbell rang. Wearily she got to her feet. Matthew must have forgotten his key.

"Hello," she said into the entryphone.

"Hi, it's Ashley."

"Ash!" Jenneen cried with delight. "Come on up."

Ashley came stomping up the stairs, and Jenneen could see that she was angry.

"Bloody men! Bloody, bloody men!"

Jenneen laughed. "What's Julian done now?" she said, as she closed the door behind her.

"Oh him!" Ashley snorted. "I don't mean him, for once. No, I've just been to the garage to fill up with petrol and oil and air, and all that palaver, and I saw two men watching me from the workshop."

"Well, surely you weren't surprised," said Jenneen. "You must get it all the time. An attractive woman and a Mercedes, any man would look."

"That's just it," said Ashley. "I'm beginning to get fed up with it. Do you know what I heard one of them say? They were looking at me, and sniggering, and then one of them said to his mate, 'Wonder where her patch is?' Of all the bloody nerve!"

"What did you say?" said Jenneen.

"Nothing. I almost gave them a two-fingered salute as I drove off, though, but I decided not to stoop to their level. Thanks," she said as Jenneen handed her a glass of wine. "It really makes me sick. A woman isn't allowed to have something nice without her being on the game to get it. Narrow-minded, pig ignorant, stupid men like that, they make my blood boil. Jealousy, that's all it is. Jealousy. I wish I'd run them over."

Jenneen chuckled.

"Whatever makes some women think they've achieved equality, I'll never know," said Ashley. "While there are lame-brains like that in the world, we don't stand a chance."

"What, of stooping to their level?" Jenneen remarked. "I should hope not."

"And to make it worse," Ashley went on, "when I was on the way to the garage I pulled up at some traffic lights, the window down, and this idiot pulled up alongside me, and shouted out, 'How much, darlin'?' And do you know what I did? I smiled, and started to laugh. I thought he was asking how much the car was!"

Jenneen burst out laughing. "Oh, I love you, Ashley Mayne. The only woman in the world who is naive enough to think that. Come on, sit down, and calm down."

Ashley sat on the settee, and picked up the skiing brochures. "Now, tell me about the filming. Where did you go? Who did you meet? Didn't know you were into skiing," she added, as she opened one of the magazines.

"I'm not. Matthew is."

"Where is he?"

"Down at the wine bar. I threw him out, he was getting in the way."

"Poor Matthew."

"What time is your friend Mr. Winston arriving?" Jenneen asked.

"Oh, I forgot to tell you, he can't come. His nephew has come to stay for a few days."

"Oh, that's a shame. He's always such fun."

"I know," said Ashley. "He was really upset to miss it. But he sends his regards."

"Well, we are still on for lunch with him at the Brasserie on Saturday, aren't we?"

"Of course."

"Good, so we'll see him then. Have you invited Keith in his place?"

Ashley shook her head and swallowed a mouthful of wine. "He's in Dorset somewhere, on some kind of a course, so he couldn't come either."

"How are things going there?"

"OK. Bit like you and Matthew, I guess. It's nice to have someone around, but I don't want any more than that. Not that I can convince Keith of it. Never again, though! Twice bitten. However, I did take it upon myself to invite someone else."

"Oh?"

"Giles Creddesley."

"Giles Creddesley! *The* Giles Creddesley? Whatever made you do that?"

"Basically, because I was stuck."

"But I thought you two couldn't stand the sight of one another."

"We can't normally. But he's been so nice lately, he didn't even ride roughshod over my creative review. And as he so gallantly escorted me to the awards ceremony the other night, where Frazier, Nelmes won an award for their Newslink campaign . . ."

"Ashley!" Jenneen cried. "Oh, congratulations. Did you bring it? What was it? What did Julian say? Jesus Christ, that's wonderful. Here, have some more wine. We should be having champagne."

Ashley laughed. "Wine is good enough, thank

you. I drank enough champagne to sink the *QE2* the night we won. So anyway, as I was saying, I thought, as Giles wasn't doing anything this evening, I'd ask him along. You don't mind, do you?"

"Not if you don't."

"Kate should be pleased. She's been interviewing him today, for an article about men in the media. That will have flattered his ego no end."

"Oh God, he'll be unbearable," Jenneen groaned.

"Well, it'll give us all a laugh, if nothing else."

"You don't think he'll bring that revolting pipe, do you?"

"Probably."

"Ugh! I don't know what he puts in it, but it smells like something he's swept up in a farmyard."

"Don't tell him that," said Ashley. "He thinks it turns us all on. Condor man, and all that."

Jenneen pulled a face. "Well, he's not to smoke it until after we've eaten."

"Don't worry, I'll tell him."

Ten minutes later Kate came bursting in through the door. "I'll kill him!" she cried. "I'd like to stuff his head right down his bloody pipe!"

"Come in," said Jenneen. "My, we are all feeling fond toward the opposite sex tonight. Who's upset you?"

"Giles bloody Creddesley!" she said. "That's who!"

"Oh dear," said Jenneen, "now that could be a problem. Come through to the lounge, Ashley's already here."

"Good. I've got a bone to pick with her."

"Kate," Jenneen announced to Ashley, as she pushed open the door to the lounge. "Steel yourself," she added under her breath.

Ashley looked up. "Hi," she said to Kate. "How are you?"

"Bloody livid, that's how I am."

"Why?"

"Piles Cretin, that's why!"

"Giles. Why? What happened?"

"I don't know how you could have put me on to someone like that, Ash, really I don't. He's an asshole."

Ashley raised her eyebrows.

"I've never been so insulted in my entire life," Kate went on. "How do you stand working with him?"

"Only just."

"He's abominable! Sitting there with his pink bow-tie covered in green spots, and blowing clouds of manure into the air through that Dickensian effort he puffs away on, he's an insult to the human race!"

"I quite agree," said Ashley, "but did you get your interview?"

"Did I get my interview! Darling, just let him wait till it comes out. Then he'll know the wrath of a woman. I'm going to crucify him."

"Just exactly what did he say?" Jenneen asked.

"Not much, and what he did say was of no use to me. Now he'll find out just how much use it is to him. I asked him something, I can't quite remember what it was, and he said, 'My dear, I can't write your article for you.' Of all the cheek! Then I asked him something about art directors, and he puffed on his pipe, looked me up and down, and said: 'Oh dear, you really don't know very much at all, do you?' At that point, I almost got up and strangled him with his dicky bow."

"He doesn't like it to be called that," Ashley said seriously.

Jenneen burst out laughing. "Were you rude back to him?"

"I told him that if I knew everything then I wouldn't be there asking him, would I?"

"What did he say?"

" 'Next question.' So I asked him which particular bit of the woodwork he had crept out of this morning."

"And?"

"He said that he didn't understand the question. So I explained. And he laughed. 'Oh my dear,' he said, 'you really shouldn't get so upset. This is where so many of you women fall down these days, you know, now that you are all striving for equal rights and status. You're all far too emotional.' I very nearly screamed."

"You didn't, though, did you?" said Jenneen.

"No, I picked up my pen, wrote asshole in large letters across the notes I had taken, and smiled at him sweetly. Then I picked up my coat, told him it had been an experience, and left."

"He would take that as a compliment," said Ashley.

"I'm sure he would," said Kate, "he's stupid enough to. I'd like to knock that pipe of his right down his patronizing throat."

"Well, I think you're going to get the chance," said Jenneen.

Kate looked at her with alarm. "What do you mean?"

"He's coming here for dinner, tonight."

"What! Giles Creddesley is coming here? Why? How? Oh Jenneen, how could you?"

"I invited him, I'm afraid," said Ashley.

"Are you mad?"

"Probably. But he'd been behaving so well lately, I thought it would be all right."

"Just don't sit him anywhere near me," said Kate. "I won't be responsible for my actions. Any wine going? I could do with something to calm me down."

"Help yourself," said Jenneen. "I'd better go and see how the dinner is coming along."

FOURTEEN

THE EVENING WAS GOING WELL. JENNEEN'S NATURAL TALENT for the unexpected ingredient went a long way toward making her dinner parties a success and even Maggie had managed to slurp her way through the soup. As Matthew cleared the table, Jenneen glanced in Maggie's direction and saw that her chin was still resting comfortably on her collar bone and for the moment, thank God, she was too drunk to speak.

The men, Giles in particular, had dominated the conversation for most of the evening. Where was it, Jenneen mused, that she had read those statistics about men talking eighty percent of the time when in mixed company? She turned with relief to listen to Ellamarie as she demanded that Kate tell her how much she had lost at the casino in Monte Carlo. Ellamarie gasped when Kate told her. But had Kate seen anyone when she was there, you know, anyone famous? Jenneen shifted in her chair, and leaned forward to say something to Bob. Kate answered that she had only seen Prince Albert, darling, and she thought Stephanie too, but she hadn't been too sure.

"But hey, hang on a minute," she cried suddenly. "I thought I saw you, Jenn. Do you remember?" she said, turning to Joel. "There was this woman in the casino, she was with an Arab, disgustingly wealthy-looking he was too. But anyway, this woman, she looked just like you, Jenn. So much so I even called out to her. God it was weird. They say everyone has a double somewhere, and I could have sworn it was you at first. Don't know any rich Arabs, do you, by any chance? Not hiding him from us are you?"

Jenneen caught Matthew's eye across the table and could do nothing to stop the rush of blood to her face.

"She's blushing!" Kate cried. "So you do have a guilty secret. Come along now, out with it!"

Jenneen's eyes were riveted to Matthew's as he smiled and picked up a bottle of wine to refill the glasses. "No, Jenneen doesn't have a double, do you, Jenn?" he said, smoothly. "No, what Jenneen has is a Doppelgänger."

"Oh Matthew!" Kate shuddered. "That's a horrible thing to say."

Jenneen's eyes flashed, but she was smiling as she said: "Which is no more than one can expect from the likes of him," and the others started up a barrage of lighthearted abuse in her defense. Matthew took it goodnaturedly and Jenneen felt almost sick with relief as the moment passed.

Ellamarie was watching the way Kate was behaving with Joel. It made her mad as hell sometimes to see the way Kate hung onto his every word. The man was no good, Ellamarie was certain of that. She put a lot of store by a person's eyes, and Joel Martin's were cruel. Catching Ellamarie looking at him, Joel smirked and raised his glass. Ellamarie returned the smile. She hadn't got his measure yet, but even if she had, she knew it would make no difference. Kate would have to find out for herself what he was like—there was nothing the rest of them could do. She turned away as she felt Bob reaching for her hand. Joel Martin left a bitter taste in her mouth.

Bob was enjoying Giles Creddesley's company immensely. The more drunk Giles became, the more pompous and self-congratulatory he was. He seemed blissfully unaware of the suppressed guffaws of the others. He knew everything there was to know about absolutely everything, and his opinion, which was blasted into the conversation with voluminous regularity, was unmitigated and indisputable.

Bob, and then Matthew, did all they could to encourage him. Joel sat back to listen, sometimes remembering a little too late to straighten his face whenever Giles addressed him. Ashley was sinking deeper into her chair, suffering all the embarrassment Giles should have been suffering, had he had the sensitivity. At one point she heard Kate whisper to Jenneen that Giles must be the absolute ultimate in "Hooray," which was promptly confirmed by Giles himself, as he began the hunt for a "window" in his Filofax, saying that he simply had to go and see *Twelfth Night,* old chap. And *Don Giovanni* too, of course. Oh hell, *Don Giovanni* clashed with Badminton, that was just too bad. He had to go to Badminton, naturally—though he didn't say why. But then *everyone* went to Badminton, didn't they?

Unlike the men round the table, Jenneen soon became bored by Giles and turned to Kate to ask her how the novel was coming along. It was a mistake. Giles, who appeared to have ears any self-respecting bat would envy, was writing a book too. Joel caught Bob's eye, and Matthew replenished the glasses.

Bob listened with awe-inspired interest as Giles unfolded his less than intricate plot, and Ashley gritted her teeth as Bob, leaning back in his chair and draping an arm round Ellamarie, asked if the book was in any way autobiographical.

"Autobiographal?" Giles repeated.

"Well, what exactly is it that you yourself do in advertising?" Bob asked.

Giles sucked noisily on his pipe. "Me!" he said, failing in his attempt to sound modest. "Well, where to begin?" Ashley winced as with the greatest of ease Giles found his starting point, and, encouraged in the main by Bob, went on to discard all "false modesty" and admit how outstandingly accomplished he was in his field, and how actually . . .

Jenneen regarded him with increasing antipathy. He was not one of the world's most attractive men when he had his mouth shut, but with it open . . . words failed her. It was a shame they didn't fail him too. She yawned, and allowed her mind to wander, until several minutes later she noticed that Bob was speaking. Bringing herself back to the present, she turned to listen to what he was saying.

"Oh, I agree with everything you say, Bob," Giles interrupted as Bob paused to draw breath, "our class system is indeed archaic." At what point had the subject changed? Jenneen wondered. "But nonetheless," Giles went on, "one has to admit that it still exists, and indeed does have its merits. I mean, we couldn't have just any old chap, or," he chuckled, "chapess, sauntering into the boardroom, could we? One simply shudders to think what might happen if the peasants found their way in." He grinned through a fallen halo of pipe smoke, creating such a disturbing image that Jenneen found herself wondering where he spent Hallowe'en.

"Giles, shut up," Ashley groaned.

"No," said Ellamarie, "no, I'm interested. Go on, Giles. Just what do you think would happen if the peasants did find their way in, or," she shot a glance at Ashley and shuddered, "God forbid, chapesses!"

"Oh, chapesses, er, women, belong just as much as men to the class structure," Giles answered, managing to sidestep the question. "And if their background is right, if they are of the right stock, then they can be well suited, and actually surprisingly efficient in the positions they hold."

"And if they are not from the right class, the right *stock*," said Jenneen, who was by now utterly sick of the sound of him, "and yet they hold a good job, what then?"

Giles shrugged. "Oh, hysterics, sickness, I don't know, you name it . . ."

"Shit, I can't believe I'm hearing this," said Ellamarie.

"Personally speaking," said Jenneen, "I'm both a chapess and a peasant, and although I can't claim to be on the board, I don't generally regard myself as a failure, so where would you say that I fit in? Perhaps you would like to call me an hysterical success?"

Giles shrugged and sucked on his pipe.

"Well, she must be something," Kate prompted. "So must we all. Just where do women like us fit into your class structure, Giles? We're all from different backgrounds, and yet we all lead the same lives now. Successful lives. So, where do we fit in? Exactly what are we?"

Giles shrugged again, as if the question were of no importance. "Call yourselves what you like."

With delight Bob saw Jenneen's eyes narrow. "I'll tell you what we are, Giles," she said, trying not to slam her hand on the table, but failing, "we are something that the likes of you will probably never understand. Something way beyond your pomposity and powers of comprehension. There's another class now, Giles, and you and your type don't even know it, and are too *stupid* to be a part of it. It is a class of awareness, Giles; without discrimination or prejudice, that nurtures the seeds of ambition and ultimate success, regardless of background or birth. It does not belong to the dried up, retrogressive class system that you, I am sorry to say, are so ignorantly and laughably proud to be a part of. It is an elite, Giles, deserving of its merits and superiority, and above, below and independent of your system; it is, and we are, a class apart."

Ashley, Kate and Ellamarie gave her a round of applause. Giles looked at her, then let go of a cloud of smoke.

"I think you're in a bit too deep, old man," said Joel.

Giles clutched at the barrel of his pipe.

At the unexpected lurch of a hiccup everyone turned to look at Maggie. She hiccuped again as her eyes reluctantly gave up on the task of trying to out-stare one another and fixed themselves on Giles. "That stuff stinks," she slurred, after deciding that the aroma was coming from him. It was the first thing she had managed to say all evening, and she looked now as though she were going to be sick. Bob, unable to contain himself, roared with laughter.

An hour later Joel looked at his watch and announced that it was time he was going. "Got to be up early in the morning," he grumbled. Seeing Kate reach out to pick up her handbag he caught her by the arm. "No," he said, "you stay. No need for you to leave now."

"It's all right," said Kate, blushing as she became aware of everyone watching her, "I don't mind."

"No, I insist. Stay, and enjoy yourself. You don't have to be up early."

Jenneen came to the rescue. "Why don't we all go and sit down a little more comfortably to drink our brandy," she said, getting to her feet.

Kate and Joel stayed by the table. "Why are you going now?" she whispered.

"I told you, I've got to be up early in the morning."

"Then I'll come home with you."

"There's no need. I have to get a good night's sleep tonight, so I thought I'd go home to my place."

"Then I'll come with you."

"No. Stay here, with your friends. I'll ring you to-morrow."

Kate caught his hand as he turned away. "I thought we could, you know. . ."

"That's what I mean," he said. "I have to get some sleep. I'll ring you tomorrow, OK?"

"Will I see you tomorrow night?" she said, hating herself for asking.

"I don't know. Yes, probably."

"I'll walk to the door with you."

Out in the hall, Joel took her in his arms. "Don't look so miserable," he said. "It's only for one night. But honestly, Kate, I have to sleep sometime. You're insatiable, you know."

"I thought we might start using the cane again," she whispered, as he started to put on his coat.

He stopped, and turned to look at her. She noticed that his eyes were suddenly bright, and waited for him to speak. Taking her face in his hands, he pressed himself against her. She could feel the bulge thickening in his trousers.

"Will you come home with me now?" she said.

"Darling," he groaned, "I want to. More than anything, I want to. But I have to get home tonight. I've such a lot to do before I leave in the morning. But I will be round tomorrow night. Promise. Have it waiting, eh?"

"I love you, Joel."

"Mmm," he said, as he kissed her again. He pulled his coat together, and reached out to open the door.

"Aren't you going to tell me you love me?" said Kate.

He turned back. "You know I do."

"I wonder sometimes."

"Then don't. You haven't told anyone, have you?"

"That you love me?"

"No, about our little secret."

"Of course not."

"Good girl." He tweaked her nose, and gave her a smile. "Be in touch," he said, and left.

Kate closed the door behind him, and leaned against it. Everything had been so perfect when they had been in France, but now, since they had returned, he had become cool and aloof again. She wished she knew what it was that made him tick. She heard the others burst out laughing at something in the other room, but made no move to join them. She was so obsessed by Joel now that it was hard even to think about anything else.

Jenneen woke very early in the morning. She had been careful not to drink too much the night before, but her head still felt heavy. She tried for a while to go back to sleep, but finally she gave up, and got out of bed. Matthew was still sleeping peacefully, and she made sure not to make any noise as she left the room.

Rain was beating against the windows and every now and again she could hear the swish of a car passing by. The heating had not long been on, and it was still chilly in the flat. She wrapped her robe tightly round her while she waited for the kettle to boil.

The kitchen was tidier than she had expected it to be, Matthew must have done it before he came to bed last night. The washing up was still in the sink, however, and the dining area of the lounge looked as though a bomb had hit it.

Ignoring the mess, she settled herself down on the settee with her coffee and picked up one of Matthew's skiing magazines. In truth, the idea rather appealed to her, but she was angry that he had broached the subject in the way he had, as if she couldn't see through him and know what he was up to.

Sooner or later they were going to have to face facts. It was not working out for them. Or, more to the point, it was not working out for her. She knew that he had been trying hard since Christmas, but it wasn't enough. She wanted more. But more of what? In the main Matthew was kind and considerate, did everything he could think of to make her happy, yet still she didn't trust him, still she wanted more.

She had hoped that once things had settled down a little with Matthew, the burning obsession of her alter ego would cease to exist, but she had only to look at what had happened in the south of France to know that Mrs. Green was still with her, and perhaps more now than ever. That there was something seriously wrong with her was now an almost constant fear. She didn't need anyone to tell her that it wasn't normal to assume another identity, and for that identity to make her behave in a way that was so completely alien to her true nature. Why, when she had Matthew, did she still need to satisfy Mrs. Green? She had no answer to the question. A macabre pattern was beginning to emerge. By day she was Jenneen Grey, television personality, and by night—almost every night—Mrs. Green, alter ego and nymphomaniac!

There! She had said it. Nymphomaniac. She was a nymphomaniac. But what was nymphomania? The dictionary definition was a morbid and uncontrollable sexual desire in women. But Jenneen wasn't even sure it was a sexual desire; she got no pleasure from it. Ah, but Mrs. Green did, therefore Jenneen did surely. But she hated it. She hated herself, and she hated the men. And most of all she hated the act itself, the shameless violation of her own body, taken over by the sinister character of Mrs. Green.

She had toyed with the idea of trying to get help, but how could she? If the press were to get hold of it they would have a field day. She could see the headlines now. "Jenneen Grey, hospitalized for sex problems." "TV double personality." "Mrs. Green or Ms. Grey?" And then there was the night that she had spent with a woman, feeding her insatiable appetite again—it would all come out and it would mean the end for her. She would never be able to hold up her head in public again. No TV company in their right mind would give her a job, no employer would be prepared to take the risk of such a scandal. And, perhaps even worse than that, was what it would do to her parents.

But surely she could sort this out. If only she could

discover, somewhere deep inside herself, what the real problem was, then she would be able to deal with it. Was it that she couldn't cope with her success? Was there something inside that was trying to push her into destroying herself? Dear God, why was she doing it? If only there was someone she could talk to, but there was no one.

The bitter tears of frustration, pain and confusion were stinging her eyes as she looked up and saw that Matthew was standing in the doorway, watching her.

She rubbed the back of her hand across her eyes and sniffed. "Morning," she said. "I didn't see you standing there."

"You're up early."

"I couldn't sleep."

He picked up the packet of cigarettes lying on the table and lit one. "You were miles away."

"Was I?" she said. "I've been trying to get together a commentary for the films we shot in Europe. For some reason the words seem to be evading me."

"Well, you won't find them in there."

Jenneen looked down at the brochure she had forgotten she was holding, and saw that it was torn and twisted.

"More coffee?"

She nodded, and handed him her empty cup.

"Are you going in today?" he called out from the kitchen.

"Yes, I'll have to. I've got a lot to do."

"Can't you ring in sick? You look awful, you know."

"No, I'm just tired. I'll get an early night tonight."

When he came back with the coffee he sat down on the settee opposite her. He was still watching her, and she wished he wouldn't. She guessed he was probably concerned, but she didn't want his concern. The truth was, she didn't want him at all.

"There's something else bothering you, Jenn, isn't there?" he said. "I mean besides the commentary."

She didn't meet his eyes.

"What is it?"

She shook her head. "Nothing," she said. "There's nothing."

"It might help if you talked about it."

"I told you, Matthew, there's nothing." She hadn't meant to sound irritable.

He shrugged. "OK, have it your way."

They sat in silence, drinking their coffee. She tried not to look at him. Now probably wasn't the time to tell him, but she knew she couldn't put it off much longer. She couldn't carry on living this lie. There were too many lies in her life already.

"Think I'll go and have a shower," she said eventually, and stood up.

"Jenn, don't."

She looked at him, and from the way he was looking back at her she knew that he wanted some answers. "Not now, Matthew," she said. "Please."

"Then when? We have to talk, you know we do. There is something wrong, and I need to know what it is. I need to know if it's me, or if it's something else."

"We'll talk later."

"No!" he shouted. "That's what you always say, but we never do. I've been trying to get through to you for weeks, but you just keep walking away. I want to talk now!"

She ran her fingers through her hair and heaved a long and tired sigh.

"What can I do, Jenneen? Just tell me, what do I have to do to get through to you?"

She sat down again, and covered her face with her hands.

"Look," his voice was almost pleading, "you know how I feel about you, but I can't go on like this. I want to be part of your life, I want to share things with you, so why won't you let me?"

"Do you, Matthew? Do you really want to share things with me?" she said, her hands still over her face.

"Jenneen," he said.

"Matthew." She uncovered her face and looked up. "There's no point pretending any more, is there? There's no future for us, you know it, and I know it. So let's end this pretense now."

"But why?"

"I don't love you, Matthew. I can't love you. I have tried, God knows I have tried. But I can't."

"But you've hardly given us any time."

"I don't need time to know. It can't work, it won't work."

"It can if we make it."

"It can't, Matthew. And if you were being honest with yourself, you know it too."

"Have you met someone else?"

"No."

"Then I don't understand."

"There's nothing to understand. It's simple, I don't love you, and I can't carry on like this."

"But I love you," he said.

"No, you don't. I know you say you do, but it's not true. These past weeks between us have been a lie."

He looked away, letting her words hang in the air. "Are you saying that you want me to go?" he said, finally. She didn't miss the slight tremor in his voice.

"Yes."

His feelings were forming in a clump at the base of his throat. "When?" he finally managed to ask.

"As soon as you can."

"Just like that?"

She shrugged. "I suppose so, yes."

"I don't have anywhere else to go."

"You can always stay with friends."

He watched her face as she spoke, and his lip

began to curl. "You really don't give a damn about me, do you?"

"You know that's not true," but she couldn't meet his eyes.

"No, I don't. For once you have someone who cares about you, someone to love you, who wants to be with you, and all you want to do is throw it all away. That's not caring, Jenneen."

"All right then, I don't care."

She saw the flush spread across his cheeks as he got to his feet. "As far as you're concerned there was never anything there in the first place, was there? You've used me, like you've used everyone else in your life. You don't care about anyone, except yourself, do you? And now I've served a purpose, whatever that purpose was, you're going to toss me to one side, just like you do with everything else. I feel sorry for you, Jenneen, you're a coward and you're a bitch. A cold, unfeeling bitch. You'll never have anything good in your life. Never!"

She was staring into her lap. She didn't want to see the anger in his face. She didn't want to listen to him. Everything he was saying was the truth, she was a coward, and she didn't care—at least not about him—and she never would.

"You're sick, you know that, don't you? You're sick in the head." He saw the alarm in her eyes as she looked up at him and he laughed. She was remembering the comment he had made the night before about her having a Doppelgänger. "Yes," he said, "yes, you do know it. And you don't even care about that, do you?"

"Matthew, please," she said. "You don't know what you're talking about."

"Oh, don't I? Don't think I don't know about you, Jenneen. I know everything there is to know about you. I know just how sick you really are."

She was shaking, and felt as though she was going

to throw up. "You don't know what you're talking about." Her throat was dry and her voice came in a whisper.

"I know what I'm talking about all right," he sneered. "I know what you get up to. I've known all along. And that's why you flinched when I said you were sick, wasn't it? Because you know it too. You're sick and disgusting, and God help me, I'm in love with you."

"Shut up, Matthew. Just shut up!"

"Can't face the truth, Jenneen? Well, it's about time you did. You need treatment. You need a psychiatrist. You're not normal. People don't go around behaving like you."

"I said shut up! Shut up! Just go! Get out of my life, I don't want you here any more. Do you hear me? I don't want you here!"

"Oh yes, I hear you all right. The almighty Jenneen Grey has spoken. Or should I say Mrs. Green?"

Jenneen's face turned white. How long had he known? How long had he been storing this up, just waiting for an opportunity to throw it in her face?

Under his cold, mocking eyes she felt herself begin to crumple inside, and she slumped forward. "I might have known," she said in a quiet voice. "You haven't changed one bit really, have you, Matthew? It's all been an act. And now we're beginning to see the real Matthew again. Well, you might be right about one thing, I might have a problem, but before you start casting stones at me, why don't you try and get your own life sorted out."

"Fine words, from a pervert. Tell me, it was you Kate saw in the casino, wasn't it? No, don't bother to deny it, I saw your face. So where's the wig now, Jenneen? Where do you keep it? When are you planning your next excursion into the world of filth and degradation? The world where you belong. Or have you turned to women again? Who's going to be next, Mrs. Green? Is it Ashley? Kate? Ellamarie? Who's next?"

Every fiber of her soul cried out in protest at what he was saying, and she began to shake violently.

"Well, Mrs. Green," he jeered. "Who next? Kate is very attractive, isn't she? Oh, not Kate? Not your type, is that it?"

"You bastard!" she cried. "You filthy, disgusting bastard. Get out of here, and take your filthy mind with you."

"Filthy mind? Oh come on, Jenneen, don't tell me you've never thought about it. I've seen the way you look at her. She's beautiful, isn't she? And Ashley, perhaps she's more your type. So tall, with those sexy black eyes of hers, and those full lips. I'll bet you dream about running your fingers through that shining black hair. I wonder what she's like in bed, Jenneen. But then, I expect that's something you already know, in that warped, fantasy mind of yours?"

"You bastard! How could I ever have been taken in by you? It's you who's warped, Matthew. You! You're no good, you're a loser, and you'll never be anything else."

"That's rich, coming from a nymphomaniac, and a lesbian nymphomaniac at that. At least my sexual tastes are normal."

"Normal! Normal! You're so fucking sexless . . ."

"Compared with what you're used to, I'm not surprised you think that. But I didn't hear you complaining last night. I'll sink to any depths for you, Jenneen, hadn't you noticed? But of course, I'm lacking the vital organs, aren't I? I don't have tits. Or a nice soft . . ."

"You're disgusting. *Get out of here!* I never want to see you again. Not ever!"

"Don't worry, I'm going. But I'm warning you now, Jenneen, you'll never find anyone else. I love you, you bitch, knowing everything I do about you, I still fucking well love you. And you want me too, because

I'm all you're ever going to get. It's not often in my life that I give as much to someone as I have given to you, Jenneen Grey, and you've turned on me again, just like you did the last time. Well, you'll pay for this, mark my words, you're going to . . ."

"Forget it! You'll never get anything from me. And don't think you can blackmail me, because I'm through with it, Matthew. And you don't even have the guts to . . ."

"Just try me, Jenneen, just try me. No one throws me out, especially not the likes of you, you whore! But I've got so much on you now you're going to be paying for the rest of your life. And I'm telling you, if I can't have you, then I'm going to make damned fucking sure that no other bastard ever does."

Suddenly she found herself picking up the cup that she had put on the table, and with all her might she flung it at him. "Get out!" she screamed. He ducked and the cup broke against the wall behind him. She stooped to pick up another, but he grabbed her hand and shoved her back onto the settee.

"Don't ever try that again," he yelled into her face, showering her with saliva.

"Let go of me! Let go!"

"Look at you," he spat, "you're ridiculous. Ridiculous and sick!" and he flung her hands to one side and drawing back his fist he brought it down hard against her jaw. "I'll leave you with that, and let it be a lesson to you. No one, do you hear me, *no one* throws me out on the streets, least of all you! I'll be back," and he stormed out of the room.

As he walked into the hall he almost fell over Maggie who was lurking behind the door. He glared at her a moment, then suddenly he began to laugh. There was no doubt from the look on Maggie's face that she had heard everything.

"Where are you going to go?" she said to him.
He shrugged.

"Take *her* with you," Jenneen yelled. She was standing in the doorway, a thin line of blood trickling over her chin. "I don't want her here."

Matthew looked at Maggie's pale and frightened face. It had already occurred to him that as she now knew about Jenneen he had to take her with him.

"Well, what are you waiting for?" Jenneen said. "Get out! Go on, both of you, get out!"

Maggie looked at her, afraid and not knowing which way to turn.

"Come on, kid," said Matthew, putting his arm round Maggie's shoulder. "Get your things. I wouldn't leave you here with her, you might not be safe."

Maggie looked at Jenneen. "Just wait until I tell everyone at home about you," she said slowly, "there'll be no more of your airs and graces then, Mrs. Green!"

Jenneen closed her eyes and fell to her knees. Dry, choking sobs convulsed her body, and the excruciating grip of fear seized her brain as Maggie's words hit home. It was inevitable, she had always known it would come, always known that Mrs. Green would win. And now, for Mrs. Green, victory was at hand. For Jenneen Grey this must be the beginning of the end.

FIFTEEN

KATE WAS SINGING TO HERSELF IN THE KITCHEN AS SHE spooned coffee into a jug. She was unaware of the way that her eyes were shining, but it wouldn't have sur-

prised her to have known. It was the first time in weeks
that she had felt happy.

She had just returned from a marvelous evening
with Nicholas Gough—the third in less than two
weeks—and she couldn't remember enjoying herself so
much in ages. They had been for an after-theater dinner with Ellamarie and Bob, who were so terribly in
love these days that they had left early. Nick and Kate
had laughed at them, and Kate hadn't missed the look
in Nick's eyes as he had turned back to her, but he had
only suggested, in a friendly way, that it might be time
that they were leaving too.

He was standing at her desk when she took the
tray in, and she was relieved that she had nothing in
her typewriter. It wouldn't have mattered if it had been
a page from an article she was writing, but she didn't
want him to see her book—what little there was of it.
After all, he was a Shakespearean actor.

"Coffee's up," she said, putting the tray on the
table. "No cream, I'm afraid. Mrs. Adams, my nosy
neighbor, came down earlier and wolfed the lot."

Nick smiled and waited for her to pour. "You
know, you've talked about practically everything else
this evening," he said, settling himself down on the settee and stretching out his long legs, longer and perhaps
more muscular than Joel's, she noted, "but you haven't
mentioned a thing about your book."

"Ah, I was afraid you were going to say that." He
waited for her to go on. "The truth is, I haven't talked
about it because there's nothing much to tell."

"I see. Are you sure you're not just being modest?"

"No," she said. "Honestly, there's really nothing
to tell. I've hardly written a thing."

"But Ellamarie seems to think that it's coming
along in leaps and bounds."

"Because that's what I've told her."

"And it's not?"

She shook her head.

"What's the problem? Time, I suppose."

She sighed. "No, I don't think it's anything to do with time, at least not where I'm concerned. I've been afraid to admit it even to myself, but the real truth is, I just simply don't think I can do it."

"I find that difficult to believe. How long have you been trying?"

"Oh ages! Four months, maybe longer."

He laughed and nodded. "Ages!"

She smiled, and a faint color spread across her cheeks. "I think it is."

"Just because some people churn out books in a matter of weeks, doesn't mean everyone has to."

"I know that. It's just, well, I imagined, you know, as a journalist and with writing being my trade, as it were, that I would be able to do it, that it would be, well, rather easy really. But it's not."

"Will you keep trying?"

"Yes, I suppose so. I don't know. Oh, I have to really. My father will be so terribly disappointed if I don't. He's really excited about it. He hardly talks to me about anything else these days."

"Have you told him that you're having problems?"

"Oh God no. He thinks the same as everyone else, that it's coming along simply wonderfully. He'd be really upset if he knew. So you see I have to persevere."

"What does Joel say about it? He is your agent, isn't he?"

She shook her head. "No. Joel has made it perfectly clear that he doesn't want to know, at least not until I've finished it. Besides, I haven't seen him since Jenneen gave the dinner party I was telling you about. Anyway," she forced a smile and tried to put a lightness into her voice that she was far from feeling, "not to worry, I'm sure everything will sort itself out."

He could see that she was upset. "Sorry," he said, "I didn't mean to pry."

She reached out to pick up her coffee. Nick was watching her and she couldn't help but wish that Joel would sometimes look at her in that way. "Perhaps it will do me some good to admit the truth, for once," she said.

"Have you tried ringing him?"

"Yes. But either I don't get a reply, or I'm told that he's in a meeting. It's all pretty humiliating really."

"Is that why you rang me? No Joel?"

"I'd be lying if I said it wasn't. But I'm glad that I did."

"Me too."

She smiled.

"Sunday," he said. "I've got the whole day off, perhaps we could go somewhere together. Take a trip out to the countryside, or something." She looked hesitant. "You can't wait around for him for ever, Kate."

"I know." She looked away, embarrassed that he had seen through her so easily.

"Anyway, time I was going. Mr. McElfrey doesn't approve of us actors having late nights. And we're doing a read for the *Queen of Cornwall* tomorrow."

"Is he such a tyrant?"

Nick laughed. "Sometimes. But it's not a bad thing, I suppose. He sets standards for himself, and expects them to be taken up by those around him." He stood up and put his cup back on the tray. "If you change your mind about Sunday, then the offer still stands."

When he had gone she regretted not saying she would go, but if Joel did ring, well, she just had to be free.

She went into the bedroom and closed the curtains before she turned on the light. This was becoming a habit now, for two reasons. One so that she could see out easier, in the hope that she would see Joel pulling up outside in his Range-Rover, and the other so that no one could see in.

The mysterious phone calls were becoming more frequent lately, and once or twice she had thought that she had recognized the voice, but she couldn't place it. But who did she know who would do something like that? The calls weren't threatening in any way, in fact quite the reverse. They were hurried and brief, and she could tell that the caller was holding something over the mouthpiece in an effort to disguise his voice. She had thought for one mad moment that it was Joel. But that just wasn't his style.

She sat down in front of the mirror and began to cleanse the makeup from her face. Every time a car pulled up outside she tensed, waiting for her bell to ring, but it didn't.

She looked at the cane, standing innocently in the corner, and felt a sudden surge of anger. Like a dog, too eager to please its sadistic master, she had told him he could use it again, and then he hadn't even bothered to ring her. She was tempted to break it to pieces and send it to him, but she was afraid of making him angry.

But sooner or later she would see him again, of that she was certain. She laid her hand on her tummy, and smiled at her reflection. She was sure that Joel would enjoy being a father, once he got used to the idea.

Ashley shrieked and covered her face just a second too late as a snowball came flying through the air and caught her full in the face.

"Oh, just you wait," she cried, and scooping up a pile of snow, she started after him.

"You'll have to run faster than that," Keith shouted, as he dodged behind a tree. Then he gave a sudden yell as Alex popped up behind him and tossed a snowball into his face.

"That was cheating," Keith laughed, wiping the snow from his eyes. "Come here!"

But Alex ran off before his father could catch him.

"Hey!" Ashley yelled.

Keith turned round, and was caught again.

"This isn't fair," he complained, wiping the snow away again. "Two against one isn't allowed."

"Yes it is," said Alex. "You're bigger than us."

"Exactly," said Ashley, as she aimed another snowball, and missed.

"Right, you've asked for it now." Keith tried to stock up on his ammunition and at the same time shake off Caesar who was getting far too excited on behalf of the opposition.

Ashley and Alex were quickly stocking up on their own line, and then the battle was on.

"Got you!" Alex shouted, as one of Ashley's snowballs hit Keith on the back. "And again!" he yelled, as she threw another.

With so many snowballs raining down on him, Keith hardly had a chance to aim any himself. But Ashley and Alex ran out of ammunition far too quickly, and they had no alternative but to resort to their only other means of defense; they ran away. Seizing his opportunity, Keith went in pursuit. He caught Ashley round the neck, and jammed a snowball inside her jacket.

"Oh no!" she gasped, as the snow began to melt against her skin. "That's not fair."

Alex was jumping up and down in delight. "Got you, Mum!"

Ashley looked down at him. "Just whose side are you on?" She picked up a handful of snow and threw it at him.

"Come on, Alex," Keith shouted as she ran off. "After her!"

Ashley was laughing so much that she didn't get far before they caught her again.

"No," she yelled, as Keith picked up more snow. "No!"

"Go on, Dad!"

Caesar was barking, and running in and out of the trees delightedly.

Keith held onto Ashley and looked into her face, a ball of ice-cold, sparkling white snow in his hand.

"No," she laughed, "No, don't you dare."

Slowly he brought his hand toward her, and she tried to bury her face in his shoulder. She was too late.

"OK, OK," she spluttered, wiping the snow from her eyes, "I admit defeat."

"Did you hear that, Alex?" Keith cried. "We've won!"

"Hooray," Alex shouted, jumping for joy.

Keith turned to Ashley. "Do you want to go back? Dry off?"

"Oh no!" Alex groaned.

"No, I think I'll survive. No thanks to you," Ashley added, looking at Alex. "Come on, let's walk on to the stream, see if it's frozen over."

Alex whooped with delight and Keith picked him up and swung him round. Alex gave his father a big hug, then called out to Caesar and ran on ahead, sticking out his arms pretending to be an airplane.

"You sure you're all right?" Keith said, turning back to Ashley.

"Sure. Just a bit damp."

He laughed, and put an arm across her shoulders.

It had been a surprise to wake up this morning and find that it had been snowing, so well into spring. None of them minded. She had always enjoyed walking in the woods when everything was covered with snow. It gave her a romantic sort of feeling, as if she were walking into a Christmas card.

They stopped at a bench and sat down to watch Alex and Caesar playing on the frozen stream. Caesar was slipping and sliding all over the place, not knowing what to make of this at all.

"Come on!" Alex called out to them. "It's great!"

"Your mother can't skate. She doesn't know how."

Ashley looked at him. "Who says?"

"I do," he said, the challenge in his eyes.

"Then just you watch," and she started to climb down over the bank. She gave a loud yell as suddenly the snow gave way beneath her, and she slid the rest of the way, ending up sitting on the ice at the bottom.

"I take it back," said Keith, when he had managed to control his mirth. "That was quite some performance."

Ashley threw a snowball at him again, and missed.

"Why don't you give up?" said Keith. "Apart from anything else you're too old."

"Just you wait till I get back up there. I'm going to think of something mean and nasty, and very slow, to do to you."

"Can't wait," he grinned, as she struggled up the bank. At last she made it, and flopped down on the bench beside him.

It began to snow, only a light fall, and everything around them looked so beautiful, and peaceful, reminding her of the little paperweights she used to buy for her mother when she was a child.

Keith was stroking her arm, and she leaned against him. It felt so good to be with him. Each time she saw him with Alex these days, it brought a lump to her throat. There was little doubt that Keith really did love his son, and that Alex loved his father. They were like friends sometimes, rather than father and son, and it seemed to give them both so much pleasure when she joined them on their days out together. And she had to admit, she enjoyed it too. It felt right.

"What are you thinking about?" said Keith.

"Oh, nothing."

"Were you thinking about him?"

She looked up into Keith's face, and saw the sadness in his eyes.

She shook her head. "No, I wasn't thinking about him."

"How have things been there?"

"At the office? OK, I suppose."

"Do you see much of him?"

"No more than I used to. At work," she added.

"Do you still think about him?"

"Not really," she lied. "What's the point?"

Keith shrugged. "None, I suppose, unless you still love him."

She looked away.

"Do you?"

Ashley held her breath. She had dreaded Keith asking her that question. She didn't want to lie to him; perverse as it might seem, she felt it would be disloyal to Julian if she denied it, but neither did she want to hurt Keith. The truth was, that these last couple of months had been hell. She had told herself that things would get easier, and sometimes she believed that they would. But then she would see him walking into his office, or chatting with someone as he walked along the corridor, and she would know that she loved him now as much as she had ever loved him. If only things were as simple as they were in a book. A few pages, maybe only a few lines, and it would all be over and onto the next. But life wasn't like that. Rejection and heartbreak were real, and they didn't go away, not for a very long time.

"Alex, stop that!" Keith shouted. Ashley looked up to see that Alex had picked Caesar up by his front paws, and was dancing him around on the ice.

"He likes it," said Alex.

"He doesn't. You're hurting him, now let him go."

Alex ignored his father, and carried on dancing.

Keith stood up. "Alex," he warned, "you heard what I said."

"But Dad, he likes it, look."

"Let him go. Now! I won't tell you again."

"He likes it, doesn't he Mum?" said Alex, turning to Ashley for support.

"Alex," Keith said, sounding very stern to a little boy's ears.

Reluctantly Alex let go of Caesar's paws, and Caesar went running off into the woods, clearly glad to be free.

"Now come here."

Alex made no move toward Keith. Ashley watched, her heart going out to her son as he looked at his father with big, round eyes.

"I'm waiting." Keith held out his hand to pull Alex up from the stream.

"Now," said Keith, when Alex was standing in front of him. "You must understand that Caesar is only a puppy, and if you're hurting him he can't tell you. He loves you too much to bite you, so he will let you go on hurting him. You don't want that, do you?"

Alex shook his head.

"Now call him, and you can say sorry to him."

Alex turned away, a little sulkily, and called out for Caesar. The little dog bounded up, carrying a stick in his mouth. Taking it from him, Alex ran off into the woods with it.

Keith sat down again, and put his arm back where it had been before. His face was still stern, and Ashley laughed. "You're not going to tell me off too, are you?"

"No," he said. "But I ought to. You're too soft with him sometimes."

"Don't blame me. You jumped in before I did, that's all."

"But you can't deny he needs a father," said Keith.

"He's got one," Ashley countered.

"That's not what I mean, and you know it."

The silence stretched between them, until taking her gently by the chin he turned her to face him. "So what do you say, Ash?"

"What about?"

"Being together again, as a family."

She looked down at her hands, and started to

straighten her gloves. She couldn't deny that she wanted it too. But she just didn't love Keith—at least not in the way she loved Julian. But then she thought of all the lonely nights she spent now, longing for someone to put their arms round her, and tell her they loved her. And the longing to feel needed and important to someone. There was something missing from her life, and the emptiness and loneliness were becoming almost unbearable.

"Well?"

She looked up at the sky and sighed.

"It makes sense, Ashley, you know it does. We've been getting along so well these past months, and you know how I feel about you. Can't we give it a try?"

"Oh Keith, I only wish things were that easy."

"But we can't go on like this for ever. We're just wasting time."

"I know," she said, "but I feel so confused at the moment. I don't want to lose you, I know that. But I just don't know if we would be doing the right thing."

"You'll never know, unless you try." He turned her to look at him again. "I love you, Ash. I love you more than anything else in the world."

He lowered his head and touched her lips with his. She squeezed her eyes tightly, not wanting him to see the tears that were in them. If only she could stop thinking about Julian.

"Tell me there's a chance," he said, as she pressed her face into his shoulder. "Please, just tell me there's a chance."

When she didn't answer he pulled away so that he could look into her eyes. She looked back at him, hating herself for wishing he was another man.

"Well?"

She smiled a tired smile, and there was the smallest suggestion of defeat in her eyes. "Give me a little more time, Keith. Please, just give me time," and she got up from the bench and walked back into the woods.

He watched her go, and knew that it would not be long now before he would have his son back again.

SIXTEEN

LINDA PUT THE PHONE DOWN AFTER SPEAKING TO VIOLET. She glanced out of the window and noticed it was beginning to get dark outside. It was Friday afternoon and Bob would be arriving home any time now. Her heart skipped a beat. As the weeks had gone by, since the phone call from Maureen Woodley, she had become increasingly nervous at seeing her husband. Her weeks began with a feeling of relief that he had gone back to London and that nothing had been said over the weekend, only to build, sometimes almost into a frenzy of terror, that the coming weekend would see it all come to a head, and he would tell her he was leaving.

At first she had wanted to find out who the other woman was, but she didn't. It was the coward in her that stopped her, a side to her nature that she had never known, until now, had existed. But she was afraid of what she would find. Perhaps fighting against the unknown was not the way to do it, but if she knew who the other woman was, and if she could see why Bob loved her, and if she was beautiful and sophisticated and intelligent, and moved so easily in his London circle, Linda was afraid she would feel ordinary and dull in comparison, and unable to compete.

Her suitcase was sitting on the floor beside the bed, packed and ready to go. Her coat was lying on top of it, so she picked it up and put it on. She wasn't running away exactly, at least that's what she told herself, but she couldn't face him this weekend. She didn't know how much longer she was going to be able to hold on. He knew that something was wrong, that she had changed, and he wanted to know why, but she hadn't been able to bring herself to tell him. The only way she seemed to be able to cope was to pretend that this wasn't happening, or at the very least that it would all go away. But for now, she was going away. Not far, at least not far from the bosom of the family. She was going to stay with Violet for the weekend. Violet had flu, and Linda would give that as the reason for not being here when he got home.

She had tried to ring him earlier at the mews house, but there was no reply. She hadn't really expected there to be, but it hurt nevertheless. She wondered if he would join her at his mother's, or if he would stay here, in the farmhouse, alone. There was always the chance, of course, that he would return to London, to her, but she didn't want to think about that.

She picked up the wedding photograph that they kept on the windowsill of their bedroom. They had been so much younger then, so much in love, and full of what life had to offer. He had bought her this house as a wedding gift, where she could keep her own horses, and train others. In those days she had had almost to fight with him to get him on the train back to London at the end of the weekend. And it was never a surprise to see him at home on Thursday instead of Friday. He had invited people to the house then. Writers, producers, actors, art directors, all sorts of people had come for the weekend. But now he did all his business in London, and it was seldom that they had anyone to stay. She wondered if it was her who had driven them away, and she started to cry. They had shared so much together, and now this other woman, whoever she was, was going to take it all away.

She touched his face in the photograph, and a tear splashed onto her fingers. "Please don't let it be too late," she whispered. "Please don't go away."

Robert Blackwell's parties were renowned for their wild, sometimes ostentatious extravagance, outlandish style, and several unmentionable things besides. Everyone came to have a good time, and Robert Blackwell did everything humanly possible to ensure they got it. No expense was spared, no fantasy left unfulfilled.

Ellamarie turned the car from the country lane into the drive that twisted through the trees and up to the big house. Lights had been rigged along the route, and the field at the side of the house had been given over to a car park. As the house came into view, all four of them gasped.

"Will you look at that!" Ellamarie cried.

"Isn't it romantic!" said Kate, clasping her hands together.

Ashley was sitting in the back with Jenneen, who had said very little during the journey down and now seemed to have lost her tongue entirely. Ashley put her hand on her arm. "Are you all right, Jenn?"

Jenneen nodded and Ashley heard her swallow in the darkness.

A butler was waiting to greet them, very smart in his uniform of black tie and tails, and the austere, almost overpowering entrance hall was lined with footmen, who took their coats and overnight bags, then handed them champagne as they ushered them into the party.

"Wow!" said Joel, breaking free of the crowd and coming over to greet them. "You look terrific, all of you."

Kate glowed as he put his arm round her and kissed her.

"How have you been?" he whispered.

"Fine. I've missed you though."

"And I've missed you too. We'll make up for it later, eh?"

She smiled into his eyes, and nodded. Just seeing him standing there made her knees turn to jelly. Any thought of Nicholas Gough, and letting him down yet again, was wiped from her mind.

Joel had rung her the night before to invite her to this party, and had insisted that she bring her friends along too. It had been the first time in weeks that she had heard from him—since the night of Jenneen's dinner party, to be exact.

"Sorry I couldn't bring you down myself," he said. "But I've been here all day. There's been so much to do, besides this party. Where's Bob?" he added, looking past Kate to Ellamarie.

"Too much work," Ellamarie answered, a little too quickly. She wasn't about to tell him about the fight she had had with Bob because he had refused to come. But what she hadn't known, because Bob had been unable to tell her, was that he couldn't go to the party with her, as he had already been invited, with his wife. When he found out that Ellamarie was going, he heaved a sigh of relief that Linda had already sent their excuses.

Kate nudged Ellamarie and nodded toward a couple who were passing. "Prince Dimitri of Yugoslavia," she whispered. "Isn't he simply divine?"

Ellamarie's eyes came out on stalks.

Indeed, the rich and famous were out in force: aristocrats, pop stars, actors, businessmen. The champagne corks were popping all over the room, the lights were low, and the music floated through from the ballroom.

Ashley soon became in grave danger of finding herself on the wrong side of Robert Blackwell's girlfriend, as Robert Blackwell was doing very little to hide his desire for Ashley. But the more champagne Ashley consumed, the more reckless she became, until she knew it wouldn't be long before she succumbed to his desire.

Ellamarie was whisked off her feet by a "Greek God," making the others laugh as, disappearing into the ballroom, she threw a look of pure lust over her shoulder.

Jenneen stood on one side, hardly daring to move. Her eyes flicked over the many faces, designer gowns, glitter and jewels. There was so much noise in the room she could hardly hear anything anyone was saying. She looked at the curtain beside her, and was tempted to disappear behind it. She hadn't wanted to come, and now she was here she regretted giving in. She was afraid of what she might do. She was afraid that at any moment Mrs. Green might take over, and disgrace her. She had no control over her now, she could emerge at any moment. She looked around again and half expected to see Matthew's face in among the crowd. She hadn't seen or heard from him since that terrible scene they had had, and his silence frightened her even more than his threats.

Shrieks of laughter from the other side of the room made her look up. A fountain had sprung to life in the corner. It was a fountain of champagne. She looked at her empty glass. Well, why not? She couldn't stand there all night, after all.

As she weaved her way through the crowd, she listened to the little snippets of conversation as she passed by.

". . . the photographs from Cannes, darling," said one, "they were . . ."

". . . we had the car stolen, and all the luggage was gone, haw! haw! haw!" laughed another. Jenneen glanced at him in surprise.

". . . they float in July. Buy! I'm telling you. Buy!"

As she approached the fountain, Jenneen felt very alone. She looked at the crowd that was grouped around the fountain and was unsure of what to do.

Feeling that someone was staring at her she looked up.
A pair of blue eyes were regarding her with a lazy interest. She recognized him immediately. It was Paul
Deane. She didn't actually know him, of course, but
that he played cricket for England, she did know.

She smiled.

"That's better," he said, taking her glass. "Allow
me."

She waited while he filled the glass from the fountain.

"Let me introduce myself," he said.

"I know who you are," she answered. "Though I
have to admit I've never seen you play."

"I should be hurt," he smiled. "And don't I know
you from somewhere too? Your face seems familiar."

"Jenneen Grey," she said, holding out her hand.

"Of course. My wife watches you every week."

Jenneen raised an eyebrow, and looked around.

"She's not here. At least, not yet." He lifted his
glass and tapped it against hers. "Here's to you."

"Thank you," she replied, her eyes beginning to
dance. "And to you."

He was even more good-looking than he appeared
in his whites. His blond hair curled round his collar,
and his lean tanned face smiled in an ironical sort of
way.

"Why so sad?" he said, leading her away from the
fountain.

Jenneen looked at him in surprise.

"You looked so unhappy, alone in a crowd, so to
speak. You brought out all the protective male instinct
in me."

"Do men still get that?"

"Of course. I'm surprised you doubt it."

She shrugged.

"You know, you reminded me of a daisy, you
could so easily have been crushed. Are you ephemeral,
Jenneen?"

"Are you sure you're a cricketer?"

"So they tell me. But being a sportsman, you know, doesn't make one immune to the nicer things in life. The special things in life. I suspect, Jenneen Grey, that you are very special."

"And I suspect, Paul Deane, that you are flirting outrageously with me."

His look was one of mock surprise. "Do you blame me?"

She laughed. "Now I can hardly answer that, can I?"

"Did you come alone?" he asked, running his fingers across her hair.

"Not exactly."

"Not exactly? Does that mean you've mislaid your escort for the moment? Or does it mean you came by taxi?"

"It means I came with some friends, who are all dancing at the moment."

"Paul! Darling!" Jenneen turned to see a beautiful woman, the same blonde curls as Paul's, and dark humorous eyes, bearing down upon them. She was obviously delighted to see him.

"Vicky!" Paul's face lit up.

"I didn't know you were coming," she said. "Why didn't you tell me?"

"Because I don't tell you everything I do." He looked at Jenneen, and saw that she was watching them curiously.

"Jenneen, allow me to introduce Victoria Deane, my cousin. Vicky, meet Jenneen Grey."

"Hello," said Vicky, taking Jenneen's hand. "It's so nice to meet you."

"And to meet you," said Jenneen.

"You are a little bit of a surprise," said Vicky. "You are so much smaller than you seem on TV. Oh, I'm sorry," she said, covering her mouth, "I hope I haven't offended you."

Jenneen smiled. "Not at all."

For no accountable reason she liked this woman on sight. Her blonde hair was a little chaotic, and she had an air about her that made her appear to be in a rush. But her smile was soft, and genuine, and her eyes sparkled with interest.

She took Paul by the arm. "I expect he's been trying to sweep you off your feet, hasn't he?"

"I hadn't got that far yet," he said.

"Oh look!" cried Vicky. "A champagne fountain! Be right back," and she went off to fill a glass for herself.

"Completely nuts!" said Paul. "And I adore her." He reached out to take Jenneen's glass. "Would you like to dance?"

A surge of panic almost overwhelmed her, and her fingers tightened round the stem of her glass as she opened her mouth to say no. But at the last minute she managed to pull herself together, and straining to keep her smile in place she followed him into the ballroom. Inside she was aching with fear as she told herself that no matter what happened she must not try to seduce this man, not now, not ever.

As they started to dance, Jenneen saw Ashley go floating by in the arms of Robert Blackwell. And there was Ellamarie, still swaying from side to side in the arms of the Adonis, listening to what he was saying, and giggling.

Robert Blackwell looked down into Ashley's eyes, and ran the backs of his fingers across her breast. It was the third time he had done it and her nipple was straining hard against the flimsy material of her dress. She looked up into his face, her lips moist and slightly parted.

"I am going to make love to you this evening, Ashley, you know that, don't you?" he whispered.

She closed her eyes as his mouth pressed gently

against hers. She knew she had had too much to drink, but she was past caring. His sexuality was overpowering, and she molded her body closer to his feeling the thrill of his hardening penis as it pressed against her.

As he pulled away she looked up at him, waiting for him to speak, but he was looking past her.

"Sean!" he cried. "I thought you were in the States."

"Flew over earlier than we intended."

Ashley turned round in disbelief. She would recognize that voice anywhere. She almost melted as she looked into those laughing eyes, and Sean Connery chuckled.

Kate was watching her with envy. What she wouldn't give to meet Sean Connery. Joel found this amusing, but was in no position to make the introduction, so he led her back into the next room, and fetched her another glass of champagne.

"There's someone over there I have to see," he said. "Don't move, I'll be right back."

Kate was a bit put out that he didn't take her with him, but there was so much going on around her, she was content to stand and watch for a while.

Ellamarie was laughing up into the face of the Adonis. "I don't believe you," she said.

"It's true. I have seen everything you've ever done," and he tried to pull her closer. "You are the most beautiful creature God, in his wisdom, has ever created."

"Oh, I don't think I would go quite that far."

"I'd go much further."

"Please, don't," she said, covering his mouth with her fingers. "I'm not sure I can take any more."

"I watch you every night." He took her hand and kissed it. "Every night. I feel like I know you. Like I know every inch of you. I've kept everything that's ever been written about you, every picture that's ever been taken of you."

"You're kidding me."

"I could show you, if you let me."

She laughed a little nervously. There was something about his manner and what he was saying that made her uncomfortable. To be complimented and flattered was one thing. But to be adored, idolized even, by a total stranger, well, it sent shivers down her spine. He was watching her closely, his pale eyes almost smothering her face, and she looked away.

"Don't," he said, pulling her close, and he started to cover her face with light kisses. He lifted her hair from her neck, and gently kissed that too. His hands were stroking her back, tantalizing her, and she could feel his breath, warm and moist on her skin.

"Please, don't," she protested, weakly, and tried to push him away.

He looked into her eyes, and she thought his expression curious, odd even. "I want to kiss you all over, just like that," he whispered. "Every inch of you." As he smiled the light in his eyes gleamed, almost hungrily, belying the softness of his voice. He bent his head to hers, and ran his tongue across her open mouth.

"Please," she said, "you're embarrassing me." She wished that Bob was here so that he could rescue her from this strange man.

"Let me take you somewhere, where we can be alone." He took her hand and, unable to stop herself, she began to follow him out of the room. She watched him as he walked in front of her, and wondered why she was following him. Why was she allowing this stranger to take her away, where he could be alone with her, and . . .

"Ellamarie!"

Ellamarie swung round to see Kate waving at her. The Adonis tightened his grip on her hand, but she pulled away.

"Excuse me," she said. "That's a friend of mine over there. I really must go and see if she's all right."

"You can see that she's all right," he said. "You don't need to go to her."

"No, really, I must. Please, let me go."

He kept hold of her hand. "I'll be waiting, Ellamarie," he whispered.

Ellamarie tugged her hand free and turned abruptly toward Kate. The Adonis watched her as she almost ran across the room, but Ellamarie didn't look back.

"Thank God you were here," said Ellamarie. "I dread to think what might have happened if you hadn't called out."

"You're complaining?" said Kate. "He's divine."

"He's weird!" Ellamarie shuddered. "Where's Joel?"

"Over there, talking to someone, don't ask me who. But have you seen Ashley? She's only talking to Sean Connery."

"Are you kidding? Where? Where is he?"

"In there." Kate pointed toward the ballroom.

"Can't we be introduced as well?"

"I think not, unfortunately. She's with Robert Blackwell, honored guest and all that."

"Pity. Seen Jenneen anywhere?"

"Thought I saw her dancing with Paul Deane— you know, the cricketer. My guess is she's up to no good by now."

Ellamarie laughed. "It'll be what she needs."

"Has she said anything to you? About Matthew?"

"Not a word. All I know is he's not living there any more. Do you know what happened?"

"Not a clue. I asked Ashley earlier, but she doesn't know either."

"I wonder why she won't talk about it?"

Kate shrugged. "Well, Paul Deane was really making her laugh when I last saw them, so at least that's something."

"Isn't he married?"

"Mmm, I think so. But when did that ever stop anyone?"

Ellamarie threw her a look. "Touché," she grinned. "How are things going with Joel? Did he say why he hasn't called for ages?"

"Not a word—sssh! Here he comes," said Kate, her face lighting up as she looked past Ellamarie.

"No one swept you off your feet yet, Ellamarie?" Joel grinned, planting a kiss on Kate's cheek.

"Why, are you offering?"

"Of course." He turned round and Kate noticed that someone was making their way across the room to join them. "Oh no," she muttered, under her breath.

"Ladies," said Joel, "I believe you have already met Conrad Frazier. Conrad, Ellamarie and Kate."

Conrad nodded abruptly. His manners haven't improved any, thought Kate and Ellamarie in unison, and they both gave cold nods in return.

"Ready, Ellamarie?" said Joel, offering her his arm, and he took her off to the dance floor.

Kate looked at Conrad, but Conrad was watching the people at the fountain, pouring champagne into their shoes. He laughed as a very drunken, astonishingly beautiful woman disentangled herself from the crowd and teetered her way toward him.

Kate found herself studying Conrad's face as he lifted the straps of the woman's dress back onto her shoulders and smiled down into her eyes. Despite her dislike of him, Kate felt her heart turn over. Dear God, he was so handsome. The woman kissed him, full on the mouth, and unashamedly Kate watched as he kissed her back.

"Candy, darling," she heard him whisper, "I think you've had a little too much."

"Oh nonsense," Candy slurred, in a Southern drawl, and she staggered back to the champagne fountain. Conrad turned back to Kate, who blushed as she realized that she hadn't taken her eyes off him once. He smiled at her, and involuntarily she smiled back.

"What brings you here?" she asked, having to shout over the cacophony of laughter coming from the fountain.

"I was invited," he said, taking a sip of champagne.

She raised her eyebrows. "I gathered that. But don't you live in New York?"

"Sure," he said. "But I had business to attend to in London, so I thought I'd combine the two."

"Julian isn't here, is he?" Kate asked, quickly.

"Not that I know of."

"Thank God for that."

Conrad seemed amused. "Don't tell me, yours is another heart broken by the devastating Arbrey-Nelmes charm?"

"Actually, no!" Kate snapped.

Conrad shrugged, and seemed to lose interest in her.

"Are you always so rude?" she said, walking round to stand in front of him.

"Me?"

"Yes, you!"

He seemed to think about this for a minute. "Yes," he said, finally. "Yes, I probably am."

"Don't you care about offending people?"

"Not really. These sort of parties bore me, and so do the people that come to them."

"Of all the . . ."

"Kate!" cried Ashley, coming toward her. "You'll never guess who I've just been talking to."

"Sean Connery," said Kate, turning round, "and I could kill you. If I don't kill him first," she added under her breath, jerking her head toward Conrad.

Ashley paled as she saw him, and he grinned. He held out his hand toward her and said, "I'm afraid I've forgotten your name."

The flash of indignation that shot through Ashley's eyes did not go unnoticed, but it only seemed to amuse him further.

"Conrad Frazier," he said, introducing himself.

"Yes, I know who you are." Ashley ignored his hand.

"Are you going to remind me who you are? Besides being my partner's mistress."

Ashley gasped. How dare he! She turned her back on him. Kate took her by the arm and they walked away from him.

Conrad watched them go, a thoughtful smile playing around his lips, and then turned to see what had caused the shrieks of delight behind him. Candida was pouring tiny rivers of champagne over her naked body. As he reached her side, she looked up into his face, as if waiting for his kiss, then with a hiccup, punctuated by a long sigh, she collapsed into his arms.

Bob pulled his car to a halt in the country lane, and switched off the engine. Looking out along the drive he could see the bright lights from the house glowing through the trees. He knew that Ellamarie was inside, that was why he had come. So why had he stopped now? Why didn't he just drive in, and go and find her?

He turned on the radio, but the sound irritated him, and he turned it off again.

He leaned back against the head-rest. What a bloody mess that was all turning out to be. He didn't know what was happening to his life, or what he wanted from it any more. He had tried to do some work on the *Queen of Cornwall,* but he had been unable to concentrate. Visions of their faces seemed to block everything else from his mind. Ellamarie, shouting at him, trying to hide the hurt and bewilderment she felt inside. Linda, silent, trying to be strong, but he could see the pain and confusion she was in. And in both their eyes he could see the love they had for him. And his heart was weighted with the love he felt for them.

What was he going to do? What could he do? All he knew was that this couldn't go on. It wasn't fair on either of them, and he couldn't cope with it much longer himself. Had he come here with the intention of telling Ellamarie it was over? Or had he come here because he couldn't stand being away from her? The confusion was twisting his mind, and nowhere could he find the answers he needed. Whatever he did, someone was going to be hurt. And he would be hurt too. But he didn't care about himself, he only cared about them. Which one of them was it to be? Whom should he walk away from, and never see again?

He thought about Ellamarie. She was probably dancing with someone inside, laughing and flirting, completely oblivious to him sitting here, contemplating whether to put an end to her happiness. But what was the point in even thinking about it? He wasn't going to do it, so he might as well stop tormenting himself like this. Just go in, he told himself, find her, and tell her you love her.

But what would he say to Linda? Linda, I've fallen in love with someone else. Our marriage is over, and I'm leaving you. He shuddered, and knew that he could never say it. Linda, I love you, I'm sorry for all the hurt I've caused you, but it's over now, I'm here, and I will never do anything to hurt you again. She would ask no questions, she would just take him in her arms, and hold him, and tell him it was all right, as long as he was there.

Dear God, which was the right way to go?

He turned the key in the ignition, and reversed the car. Weak he might be, but he couldn't make the decision—not now. Probably he never would. Instead, he would let fate decide what was to become of them all. Yes, let fate take the insupportable burden.

SEVENTEEN

Conrad walked back into the room. After Candida had passed out he had taken her upstairs and put her to bed. For a moment he had toyed with the idea of staying with her, but there was some unfinished business he had to attend to. He looked around for Robert Blackwell and saw that he was talking to Ashley. Her eyes were bright and feverish and Conrad gave a smile. Robert always was a fast worker—and as if to confirm this, he turned and started to walk toward the door that led outside to the pool. Ashley placed her glass on the tray of a passing waiter, then gathered up her handbag.

Conrad moved swiftly, and caught up with her as she was about to disappear through the door. Ashley spun round as she felt the hand close around her wrist.

"Dance!" said Conrad.

"Let go of me!" she demanded, glaring first at his hand, then at him.

He smiled, "I said dance," and keeping a tight grip on her wrist, he all but dragged her into the ballroom.

"How dare you!" she hissed, pulling away from him, but his hold remained firm, and she couldn't break away. She trod heavily on his foot, and enjoyed the expression of pain that shot across his face.

"Don't do that again," he said.

She glared at him. "What are you playing at?"

He lifted an eyebrow, and looked down at her, his

mouth angled in that lopsided grin that she detested so bitterly. "Robert Blackwell was inviting you to take a swim, was he not?"

Ashley looked at him from beneath her eyelids.

"Just as I thought," he said. And didn't enlarge.

"I don't call that an explanation." She tried to tread on his foot again, and failed.

"Have you any idea what is going on out there in the pool?"

"I imagine that people are swimming."

"They are doing a lot of things in the pool, but swimming is not one of them."

"And what is that supposed to mean?"

"I'm sure not even you are that naive," he said.

"Don't be so damned pompous," she snapped. "Whatever is going on out there in the pool, I fail to see what it has to do with you. Now let me go."

"It has nothing to do with me, as I have no intention of joining in. But as you do, I have taken it upon myself to stop you, for Julian's sake. The idea of his mistress floating around in an orgy of cavorting bodies is not one that either he, or I, would relish."

"I beg your pardon?"

"Julian is to marry my cousin in less than two weeks, and I should hate for her to develop something . . . well, shall we say something unsavory, while away on her honeymoon."

Ashley dealt him a stinging blow across the face, which forced him to let go of her and take a step backward.

"For your information," she spat at him, "I am no longer Julian's mistress, as you like to call it, so save yourself the bother of coming near me again. Ever!" And she stormed off, her face white with rage and her hand stinging from the force of the slap.

Across the room Kate and Joel laughed. "No more than he deserves," said Kate. "I only wish I could have heard what he said to her."

"Or what she said to him. She's quite something," Joel remarked.

"Isn't she?" said Kate, not seeing the look in Joel's eyes as they watched Ashley leave the room.

"So," he said, turning back to Kate. "What do you say?"

She blushed as she remembered what they had been talking about. "OK."

"My room's on the first floor."

"Actually, there is something I want to tell you first."

"Why don't you let it wait? I've been dying to get you alone all night."

"Oh Joel, you've hardly spoken to me all evening."

"I've had a little work to do, I admit, but when I haven't been attending to that, I've been at your side every minute. Kiss me," he said.

She slipped her arms round his neck, and opened her mouth in readiness for his embrace. His lips were firm against hers, and she could feel him becoming aroused. He pulled her body fiercely against his, and began to move against her, running his fingers through her hair, pressing his mouth harder and harder into hers.

She clung to him, breathless, as he let her go. His eyes were shining, and he looked across the room. He grinned as he saw Ashley slipping in through the door that led to the pool, and his eyes took on a dark glow. By God, she was a beautiful woman.

"Go on up," he said. "The Butler has put your things in my room, he'll show you the way."

"But aren't you coming now?" she protested.

"I want to think about you getting ready for me." He moved in front of her and cupped his hand between her legs. "You're wearing underwear," he murmured, "make sure it's off by the time I get there." He kissed her again. "Not a stitch, OK?"

She nodded and went off to find the butler.

Jenneen giggled. "Looks like Kate is going to be up to no good any minute now."

"Lucky devil," said Ellamarie.

"Her, and Ashley."

"Ashley?"

"I saw her going off to the pool. Have you seen what's going on out there?"

Ellamarie shook her head. "No, but I can guess. Who is she with?"

"None other than Mr. Blackwell himself. Don't look now," she went on, "but you're being watched again."

"Oh no," Ellamarie groaned. "Not that creep again?"

" 'Fraid so. He's over by the door, can't take his eyes off you."

"Whatever you do, don't leave me on my own. He's been watching me all night, like some kind of spook."

"Well, better brace yourself, I think he's coming over," said Jenneen.

"What am I going to do?"

"The ladies'."

"Where is it?"

"No idea, let's try this way," and before the Adonis could reach them, they disappeared in the opposite direction.

A haze of thick, swirling steam rose from the pool, and Ashley could hear the laughter and shrieks coming from within. Every now and again she saw a naked body emerge, and she was put in mind of a host of gods at play in the clouds. The cold night air bit sharply into her skin, and she shivered. The bikini she had found in the small changing room at the side of the garden covered very little.

She stood above the lights that edged the pool and watched the steam curl around her body. Then, without a second thought, she plunged through the mist and into the water below. She swam to the other side, then jerked herself upward, turning in the steam, and thrilling at the exhilaration of cold and warm air, brushing like a caress, against her skin. Diving back into the warm water again she felt a reckless tingling of excitement surge through her veins. She, Ashley Mayne, was going to do anything Robert Blackwell wanted her to do tonight, and the very thought made her catch her breath with anticipation.

She swam back to the other side of the pool. Someone came up behind her, reaching round her and cupping her breasts in his hands. Ashley threw back her head, her lips open, and groaned as the man buried his tongue in her mouth. When he swam away she turned to watch him go, but she could see nothing through the silvery vapor.

The lights went down, and the water lapped against her body in warm and erotic waves. Holding onto the side, she let her legs float to the surface, moving them up and down gently to keep them afloat.

And then he was beside her. She knew it was him, the sheer magnetism of his body drew her to him. He pressed himself against her back and she could feel his nudity penetrating the flimsy scrap of material that covered her. She returned the pressure and he pulled her head back onto her shoulder, pushing his tongue against hers, his mouth wide and demanding. His fingers fumbled with the catch at the back of the bikini, then he jerked it down over her arms, and let it float away. She reached up behind her, drawing her breasts from the water. Her nipples were achingly aroused, and he took the swollen buds between his fingers.

Lowering her reach, she lifted his erection from his belly, and her insides lurched as she heard him catch his breath. With one hand he lifted her away from him, while he drew the bottom of the bikini down over her legs. Quickly he slipped his hand between her thighs and pushed her forward. She gripped the edge, holding her breath waiting for him to come to her.

Gently he eased her legs apart, and with one thrust he entered her, pulling her down, handling her breasts, first with tenderness, then with passion.

His thighs moved determinedly against her buttocks, and she held onto them, pulling them to her, and sinking beneath the surface of the water. She floated away from him, and he pulled her back, this time thrusting himself into her so hard she cried out. His hands moved over her body, and she reached up and pulled his head down to hers. He kissed her again, burying his tongue deep in her mouth, and all the while he was thrusting into her.

Finally, with a strangulated groan, he pushed her hard against the side and ground into her, rotating and jerking his hips until he was spent.

As he pulled free of her she turned to take him in her arms, but he was swimming away. She smiled to herself, and ran her hands over her breasts. This was how she wanted it to be too. No complications, no declarations, only the coming together of two bodies.

She climbed out of the pool, small clouds of wispy moonlight circling from her body. Her limbs felt weak, and her knees were shaking. It was the first time in her life she had ever done anything like this, and she didn't regret one moment of it.

As she walked back toward the changing room the door opened and a shaft of light fell across the garden. She stopped as she saw Joel leaning against the wall, naked and dripping wet; a smile came over his face as he saw her watching him in the semi-darkness. Then a woman appeared at his side and wound her arms about his neck. Just before the door closed again Ashley saw him bury his tongue in the woman's open mouth, but his eyes were still on her.

She walked on into the changing room, dried herself off and redid her makeup.

As she rejoined the party Jenneen spotted her and waved. Ashley started across the room toward her friend.

A waiter passed, and she reached out to take a glass of champagne. It was then that she saw him. Her eyes rounded with horror. There, standing beside the champagne fountain, idly caressing the nearly naked breast of his girlfriend, was Robert Blackwell. Ashley stayed rooted to the spot, trying to deny the suspicion that was struggling to give some sense to the scene, but as he looked up and saw her watching him, the expression of regret that came into Robert's eyes confirmed the unthinkable. Whoever it had been in the swimming pool, it had not been him.

Ashley looked around in panic. If it wasn't him, then who? Who had it been? Joel! She closed her eyes. Dear God, it must have been Joel. She had made love with her best friend's boyfriend! And there was Conrad, standing with his back to the door of the pool, watching her, that detestable grin on his face. From the way he was looking at her she could tell that he knew what had happened. His smile widened a fraction as he saw the panic in her eyes and he raised his glass to her. She hated him more then than she had ever hated anyone. She turned away and started to walk blindly across the room. Whatever happened, Kate must never know. But Conrad Frazier knew. Surely he would never tell Kate. She stopped, half-turning back to Conrad. He was still watching her. No, she couldn't ask him. Not ever! She would rather die than give him the satisfaction.

Kate lay back in the luxury of the Karin Kinsella sheets and stared up at the ceiling. She should be happy, she knew she should. Their love-making had been probably the best ever, and she had thought that Joel might explode when he had finally reached his climax. It had been a long time in coming, he had been holding back and savoring every moment. She had given him that exquisite pleasure he craved, and he her, but somehow she felt that the fact that she gained pleasure from their love-making was purely incidental, and of no importance to him. She smiled bitterly.

She had waited for almost an hour, sitting naked on the bed feeling pathetic, looking at the cane that she had brought with her, feeling ridiculous and dreading someone coming into the wrong room.

When finally he came he was smiling, a smile that she didn't quite like, and his hair was wet. She asked him what had kept him. He gave her that smile again, and asked her if she was angry. She could tell that he wanted her to be.

And then he stripped off his clothes, and took the cane from her. But she snatched it back, she didn't want him to beat her. She was amazed at the excitement in his face as she snatched it from him, and then he asked her to beat him. So she did, it was her only way of giving vent to her hurt and anger. She had beaten him so hard she left marks all over his thighs and buttocks. But it only served to arouse him all the more.

She smiled. Yes, she had got pleasure from hurting him, like he hurt her. And after, when their love-making was at an end, he had rolled over, and now he was snoring gently beside her.

She looked at him. His hair, blue-black against the white of the pillows, his eyes closed, his mouth half open. Asleep he looked almost vulnerable, and she felt sad that when awake his face was so often cloaked in a sultry arrogance, and his mouth sometimes almost cruel. She wished with all her heart that it wasn't like this. The way she would lie awake after their passion was spent, feeling alone, and dispensable. If he knew how much she loved him, then surely he wouldn't treat her like this. But she had told him often enough, and it had changed nothing. He seemed to enjoy humiliat-

ing her and teasing her. Was that really all he wanted
from her? Just to beat her, or to have her beat him, so
that he could achieve the earth-shattering climax it
gave him? Couldn't he see that there was more to her
than this? That she was a woman, with feelings and
a heart that needed satisfying too?

She got out of bed and went to sit in front of the
mirror. Her hair was a mess, and the jewels that had
decorated it so becomingly earlier were caught in a tan-
gle at the nape of her neck. She took her brush out of
her bag and began to repair the damage.

"What are you doing?"

She turned to look at him. He was propped on one
elbow, watching her.

"Are you all right?" he asked, and his eyes were
gentle.

She smiled, and nodded.

"Love you," he whispered.

Her heart soared. It was the first time he had said
that for so long.

"Do you really mean that?" she said, going back
to the bed.

"Of course I do," and he stroked her face. "You're
beautiful. I've never shared anything like this with
anyone before, you know."

"Me neither," she said, and she lowered her face
to his, and kissed him.

He sat up and pulled open the covers for her to get
back into bed. She rested her head on his shoulder, and
snuggled in closer as he wrapped his arms round her.
He ran his hand down over her shoulder and across her
breast. It wasn't a sexual move, more of a closeness really. And then he moved his hand to her tummy, and
began to stroke the skin around her navel. She looked
up into his eyes and he smiled and kissed the end of
her nose. She sighed and lay back. It was as if he already knew.

She wound her fingers between his. "There's something I must tell you."

"Oh?"

"Something, well, something special."

He hugged her, and waited for her to go on.

She took a deep breath, then stopped. Now that the moment had arrived she was even more nervous than she had thought she would be, and the words seemed to evade her. He hugged her again, and kissed her cheek.

She held his hand to her face, liking the rough feel of his skin. "I'm going to have a baby," she said, her voice coming in a broken whisper.

Immediately she felt him tense.

"I know it's a bit of a shock," she rushed on, not daring to look at him yet, "but well, I hoped that when you got used to the idea, that, well, I don't know, well, that you would be pleased."

He pushed her away and got out of bed. He walked over to the window, his back to her, staring out at the darkness, and said nothing.

She waited. "Joel."

His back stiffened.

She got out of bed and sat on the edge. "Aren't you going to say something?"

He turned, and she drew back at the look in his eyes. "Just what do you expect me to say?" His voice was cold and sarcastic.

She looked down at her hands, and shrugged. "I don't know really. I suppose I hoped you would be pleased—once you'd . . ."

"Pleased? Pleased! For Christ's sake, you expected me to be pleased that you're pregnant? Are you mad?"

She reached for her robe. Her hands were shaking, and she was afraid she was going to break down.

"How did it happen?" he snapped.

She looked at him.

"I mean, I assumed you were taking the pill or something."

She shook her head.

"Bloody hell!" he shouted. "Are you mad? You must have known this would happen."

"I was taking the pill," she said. "It must have been that I just forgot to take one."

"Just forgot," he sneered. "Just forgot. You mean you meant to forget . . ."

"That's not true," she said. "It was an accident. I didn't mean it to happen. Really, I didn't."

"Liar!" he shouted. He slapped his hand against his forehead. "Christ, I should have known that something like this would happen with you. I should have known that I couldn't trust you. Bloody hell! What a mess!"

He looked vaguely ridiculous, standing there naked and furious. He drew his fingers through his hair. "You'll have to get rid of it."

"No!" she gasped.

"For God's sake, don't tell me you're actually so stupid you're considering having the bloody thing."

"Of course I'm going to have it, why shouldn't I?"

"Because I have no intention of having a child, that's why not!" he shouted.

"Look," she said, "I know you're angry now, I understand . . . I know it's a shock. But when you get used to the idea, well, you'll see that . . ."

"Get used to the idea? I have no intention of getting used to the idea, so you can get that out of your head now."

"But . . ."

". . . and if you've got some fancy notion that I'm going to marry you, then you can forget that too. Jesus Christ, I don't believe this."

"B-but I thought you loved me."

"Oh, for God's sake, grow up."

She began to cry.

"And stop bloody well crying, that won't solve anything."

She wiped the back of her hand across her eyes.

He started to pace up and down. "What is it with you women? Just what is it?"

"Look," she said, "it'll be all right. Really it will. We don't have to get married, not if you don't want to. We could . . ."

"You're damn right I don't want to."

"We could live together. I could sell my flat and move in with you. We don't have to be married. But it is your child as well, Joel, surely that must mean something?"

"No!" he yelled. "No! Are you listening to me? No!"

She turned away. After a while she said: "I'm sorry. I'm sorry, I've got it all terribly wrong. I thought you meant it when you said you loved me, and I thought you might be happy that we were going to have a baby. I can see now how stupid that was. I'm sorry."

"Stop being so bloody pathetic," he growled.

"I don't know what else to say."

"Jesus, you're just like the rest of your sex. You only see what you want to see, and you pretend that the rest doesn't exist. Well, it's no use pretending any more, Kate. I'm not marrying you, I don't want the child, I don't want you, in fact. I want nothing to do with this whole damn farce, and you know why."

Her face was white as she shook her head.

"I'm already living with someone, that's why. And don't tell me you didn't already know because I won't swallow it."

Kate caught her breath, and clutched the end of the bed to steady herself. He was still speaking, and she tried to stop herself from listening.

". . . Jenneen knew, and she must have told you. All this pregnancy bit, it was to try and make me change my mind, wasn't it? Well, I'm telling you here and now, nothing will change my mind, and certainly nothing calculated to trap me like this. Anyone would think we were living in Victorian times. You can't go around using your womb to catch men any more, don't you know that?'' He turned back to the window. "I'll give you the money, if that's what you want, and you can get rid of it. But if you decide to keep it, that's up to you, but I'll deny it's mine, and you'll never see me again. The choice is yours."

Her mind was spinning. So all along there had been someone else. She should have known, of course, from the times she hadn't seen him for days, sometimes weeks on end. But he had said that Jenneen had known. So why had Jenneen never told her? This was a nightmare. She had made a fool of herself, and Jenneen had let her go ahead and do it. But no one was going to take her baby away from her, no one.

He was getting dressed, his face still dark with fury.

"Where are you going?" she said.

"I don't know. Anywhere. Anywhere away from you. You're stifling me."

The tears were streaming silently down her face, and she did nothing to stop them. Finally he picked up his jacket and came to stand in front of her.

"You're a stupid, stupid child, Kate." His voice was less heated now. "If you take my advice you'll get rid of it. If you want the money, I'll give it to you. Abortions aren't difficult to get these days. But we're through. I don't want to see you again."

"Joel!" she cried, reaching out and taking his hand. "Please, don't go like this. Please stay. Let's talk, we can sort something out."

He snatched his hand away. "There's nothing to talk about. I'm in love with someone else, Kate. What we had was just a fling. You knew that, and I never pretended otherwise."

"But you said you loved me."

"Words, Kate, only words. Don't you know that people don't always mean everything they say? You take everything so damned literally. You knew there was someone else, you must have."

She shook her head.

"Well, ask Jenneen, she'll tell you. And with any luck she'll be able to talk some sense into you and persuade you to get rid of it. I'm going now."

She watched him walk to the door, wishing she could die. She had known that he could be violent, cruel even, but not like this. To cause her such pain, to throw such brutal words at her. He had called her a child, and maybe he was right, she was a child. To have believed him, to have suffered the indignity of his passion, and the indifference to her feelings, and yet still to have loved him. Yes, she was a child but even worse than that, she was a fool, with no dignity and no pride left to her.

Kate was still sitting on the bed, holding onto the edge, when the door opened and Ashley put her head round.

"All right to come in?"

Kate didn't answer so Ashley closed the door quietly and went to sit beside her on the bed.

"What is it? What's happened?"

Still Kate didn't answer, but two large tears trickled from her eyes and rolled unchecked over her cheeks.

"I saw Joel," said Ashley. "He told me to come up. What's the matter? Tell me what happened?"

"Nothing." Kate shook her head. "Nothing's happened."

"But it must have, or else why are you crying?"

"Am I?" said Kate, and she seemed genuinely surprised.

Ashley took her hand. "Did you have a fight?"

Kate laughed, a mirthless, dry laugh. "No, no, we didn't have a fight. Not exactly."

"Then what?"

"It's over," said Kate. "He never wants to see me again."

"But why?"

Kate looked down at her hands. "Because I'm going to have a baby."

"What?" Ashley gasped. "But why didn't you say something before?"

"I wanted him to be the first to know. Can you believe that? I wanted him to be the first to know."

"What did he say?"

"He said that I was childish, that I had planned it to try and trap him, and that I had to have an abortion."

"Oh my God. How long have you known?"

"Not long. A couple of weeks."

"What are you going to do?"

"I don't know. But I don't want to get rid of it, Ash," she said, turning to face her. "I want to keep it. I can't get rid of it. You understand that, don't you? You're a mother."

"No one's saying you have to," said Ashley, trying to comfort her as the tears started again.

"Joel is. If I have it, he says he'll deny it's his. Oh Ash, how could he say such things? How could he be so cruel? It's his child too, why doesn't he care?"

"I'm sure he does," said Ashley. "It's just come as a bit of a shock, that's all. He'll come round, you'll see."

Kate shook her head.

The door opened again and Ellamarie and Jenneen came in. Jenneen was carrying a bottle of brandy and four glasses. "Thought we might find some use for this," she said.

As Kate fixed her eyes on Jenneen, Ashley felt her tense.

"How could you?" said Kate, her voice almost a snarl. "How could you, Jenneen?"

Jenneen looked at her. "It's only brandy," she said, weakly.

"I don't mean the brandy. You know what I mean. You knew, didn't you? You knew all along, and you never said a thing. You just let me carry on humiliating myself, and crying over him, waiting for him to come, when you knew all along he wouldn't. No wonder you were all so in favor of my seeing Nicholas Gough. You knew, didn't you? You all knew!" She spun round, her face rigid with anger. "And not one of you told me."

"Told you what?" said Ellamarie. "Knew what?"

"About Joel," Kate snapped at her.

"What about Joel?" said Jenneen.

"That's rich coming from you, who knew from the start. You knew there was someone else in his life, didn't you? He told me you knew. I'll never understand how you of all people could lie like that to me! I'll never be able to forgive you for this."

"I don't know what you're talking about," said Jenneen.

"Don't pretend!" Kate shouted into her face. "You were the one that introduced me to him. You were the one that persuaded me to meet him, when all along you knew there was someone else. God, and you call yourself a friend! I'll never trust you again."

"Kate," said Jenneen, "I didn't know. I promise you, I didn't know."

"It's too late, Jenneen, the damage is already done. I suppose it was all just a game to you, because you never think about anyone else, do you? Going around with that working-class chip on your shoulder, so above the rest of the human race. You make me sick! Do you know that? I don't know what it is that goes on in that twisted mind of yours, but whatever it is, it's poisonous. I never want to see you again. Now get out of here, all of you. Just get out of here and leave me alone."

"Look, hang on," Jenneen protested.

"No! I won't hang on. Get out, Jenneen, get out!" Ashley went toward her. "Kate . . ."

"Don't touch me," said Kate, recoiling from her. "Just go! I'll ring for a taxi, I'm going back to London."

"I'll drive you," said Ellamarie.

"No!"

"Look," said Ashley. "You're upset, shocked, but we want to help you, Kate, we care about you."

"Don't make me laugh!" Kate spat the words into Ashley's face. "If you were so keen to help then why didn't you say something before I went and got myself pregnant."

Jenneen gasped.

"Yes," said Kate, turning to her. "Pregnant! Now how do you feel? If you had been honest with me from the start this would never have happened. You're as much to blame as anyone, Jenneen Grey, and I never want to see you again. Not ever, do you hear?" And she caught Jenneen by the shoulders and pushed her out of the room. "Now you as well," she snapped, turning to Ellamarie and Ashley.

"Kate, listen, please," said Ellamarie.

"Get out! Get out! Get out! Can't you hear me!" Kate screamed at the top of her voice. Seeing that for the moment there was no more they could do, Ellamarie and Ashley followed Jenneen out into the corridor.

Jenneen's face was white, and the others could see that she was on the point of tears.

"Don't worry," said Ellamarie, putting an arm round her, "she'll come round, you'll see."

"But she's pregnant," said Jenneen.

"Did you know, Jenn? About Joel I mean," Ellamarie asked.

Jenneen shook her head.

"Well, she's too hurt to listen to reason now," said Ashley. "What are we going to do?" They looked at each other.

Ellamarie pulled herself together. "Look, you two take a taxi back to London. I'll wait here till she comes out," and she started to usher them to the top of the stairs.

Jenneen wiped the tears from her eyes. Everything was so awful. Her life was already a mess, and now, because of her, so was Kate's. She loved her friends, she needed them, but she would never be able to tell them that in truth, she had known. She had known about the other woman in Joel's life, but she had never said anything because she hadn't realized that it was so serious. And when she had seen the way that Kate was falling for Joel, she had hoped that Joel would fall in love too, and that it would all work out in the end. How does anyone ever tell their best friend that the man they love could be in love with someone else? So she had let Kate carry on, and she had told herself that, in the end, it would work itself out. She had never dreamt that Kate would go and get herself pregnant, the possibility had never crossed her mind. And that was why she was no friend. She knew Kate so well, she knew how desperately she wanted to have children. If only she had thought, then she could have stopped all this from happening. Dear, dear Kate, who so longed for a baby, and now to have one like this.

"Come on," said Ashley, taking her arm. "Let's go and find our things. You can stay with me tonight. Will you be all right?" she asked, turning back to Ellamarie.

Ellamarie nodded. "I'll call you tomorrow."

Once they had found their luggage, Jenneen and Ashley waited in the hall for a taxi to arrive. They sat in silence, and Jenneen was dreading that Kate would come down the stairs with Ellamarie and find her still sitting there. Ashley held onto her hand, and every now and again she gave it a reassuring squeeze. The footmen turned a blind eye, politely not noticing them.

"Ah, there you are!"

Jenneen looked up, and Ashley was shocked to see

the look that descended on her face. It was so brief Ashley wondered later if she had imagined it.

"I've been looking all over for you," said Paul. "Where have you been?"

Jenneen didn't answer, but Ashley could see that she was gritting her teeth.

"You're not going are you?" said Paul, seeing their luggage on the floor beside them. Jenneen nodded. "But this is going on all weekend," he protested. "I was hoping that perhaps we could . . ."

"No," Jenneen snapped, interrupting him. "Something's come up, we have to go back to London."

She had known that he was on the point of suggesting that they repeat their earlier performance, when she had dragged him and two other members of his cricket team out of the ballroom and into a small room, hardly more than a cupboard, beneath the stairs at the back of the house. There she had proceeded to strip off her clothes, and sit astride him, his friends looking on, among all the paraphernalia of hunting gear. He had been astonished by her ardor, and her expertise at taking on three men in the way she had, but even more surprising was how cold she had been afterward, before she had disappeared.

Luckily the taxi arrived at that moment.

"Well," he said, as she stood up to go, "perhaps I could give you a ring sometime, in London."

She muttered something that he couldn't quite hear, and went to walk past him. Ashley went on ahead with the footmen, who were carrying their luggage out to the taxi.

Paul caught hold of Jenneen's arm. "I'd like to see you again," he whispered. "You're quite something, you know."

Jenneen looked at him, and he drew back to see the contempt and loathing in her eyes.

"Going so soon?"

Jenneen turned to see his cousin Victoria coming

toward them, hiccuping and balancing a glass of champagne rather precariously between her fingers.

Jenneen gave a sad smile. What was it like to be her? To have fun, and get merry like that, without the haunting presence of Mrs. Green, just waiting for an opportunity to seize her and bury her in the gutters of shame and degradation.

"Yes," said Jenneen, "I'm afraid something's come up, and we have to get back."

"Oh, what a shame," Vicky slurred. "And we didn't even get a chance to get to know one another. Oh well, never mind, maybe next time," and she teetered off again, taking Paul with her.

The following day Ellamarie received the first spray of flowers.

EIGHTEEN

KATE SHRUNK AWAY FROM THE HURT AND ANGER ON HER father's face. Finally, out of sheer desperation, she had turned to him for help. After weeks of agony and indecision he had been the only one left that she could turn to, but now she regretted it. Seeing him standing there, his face clenched, fighting with himself not to say the terrible things he wanted to say, Kate wanted to run away and never see him, or anyone else, again.

He wanted to hit her, beat her—anything rather than have to admit and face up to what she was telling him. He turned away and leaned his hands against the mantelpiece. She watched his knuckles turn white as his grip grew tighter, and she was afraid.

In the end they had all let her down. Joel, her friends, and now her father. Not one of them cared about her, or what she was going through. Not one of them thought about the pain that filled each day, and the terror of facing things alone. She hated them now, Jenneen most of all.

She looked up as her father began to speak, and the sound of his voice was as if someone had a grip on his throat and he had to fight to get air. "He's right of course," he was saying, "you'll have to get rid of it. You can't even think about having it."

Kate stared at him and felt that she didn't know him. "Do you know what you're saying?" she whispered. Her face was white, and there were dark circles beneath her eyes. "You're asking me to kill your own grandchild."

He spun round. "It's not a child, Kate. Not yet." It was clearly an effort for him to keep his voice under control.

"It is!" she cried. "Of course it is. It might not be born yet, but it's still alive, a human being."

"No!" he growled.

After a long silence he took a deep breath. "This is getting us nowhere. We have to be rational about this, think things through and decide what is to be done. There's still time, it's not too late yet. If we contact the doctor today, he will be able to fix you up. Maybe by the end of . . ."

"Stop it!" she shouted, jumping to her feet. "Stop it! I'm not having an abortion. I'll never have an abortion. This is my baby you're talking about. Mine, do you hear me? I want it. I love it."

"You're talking nonsense," said her father. "How can you love it? It's not anything yet to be loved."

"Is that what you thought about me, when Mum was pregnant? Is that how you thought? That I was nothing, that I couldn't be loved, just because I was still in the womb?"

"Of course it wasn't," he snapped. "But you were planned. Your mother and I wanted you."

"And I want my baby."

He closed his eyes and ran his fingers back and forth across his forehead. "This is no way to bring a child into the world, Kate," he said, after a while.

Kate clenched her teeth, and tried to sound calm. "You're not listening to me. I will love it, I will look after it, it will want for nothing. I thought you would help me, but I can see now that I was wrong. But let me remind you again that this is your flesh and blood too, it is your grandchild."

"And Joel Martin's bastard."

She turned away, disturbed by the venom in his eyes.

"Have you thought of what this will do to you?" he went on. "To your life? You'll be carrying his bastard around for all the world to see. You will have no freedom, no time for yourself. You can forget your novel, something you've always wanted to do. You can say goodbye to your friends, there will be no time for them. And you can say goodbye to me."

"What!" she gasped.

"You heard what I said. If you have this child, I want nothing to do with it. I couldn't stand to see it, or you, my own daughter, as the used and discarded instruments of Joel Martin."

"For God's sake, why do you hate him so much?"

"How can you sit there and ask me that? Don't you realize what he has done to you? You are soiled and labeled. I could never look at that child and forget what that man has done to you."

"It's not entirely his fault, you know. It takes two to make a baby."

"Don't be disgusting!" he spat. "Don't ever let me

hear you talk like that again. I don't want to hear it, any of it."

"All right, all right," she said. "But you can't just pretend that there isn't a baby . . ."

"A child without a father? Is that what you want?"

"Of course it's not what I want, but it's what I've got. Besides, who knows, once it's born Joel might come round."

"Stop fooling yourself, Kate. You won't see him again, he told you as much, and you have to believe him. If anything, you should be thankful to him for getting out of your life."

"Thankful?"

"Yes. You only saw what you wanted to see in him, and you fooled yourself into believing that he loved you. Well, he didn't, and you're going to have to face up to that. He doesn't want you, or the child."

Tears were streaming down Kate's face now. "Don't say that," she cried. "Don't say that."

"For God's sake, Kate, what's got into you? You can't ruin your life, not now."

"I'm not ruining my life. Why won't anyone listen to me? Even if it does mean bringing it up alone, I still want to have this baby."

He sighed wearily and went to sit down beside her. "Look," he said, putting his arm round her shoulders, "it's difficult for you to see things clearly right now, you're too emotional, too upset. But you will, in time, you'll see that it's the only sensible answer. Darling, I love you, you know I do. Do you really believe that I would ask you to do something that I felt to be wrong? I am only asking you to do this for your own sake. It would make me very unhappy to see you bringing up the child of a man who doesn't even want to see you. And, I've been thinking this for some time now, and now that this has happened, well, perhaps you will see that it's not such a bad idea. I want you to come home and live here, with me. I get lonely when

Mummy's away in hospital, and she's away such a lot of the time now. And there's no real need for you to be in London, not now that you're freelancing, is there? You'll be able to write here, undisturbed. And then later, when things are, well, more settled, then we can think again, and who knows, perhaps then it will be the right time to have children. But not now, Kate. Not now, when everything is going so well for you."

"But things aren't going so well for me," she said. "That's just where you're wrong. I didn't want to tell you, but now it looks like I'll have to. I can't write a book, I'll never be able to write a book. I just don't have it in me."

"Of course you don't, at the moment. But that's because Joel Martin has been messing up your life for the past few months. But you will, you'll see. You will write, Kate, and I will do anything I can to help you. But you won't be able to do it surrounded by nappies and crying babies. Now what do you say? The operation can be done in no time at all, and then we can begin again. Here at home, like we used to be."

She shook her head and wiped her eyes with her hand. "Please stop it, don't say any more."

"All right, you're tired, I can see that. Why don't you go up and have a lie down, think about it for a while? You'll see that what I'm saying is for the best."

"I won't!" Kate yelled, and she pushed him away. "Please, please listen to me, I beg you. I'm going to have this child, and if you're not going to stand by me, Daddy, then I'll have it alone. I can see now that none of you care about me, that all you're thinking about is yourselves, but I'm thinking about *me*. Me! Do you hear? And my child. We don't need any of you, we can make it without you. I hate you, I hate all of you . . ." and she fell onto the arm of the settee, shaking and sobbing.

Her father pulled her head up onto his shoulder. "All right," he said. "All right. We won't discuss it now. Let me take you up to bed. You're tired. You'll see things differently when you've had some sleep."

Kate wanted to scream at him, but she was too weary. Her nerves were taut, and she had been on an emotional see-saw ever since Joel had walked out on her. She had rung him several times, but he had refused to speak to her. Jenneen had rung, but Kate had refused to speak to her, and had hung up on her. And neither would she see Ellamarie or Ashley. She didn't want anyone. She had only wanted her father in the end, but even that had been a mistake.

She allowed him to lead her up to her room, where she lay down on the bed. Her father sat with her for a while, saying nothing as he stroked her hair, and held her hand. She would make him see, she had to make him understand. She must have this baby. She loved Joel, it was his child, their child, and she couldn't kill it. He would come round in the end, they all would. They had to.

Ellamarie came back into the room and handed a glass to Jenneen. "Have either of you heard from her? Spoken to her at all?"

"Not a word," Ashley answered.

"She hangs up on me every time I ring," said Jenneen, and Ellamarie could see the hurt in her eyes. "I keep trying, but it's no use, she just won't speak to me. What about you, Ellamarie? Have you spoken to her?"

Ellamarie shook her head. "No," she said. "Like you, I've tried, but she won't listen. I have spoken to Joel though."

"When?" said Jenneen.

"This morning. I rang him. I wondered if perhaps he had spoken to her."

"And has he?" Ashley asked.

"No, and no more does he want to, by the sound of it."

"What did he say?"

"He said that she'd tried to ring him a couple of times, but that he really didn't see any point in going over things again."

"The bastard!" Jenneen muttered.

"Precisely," said Ellamarie. "But we have to do something. I think one of us should ring her father."

They looked at one another, none of them relishing the idea of speaking to Mr. Calloway. Ellamarie went on. "I thought that as I spent Christmas with them, then maybe it should be me. I just wanted to know that you were in agreement."

Ashley and Jenneen nodded their heads slowly.

Ellamarie went into the hall to use the phone. Jenneen and Ashley sat in silence, waiting for her to come back, dreading what she might have to say. Jenneen felt so responsible, and so wretched about everything; not for one minute had she stopped blaming herself.

At last Ellamarie came back into the room. They both looked up, waiting for her to speak.

"She's with her parents. She's been there since before the weekend. Her father said that she's all right— as well as can be expected at any rate. Her mother's home as well."

"He knows about the baby then?" said Ashley.

Ellamarie nodded. "Sure, he knows all right."

"Did you speak to her?" said Jenneen.

"No. She wouldn't come to the phone. I only spoke to her father."

"Did he say anything else?"

Ellamarie hesitated, and there was something in her manner that made the silence before she spoke ominous. "She's going to have an abortion, on Friday," she said, finally.

"Oh my God!" Jenneen gasped. "She can't! She can't do it. She wants that child."

"Not any more, apparently. Her father said they'd spent all weekend talking things over, and they've decided it's for the best."

"I don't know what to say," said Ashley.

"I know," said Ellamarie. "Her father asked if we'd go and see her tomorrow. Can you make it?"

"Of course," said Jenneen. "I'll cancel everything."

Ellamarie looked at her. She knew how personally Jenneen had taken all of this. How she blamed herself. And Kate didn't want to see her. She would only agree to seeing Ellamarie and Ashley. But not Jenneen. Ellamarie didn't know how to tell her.

"I'm sorry," she whispered.

Jenneen leaned forward and put her glass on the table, her hand was shaking. "She doesn't want to see me?" she asked in a small voice.

Ellamarie shook her head.

Jenneen closed her eyes and swallowed hard against the lump that had risen in her throat.

"I'm sorry," Ellamarie said again, and put her arms round her.

Jenneen cried into her shoulder. What had she done? Everything she touched she spoiled. But Kate. Kate couldn't turn her back on her. She loved Kate, all she had been trying to do was make her happy. To give her something that she thought she had wanted. She would never meddle in anyone's life again, everything she did turned to disaster. And now Kate was going to give up her baby; she would never be the same again. And for the rest of their lives, both of them would know that Jenneen might have saved her from this, and didn't.

Later that night, as she was leaving the theater, more flowers arrived for Ellamarie.

It was Friday morning, and Mr. Calloway stood in front of the old Victorian building in Kensington Square looking up at the windows. He checked the address that he had written on a piece of paper before he pressed the bell. As he waited he gazed sightlessly around the square. Spring had arrived. Birds chirped merrily from tree to tree, and the sun was breaking through the clouds.

A female voice spluttered onto the entryphone, and he replied with his name.

"Is Mr. Martin expecting you?" said the girl.

"He should be."

There was a silence, and Calloway waited, looking at the intercom. Suddenly a buzzer sounded, and the catch on the door was released.

"Third floor," said the voice, as he began to close the door behind him.

He took the stairs one at a time. There was no hurry. He passed a few people on the way up, but he looked at no one. His face was grim, but not even by the flicker of a muscle did he betray the blinding rage that burned inside him.

Half an hour ago he had left Kate at the hospital. She had wanted to go in alone. At first he had thought that she was going to run away as soon as he had gone, but she had smiled, that empty smile he had come to know this last week, and had assured him that he was right, that this was the only thing to do.

In truth he had been glad to leave her. If he had stayed he might have broken down. Her eyes had reflected her helplessness and solitude, and set a barrier between them that had never been there before. He remembered when she'd been a child, always his special child, and he had done everything he could to protect and shelter her from the nastier side of life. But nothing could have prepared him for this. The killing, or perhaps one should call it the murder, of his own grandchild. But how could he even think about her carrying this man's child? He had been deeply shocked when she had told him, and had fought hard to hide the repulsion he had felt to imagine another man's hands touching his precious little girl. But this man had soiled her, and hurt her, and now he was going to pay for it.

At last he reached the door on the third floor which gleamed Joel Martin and Associates from an overpolished brass plaque. He knocked gently, then as the female voice called out for him to come in, he pushed the door open.

The girl looked up. She was a young girl, probably only just inside her twenties. Did she have any idea what kind of monster she was working for? But she wasn't his problem. He only cared for his Kate, and what the animal the other side of that door was putting her through at this very moment.

"Mr. Martin will be with you in a minute," said the girl. "Would you like to sit down while you wait?" She indicated a large, overstuffed sofa beneath the window. Calloway had plenty of time. Yes, he would wait.

He kept his hands in his pockets; they were shaking. He refused the offer of a coffee, and looked around the room. He saw nothing. Nothing, that was, except the face of his daughter when she had told him she was pregnant. Her face when she had told him that Joel Martin had impregnated her then abandoned her, never wanting to see her again. His Kate. His precious little Kate, violated by that raping bastard in there, who didn't give a damn.

"Nice day, isn't it?" said the girl.

Calloway nodded, and pointedly looked away, discouraging any idle chat from the secretary.

A few minutes later a buzzer sounded on the secretary's desk and she looked over. "Mr. Martin will see you now," she said, getting up and going to open the door for him.

He crossed the room and walked into the adjacent office. As he looked at the dark-haired man seated behind the mammoth desk, looking up at him, the whole world seemed suddenly to pause in its business and hold its breath, waiting for the onslaught of a storm.

There was a half-smile on Joel's lips, but his eyes were wary. "Mr. Calloway," he said, getting to his feet.

"This is a surprise." He held out his hand, but it was ignored. "Won't you sit down?" Joel waved his hand toward the chair at the other side of his desk.

"A surprise?" Calloway loosened his tie. He must try and keep control.

"Well," said Joel, looking more than a little uncomfortable. "I really didn't expect to see you. Not here, anyway."

"Oh? Then where?"

"Well, not anywhere, I suppose."

"No," said Calloway. "I don't imagine you did. Or my daughter."

Joel flushed. "How is Kate?"

"Don't ask questions to which you have no wish to know the answers."

Joel looked back at him. He wasn't used to being spoken to like this, particularly not in his own office, and his visitor's manner was beginning to annoy him. "Just why are you here, Mr. Calloway? Is it money you want? Because if it is . . ."

Suddenly Calloway had him by the throat, up against the wall. "I'm not a young man, Martin," he snarled, "but so help me, I could kill you. Do you know where Kate is now? Do you? But no, of course you don't, and you don't bloody well care either, do you? Do you? Do you?" He was shaking Joel, banging his head against the wall.

Joel flexed his arms, and managed to push him away. "I think you'd better leave, Mr. Calloway," he said, barely managing to control his own temper.

"I'll leave when I'm good and ready," said Calloway, spitting out the words, one at a time. "My daughter is in the hospital right now, murdering a child. Your child. I don't know how it happened, and I don't want to know, but what I do know is that you are the lowest scum on God's earth. I don't know what you said to her to make her like she is, but by God you've taken everything from her. Her self-respect, her

dignity, her pride, and now her child. You've left her
with nothing, Martin, and so help me I'm going to see
that you suffer for it."

"Oh come on," said Joel, half laughing, "this isn't
the movies. You can't go around threatening people
like that."

"Shut up! I have no interest in anything you have
to say. I have come here for two reasons. One, to tell
you that, as of today, the five largest publishing houses
in this country will cease doing business with you. Tomorrow the others will follow suit."

For a moment Joel looked uncertain, then he
sneered. "You can't pull that one on me."

"I can and already have. The authors who have the
misfortune to be represented by you will be found
other agents, and the publishers, as I said, will no
longer recognize you."

"You haven't got that sort of power, Calloway, nobody has."

"You're wrong. But, if you don't believe me, try
ringing one of them, now." He picked up the telephone
and handed it to Joel, but Joel didn't take it.

Calloway put it down again. "Now for the second
reason I am here," he said, his voice icily calm. "I ought
to kill you for even laying one finger on my daughter,
but I have no intention of going to prison for filth like
you. I just want you to remember this, don't ever try
to come near Kate again, do you hear me? Not ever. She
is mine, and no one, *no one* lays a hand on my daughter
without feeling the consequences."

Joel looked at the older man and his lips began to
quiver with disgust. "You're sick!" he snarled. "I suspected it when I first met you, but I had no idea just
how far the rot had set in. It's not just me, is it? You
can't stand to think of *any* man touching your precious
daughter, can you? The very thought makes you curl
up and hate inside. It's like a worm, isn't it, eating away
at your gut, Kate with another man. You're in love with

her, you perverted bastard, aren't you? You're in love with your own daughter. God, you're disgusting! It doesn't matter whose child she's carrying, does it? All that matters is that it isn't yours. You're twisted, Calloway. Perver . . ."

The blow to his jaw landed so hard that Joel crashed to the floor. Calloway stood over him, his face twitching with fury. "I'm warning you, Martin! If I so much as even hear of you again, I'll kill you. Do you hear me? I'll kill you!" Turning abruptly he walked from the room.

So this was how it felt to have murdered your own baby. In fact it felt like nothing at all. Nothing. It was there one minute, the next it was gone. Nothing inside any more, no tiny whispering of life, just nothing. Empty and painless. There were no feelings, no care, no love, no hate. When they had taken the baby away, they had taken her soul away too. Her body was an empty shell now.

Sometimes she slept, but it didn't seem like often. Sometimes she opened her eyes, but there was nothing to see. People came in and out from time to time, but she didn't know who they were. They held her hands, kissed her on the face, and she felt she should know them, but they were strangers, and they frightened her. She didn't speak to them, she had nothing to say, because there was nothing left to say.

But one thing puzzled her. Why wouldn't the baby stop crying? Why were they letting it cry like that? Did no one care? Someone was talking to her. Couldn't they see that she couldn't hear them? Why didn't they help the baby? Why didn't they stop it crying? She knew that it was her baby. The one she had killed. It was dead, and it was crying because she had killed it. It would cry like this now for ever. There could be no comfort for her baby, no loving arms to hold it, no breast to feed it. There would be nothing for her baby now, only tears. Tears for the life that it would never have. The life that she had taken from it.

The voice went away, but the crying went on. She heard a door close, somewhere in the distance, but still she could hear the crying. A child's cry, echoing through the hollow of eternity. Crying because its mother had killed it, had robbed it of life. But she would die soon, and then she could comfort it, then she could love it, and feed it the milk of eternal life. Yes, soon she would die, and then she could hold her baby.

"It's no good," said Ellamarie, going back into the room. "She still won't say anything."

Kate's father looked up. His face was strained, and the lines around his eyes had become deeper these last two days. Ever since he had brought her home, Kate had simply lain on her bed, and said nothing. She didn't eat, she didn't cry.

He ran his fingers through his hair, and Ellamarie saw that they were shaking. "I don't know what to do," he said. "God help me, I just don't know what to do."

"I think we should call the doctor back again. She can't go on like this, she must have some food."

"OK," he said wearily. "Where's the number?"

"Don't worry," said Ashley, "sit there, I'll do it."

When she had gone, Ellamarie went to sit beside him, and put an arm round his shoulders. Bob went to the cupboard and took out a bottle of brandy. As he poured them all a drink, he noticed the barely started manuscript of Kate's book, lying beside her typewriter on the desk. He was suddenly overcome with sadness, and wondered if she would ever finish it now. He handed the drinks round.

"It's so good of you all to care like this," Calloway said, very near to the end of his tether.

"We all love her," said Ellamarie. "We want to help."

"It's only depression," said Calloway. "She'll get

over it. She just needs time. She will get over it, you know." He looked at Bob and his eyes were pleading.

Bob smiled, trying to give him the assurance he needed. "Of course she'll get over it. These things always take time. But she'll be fine again, soon."

Ashley came back into the room. "The doctor's on his way."

Calloway reached out for her hand. "Thank you, my dear. You've been so kind. I don't know what I'd have done without you all."

Ashley pressed his hand to her face. "We all care about her a great deal, Mr. Calloway," she said. "I only wish that there was more we could do."

There was a long silence which was finally broken by Kate's father. "Did you see Jenneen earlier?" he asked, looking back to Ellamarie and Bob.

Ellamarie looked at Bob before turning back and nodding.

"How was she?"

"Not good, I'm afraid," said Bob. "She still blames herself. She thinks it best that she stays away for the time being. That coming here will only upset Kate more."

"Please tell her, she really mustn't blame herself. It wasn't her fault. She mustn't hold herself responsible. Kate is a grown woman, she can make up her own mind." But there was no conviction in his voice. He blamed himself.

"To tell you the truth," said Ellamarie, "we're not sure that it's only Kate that has made Jenneen like this. There might be something else."

Calloway looked at them, the question in his eyes giving voice to his need to think of something else, if only for a moment.

"She won't tell anyone," said Bob, "but she was depressed before all this happened. I spoke to her editor today, and apparently things haven't been going too well for her at work either. Bill was really quite worried about her."

"Is there anything I can do?" Calloway asked.

Bob shook his head. "I think you've got enough to do here. Kate needs you now. We'll look after Jenneen, don't worry."

Finally the doctor arrived. He went straight in to Kate, and again they waited, saying nothing, until he came out. None of them were surprised when he said he was taking her back into hospital. She needed the kind of care that she couldn't get here.

Calloway carried his daughter down the stairs to the car, and sat her in the back seat. Ellamarie got in beside her, taking her hand and telling Bob she would see him later.

"Please God," she prayed silently, as they passed through the busy streets of Kensington, "please God, let her be all right. Help her to get over this."

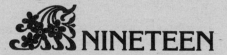

NINETEEN

J ENNEEN FINISHED READING THE LETTER. IT HAD BEEN A LONG time in coming, she had been expecting it for weeks. She read it again. Irony, pure irony. It contained nothing of what she had expected, nothing at all. But she didn't feel the relief she should feel, only the realization of what she should have known before, if only she had thought.

Her mother had begun her letter in the usual chatty way. Gran had had a win on the bingo. Fifty pounds, so she was planning to take a short holiday in Skegness at Easter. Dad was well, so were her brothers; as usual, her mother said nothing about herself. Then she had gone on to tell her that young Maggie Dewar had never returned from London, and had telephoned her mother to say she was staying with a friend, called Matthew Bordsleigh. Wasn't he the actor that Jenneen used to know?

That was really all her mother had to say, except that she loved her very much and hoped she would be able to get up to see them again soon. And she had enclosed a tatty little photograph Gran had found of Jenneen playing on the sands at Blackpool, aged four. Jenneen turned it over, half expecting something to be written on the back, but it was blank. She tucked it back inside the envelope and turned to the letter again. There had been no other mention of Maggie or Matthew, so obviously they hadn't carried out their threat. Of course, it all fell into place now. The demands for money had increased. Matthew was no longer asking for twenty, maybe fifty pounds at a time. No, now he was asking for a hundred, sometimes even two hundred pounds. And it made sense. He was supporting Maggie as well. Correction, Jenneen was supporting Maggie as well. Such twists and turns in fate. She had brought them together, and now, together, they were bleeding her dry.

Blackmail. The cruelest torture known to mankind. You never knew that, of course, until you were the victim. The terror you had to live with, each day, all day. To dread the wrath of your persecutor, never to know if he would keep his word, and not tell. Never to know when he would show; to live in fear of the door, the phone, the mail.

She picked up her coat, and left the flat. She would be late if she didn't hurry, and she had been late too often these last few weeks. The crew were meeting at nine-thirty at Earls Court. The London mid-season fashion shows were well under way.

They were waiting for her when she arrived, sitting in the coffee bar, having breakfast. She looked at her watch. It was twenty-five minutes past nine. Good, she wasn't late. The director was sitting with his PA at a separate table. After saying good morning to the crew, Jenneen went to join them.

"Morning," she said, sitting down beside Patsy.

They both greeted her with what to her seemed to be an unusual amount of warmth, and immediately, as she so often did these days, Jenneen began to panic. Why were they being so kind? Did they know something she didn't? Was that pity she could see in Patsy's eyes? Matthew must have broken his word—where were the morning papers? But Brian, the director, started to talk to her quite normally about the day's shoot, and Patsy went off to fetch her a coffee, as usual. Gradually Jenneen began to relax again.

The morning dragged and she ran up to eight takes to do her opening statement to camera, before she finally managed to get it right. Although he didn't remark on it, she knew that Brian was surprised; it wasn't like her to need more than two takes as a maximum, for anything.

At lunchtime she decided to go for a walk. She was too on edge to sit with the crew and make idle chat about putting the company to rights. The letter this morning had disturbed her more than she had realized. Matthew alone she felt she might be able to control. But Matthew egged on by a scheming young twenty-year-old, that was a different matter. And with Maggie coming from her home town, it was all too close for comfort. What was she going to do? But no matter how much she thought about it, she knew that she was at their mercy.

She thought about the last time she had seen Matthew, when he had forced his way into her flat. She had been crying and, desperate to talk to someone, she had tried to tell him about Kate, tried to find that other side of Matthew that had seemed to care for her once. But he had laughed at her and ridiculed her. He told her that perhaps now she could see herself for the selfish bitch she was. She had even betrayed her closest friend. Why? And he had answered the question. Because she was jealous. Because in her perversion she lusted after Kate, and a mind sick like hers could only think of that one, all-consuming perversion.

She had begged him to stop, pleaded with him to understand and help her, but there had been no pity in his eyes, only scorn. Finally she had given him the money he had come for, and he had left.

And now, as she walked, she found herself thinking about Kate. More than anything else in the world, she wished she could be with her, to see for herself how she was. She wanted to hold Kate, and tell her that she was sorry, and to ask for forgiveness. She longed to hear her soothing voice, telling her that it would be all right. That things were never as bad as they seemed to be, and that she no longer blamed Jenneen for anything. But Kate was in no state for Jenneen.

Looking up, Jenneen found herself outside of the Cromwell Hospital. She studied the aquamarine blinds at the windows, and wondered which one Kate was behind. She wanted to go in, she longed to go in, but she couldn't Each night she rang Ashley or Ellamarie to find out how Kate was progressing, but she never visited her herself. It wouldn't be long now, Ashley had told her last night, before Kate would be going home again. The progress was slow, but what there was of it, was good. Jenneen didn't ask if Kate mentioned her, she already knew the answer.

And the bitter irony of it all was that if there was anyone that Jenneen might have been able to talk to, go to for help, and hopefully understanding, it would have been Kate. She was surprised to find herself thinking that. Normally they all turned to Ellamarie for strength and courage, but there was something in Kate that Jenneen knew was as confused and lonely as the emptiness she felt inside herself.

She turned away from the hospital, and back along the Cromwell Road toward Earls Court. Several passers-by threw her odd looks as she brushed past them. She didn't realize that tears were streaming down her face.

After a while she stopped and looked around. She was dimly aware that her heart was beginning to beat faster, and her mind was slowly starting to whirl. Then, strangely, she could see Matthew's face, laughing at her. Then she saw Kate's face, and she could feel all that Kate was feeling. And there was Mrs. Green, ruthlessly pushing her into acts so degrading Jenneen could never bear to think about them. There were her parents, and she could see that they knew; their faces were full of anguish and pain at the shame and humiliation she had caused them. And there was Kate again, and Matthew, and then they were all there, watching her with still faces, watching and waiting. Those whose lives she had already ruined, and those whose lives she was yet to ruin. And it was too late now to change anything, there was nowhere left for her to turn.

The trucks thundered by, and the cars speeding at sixty maybe seventy miles an hour blew gusts of wind around her which floated away in clouds of dust. She closed her eyes, and the faces were still there, watching and waiting, and she listened to the traffic. Slowly she opened her eyes again and the pounding of her heart pushing her blood round her body cleared her mind; she was no longer afraid. Everything seemed so very simple.

She felt she was moving in a dream, slowly and deliberately; the noise around her became a cacophony of mystical, sublime and ineffable sounds, as if it was all happening above the surface of a deep, deep pool, far away, too distant to hear. Yet it was there. And it was like drifting off into an unsteady sleep, where far-off sounds grew and faded in volume.

There was a softness, a strange beckoning, that pulled her forward, telling her it would be all right. And then she was standing, as if apart from her own body, watching herself and what she was doing, smiling that soon it would all be at an end. Just one final step, and it would all be over. No more Matthew, no more Mrs. Green, no more rejection, no more loneliness. Just one final step.

There was a deafening screech, and the sound of an angry horn. She expected pain, she wanted the pain; it would be over quickly—very soon now. Her shoulders were squashed, pushed together so hard she could hardly breathe. She rolled over and looked up at the sky, and watched the clouds passing overhead. Everything was silent.

She continued to watch the clouds, so peaceful on their celestial journey. The unconquerable sky mountains, some gray, some white. And then there were faces, worried, anxious, and hands pulling at her, voices speaking to her.

She blinked, confused; she tried to focus her eyes, but the faces kept fading away, slipping from her, then returning. Then there were soft hands on hers, and a warm, comforting voice crept into her mind. She turned her head, and she saw a woman kneeling beside her. She felt she should know her, but she couldn't think.

"Call an ambulance," she heard someone say. And the spell was broken. She struggled to get up. "No," she wheezed. "No, please."

The woman was holding her again, and Jenneen leaned against her. Was it Kate?

"Jenneen?" said the woman. "Jenneen?"

Jenneen turned to look at her. Yes, she did know her, but who was she?

"I've got to get back to work," said Jenneen. "They'll be waiting for me. I mustn't be late again."

"Ssh. We're calling an ambulance."

"No," Jenneen cried. "Please, don't. I'm all right, honestly, I'm all right." She tried to get to her feet.

Her legs were weak, but they supported her, with the help of this woman, whom she should know. She allowed herself to be led to the pavement.

Everything started to spin, and she thought she was going to pass out. But she couldn't pass out. She must hold on.

"Take me home," said Jenneen. "Please, take me home."

She saw the woman turn away, and then was vaguely aware of her talking to a man. Jenneen looked at his face. It was white with fear, and shock, and he kept looking toward her. Finally he went away. She wanted to call out to him, and say she was sorry, but she couldn't find the words. The woman turned back to her, and gently, very slowly, led her back down the street and round the corner. She stopped and, taking out a key, let them into a big house.

It must have been several hours later when Jenneen finally woke. It was dark outside, and she could see the moon through the open curtains. She looked around at the strange room, and wondered where she was, how she had got there. The bed was comfortable and warm; she turned over, and closed her eyes again.

She lay quietly, listening to the sounds from outside. A dog barking, someone hammering in the distance. Footsteps and the sounds of traffic. Traffic. Her eyes flew open as it all came flooding back. She turned onto her back and stared up at the ceiling. She had tried to kill herself. She had tried to take what she thought would be the only way out. Suicide. The most selfish act open to mankind. Suicide and blackmail. What had happened to her life? Where had it all gone wrong?

She sat up. Then she remembered the woman at the side of the road, and being led to a house. She looked across the room as the door opened. The same woman came in, and looked surprised to see her sitting up.

The woman smiled, and again Jenneen wondered who she was. She tried to think back. Where had she seen her before? But her mind was a blank.

"How are you feeling?"

Jenneen nodded and gave a weak smile. "OK, I think."

"You're very pale, maybe you should have gone to the hospital."

"No, I'm all right, really."

The woman came to stand beside the bed.

Jenneen looked into her face. "I feel as though I should know you."

The woman laughed, it was a girlish laugh and she looked younger suddenly, almost teenaged. "We met at Robert Blackwell's. My cousin introduced us. Paul, remember? I'm Victoria Deane."

"Oh yes, of course," said Jenneen. "I'm sorry, I just couldn't think."

"It doesn't matter," said Victoria. "Why don't you lie down again and I'll go and get you some tea. I've just made some."

She left the room, and Jenneen stared at the door. She must get up. She couldn't stay here any longer. Victoria had been very kind, but she was probably longing to be rid of her by now.

She climbed out of bed and looked around for her clothes. They were lying on the back of a chair, neatly folded. Quickly she slipped into them, and then she remembered that she should have been filming this afternoon. She must ring Bill. He would be furious. He had warned her only last week that questions were being asked, and she couldn't keep letting them down. Soon the people at the top would want answers to those questions. Answers she could never give.

She found Victoria in the kitchen, pouring the tea.

"Could I ring for a taxi?" Jenneen asked.

Victoria turned to look at her, her face unsure. "I really don't think you should go anywhere tonight," she said. "At least not on your own. Is there anyone you can call?" Jenneen's eyes fell and, sensing that she didn't want anyone to know what had happened today, Victoria went on. "You've had quite a shock, you know. Why don't you stay here . . ."

"But . . ."

"No, don't argue, please. I'd like you to stay. Maybe we could have that chat we never got round to at Robert's."

She handed Jenneen a cup. Jenneen took it and smiled her thanks. She wanted to stay.

"In here." Victoria pushed open the door to the sitting room.

"I really should ring my editor," said Jenneen, sitting down on the settee. "I was supposed to be filming this afternoon."

"It's all right, I've already done it. And don't worry, he was quite understanding, and told me to tell you not to worry, and he would ring you tomorrow."

"You didn't tell him . . .?"

Victoria shook her head. "No."

"Thanks." And then Jenneen groaned. "I'm really going to be in for it this time."

"You can worry about that later," said Victoria. "Now come on, drink your tea before it gets cold."

They didn't say anything for a while, Jenneen sipped her tea, and looked around the room. She was touched to see so many photographs of Paul. The two of them were obviously very close.

"Why?" said Victoria finally, and so softly Jenneen hardly heard.

"Why what?"

"Why were you going to do it?"

Jenneen felt her hand begin to shake, so she put her cup on the table beside her.

"I'm sorry. It's none of my business. I shouldn't have asked."

"No," said Jenneen. "Please don't be sorry. You have every right to ask. After all, you saved my life, and I suppose I should be grateful."

"Not grateful. Relieved. It's no answer, you know."

"Isn't it? It would have solved so many things."

"Not really," said Victoria. "Nothing can be that bad."

"Oh, it can, it can."

"Do you want to talk about it?"

Jenneen shook her head.

"It might help."

"No, it won't. It's something I have to sort out for myself."

"OK, but if you change your mind."

"Thanks."

Victoria got to her feet.

"I've made us something to eat, it should be ready about now. I hope you're hungry."

Jenneen got up too. "You really are being very kind."

Victoria pulled a face.

Jenneen followed her out of the room. "Can I help?"

"No. You are to be pampered and spoiled this evening, and that's an order. Now, you're to go back in there and sit down, and I'll call you when it's dished up."

Jenneen did as she was told and went back into the drawing room. It was quite a surprise to see Victoria in this role. When they had first met she had given Jenneen the impression of a dizzy blonde, who lived life just for fun. But this was another side of her, warm and caring, and Jenneen decided that she really did like her.

As they ate their meal they talked, and laughed, about so many things, but they never mentioned what had happened earlier, and Jenneen began to relax. It was so good to be away from home, comfortable, and in a place where she had nothing to fear.

Victoria told her all about her life, and Jenneen watched her face as she chattered on. It was a young face, full of energy for life, and Jenneen marveled at the soft sound of her voice, which sometimes burst into a bubble of girlish delight.

She told Jenneen about the string of boutiques she owned, all over London. Boutiques where Jenneen had shopped many times. Vicky, as she told Jenneen she liked to be called, had been left a little money in her grandfather's will, and with the help of her mother and father, they had made an extraordinary success of the business, far and away beyond anything they had ever imagined in the early days.

It was so good to listen. To hear about the life of someone who was happy, living in a straightforward and uncomplicated world. But Jenneen didn't envy her, she only liked her the more for it.

Later they went to sit in the drawing room again, and Vicky opened a bottle of brandy.

When she looked back on this night in later weeks, Jenneen would smile, and still wonder how it had come about that she had poured out the whole story, the whole sordid story, to someone who was, in truth, no more than a stranger.

But Vicky listened, and never said a word. She watched Jenneen's face, saw the pain and the confusion. Her heart went out to Jenneen as she heard about Mrs. Green, and Matthew, and then Kate. Looking at her sitting there, so frail, and so innocent-looking, it was difficult to believe that the monstrous character of Mrs. Green lurked somewhere beneath the surface. Or that someone would want to cause her such pain, as Matthew had. But Kate would come round, Vicky was sure of it.

Finally, when Jenneen was all talked out, she looked at Vicky sitting across the room in the shadows, and was sure she could feel her withdrawing. It was what she had expected. But when Vicky leaned forward to pour more brandy, Jenneen could see that she was smiling, a sad and compassionate smile.

"You shouldn't be trying to bear this alone, Jenn," she said.

"I don't know what else to do."

"You need help, maybe professional help."

"No, I can't."

"But it is destroying your life. You need someone to talk to, Jenneen, someone who understands and can help you."

Jenneen screwed up her eyes and ran her fingers through her hair. "I shouldn't have told you any of this."

"But you should. You've been bottling it all up for too long. Do any of your friends know?"

"Good God, no," said Jenneen, shuddering at the very idea.

"Look, honestly, it's not as bad as you seem to think it is. OK, I know that's easy for me to say, but it can be worked out, as long as you give someone a chance to help, even if it's only a friend to begin with. And, if you feel as though you can't talk to someone you know, then why not let me try? After all, I know most of it now anyway."

Jenneen felt like crying. "But there's nothing you can do," she said. "You must see that. There's nothing anyone can do."

"Maybe not, unless you are prepared to help yourself."

Jenneen's breath caught in her throat.

"You do want to help yourself, don't you?"

Jenneen looked down at her hands and shook her head. "I don't know," she said. "I just don't know. Yes, I suppose so."

"Well, you can always begin by trying, and I'll help you if I can."

Jenneen frowned, and looked across the room at her. "But why? I don't understand. You hardly know me."

Vicky smiled. "That doesn't matter. There are times in all of our lives, when we need help. Times when we feel that there is no one to turn to, just when we need someone most. I know what it's like to feel like that. So confused, so terribly alone, that life doesn't seem worth living any more. That even if there was someone there, they wouldn't understand anyway. Everything seems hopeless, and without purpose, and you grope around in the dark, trying to find an end to it. Trying to find something that might give meaning to your life again, but there seems to be nothing there in the darkness, nothing but an empty space, with no sides, no ceiling and no bottom."

Jenneen was watching her, and Vicky smiled to see the surprise on her face. She nodded. "Yes, Jenn, I've been there too. But then, at a time when I felt that there was never going to be anything, that there really was no hope any more, someone came into my life, and they cared. They helped me to accept myself for what I am, and to believe in myself, and to feel no shame. It was a long, and sometimes difficult journey, but never once did he waver in his affection or support. And now I know that to truly appreciate life, to truly believe in it, you have to accept and deal with whatever it puts your way. I am a richer person now, true to myself, and true to my life. It seems to be life's way of forming you, as a person, as an individual. To deliver the hurt, and so much pain until you think you can take no more, and then, and only then, does life turn, and take you back again. And when you come back you understand so many things you never knew before. You can feel the pain of others, and the joy of others, and at last, at long last, you are complete, but somehow different. Many of us have to experience this, Jenneen, so many of us. And you can never question the hand of fate, or God, whatever you want to call it, because you will never find the answers. But in the end it is good that you have experienced all that you have, because in turn you can help others, when they too come to know what you have known. I suppose that is why I want to help you now."

"And it doesn't matter that you don't know me?"

"Sometimes it's easier that way," Vicky answered. "Sometimes the people closest to you are the most difficult to reach, and the ones who, maybe, don't know us at all."

Jenneen shook her head, very slowly, and thought about what Vicky had said. "No," she said, finally. "No, maybe you're right, they don't."

On the other side of London, as her performance was about to begin, Ellamarie was frantically trying to get hold of Jenneen. She hadn't heard from her in days and now she wasn't only worried, she was afraid. Finally, when there was still no answer from Jenneen's flat, Ellamarie had to run to make her entrance on time.

After the performance, when she returned to her dressing room, she could barely get through the door, there were so many flowers. And again, just like all the other times, there was no card.

Kate was sitting up in the hospital bed, alone in her private room. It had been almost three weeks since she had been brought back to the hospital and during that time she had had very little idea or understanding of anything that was going on around her. Vaguely she had been aware of tubes, one into her wrist and another into her nose, but she hadn't known, or even cared, why they were there. A doctor came in to see her every day and she would watch his mouth and the crooked teeth behind his thin lips as he spoke to her, and his gray, solemn eyes as they blinked spasmodically. After a while Kate didn't mind answering his questions, but at first she had minded—she had hated it.

And then one day the baby stopped crying, and from then it seemed that the worst might be over and the tubes had been taken away. Her father brought in a TV for her to watch. Her friends came, but Jenneen was never there. It had taken a while for Kate to remember, but when she did, she couldn't bring herself to speak about Jenneen and what had happened between them.

She stared at the TV set but she wasn't watching it. She would be going home tomorrow, and she was pleased. She really did feel stronger now. She didn't think about the baby often, not any more. She had coaxed it to the back of her mind, where it must stay. She didn't tell anyone, but there were times, only ever in the dead of night, when tiny screams would pull her from the hollow depths of nightmare. But that's all it was, a nightmare. She knew that now, and knew that it would pass.

She stared down at the bed. The soft blue cover was wrinkled around her legs, and her hands were lying lifelessly across her body. Then she looked at the flowers, beautifully arranged, and placed about the room, sent in an effort to cheer her. And in a way they did. Most of them were from Ellamarie, she had plenty to spare these days. Kate smiled as she looked over at the latest bunch Ellamarie had brought in. Bob had been with her, and watching them together Kate had felt sad that she didn't have Ellamarie's inner strength. Ellamarie would never have got herself into this mess, and Kate knew that it would very likely be Ellamarie who would get her out of it.

The music changed on the TV, and Kate looked

up. She watched the familiar opening titles for the next program, and thought of how often she had admired them. The picture changed, and there was Jenneen.

Quickly Kate reached for the remote, and switched off. Her hand was shaking, and she caught it to her, trying to calm herself.

She couldn't look at Jenneen. She couldn't bear to see her face. She had thought that she had seen pain in Jenneen's eyes, and she wondered now if she had, or if she had only wanted to. Jenneen, dear, dear, Jenneen. All those terrible things she had said to her. All the blame she had thrown at her, trying to hurt her with the pain she herself had felt at the time.

She wanted to ask Jenneen to forgive her, but would it ever be the same again for them? So much had happened in such a short time, and all of their lives were changing. Would they grow apart? But no, they must never grow apart. She must see Jenneen, beg her to forgive her for saying all those terrible things. She must save their friendship. It was the only thing now that was worth saving.

Jenneen had been so dreadfully sad. Even before everything that had happened, she had been sad. The only one of the four of them who was lonely, even when they were together. Jenneen had no one, she turned to no one; she stayed remote, in her own private hell.

A private hell. Just like the one Kate had been through. Where an existence remained unrealized, and life, as yet, undiscovered. They must help one another now. Together, they would pull through.

But it might already be too late to hope. Would Jenneen ever be able to forget? Even if she forgave, would she be able to forget how Kate had so cruelly fueled the flames of confusion and torment that burned in her heart? How, blinded by her own suffering, Kate had lashed out to hurt those around her, never stopping to think that they, too, might be suffering.

She turned her head to one side and her tears fell onto the pillow.

"Oh Jenn," she whispered. "Jenn, please forgive me. I love you so much, please, please, forgive me."

She didn't hear the door open, did not realize that there was someone in the room until she felt a hand touch hers and lift it from the bed. She looked at the hand. It was a man's hand, dark with long slender fingers and short hair on the backs of the fingers. It held hers, not too tightly, and she wondered at how tiny and white hers seemed against it. And then her heart turned over. It was Joel. He had come back to her, just like she had always known he would.

She looked up and saw that it was Nick, standing over her, smiling down at her. She closed her eyes, then tried to smile. So many tricks, would they never end?

"Hello."

She opened her eyes and looked at him again. His face was almost exquisitely beautiful, but with the cragginess of a man, which lent a hardness to the beauty. His dark hair curled over his collar, and his blue-black eyes, which crinkled at the corners when he laughed, were smiling down at her and searching her face. She saw that he had a mole beneath his right eye; she had never noticed it before. She liked it. It was an imperfection on a perfect face.

"Hello," she said.

He reached for the box of tissues beside the bed, and handed them to her. She took them, and wiped her eyes.

"I'm sorry." She tried to laugh. "I seem to be doing a lot of this lately."

"Then maybe it's time you stopped," he said, gently. "Unless it makes you feel better, of course."

She smiled, and struggled to sit up. "I'm not sure that it does, but I do it anyway."

He pulled her forward, and adjusted the pillows behind her, then pushed her back against them.

When she looked at him again she could see that he was trying not to laugh.

"What is it?"

"Only that I feel completely absurd," he said. "Coming in here, trying to play nurse, and now can't think of a damned thing to say."

"And that's funny?"

"Not really," he laughed.

She laughed too.

He pulled up a chair, and sat down beside the bed. "So you're going home tomorrow?"

She nodded. "And not a day too soon. Being in here only reminds me."

He looked away, and she wondered if he was uncomfortable, talking about it. She wouldn't mention it again.

"I didn't expect to see you again. I mean, after the last time we spoke. I shouldn't have let you down, and I'm sorry. You sounded awfully cross."

He chuckled. "I was. But it doesn't matter now."

Suddenly she wanted to touch him. "Would you like some grapes?"

He looked at the fruit beside her bed.

"I know," she said. "I've been seriously considering starting a winery when I get out of here. How are you at treading?"

"Terrific!"

"Then you've got a job. I was thinking of calling it Kate's Carafes. What do you think?"

"I think I'm glad to see you."

She blushed. "I look dreadful," she said, running her fingers through her hair.

"Mmm, I must say I have seen you looking better."

"Such chivalry."

His face became serious. "How are you, really?"

She looked away, and her eyes began to fill with tears again.

"I'm sorry," he said. "I've upset you. I shouldn't have asked."

"No. No, I'm fine really. I have moments when it all seems so terrible that I think I can't carry on, but they pass."

"Have you seen him at all?"

She turned back to him. "Joel?"

He nodded.

"No."

She saw the muscles tighten in his face, and she thought for a moment that he was angry. But then his expression softened again.

"Maybe, when you're feeling better, that is, we could have that day out we talked about?"

She looked into his eyes, and he looked back. Then she lowered her head. "I don't know, Nick, I'm not sure if I want anyone in my life. Not now, anyway."

There was a long silence before he spoke. "OK. But if you change your mind, will you promise to ring me?"

"You'll be the first," she smiled. "I promise."

The look in his eyes was one of such tenderness, that again she wanted to reach out and touch him.

"Thank you for coming, Nick."

He smiled. "I'll be waiting," he said, and getting up from the chair, he left the room.

TWENTY

STOP WORRYING," SAID BOB. "THIS SORT OF THING HAPPENS all the time to actresses, you're not the first and you won't be the last." He was sitting in the canteen at the back of the theater, talking to Ellamarie and Nick. His denial that there was anything to be alarmed about in receiving so many anonymous bouquets was not ironing out the frown on Ellamarie's face. "Look, the time to worry is when you get threatening letters, but there's hardly anything threatening in a bunch of flowers, is there? If anything you should be flattered."

"Well, I'm not," Ellamarie retorted.

"All right, you're not. But I'm here, aren't I? I won't let anything happen to you. Anyway, it's not going to, so you can stop worrying."

Ellamarie looked up at Nick and grinned. "My very own superman."

Bob went on: "He's probably very lonely and shy. Who knows, it could be that you remind him of his mother."

Nick burst out laughing at the look on Ellamarie's face. "I'll take a swing at you in a minute," she said to Bob, and he ducked as she did.

"No one serving coffee or anything yet?" said Nick, looking at his watch.

"Still early," said Ellamarie. "Aren't you going to sit down?"

275

Nick walked over to another table and picked up a chair. When he turned back again he saw that Bob was running his fingers over Ellamarie's face, and whispering something to her. He sat down at their table and tried very hard not to feel like an intruder.

"Cheer up," said Ellamarie, looking at his gloomy face.

He smiled. "I don't know what it is, but every time I see you two together I think I feel jealous."

"Well, I'm sorry," said Bob, "but you can't have her. She's mine."

"I didn't mean that."

"Well, you sure as hell can't have him either," said Ellamarie.

"Maybe that's it," said Nick, "you two are always so happy and relaxed with one another. Whenever I look at you I wonder what it's like to be like you. Is life really as wonderful as it seems, in your world?"

Bob looked at Ellamarie, and she looked back at him. Then Bob shook his head. "No," he said. "No. It's even better than it seems."

Ellamarie giggled, and turned back to Nick. "He's so romantic. I wouldn't even trade him in for a newer model."

Bob pinched her, and she shrieked. "Well, maybe I would," she said.

"As things go, I think you two must be the perfect couple."

Bob looked him straight in the eye. "Not quite."

Nick was immediately embarrassed. How stupid of him to have said that. "Sorry, I wasn't thinking."

"Hell, it doesn't matter," said Ellamarie. "We all have our crosses to bear. Have you seen Kate at all?"

Nick shook his head. "Not since she was in the hospital. How is she?"

"Not good, I'm afraid. Still depressed, but I suppose it's only to be expected. I'm taking her off to a little place we know in Scotland for a couple of days tomorrow. I think she could do with a break."

Nick didn't say anything.

"Why don't you call her?" said Bob.

"No, she knows where I am if she wants me. I don't want to push it."

Bob shrugged. "Up to you. But make sure you don't leave it too long."

He pulled out the script for the *Queen of Cornwall,* and the three of them began to discuss it. Although they had done their first read several weeks ago, it had only been with stand-in actors, to try the script out. Bob and Adrian Cowley, who was to produce the film, had had several meetings with bankers and business-men and other possible investors. Interest was mount-ing, largely due to the fact that Bob's name was attached to it.

"I shiver all over every time I think of myself, up there on the big screen," said Ellamarie. "I can hardly believe that it's going to happen. I never realized until now how much I've always wanted to do a movie. Well, I knew I wanted to, but now that it's actually going to happen, I just can't believe it. Me, a movie star! Just wait till . . . you're laughing at me," she said, look-ing at Bob. And he was.

He leaned across the table and dropped a kiss on the end of her nose. "Love you," he said and winked at her.

"Are you staying for tonight's performance?" she asked.

"Can't, I'm afraid. I told Adrian I'd meet him at seven to talk over a few things, then I have to go to the Coliseum. But I'll be back in time to pick you up."

Elsie the canteen lady walked in at that moment and Ellamarie got up to get them all a coffee.

Standing at the counter watching the two of them, Ellamarie was thinking about Nick and Kate. She was sure that Nick was half in love with Kate. And there was no doubt that Kate needed someone right now. She needed her confidence and self-esteem putting back together. Maybe Nick was the right one to do it. She would talk it over with Ashley tonight, before she and Kate left for Scotland. Ashley would know what to do.

Elsie handed her three coffees, and she took them back to the table. She was looking forward to going to Scotland tomorrow. She knew she wasn't only doing it because she thought it would do Kate some good—though she prayed to her Catholic God that it would. She was also doing it because *Twelfth Night* was to break for a week. Bob would be busy at the Coliseum with *Don Giovanni,* and Nick was going back into rep at the National with *Lady Windermere's Fan.* Most of the rest of the cast were appearing in other reps around the country too, and as there wasn't even as much as an audition on the horizon for her to look forward to, she had decided it might be better for her to be out of London, where she didn't have to dwell too much on the lack of parts that were coming her way. Bob hadn't been too keen on the idea, saying that he would miss her, but Ellamarie knew that he'd be too busy really to notice, and told him that right now Kate's need was greater. She was going to take Kate to the place that Bob had taken her not long after they'd first met. It was where he had told her he loved her, and where they had first made love. She wasn't too sure why she had chosen to take Kate there. As it was a special place for her, maybe it could be special for Kate too.

She pretended to listen as Bob and Nick went over the opening lines of the *Queen of Cornwall,* but her mind had wandered on to what Nick had said about her and Bob. Did they really seem to be the perfect couple? Sometimes she felt as if they were. But she couldn't shake off this feeling of dread that it wasn't going to last. That something terrible was going to happen, and she would lose him. How deceiving people can be sometimes, she thought. To look so happy, so at one with each other, but always there was something. Was there really any such thing as the perfect couple, with perfect happiness?

Blanche stirred in her sleep, and turned over. Her hair fell back onto the pillows, and the early morning sun cast a pool of light across her face.

Julian brushed his finger lightly against her cheek, he didn't want to wake her. He was sitting up in bed beside her, watching the sun rise and wishing that he, too, could sleep so peacefully.

He had been woken again in the early hours, by that same nightmare. The one that haunted him every night now, where he found himself standing at the altar with Blanche. The vicar was asking if anyone knew of any reason why these two people before him should not be joined in holy wedlock, and every time a voice would shout that it was wrong, that he loved another, that he must not marry this woman. He knew that the voice was his own, shouting from within, warning him to stop now, before it was too late, And then he would wake up, sweating, confused.

But I love Blanche, he told himself. I really do love her. She makes me happy, she is everything I could want in a wife. So, said the voice, why are you restless?

He knew the answer. In his heart, he knew why, but until now, he had been unable to face the truth. But the truth will follow you, wherever you go, said the voice. You can never hide from the truth. Admit it. Admit that you love someone else, even more than you love Blanche. Admit that you have made a mistake. Admit it now, before it is too late.

He got out of bed, and went to stand at the window. The sun was up now, and the dawn chorus was in full flow. It was going to be a lovely day. One of the first days of spring.

The wedding was only one week away. One week, and Blanche would be his wife. He looked at her again.

His face remained expressionless, and he didn't wonder if she had doubts or fears. He knew she didn't. He knew her so well that sometimes he knew what she was thinking, even before she said it. He had believed that this was an illustration of true and complete love, to know what was in another's mind. But now he knew that it was an illustration of the sort of love shared between brother and sister. To know the depths of another's mind was to know them completely, with no mystery, and no excitement left for lovers. And that was what he felt for Blanche. A brotherly affection, deep and lasting, and safe.

Stop running away, said the voice. Face it. Face it now, and accept the truth.

Ashley. Where was she now? What was she doing? He wondered if she dreamt of him, if she thought about him still. Yes, it was her who haunted his dreams, and it was because of her that the silent voice in his mind was driving him to face reality. And suddenly he felt like a great weight had been lifted from his shoulders. He had admitted the truth. He loved Ashley, and he always had, and in trying to deny it, he had only been lying to himself, and to her.

He longed to touch her, to see her smile, feel her softness, and smell her. That was why he was afraid. He was afraid he would never be able to hold her again, never see her smile for him again, never make love with her again. He was afraid, because if he would not be true to his own heart, his heart might never forgive him.

He turned back to the bed, and looked at Blanche. He would tell her, he had to tell her. When he took his marriage vows, there was only one woman he wanted at his side, and the sorrow he felt that that woman was not Blanche, he knew she would never understand.

The rain had come from nowhere. No warning, no fresh breeze, nothing; it had simply started to pour. Keith and Ashley quickly found that they had walked further than either of them had realized, and the run back to the village was a long one.

Keith kept laughing at her, tangled up in a hood, scarf and hat, unable to see where she was going. In the end he took her by the hand and almost dragged her back to the inn at Long Melford. By the time they arrived the rain had stopped, but they were soaked right through.

Quickly they ran upstairs to their room, which overlooked the main road through the village, and began stripping off their wet coats. All the time they were laughing, and hitting one another with their towels.

"You're a bully!" Ashley cried, as he pushed her and she fell back onto the bed.

"Speak for yourself," said Keith, laughing as she ducked away from him.

He threw the towel round his head, and rubbed at his hair. When he took it off again he was such a peculiar mess that Ashley yelled with laughter.

"Try looking in the mirror," he retorted, and flopped into a chair beside the window.

"Where's that brandy you bought on the way here?" said Ashley. "I think I could do with some."

Keith went to his suitcase to get it. "Great idea," he said.

They had come away for the weekend for one reason, and one reason only—or so they told themselves. Alex had gone camping with the Scouts, the first time he had been away from home. Ashley had been very nervous about his going, but Keith and her father had insisted. Alex was delighted at the idea of going away on an adventure, and Ashley had had to hide the hurt she felt, that he was so willing to go. But Keith had been firm, and although he too was a little hesitant about the idea, he had hidden it from Ashley. That was until Alex had left, the day before.

Keith poured some brandy into a tooth glass, and passed it to Ashley. She was sitting up on the bed, looking out of the window at the gloomy afternoon.

Alex would have been outraged to learn that his parents were so close at hand. But Keith had rung the farmhouse at the camp and spoken to the Scout leader to let him know that they were going to be nearby, in the unlikely event that Alex should become homesick.

"Wonder what he's doing now?" said Ashley, not looking up as she took the glass.

"Probably sitting round a camp fire, cooking sausages, and making a thorough pig of himself," said Keith. "I only wish I was there." He put his arm round her. "He'll be all right. He won't think about us once, he'll be too busy enjoying himself. So why don't we do the same?"

"You're right," she said, and looked up at him. She caught her breath to see the expression on his face, and didn't move as, very slowly, he lowered his head to hers and covered her mouth. She lay back, her eyes closed, and kissed him back. He began to unbutton her shirt.

For so many months they had been together, so many times, when perhaps this moment might have stolen upon them, but it never had, until now. And she knew she wanted him.

Swiftly he stripped off his own clothes, watching her face and feeling himself respond to the look in her eyes. As his fingers moved from her throat over her shoulder, and across her breast, she shivered and reached out for him, whispering for him to come to her. His eyes darkened and narrowed, and he pushed her back and moved his body above her. And then he was inside her, gently probing, and pulling, and looking down into her face. She wound her arms about his neck, and ran her tongue across her lips. He groaned and held her to him, forcing himself deeper inside her. And as his passion rose, carrying him on a tide of fulfillment, he pushed harder, held her tighter, until finally he fell heavily against her, breathing loudly and clutching her to him.

They lay together for a long time, before finally he lifted himself from her, and pulled her up to sit facing him.

"You didn't, did you?" He brushed her hair from her face.

She lowered her eyes and whispered that it didn't matter.

"It does to me."

She took his hand and lifted it to her mouth. "It shouldn't."

He knew that she was pulling away from him. That he was losing her in the depths of her own thoughts, and he wished he could ask what she was thinking.

"Where are you going?" she asked, as he got up from the bed.

"To bathe before dinner." And he left the room.

Ashley lay back on the pillows, and looked up at the window. It was dark outside now, and a lamppost outside was the only light that lit the room. She shivered, and pulled a blanket round her. She was crying before she even knew she was crying. She tried not to call his name, but it was on her lips, and in her heart. She missed him so terribly.

Just one week, and he would be married. Just one week. No amount of pretence could change that. No amount of longing for him would bring him back to her. She still thought of him, every day, every night. She still loved him, and dreamt of him, and tortured herself with him. Giving herself to Keith had not changed that. She could not allow herself freedom in their love-making, because all the time, in her heart and in her mind, she was making love with Julian, and she was afraid she would cry out his name. Time had not healed the wound, it had only nurtured it.

She sat up abruptly, and tried to pull herself together. Tears would not change anything.

"How about a walk?" said Keith, glancing at his watch. He looked happy, and a flood of affection filled her heart. She was glad that she had made love with him. Maybe next time it would be better.

"What time is it?"

"Ten o'clock. We could wander up the street, and have a nightcap at the Bull."

The night air was filled with the aroma of damp streets and freshly mowed lawns. It was a rich, wholesome smell, and Keith breathed it in deeply, letting out a long and heavy sigh.

Ashley watched him, and smiled.

He planted a kiss on the end of her nose. "I love you, Ash. But you already know that, don't you?"

She nodded.

He put his arm round her shoulders and they strolled on toward the pub.

"And I love you," she said.

He stopped. For so long he had waited for her to say those words. Just those few words that might bring both her and his son back to him, and now, when he had almost given up hope, she had said them. He turned to her and put his hands on her shoulders. "Do you know what you're saying?"

She nodded again. "Yes, I know what I'm saying."

"Then you know what I'm going to ask you now?"

She smiled, and the dim streetlight caught the moisture in her eyes.

"What's your answer?"

"My answer is yes," she said.

He pulled her close, and held her tightly beneath the lamppost in the cobbled street. And then she knew that he was crying. She stroked his hair, trying to soothe him. And she told herself that what she was doing was right. Right for Keith, right for Alex, right for her.

TWENTY-ONE

ASHLEY HAD NO WAY OF KNOWING THAT THINGS WERE GOING to turn out the way they did. If she had, then she knew she would never have agreed to marry Keith. But perhaps it was in saying that she would that she finally, only days before Julian was to be married, came to know her own mind.

It was seven-thirty when she at last arrived home after a long and trying day on location. They were now more than five hours behind schedule on the fourth in the series of commercials for Newslink, but there had been nothing more they could do that day; they had lost the light.

She was exhausted, and badly in need of a drink. She started the usual hunt in the kitchen for the lemons. Sophia, her cleaner, had several hiding places for them, and on this particular occasion they were in the freezer. Ashley muttered angrily as she took out the solid bag; there was nothing for it, she would have to have a gin and tonic without the lemon. It was a small thing, but it irritated her beyond anything else that had happened that day.

She had just settled down in front of the TV, nursing her drink, prepared to be swamped by game shows and soap operas, when there was a knock at the door.

She toyed with the idea of pretending she wasn't in. It would probably be Keith, and she felt guilty that

285

she was trying to avoid him. Ever since they had returned from their weekend, two days before, he had called her at every opportunity. She had been expecting him to turn up at the flat at any time. It wasn't that she didn't want to see him, but she was tired, and he would want to discuss plans for their future. She didn't regret saying that she would marry him. How could she, when she had seen how delighted everyone had been? Her mother had wept, and her father had walked around all Sunday afternoon looking like an honorary student of the Cheshire Cat. And she was pleased it was going to happen; she just needed some time to get used to the idea, that was all.

He knocked again. She closed her eyes, knowing that her guilt was beginning to get the better of her conscience. She would have to answer it. She went to the door, preparing herself to look pleased, but as she opened it she felt her heart twist, and her mouth fell open. It was Julian.

He asked if he could come in; unable to answer, she stood back to let him pass. After closing the door, she followed him into the lounge.

He looked around the room. It felt like such a long time since he had last seen it. Nothing had changed, and he was surprised that it hadn't. He turned to look at Ashley. Her face was drawn in confusion and, he thought, maybe anger. He felt awkward. He didn't know what he was going to say. Or at least, he didn't know how he was going to say it.

"How are you?" he asked.

"Fine, thank you."

"You're looking good."

She shook her head and shrugged. "Would you like a drink?"

She poured him a gin and tonic, and handed it to him, waving him toward a chair. She stood by the table, awkwardly, waiting for him to speak, but he seemed to be in no hurry.

"This is a surprise," she said, breaking the silence.

"Did you never think that maybe I would come?"

"I've tried not to allow myself to think, Julian," she said.

"Will you come and sit down?"

"I can hear you from here."

"Please," he said. "Please sit down. I think it will be easier for me to say what I've come to say, if you're sitting down."

She walked across the room, and sat on the settee. He watched her move, wondering what she was thinking, looked into his drink, then toward the door. She followed his eyes, but said nothing.

He spoke at last.

"I've been thinking quite a lot lately."

"Oh?"

"About you."

Her heart began to beat faster; she didn't know if she wanted him to go on.

"I don't think I can go through with it, Ash."

She stared at him.

He rushed on. "Oh, it's not that I don't love Blanche, I do. But I don't love her enough, or in the right way, or, oh hell, I don't know. I just know that it's not right."

"Have you spoken to her about it?"

"I can't." He looked up. "I had to speak to you first."

She felt the room begin to move.

He got up from the chair, and came to sit beside her. He put his drink on the table in front of them.

"Do you know what I'm trying to say?" he said, taking her hand.

Her eyes were wide as she looked back at him, and she shook her head. "No!"

"Then I'll tell you."

She snatched her hand away. "No," she said,

jumping to her feet. "No, don't tell me. Please don't tell me."

He stood up, and caught her before she could move away from him.

She covered her ears. "I don't want to hear it, Julian. I can't. I can't."

He pulled her hands down to her sides, and waited for her to look up at him, but she didn't.

"It's you I love, Ashley," he said.

He felt her begin to shake, and realized that she was crying. He put his arms round her, and held her against him.

"I'm sorry. I should have told you a long time ago, I know. But I don't think I knew myself, at least not how much. Not until now."

She was still crying, and he ran his hand over her hair, trying to comfort her, trying to find the right words.

"Can you forgive me, Ashley?"

She tried to pull away.

"No, don't go away from me. Please. I love you, Ashley. Please, please say that you love me too. Please say that you forgive me for everything I have put you through."

She shook her head. "I can't," she said, her voice muffled by his shoulder. "It's too late, Julian."

"It's not too late. All you have to do is say the word, and I'll call the wedding off. I need you, Ashley. I want you, I love you. What more can I say to make you believe me?"

"I do believe you," she said. "But you mustn't, it's too late."

"Don't keep saying that. We can work things out. Together we can make it happen again. Like we used to. We should be together, Ashley. You know that. You knew it before I did, and I should have listened to you. But I know now. It's you that I want to marry. It's you that I want to share my life with. There's no one else, not any more."

"Oh but there is," she cried. "There is."

"Blanche? I know she'll be upset. But surely it's better that I tell her now, before things go so far that we can't turn back."

"But it's already gone too far. Things have changed, Julian."

"Do you mean that you don't love me any more?" He lifted her chin and searched her eyes with his.

"No, that's not what I mean. I told you, it's too late. Not because I don't love you, but because you're going to marry Blanche, and I too am getting married."

He let her go, his face white. "What did you say?"

"I'm getting married."

"But how? Who? Who is it?"

"I'm marrying Keith," she said.

"Keith!"

"My ex-husband."

"I know who he is, for God's sake. But have you forgotten everything that happened between you two? Damn it, the man's a drunk, a gambler, a womanizer . . ."

"Not any more," she interrupted, keeping her voice low. "He's changed, and he wants me back so desperately, and it would be good for Alex too. We could be a family again."

"But you can't do it," Julian protested. "You can't, Ashley. You'll be making a big mistake, and you know it."

"I don't know anything any more," she said, turning away. "But I have promised Keith, and I will keep my promise."

He caught her by the shoulders and turned her to face him. "You can't! I won't let you. You love me, Ashley. You know you do."

She looked down at the floor, unable to meet his

eyes. He stroked his finger across her chin and lifted her face.

"Tell me you don't, and I'll let you go."

Still she didn't answer.

"You see," his voice was pleading, "you can't say it. Admit it, Ashley. Face the truth. It is me that you love. Tell me, let me hear you say it."

"No! No, I won't say it."

"Then deny it."

"I won't deny it either. But saying it will prove nothing. And neither will it change anything. You must marry Blanche, Julian, you must. And I will marry Keith."

"Are you mad! What is this, some kind of let's play the honorable game? You'll only be hurting him more, by marrying him when you don't love him . . ."

"I didn't say that I didn't love him," she interrupted.

"But you don't love him. I can see it in your eyes, Ashley. You don't love him."

"I do, and I'm going to marry him."

He gripped her shoulders, and she flinched at the pressure of his fingers. "You won't marry him," he growled. "You're going to marry me."

Ashley felt as though she was going to faint. The world was spinning. How she had prayed for this moment. How she had prayed that he would come back to her. And now he was here, and she was turning him away. She couldn't stop herself.

There was a knock on the door. Breaking free of him, she ran to open it. Anything to get away, if only for a moment.

Keith was standing at the door, holding a large bunch of flowers, smiling all over his face. He took one look at Ashley, and dropped the flowers.

"What is it?" he said, going to her. "What's happened?"

Ashley pointed him toward the lounge and, letting

her go, Keith walked into the room. His face darkened as he saw Julian standing beside the settee.

"What's he doing here?" Keith wanted to know, addressing Ashley, yet not taking his eyes from Julian.

"Are you going to tell him?" Julian said. "Or shall I?"

"There's nothing to tell," said Ashley.

Julian turned away from her, and looked at Keith. "She's going to marry me, Keith. I'm sorry and all that, but that's the way it is."

"No, stop it!" Ashley cried.

Keith's face had paled. "Is it true?"

She shook her head. "No. No, it's not true. I'm not going to marry you, Julian. I can't. You're going to marry Blanche."

"But I explained all that."

"I think you'd better leave," said Keith, beginning to bristle.

"Look," said Julian, appealing to Keith. "Can't you see sense? It's me she loves. It's me she wants to marry. You can't want to force her into a marriage with you, when you know that all the time she wants to be with someone else. What the hell kind of life is that going to be for either of you?"

"From where I'm standing," said Keith, "I don't see that it's any of your damned business. Now, you heard me the first time. It's time you were going."

"Ashley," said Julian, "for God's sake, be honest with yourself. Even if you won't be honest with either of us."

"Stop shouting at her," said Keith. "She's in no state to take your tantrums, now leave her alone."

"I want an answer from her," said Julian, "and I'm not leaving until I get it. I know she loves me. I know it, you know it, and she knows it. Now tell him, Ashley. Tell him the truth."

Keith looked at her, waiting for her to speak, and

in turning away from him she didn't see the pain in his eyes.

"Is that good enough for you?" said Julian.

"Ash." Keith tried to take her by the arms. "Is this what you want? Is it him, still?"

She shook her head. "I don't know," she said. "I don't know, Keith. I'm sorry, I know I'm not helping anything. But please, you're just confusing me, both of you. Please go. I don't want you here. I need to be on my own. I need to think. Please go away."

"I'm not leaving you like this," said Julian.

"Please," she implored him. "Please. It's what I want."

"Ash, I love you. I will always love you, no matter what," said Keith. "And think of Alex. Think of what all this will mean to him."

"I am. Oh I am. But I need to be alone. Please, both of you go, now."

She closed and locked the door behind them, trying to block out the horrifying absurdity of it all. But dear God, what was she going to do now?

The baby was crying again, but Kate didn't mind. In fact she was pleased. It meant that she could hold her in her arms, comfort and feed her, play with her. She felt lonely when the baby was asleep, sitting there beside it, watching the tiny face crease and crinkle in dream, and the little fists open and close. But now she was awake again, and it was probably time for her feed.

Kate looked at her watch. Yes, she would be hungry again by now. She popped her head into the kitchen to check that the milk was warming, then went to get her.

She was such a tiny, warm little bundle, and as soon as Kate lifted her from the bed she stopped crying. Her little blue eyes were open wide, and Kate wondered how much she could see.

"There, there," she whispered. "Mummy's here

now. Mummy's got you. Are you hungry? Yes, I expect you are. And I think you need changing too, don't you?"

The baby whimpered, and Kate put her finger into the tiny fist. The child clutched at it greedily, and tried in her own feeble way to bring it to her mouth.

"Sorry," said Kate. "It's a clean nappie for you before you have anything to eat. We don't want you getting a sore bottom now, do we," and she smiled down into the little face.

She laid the baby on a towel on the floor, and changed the nappie. The baby had started to cry again, but Kate knew that that was only because she was hungry.

"Patience. Patience," she cooed. "It's coming."

She went to get the bottle from the kitchen, then settled down on the settee to feed her. "My, you are hungry," she whispered. "You'll get fat if you carry on like this."

The child's eyes were closed, and she continued to suck greedily and noisily at the teat.

Kate jumped as the phone rang, and then glared at it angrily. If it didn't stop soon it would disturb the baby. But it carried on ringing, until eventually she reached out and answered it.

"Kate! Where have you been? I've been trying to ring you all day."

"Ellamarie," said Kate. "Oh, I've been out and about a bit. I've had quite a lot to do."

"Well, I've got you now. How are you?"

"Oh, I'm fine."

"You don't sound it," said Ellamarie, bluntly. "Is your father still staying with you?"

"No, he went home the day before yesterday."

"Are you sure you're OK on your own? Would you like me to come round? I've got the snaps here from Scotland. There are some great ones of you."

"No, no," said Kate. "I'm fine, honestly. How are you?"

"Great! Seems like everything's going ahead with the *Queen of Cornwall.*"

"Oh good." Kate pushed the teat back into the baby's mouth.

"Are you sure you're all right?" said Ellamarie. "You sound a bit vague."

"Vague? No, I'm all right, I was just thinking."

"What about?"

"Nothing in particular."

There was a short silence.

"I could come round now for an hour, if you like."

"No, better not. I'm actually rather tied up right now."

"Oh, I see."

Another short silence.

"Nick has been asking about you," said Ellamarie.

"Has he?"

"Yes. He wanted to know how you were."

"Oh, tell him I'm fine. Tell him I'm just fine."

"He was hoping you might call."

"I've been too busy, Ellamarie. But I will, when I get the time." The teat slipped from the baby's mouth again, and the baby started to whimper. "Look, I really must go."

"What was that noise?"

"What noise?"

"I don't know. Didn't you hear it?"

"No, I didn't hear anything. Must go, 'bye," and Kate hung up.

Ellamarie was startled by the abrupt end to the call, and looked at the receiver for several seconds, before she finally put it down.

"How was she?" said Bob, coming in from the bathroom.

"I don't know. She sounded, well, she sounded a bit strange."

"Strange?"

"I don't know. Distant, vague somehow. It was almost as if she wasn't alone."

"Perhaps her father was there."

"No, she said that he'd gone home again now. Do you think I should call her back?"

"Not yet. Give her some time, ring her again in an hour. You're probably worrying about nothing. I'm sure she's all right."

"Yes, you're probably right," said Ellamarie, but the frown didn't go away.

"What time did Nick say he'd be here?"

There was a knock on the door.

"About now," said Ellamarie, and went to answer it.

"I see your admirer is still as generous as ever," Nick said, as he walked into the sitting room and saw all the flowers about the place.

"It's like a bloody funeral parlor in here," Bob grumbled. "I'll be glad when he, whoever he is, runs out of money, or passion, or whatever it is he needs to run out of. Sitting here with all these damned flowers, I feel like a garden gnome."

"He's jealous," Ellamarie said to Nick. "I've told you, Bob, you can send me flowers too if you like. I won't object."

Bob grunted, and went to sit down.

The time passed quickly as they discussed the delivery and interpretation of the *Famous Tragedy*, until Nick suddenly realized that he was perhaps encroaching upon the valuable hours that Bob and Ellamarie had together. He looked slightly embarrassed as he announced that he really must be going, and was grateful to Ellamarie for making him feel that he didn't have to rush off.

"I'll see you tonight," he said, as he was leaving.

"Last but one performance, eh? Soon comes round, doesn't it?"

"You're not kidding," said Ellamarie.

"Just one thing before I go. I meant to ask earlier, how's Kate? How did it go in Scotland?"

Ellamarie's face fell.

"She's all right, isn't she?" said Nick, looking worried.

"I don't know," said Ellamarie. "She seemed fine when we got back on Sunday, but I called her earlier, and she sounded, well, kind of peculiar. I think I'll give her a call again now."

"Say hello to her for me?"

"Sure. Look, I know you keep saying no, but why don't you give her a call yourself? I'm sure she'd like to hear from you. It will do her good to get out again."

Nick shrugged. "I don't know. We'll see."

TWENTY-TWO

NICK TURNED THE CAR OUT INTO THE KING'S ROAD, AND pulled into the traffic. The King's Road was always busy, and it took ages just to get as far as Sloane Square. He turned into Old Church Street, and drove across to the Fulham Road, which was usually marginally better. Once in the Fulham Road, he had to drive past Neville Street. And almost before he knew he was doing it, he was indicating and turning left into it.

He pulled up outside the large house where Kate had a second-floor flat, and looked up at the windows.

There was no sign of life. As he pushed the bell, he felt as nervous as a schoolboy on his first date. He didn't like calling in on people, unannounced, and he was beginning to wonder whether this was such a good idea after all, when Kate's voice came over the intercom.

"It's Nick," he said. "Nicholas Gough."

"Oh, Nick. What can I do for you?"

"Well, I thought I'd call round to see how you were."

"I'm fine, thank you," she said, and he heard her put the entryphone down again.

Strange, it wasn't like Kate to be rude. He was wondering whether he should ring again, or just go away, when someone came out of the door. The man nodded at Nick, and he caught the door before it closed again.

He climbed the stairs quickly, and then hesitated outside her door. What if she really didn't want to see him? But she had sounded strange, and Ellamarie had been worried too. Maybe he should try once more.

He knocked loudly and waited. There was no reply, so he knocked again, and still there was no reply. He knew she was there, and she must have guessed that it was him knocking, so why not come to the door? The answer seemed obvious. She didn't want to see him. He turned to go, but then something made him try just once more.

Still she didn't answer, and he pressed his ear to the door. There was no sound coming from within.

"Kate!" he called. "Kate!"

Then suddenly the door jerked open, and she was standing there. She looked annoyed, and it was clear that she didn't want him to come in.

"Yes?" she said.

"Um, I was in the neighborhood, thought I'd drop round."

"I'm sorry," she said. "It's not really convenient at the moment."

"Oh, I see. I'm sorry. I should have phoned first."

"Yes, but it was nice of you to bother."

"Don't mention it. I'll see you around, I suppose."

"Yes," she said. "Goodbye."

He turned away, feeling angry at her abruptness. And then he heard a baby cry. He was confused at first, thinking it was coming from somewhere upstairs, but it sounded closer. He turned back, and Kate, her face wide with alarm, tried to close the door. The terrible suspicion hit him like a hammer. He managed to wedge his foot against the door in time, and pushed it open.

"Let me in."

"No!" Her voice was nearly hysterical.

"I heard a baby."

"Don't be silly," she snapped. "You're imagining things."

"Then let me in."

"No. I told you, it's not convenient right now," and she started to push him out again.

The baby cried again, loud screams, leaving him in no doubt that it was coming from inside her flat. He looked at her, and saw that she was frightened.

"Oh my God," he breathed. "What have you done? Let me in, Kate," and when she tried to close the door again he pushed her roughly to one side, and marched into the bedroom.

Even though he had heard it, it was still a shock to see the baby lying there on the bed, its tiny face red from screaming, and its legs kicking around in frustration. Kate came into the room and stood beside him.

"Whose is it?"

Kate went to pick her up. "She's mine," she said, hugging her fiercely.

Nick closed his eyes. What the hell was he going to do now? He looked at her, and saw the fear in her eyes. His heart went out to her in her pain.

"Oh, Kate, she can't be yours."

Kate's face began to crumple. She hadn't really believed that the baby was hers, and she knew that eventually she would be taken away. But not yet, please, not yet.

Nick steered her into the lounge. The baby had stopped crying, almost as if she could sense what was going on around her. Nick sat them both down on the settee, then perched beside them. Tears were standing in Kate's eyes, and he was thankful to see them. Maybe she did know that what she had done was wrong after all.

"Why did you do it, Kate?"

Kate opened her mouth to answer, but he stopped her.

"I'm sorry, that was a stupid and senseless question. I know why you did it. Just tell me when."

"This morning."

"Where?"

"I can't remember."

The baby started to cry again, and Kate looked down at her. "She's hungry."

"Why don't you give her to me, and go and get her some milk or whatever it is she needs," he said. "How are you going to feed her?"

"I've got a bottle, I bought it this morning. And some nappies. I've taken very good care of her."

Nick smiled. "Yes, I'm sure you have." He went to take the baby, but Kate held back.

"Don't worry, I'm not going to hurt her."

His eyes were so kind and understanding that Kate let the baby go. She went to warm some milk, and Nick cradled the child in his arms. He was disturbed by the turmoil inside him. He had to decide what to do. He looked at his watch. Time was getting on, and he was due at the theater in an hour.

Kate came back into the room and, taking the baby from him, sat down and began to feed her. Nick didn't ask if she was giving her the right milk, he wouldn't know anyway. But what he did know was that he had to get the child back to its real mother, and quick.

"You will have to give her up, Kate, you know that, don't you?" he said, softly.

Kate didn't answer, she remained intent on the baby.

"You do know that, don't you?" Nick insisted.

She nodded.

"I think we're going to have to call the police."

Kate's expression turned to terror. "No, please! Not the police."

"But who else? We must find the child's parents."

"I know," said Kate. "I didn't mean to keep her, you know. I only wanted to hold her for a while. I just had to hold a baby. I just had to, Nick." She started to cry.

"I know," he said, taking her in his arms. "It hasn't been easy for you, has it?"

"What are you going to do?"

"I don't know. But we'll have to think of something." He looked at his watch again. He couldn't just leave her here like this. "I'm going to call the theater. I'll have to tell them to prepare my cover."

She looked confused.

"My understudy," he explained. "I can't leave you."

"No," she said. "No, don't leave me."

He rang the theater, and luckily managed to find Bob. "I'm round at a friend's," he said. "I'm not going to be able to make it tonight."

"What do you mean you can't make it?"

"Something's happened, I just can't come in. Can you prepare the cover in time?"

"I don't know where he is." Bob sounded angry. "This isn't like you, Nick. You were all right this afternoon."

"Oh yes, I see," said Nick. "Yes, yes. That's right, and if you tell Ellamarie, she'll know."

"Ellamarie?" said Bob, completely baffled. "What's she got to do with it?"

"Oh, I spoke to her about it earlier. Yes. Yes, if you just tell her I've done as she asked."

"What the hell are you talking about?"

"At the door," said Nick, willing Bob to understand.

"At what door?"

"Hers!" said Nick, through clenched teeth. He glanced back at Kate, but she was intent on the baby. "It's Kate," he whispered.

"Who?"

"Think!" Nick almost shouted.

"Did you say Kate? What about her?"

"That's right. The performance, well, I think it can be sorted out."

"Is she all right?"

"No," Nick answered, with relief.

"What's happened?"

Nick didn't answer.

"Is she there with you now?"

"Yes."

"Do you need some help?"

"I don't know."

"Can you tell me anything?"

"No."

"Oh God," said Bob, exasperated. "What the hell has happened? Shall I find Ellamarie?"

"No, not yet. I'll let you know."

"Ring me as soon as you can."

"OK, then," said Nick. "I'll see you tomorrow. Thanks. 'Bye." He put the phone down, and turned to see that Kate was watching him.

"Was that Bob?" she asked, and he nodded.

He ran his fingers through his hair, and looked at her in despair. Just what was he going to do now? As he went to sit down again he saw that the baby was sleeping. "What shall we do?" he asked, almost as if he expected the child to answer.

"I don't know," said Kate.

"Look, try starting from the beginning, tell me what happened."

Kate inhaled deeply, and caught her breath on a sob. She reached out and clutched at his hand, and he squeezed hers, trying to reassure her. "It's been so awful, Nick," she said. "Ever since I've been out of hospital it's been like one long nightmare, except when I wake up, it's still there. It just won't go away. Everyone said it would get better, that soon it would get easier, but it didn't. And I wanted my baby so badly, Nick, and I don't think I'll ever be able to forgive myself for what I've done." She caught her breath again, and Nick slipped an arm round her, in an attempt to give her some comfort.

"Daddy did his best to make me feel better," she continued, "and it was very nice of Ellamarie to take me to Scotland, but you see all I needed was to hold a child. I needed to feel one close to me. Hold its hands, and feed it. Comfort it when it cried, and give it all the love I could. Do you know what it's like, Nick, to want a child so badly that your arms ache from emptiness? To have your heart feel as though it will burst unless it can give the love it has inside. Do you know how it feels to be haunted by the tears of the child you have murdered, the child you have wrenched from life, before it even had a chance?"

Nick shook his head. What could he say?

"And then Daddy said the other day that one day we would have a baby, the two of us, and we could love it and share it, and bring it up together. And no one would hurt us any more."

Nick looked at her curiously. That was a very strange thing for her father to have said.

"So I thought that maybe, if I was going to have one one day, then why not now? Not that I ever meant to keep her, but I couldn't wait for one day to come. And now I've held her in my arms, it doesn't feel any better. It only feels worse, and if I can't keep her I feel like I'm going to die. I just want her to be mine. I already love her, like she was mine."

Nick found that he had to swallow the lump in his throat before he could speak. "Had you made any plans about what you were going to do next?"

"I was going to tell my father that we had the baby he wanted, and I thought he might be pleased. But I can see now that I was wrong, and I don't suppose I really believed that I would ever go that far. I meant to take her back, really I did. But I kept putting it off, I didn't want to let her go. And then I couldn't remember where I had taken her from. It's as if the whole thing was a dream, and now I can't remember very much of it."

"Look, I don't see that there's anything else we can do, we'll have to ring the police." He felt her stiffen, and he rushed on. "The baby's parents are bound to have reported her missing by now, they're probably going out of their minds with worry."

"But I haven't hurt her," said Kate.

"I know. But they don't know that. All they know is that she's disappeared. You must give her back to them, Kate. Think how the mother must feel right now."

Kate looked down at the sleeping child.

"Will you let me call the police?" he said. "Please."

"What will they do to me?"

"I don't know. But they will be kind to you. They won't do anything to hurt you, I promise."

"Do you think they'll lock me away?"

"No, of course they won't. They'll probably want to ask you a few questions, but I'll be here."

He watched her face, and he longed to be able to take some of the pain from her. She looked so frail and helpless sitting there, holding on to the baby, knowing she was going to lose it.

"So," he said quietly, "will you let me ring?"

She forced a smile. "You won't go, though, will you?"

"Of course not."

The police came, and then the baby's parents arrived. The mother looked ravaged in her grief and fear, and Nick's heart went out to her too. Kate sat in her bedroom, talking with a policewoman, and Nick handled everything else. It was a nightmarish experience, and he was terrified at one point that the police were going to insist that Kate go with them.

An ambulance arrived and took the baby and its parents to hospital, and the police stayed. Nick made them tea and coffee, while Kate stayed in the bedroom with the policewoman. When she finally came out, she shook her head solemnly to the others, and asked to speak to Nick alone.

"This happens such a lot," she said. "More than you think. They're usually our most tragic cases. She needs help, she needs it very much. Are you her husband?"

"No," said Nick. "No, I'm a friend."

"Can you stay with her tonight?"

He nodded.

"Good. I'm afraid that this isn't the end of it, though. Someone will be round to see her again in the morning. I think you ought to ring her doctor, maybe he can help. Anyway, she shouldn't be left alone."

"I understand," said Nick. "What do you think will happen to her?"

"I'm not sure yet. It really depends on the report of the police psychiatrist. But as she has so recently gone through such a traumatic experience it will be taken into consideration and they will treat her with care, please don't have any worries on that score."

"Will she have to go away?"

"Again, that depends on what the doctors have to say. But from talking to her, I think it might do her some good. That, or to have someone here all the time. She needs love, and care, and she needs rebuilding again. It won't be easy, but what has happened to her has completely crushed her."

Nick looked at the policewoman. "I wasn't the father."

"You're not Joel, you mean?"

"No."

"Thank God for that. Where is he now?"

"I've no idea, and I don't want to know. Look, if I say that I'll stay here, all the time, and I won't leave her alone, not even for a second, do you think they might let her stay?"

"They might. Does she have any family?"

Nick nodded. "Do they have to know about this?"

"Shouldn't they?"

"I don't think so," he said. "I can't explain, but I think it would be better if they didn't know, at least for the time being."

"OK," said the policewoman. "Well, it's over to you for now. But as I said, someone will be round again in the morning."

"Right."

"Can you give me your name?"

"Nicholas Gough." She wrote it down. "And you are?"

"Detective Sergeant Brown. And please, phone me, any time, if you think you need to."

"Thank you. I'll remember that."

When they had all gone, Nick went into the bedroom and found Kate lying on the bed, asleep. He stroked the hair from her face; she stirred but didn't wake.

*　　　*　　　*

The next day Kate was taken off to hospital again. She probably wouldn't have to stay long, the doctor assured Nick, but for the moment it would probably be for the best.

Nick went with her, and stayed with her, until finally she fell asleep. All the time she held onto his hand, as if she were terrified that he might leave her. When he was sure that she was sleeping, he slipped his hand out of hers, and went to the phone. He had promised to ring Ellamarie as soon as he could. She and Bob had rushed round to Kate's flat after last night's performance, and had sat up with him all night, only returning home when Kate had gone off to the hospital.

The telephone woke Ellamarie, but she didn't mind, and Nick told her that Kate was sleeping, and that the doctor had said that probably the worst of it was over now. He wanted her to stay in overnight, so that they could keep an eye on her, but there was nothing more they could do that love and care, and a great deal of patience, wouldn't do.

Nick decided against ringing Kate's father. The thought of Mr. Calloway left a bad taste in his mouth, and he didn't care to think about why.

He went back into Kate's room, and flopped down in the chair. He was soon fast asleep.

Kate's doctor saw the police psychiatrist, and the two of them talked for two hours or more behind closed doors. When they finally emerged, the police doctor seemed satisfied that Kate was in no danger of doing it again, and he went away.

When Nick finally woke, Kate was sitting up in bed, dipping into a bowl of soup. She smiled over at him.

"How are you feeling?"

"Bit groggy," she said. "But OK, I think."

He got up, and went to sit on the bed. "Do you remember much about last night?"

She nodded. "Yes, everything, even though it feels

like a bad dream. If only it was. I'm sorry that you've had to go through all this. Have you spoken to the baby's parents?''

He shook his head.

"No," she said. "Probably not a good idea anyway. I'm sure they never want to have anything to do with me, or anyone else to do with me, ever again. I can't blame them. I just don't understand why I did it. Oh, I know, with the, well, with the you know, that it must have had an effect. But to do something so terrible, I can't believe I did it. It was so wicked, so terrible.'' Her eyes were beginning to fill with tears.

"Don't be too hard on yourself. You weren't well. You lost control for a bit, that's all. But you're all right now.''

She smiled at him. "Thank you, Nick. Thank you for everything you've done.''

"I'd like to say it's been a pleasure," he grinned, "but under the circumstances, I think experience would be a better word.''

She pushed her soup away. He pushed it back again. "Eat!" he ordered.

"But I'm not hungry.''

"Eat.''

She made another attempt at the soup, and he watched over her, making sure that she ate it all, and trying to ignore the rumblings in his own stomach. He couldn't remember when he had last eaten; it felt like a week ago. When she had finished, he took the bowl and put it on the small table beside the bed.

"Does Daddy know I'm here?" she asked.

Nick didn't meet her eyes. "No.''

"But didn't you ring him?''

"No. I didn't want to worry him any more than he's already been worried. I would have rung him if things looked like they might get worse. But as no one seemed to think it was necessary, I thought I'd wait for a while.''

She nodded. "Probably for the best."

Nick sat down again. "The doctor said you can go home tomorrow. If you feel up to it, that is. But you'll have to register as an out-patient."

"I'd like to go home," she said. "I don't like it much in here. Right now, I feel as though I've spent my whole life here."

"There is one condition, though."

She raised her eyebrows.

"I'm afraid that you're not to be left alone."

"Well, I can't say I'm surprised," said Kate. "But that's all right. I shall go and stay with my parents, in Surrey."

Nick nodded. He would have liked to offer to stay with her, in London, but she wasn't ready for anything like that yet, and he must give her time. The thought of her back under the protection of her father made him uncomfortable, but he tried to push it from his mind.

The door opened, and a nurse came in. She picked up the bowl and, smiling at Kate, asked her how she was feeling. Kate answered politely, and Nick smiled to himself. Proper, polite little Kate. Almost like her old self again. But he knew that there was a long, long way to go yet.

"Could I have a word?" said the nurse.

Nick was getting up to leave before he realized that the nurse was talking to him.

"Yes, outside," she said, as he went to sit down again.

Kate looked at them curiously, but the nurse was already half out of the door. Nick shrugged his shoulders at Kate, then followed the nurse outside.

"This way, please," said the nurse, and she walked along the corridor.

Nick followed, wondering where they were going. When they got to the end, the nurse stopped, and opened a door that led into a small room on the right. She gestured for Nick to go through.

Nick was more than a little surprised to find Jenneen sitting by the window, obviously waiting for him.

"Jenn! What are you doing here?"

"I wanted to see Kate."

"Then why don't you go in?"

Jenneen looked into his face. "Don't you know? Hasn't Kate told you?"

"Told me what?"

"We had the most terrible fight," said Jenneen. "The night that she broke up with Joel."

"But why? What was it all about?"

Jenneen gestured for him to sit down, and she went to sit opposite him. It didn't take her very long to tell him what had happened, but by the time she had finished she was crying so hard Nick went to comfort her. "So you see," she said. "It's all my fault. This whole damn rotten mess. It's all my fault."

"It's not. How can it be your fault? No one's to blame, no one at all. With the possible exception of Joel Martin. But why have you come here now?"

"I had to see her," said Jenneen. "I couldn't stay away any longer. I don't care if she hates me, I don't blame her. I don't care if she shouts at me, but I have to see her. You do understand, don't you, Nick?"

"Of course I do," he said. "And Kate will too. Why don't you go along now?"

"Do you think she'll see me?"

"I'm sure of it. Come on, I'll come with you if you like."

Jenneen nodded. "Yes, I'd like that."

Together they walked back along the corridor until they reached Kate's room. Jenneen hesitated as Nick made to open the door. "Perhaps you should warn her first."

Nick nodded. "OK, but wait there, don't run away."

Jenneen smiled. "Don't worry, I won't."

Kate was lying back on the pillows when he went

in, but she opened her eyes at the sound of the door. She smiled when she saw him.

"You've got a visitor," he said.

"Oh? Who is it?"

"A friend of yours. Jenneen."

Kate's eyes widened, and she looked afraid.

"I think she's got something she'd like to say to you, if you'll give her the chance. Can she come in?"

Kate didn't answer, but she looked at the door. Oh, how she had missed Jenneen these last weeks. How she had longed to talk to her, to tell her everything she was feeling. Jenneen was so strong, and she always knew what to do. But she had said so many hateful things to her, Jenneen would never forgive her.

Nick went back to the door and opened it. He gave Jenneen an encouraging smile. "You can go in now."

"Aren't you coming too?"

"No." He steered her through the door, then walked away.

Jenneen stood in the doorway, and looked at Kate. Kate lay in bed, and looked at Jenneen.

Suddenly Jenneen sobbed. "Oh Kate!" she cried, and ran across the room to throw her arms round her.

"Oh Jenn!" Kate wept. "Jenn, you don't know how much I've missed you."

Jenneen hugged her even harder. "I'm sorry, Kate. I'm so terribly, terribly sorry."

"And I'm sorry," said Kate. "I should never have said all those awful things to you."

"No, sssh! Don't," said Jenneen, wiping the tears from Kate's face. "We're together again, that's all that matters."

"Oh Jenn, I love you. Now that you're here, I know that everything's going to be all right."

"It will be," said Jenneen. "Oh, it will be!"

Nick wandered outside to see if he could find himself something to eat. He was surprised when he was stopped by a strange woman. "Are you Nicholas?"

He nodded, and looked at her curiously.

"I'm Victoria Deane," she explained. "A friend of Jenneen's. Is she with Kate?"

Nick nodded.

The woman seemed relieved. "Is everything all right?"

"Yes," he said, "I think so."

"Thank God for that," she sighed, and walked away, without saying another word.

✿TWENTY-THREE

MR. WINSTON SAT BACK IN HIS CHAIR. ASHLEY LOOKED INTO his face, her eyes pleading with him to tell her what she should do. For the past twenty-four hours she had struggled to come to a decision, but it was hopeless; she was no nearer now to knowing what she wanted than she had been when Keith and Julian had confronted her. In the end she had turned to the old man.

He picked up his glass and shook his head. "It's not easy," he said. "Not easy at all."

"I know."

"And such a short time in which to decide."

Ashley nodded, and looked into his kind, old face, so full of wisdom and understanding.

"Do you really love them both?"

"Right now I don't know if I love either of them."

"Then the answer seems plain to me."

She looked at him.

"Don't marry either of them. Not until you're sure."

"But Julian . . ."

"Julian must make his own decisions," said Mr. Winston. "He cannot, and should not, rely on you to do it for him. If he doesn't want to marry Blanche, then that is his look-out."

"But what if he does marry her, and then I decide that I want him?"

"Difficult, I admit. But as you are incapable of making up your mind now, that is something that you'll have to face, should it happen."

"Do you think it will?"

"How can I say?"

"And what if it's too late?"

"I don't think it will be."

"But how can you know that?"

"I can't. But fate usually has a way of working these things out."

"I wish fate could tell me the answers now."

"Fate might well be telling you the answer now," he said. "It's just that you're too confused to see it."

"What do you mean?"

"Only what I said. Probably the answer is there, somewhere, but you won't let it out."

"But I want to," she said. "Really, I want to."

"Then think about it."

She shook her head. "All I know is that right now the only thing I want is to go as far away from it all as I can."

He shrugged. "Then maybe you do have your answer."

"But isn't that running away?"

"Depends how you look at it. Keith will wait, come what may. He is in no particular hurry. And as I said, Julian must make up his own mind. It seems to me that he is hedging his bets somewhat."

"Hedging his bets?"

"He hasn't broken his engagement with Blanche, has he?"

"No."

"Then he is hedging his bets. If you won't have him, then he'll always have Blanche. Whatever, he is determined he is not going to be left with no one."

"I never looked at it like that."

"No. And I daresay he didn't either. But that's what he's doing."

"Is that wrong?"

"What do you think?"

"I think it is," she said.

"Of course it is. He is too wèak to make a decision himself, so he is trying to push you into making it for him."

"And you don't think I should."

"It's up to you what you do. But I don't think you want to make the decision right now. Now, if he were already free, it might look different."

Ashley thought about that. "Yes, it probably would. But he isn't."

"No. So either he has to give up Blanche, and wait on your decision."

"Or?"

"Or, one way or another, he could make four people very unhappy."

"Should I speak to him again?"

"If you like. But I don't think you will change anything, not now. Julian sounds to me like someone who plays his cards very close to his chest. He will see to it that he doesn't come out completely on the losing side."

"I've never thought about him in this light before," she said.

"Maybe he's never shown himself in this light before. People always change with circumstances," and she wished Mr. Winston could have been there to hear her say it.

"But what about Keith?"

"What about Keith?"

"He's waiting for an answer too."

"Well, you've said yourself, you're not ready to give an answer to either of them. If you can go away, I think it would be best."

"For a holiday, you mean?"

"Or longer."

Ashley thought hard, then suddenly she realized what the old man was saying. He was the only one she had ever dared mention it to. "Do you mean . . . ?"

He smiled. "Yes, I do mean."

Until now it had only been a dream, but maybe, just maybe, it was the answer she was looking for. It need only be for a short while. A year, perhaps two. She would have to think about it.

"Would you like some more coffee?"

Ashley nodded, and smiled. "Yes, I'd like some more coffee. And how about a nightcap too?"

Mr. Winston chuckled. "Now you're talking," he said, and signaled for the waiter.

The following morning Ashley rang Julian. "I'd like to talk to you," she said.

He hesitated. "Does that mean that you've made a decision?"

"Yes, I think I have. But I must talk it over with you first."

"Are you going to tell me anything now?"

"No, I want you to come round."

"You're at home, I take it?"

"Yes."

"OK. I'll be there in an hour. And Ashley . . ."

"Yes?"

"Whatever your decision, I still mean everything I said the other night."

"I know," she said. "See you in an hour."

She hung up, and looked down at the phone, glad

that the call was over. She had sat up practically half the night, thinking of nothing else, and now, for the first time in months, she felt strong. At long last she had regained control of her life; she could once again see things clearly, and not through the mist of loneliness and rejection she had shrouded herself in. This odd and unexpected twist in fate had renewed her lease on life, and silently she thanked Mr. Winston for helping her to see the way.

She looked in the mirror, and studied her face. Now she was going to live her life the way she wanted to once more. Goodbye to the heartache, and goodbye to the weak indecisive woman who had staggered her way through the first part of the year. And welcome to the woman she truly was, the woman of character. She laughed. Yes, she was one of the class apart, as Jenneen had called them. She qualified. Now more than ever, she qualified.

While she waited for Julian she rang Kate. There was no reply. She toyed with the idea of ringing Ellamarie, but decided against it—Ellamarie always slept late the morning after a performance. She made a mental note to call round at Kate's later, and then tried ringing Jenneen at the studio. She was out filming, and not expected back that day.

Sitting beside the window, looking out over Onslow Square, Ashley contemplated her future. Things were going to be so different from now on, and she was excited. She was glad it was spring. Spring heralded new beginnings, and there was going to be so much to do in the coming weeks. She pondered a while over how everyone would react when she told them her news.

The hour slipped past quickly, and soon Julian was knocking on the door. He eyed her warily as she opened the door, and she could tell by his face that he already knew that she was not going to say what he wanted to hear.

"Coffee?" she said, following him into the lounge.

"No thanks."

"Sit down," she offered, clearing the newspapers from the settee.

He sat down, and waited.

"Well," she said, nervous despite herself, "I've arrived at a decision."

"Have you told Keith yet?"

"No, not yet. I wanted to talk to you first. In fact this all hangs on you rather."

He raised an eyebrow, and waited for her to go on.

"I've been awake most of the night, and I've thought this through very carefully. It wasn't an easy decision to reach, but I think it's the best one, the only one, under the circumstances."

"I have a feeling I'm not going to like this."

"No," she said. "No, I don't think you will. But I need your help, and I am relying on you to give it."

"I'm not making any promises."

"You don't have to, not yet anyway."

She took a deep breath, and braced herself. "I've decided that I want to take the position of Executive Vice-President at Frazier, Nelmes in New York."

Julian's face was incredulous. His eyes were so wide she thought they were going to burst from his face. "Are you serious?"

"Quite serious."

"Do you know what you're saying?"

"I know exactly what I'm saying."

"But Ashley, I'm asking you to marry me and you tell me that you want to go to New York. What kind of an answer is that?"

"It's the only answer I can give, Julian. I'm sorry, I know it's not what you want to hear, but I've made up my mind. I have to have some time to myself, to find myself again, and the only way I can do that is to get right away."

"But it's a bit drastic, isn't it? New York?"

"It might seem so to you, but it's what I want to do. You've already half promised me promotion in London. What I'm asking is the same promotion, but in New York. If you want to help me, then you can. If you don't well, then I suppose I'll have to think again. But I don't think you'll let me down. Will you?"

"I don't know," he said. "I have to be honest, when I came here the other night, I thought that it would all be so easy. I thought that you still loved me, and I knew that I still loved you. I thought that it would be as simple as that. But now, I just don't understand you. In fact I wonder if I've ever understood you."

She smiled. "People always change with circumstances." and she wished Mr. Winston could have been there to hear her say it.

Julian stood up and started to pace the room.

"Are you sure you wouldn't like some coffee?"

"Sure," he said, distractedly. "Look, Ashley, this is no answer, you know. You're running away. If you love either of us, I just don't see how you can do it."

She felt annoyed. He was only thinking of himself, again. "And I just don't see how you can try and push me around the way you are. You come back into my life, four days before you're going to be married, and tell me that you love me. Not only that, you tell me that I only have to say the word, and you will call your wedding off and marry me. What was I supposed to do, Julian? Was I supposed to fall at your feet in gratitude? Was I supposed to run into your arms, and tell you that I loved you, and that everything would be all right? Well, life isn't as simple as that. You hurt me, you hurt me very deeply before Christmas. Did you think about me then?"

"You know I did."

"No," she said. "No, I don't know that you did. You just walked out of my life, and never came back."

"You made me promise never to call you."

"Oh Julian," she sighed. "People in love are always breaking promises. You can't use that as an excuse."

"Look," he said, going to sit beside her. "What if I call it all off with Blanche? Now. I'll ring her from here, and tell her. I can't lose you, Ashley. I just can't bear to think of it. I love you. OK, I know it's taken me a long time to realize it, but I know it now. What do you say? Shall I call her now? Will that put an end to this madcap scheme of yours?"

"Don't be fatuous, Julian!" she snapped. "And if you could even consider calling Blanche, and from here of all places, to tell her that the whole thing is off, then I really never knew you at all. And as for my madcap scheme, as you like to call it, my mind is quite made up. I want to go to New York, and the sooner the better."

"But what about Alex? Have you thought about him?"

"I've thought about Alex more than either of you. But he will be going away to boarding school in September. He can come over to New York for his holidays, and I will come over to see him as often as I can. And, I hope you don't mind, but I have decided to sell the Mercedes, which will give me a good sum of money to start me off. I can rent out my flat here, there are always people looking for good accommodation in this area."

"God, you really have thought this through, haven't you?"

"Yes."

"Just tell me one thing, Ashley. I know it won't make any difference now, but I'd like to know all the same. Do you still love me?"

She looked at him, and she saw the sadness in his eyes. Now she regretted being so firm, maybe she could have broken it to him a little more gently. After all, he was prepared to throw up almost everything for her, and she was now rejecting him out of hand.

"I don't know," she answered, truthfully. "I thought I did. And, like you, I thought that if you did ever come back to me, that I would fall into your arms, and welcome you back. But now it has happened, well, all I can say is that my decision has surprised me as much as it has surprised you."

"Is there anything I can say to make you change your mind?"

She shook her head. "No, Julian. Please, don't even try."

He looked defeated, and she reached out and took his hand. "I'm sorry, I never wanted to hurt you, truly I never."

"I know," he said. And the whole situation suddenly seemed too bitterly ironic for words.

She stood up. "I do need to know, though, if you are going to help me."

He looked up at her, and although they were sad there was a smile in his eyes. "I've always underestimated you. I suppose that's been half the trouble."

She smiled. "Now you're keeping me in suspense."

"For the sheer cheek of it I ought to say no," he said. "Giving yourself promotion, no, demanding promotion, and in New York too. It's a big world out there, Ash, you do realize that, don't you?"

"I'm prepared to take my chances."

"And what about Conrad? Have you thought that he might want to have something to say in the matter?"

"I'm sure he will. But you can make him see it your way."

"Your way you mean."

She laughed. "OK, my way."

"I thought you two didn't get along?"

"We don't. He is arrogant, conceited, despicable, chauvinistic, and downright bad-mannered, but I shall try my best to overcome his annoying little habits."

Julian chuckled. "I wouldn't let him hear you say that if I were you."

"Perhaps not. But I'm right for the job, Julian, you know I am. If you are with me, you know that Conrad can be persuaded round."

"I don't want to persuade him round."

"I thought we'd settled all that."

He sighed.

"So will you do it for me?"

He looked at her, and couldn't help but admire her strength. "Yes," he said. "Yes, if that's what you want, I'll see what I can do."

"Thank you," she said, and put her arms round him. "Would you like some coffee now?"

"Sure."

When Ashley came back in with the coffee, his mind flashed back to the night, so long ago now, when once before she had brought coffee into this room. That had been the night he had walked out of her life. He had rejected the love she had offered him, the life she had wanted to share with him, and without a backward glance he had walked away from her. And now once again they were sharing coffee. The difference this time was that now she was going to walk out of his life.

What a mistake he had made, all those months ago. What a fool he had been. But it was too late now. Decisions were so hard sometimes, and you never knew, until maybe a long time after, whether or not they were the right ones. And what did you do if they were the wrong ones? Well, you just did what he was doing now, he supposed, accept the consequences.

They talked a little over their coffee, but she could see that he was eager to go. She walked with him to the door, and as she opened it, he took her in his arms.

"I will always love you, Ash. I'm going to miss you." He let her go and started to walk away.

"Julian."

He turned back.

"Will you marry Blanche?"

He looked at her for a long time, his face inscrutable. Then finally he nodded his head, very slightly, and turned away.

Ashley smiled sadly to herself as she closed the door. What strange twists there sometimes are in life, she thought.

And now it only remained for her to tell Keith.

"Ashley, I'm begging you not to do it. Please!"

"Keith, I have to do it. I have to get away, I feel as though I'm being stifled here."

"I'll give you some room. I won't see you, only at weekends, I'll do anything, but please say you won't go."

She tried to pull away. "Keith, you're only making it worse for yourself, behaving like this. I've told you, I've made up my mind, now please let me go."

"I can't. I can't let you go again, Ashley. Don't you see that? I don't want to live without you. You're everything to me. I love you, I *love* you."

"And in my way I love you too. But it's not enough. I want more, I need more."

"Then tell me what you need. Just tell me. Give me a chance, Ashley. Please! I'm begging you."

"Don't, Keith. Don't beg me."

"Then what can I do to make you stay?"

"Nothing. I'm going, I've made up my mind."

"But what about the people you are leaving behind? Your mother, your father, Alex. What about Alex? Don't you care anything for your own son?"

"You know I do," she said. "I care about him more than anyone else. But try to understand, Keith, I have to be true to myself as well. If Alex was old enough, he would understand that. He would want me to go."

"But he's not old enough. He needs his mother. Here! Where he can see her, talk to her . . ."

"Keith, stop!" she cried. "I've been over all this with my mother and father, and they feel the way you do. But they are willing to support me in whatever I do. And Alex knows too."

"You've told Alex? You told Alex before you even told me?"

She nodded.

"Don't you think I had a right to know first?"

"No," she said. "I'm sorry, Keith, but Alex comes first."

"Then you've got a funny way of showing it."

"I know it might appear that way to you, but what kind of mother would I be if I just married someone for his sake?"

"For God's sake, Ashley, I'm his father."

"I know, but if a child is to have two parents, he needs two parents who love one another."

"But isn't that what I'm saying? I love you, Ashley."

"But I don't love you."

His face looked stricken, and she was sorry she had said that. "I'm sorry," she said, "I didn't mean it like that. It's just that I don't love you in the way you love me. I wish I could, God knows I wish I could. Things would be so much simpler then. But I don't and there's no use in pretending."

"I suppose Julian put you up to this."

"Of course he didn't. He's no happier about it than you are."

"Then why are you doing it?"

"Keith, I'm doing it for me. I'm doing something I want to do for once."

"For once? It strikes me you always do what you want to do."

"Oh God, it's pointless going on like this. I've told you, my mind is made up. I'm going to New York, and nothing you can say will change that."

She got up and walked out of the room. Going into the kitchen she heard Alex and her father playing out on the back lawn, waiting for her mother to return from

Guildford. She sent a silent prayer of thanks that she should have the parents she had. When she had told them her plans they had been upset, and confused, but just like they always did, they had listened. And now, despite their disappointment, they were going to stand by her, and help her in every way they could. They had started by deciding that it would be for the best if Alex wasn't around when Ashley told Keith. She watched her father through the window as he chased Alex with a football—an old man with a young man's vitality. She wondered how long they had been back. But if her father had heard anything, he was making sure that Alex didn't.

She went back into the lounge. Keith was still sitting in the chair beside the empty fireplace. Her eyes rounded with horror as she saw the great shuddering sobs that were wracking his body.

"Oh Keith, Keith," she said, going to him, "please, try and pull yourself together. Alex is outside, he'll be coming in any moment. Please, stop."

Keith caught her hand, and looked up into her face. He could hardly speak. "I can't, Ash. I can't. Nothing matters any more. If I can't have you, then life isn't worth anything. I love you so much, I never knew it was possible to love anyone so much. Don't do this to me, Ash. Please! Don't leave me."

She felt a moment's panic as she remembered his threats the last time she had told him she was leaving him. She would never forget how he had threatened to take Alex away, somewhere she would never find them. But now he seemed almost defeated in his grief, and she told herself that he loved Alex too much to try and hurt them all like that again. Her own tears mingled with his as she put her arms round him. She held him for a long time, and waited for him to be calm. But it was difficult for him. He had placed everything on his future with her, it was the only way he had of getting his son back, and now his future seemed worthless.

Finally he lifted his head from her shoulder. She looked into his face, and her heart turned over to see such despair.

"When will you go?"

"I'm not sure yet," she answered. "Soon."

"Is there any chance that things might fall through?"

"I don't think so. Julian has already spoken to Conrad, and the wheels are in motion."

"And what is Julian going to do?" he asked, pathetically.

"Julian?" she said, looking at her watch. "Well, about now, Julian will be getting married to Blanche."

"I could kill him. If he hadn't come back into your life, then none of this would have happened."

"You can't say that. Maybe it would have happened anyway, sooner or later."

"I'd like to think it wouldn't have."

She hugged him, and kissed his cheek. "I know."

"What did Alex say, when you told him?"

She chuckled. "Alex thinks of the whole thing as yet another adventure. He seemed rather to like the idea that his mother was going to New York, though why I can't imagine. He's already planning his first holiday out there. That's where he and Dad have been now. Down to the library to get some books on New York."

Keith smiled weakly. "He is a great kid, isn't he?"

"Like his father."

His eyes became soft, and she thought that he was going to cry again.

"Come on," she said. "You don't want him to see you like this. Why don't you go upstairs and clean up. I'll make us a nice pot of tea, and then call him in."

She stood up, but Keith held onto her hand. She turned back. "I'll always love you, Ashley," he said. "And no matter where you are, or what you're doing, it'll always be me who loves you more than anyone else. I'll wait. You'll come back to me in the end. I know you will."

She nodded, and drew her hand away. She didn't want to answer him. There was nothing more she could say.

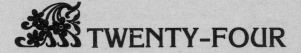 # TWENTY-FOUR

Linda stopped in the middle of the village street to check off her shopping list. Yes, she had already picked up Bob's shirts from the laundry and put them in the car. She had collected his tax return from his accountant. Violet's birthday present was ordered. She checked her bag to make sure she had remembered to pick up the new plug for the bathroom sink—Bob had been complaining about the old one for weeks. Now she had only to go to the butchers and, her heart lurched, last of all she must go to the chemist.

She looked up as someone prodded angrily on their car horn. It was Jason Arnold, her neighbor's son. Obviously he hadn't realized it was her. She moved to get out of the way, and Jason thrust his Porsche into a lower gear and accelerated off down the street, leaving a cloud of dust behind him.

Linda looked after him, wondering what his life was like. And then she saw Mrs. Plester coming out of the Post Office. They exchanged greetings, and Linda watched her walk away, wondering what her life was like.

Fixing a smile on her face, she went on about her

business. Ten minutes later she was getting into her car and driving home. She had been to the chemist. She glanced at the white paper bag, sitting on the passenger seat beside her, and felt a familiar lump rising in her throat. That morning, regular as clockwork—as they say—her period had arrived. It was all very well deciding that she would get pregnant, but it seemed that fate had other plans for her. She felt angry. What did fate know about anything? Let fate try making love with a husband whose mind was with another woman.

She pulled up outside the house and began taking the things from the car. Millie, her daily, came to take Bob's shirts. Linda watched her walk back inside, pulling the door behind her and making the trawler net that was hanging beside the door sway in the breeze. Routine. Linda shopped, Millie cleaned. Bob asked, Linda did. It was part of married life. If she needed something in London, Bob got it for her. If he needed . . . Their life was a routine. Entwined like the ropes of the trawler net. Every twine as important as the next, but each one appearing as insignificant as the next. Yet, if one gave way . . .

He'd be home tomorrow. Another weekend of pregnant silence and perfect manners. Did she, whoever she was, know what it was like to live like this? To carry on, day after day, trying to pretend that everything was normal, when all the time the earth was preparing to open up and swallow the precious routine.

And now another routine. The monthly routine. It meant they wouldn't make love this weekend, and she didn't know whether she was glad or not. Would he ask why? He hadn't asked any questions when she had disappeared for the weekend. She had left a note of course, so he had known where she was, but he had never asked her anything about it. She knew he hadn't returned to London—the stable boys had told her. How she had hated asking.

She went inside and found Millie sorting through

a pile of theater programs. "What shall I do with these?"

"I'll take them upstairs," Linda smiled, taking them from her. She had spent the previous evening going through them, reliving the memories that each one of them stored. The program for *Twelfth Night* was untouched. "Anyone call when I was out?"

"Ah yes," said Millie, remembering. "Mr. McElfrey rang."

Linda turned back in surprise. "Did he say what it was about?"

"Just wanted to remind you to pick up his shirts," Millie informed her, and abruptly flicked the switch of the vacuum cleaner.

Linda took the theater programs into the bedroom. *Twelfth Night.* She picked it up and fingered it carefully, as if she were touching a poisoned apple. She wanted to open it, but she knew that the picture—*her* picture—would be inside, and Linda didn't want to see her for the first time like that.

She put the program down again and went to look in the mirror. She had been toying with the idea for some time now, and suddenly the decision was made. She would go to the theater. She would watch a performance of *Twelfth Night,* and see her. She wouldn't tell Bob she was going, she was afraid he might try to persuade her not to. She would just turn up and sit anonymously in the audience, and watch her. She had no clear picture of what she would do afterwards; she would take it one step at a time.

Watching the fingers of the floor manager from the corner of her eye, Jenneen turned to the camera and started to wind up the program. "And that's all for this week. Join us again at the same time next week, when among others, we will be interviewing the Duchess of Westminster. Goodbye."

The studio remained silent until the closing credits

had rolled. The floor manager kept his finger to his ear-piece. "And they're off us," he said, after the usual forty seconds.

Jenneen gathered her things and waited for the director to come into the studio so that she could walk back to the office with him.

"You were on good form today," he said, as he came in.

"Aren't I always?"

"Of course. Come on, I'll buy you a cup of coffee."

They walked out of the studio and through reception toward the coffee machine. Brian dug in his pocket for some coins and Jenneen looked around the spacious reception as she talked over the following week's running order. "I think we should run the film in two sections. Gary's cutting it, I'll give him a ring and see if we can go and . . ." she stopped. Brian turned to hand her a cup of coffee and followed her eyes across to the front door, wehre there was a heated, though whispered, discussion taking place between three men, one of them Stephen Sommers.

Jenneen looked back to Brian. "That doesn't look very pleasant, does it? What do you suppose it's all about?"

"I can tell you exactly what it's all about," said Brian, taking another cup from the machine. "It's all about the little white powder."

"Cocaine?"

"Cocaine."

"What, right there, in the foyer of a major television station? It can't be."

"I can assure you it is. He won't be buying it there, now, but Sommers is in a bad way, probably owes them money and they've come to collect."

"Does Bill know? About the cocaine?"

"Yes."

"What's he doing about it?"

"Nothing, as far as I know. Nothing he can do,

until Steve comes clean and asks for help. Bill's already offered, but Steve didn't want to know. But if this sort of thing carries on at the front door, well, all I can say is, Sommers better look out for his job."

Jenneen followed Brian back to the production office. As they walked in through the door Stephen Sommers pushed past them and went to his desk. She watched in increasing fascination as the secretary with whom it was rumored he was having an affair kept her head down as she listened to what he was saying, and then dipped into her handbag and took out a small bundle of money.

"Seems I was right."

Jenneen looked at Brian.

"They've come to collect," he said and went off to speak to one of the researchers.

Jenneen sat down and wound a piece of paper into her typewriter. She looked up as Steve rushed past again, and then saw Bill follow him out a few minutes later.

She shrugged. Well, whatever was going on, it was none of her business, and she began to prepare her commentary for the film dub first thing in the morning.

"Jenneen, can you come in for a minute?"

Jenneen looked up in surprise. It was Bill, his head poking round the door of his office. She hadn't seen him go back in.

"Sure."

He was sitting at his desk when she walked in, and seeing the serious look on his face, she closed the door behind her.

"Sit down," he said, waving her to the chair opposite.

She wondered if he was going to speak to her about Stephen Sommers, but that was ridiculous, it had nothing to do with her and if she were to mention it herself, Bill would remind her of that. He never discussed the affairs of one presenter or reporter with another.

She tried to think what she had done recently to warrant this sudden summons to his office. She had no idea what Vicky had told Bill when she had called him, several weeks ago now, and Bill had never referred to it. But perhaps it had not all gone away as easily as she had thought. Try as she might, she couldn't think of any other reason for his sombre face. Steeling herself, she crossed her legs and waited for him to speak.

He was reading something on the desk in front of him, apparently engrossed, and he didn't look up for several minutes. Several minutes in which she became more and more uncomfortable.

At last, he looked up. He had a lovely face. Kind eyes, and young-looking skin for a man well past fifty. The few lines that he had were etched attractively around his eyes and projected the warmth of his personality. Jenneen was immensely fond of him. They had known one another ever since she had arrived in London, some nine years ago now, when he had taken her under his wing, and built her into what she was today.

"So, how are you, Jenn?"

"Fine," she said. "I'm fine."

"Good," and she could tell that he really meant it. "Any news on your friend, Kate?"

"I saw her yesterday. She's down in Surrey, resting for a while."

"But everything's OK between you two now?"

"Oh yes, I'm glad to say." She wondered what he was leading up to.

"Does she have many visitors?"

"Not many. Her father has become even more protective than ever. Only the chosen few are allowed in," Jenneen smiled.

Bill nodded.

Suddenly it occurred to Jenneen that Bill might be

wanting to do an interview with Kate about her experiences, and Jenneen was horrified. It was the side of her business she hated most. The delving into other people's tragedies.

"Well, I'm glad to hear that it's all been repaired between the two of you," he said, and that seemed to be it. Jenneen relaxed.

"Nothing else bothering you is there?"

She looked away. She knew she looked tired, and was only too aware of the dark circles under her eyes. But she would never tell him about Matthew. The only person she had ever told was Vicky, and Vicky had never referred to it since. It was a constant fight now for Jenneen, to accept Matthew and his foul extortion as a part of her life, and a part that she might never be rid of. But accepting it, and trying to absorb it into the channels of everyday life, was the only way she could deal with it. Providing his demands got no greater, she might just be able to manage. She shuddered to think what she might do if he became greedy, but that was a bridge she would have to cross when, or if, she ever came to it.

"You haven't answered me."

Jenneen smiled at him. "No," she said. "No, there's nothing else bothering me. But when you ask in such a fatherly way, I almost want there to be something, so that I can come to you for advice."

He chuckled. "I don't know whether to be flattered or not. But anyway, the main thing is that you have got yourself sorted out now."

"I think so," she lied. Mrs. Green was strictly taboo.

"Good. That's what I wanted to hear." He looked back at his desk, and started reading again.

"Is that it? Can I go now?"

He looked up. "No. There is something else. The real reason I called you in."

Jenneen's heart somersaulted, in the way hearts that contain a guilty secret do. "Oh?"

"Don't look so worried," he laughed. He picked up the document he had been reading. "It's about this."

"What is it?"

"You don't recognize it?"

"I can't see it."

He turned it round. "It's the program idea you gave me a couple of months ago."

Jenneen looked surprised. "Well, you've taken your time, I must say. I was beginning to think it had disappeared along with yesterday's news."

"Not at all," he said. "In fact, it's been right here on my desk, all the time."

"So, what do you think?"

He put it down again. "I think it's good. Very good, in fact. But that's almost irrelevant. What is relevant is that them upstairs think it's good too. They're quite excited about it."

"You've shown them?"

"Yes," he answered. "But more than that, I've had extensive talks with them about it."

"But why haven't you said anything before?"

He lifted an eyebrow, and looked at her.

"I see," she said. "Too many problems, and not stable enough, eh?"

"Something like that. But you seem a lot better lately, so I thought that perhaps now was the time. The budgets are being set up for next spring, and there's a chance we might be able to get it in."

"You're kidding me."

"Nope, I'm deadly serious. There's a little more to be done yet, before they can finally be persuaded to push it through. They want to know how much it's going to cost. Who you've actually approached about the idea. Whether or not you've anyone particular in mind to front it, other than yourself of course. And ba-

sically how many contacts you have in the film world
that will make this stand up."

"When do they need to know by?"

"As soon as you're ready. But I'd make it soon. If
this company can be praised for anything, it's the speed
with which they present their budgets. Not perhaps always so hot on programs, but budgets, well, that's a
different story."

She smiled. "I'll need some time."

"How much?"

"A couple of weeks, minimum. There are a lot of
people to see."

"Have you spoken to anyone at all?"

"Only a few."

"What about the critics? If you're going to ask
them to justify their reviews, you have to be sure
they're willing to participate. Without them, you don't
have a program."

"I know a couple already who have said they will.
But basically I'm relying on their conceit. An army of
little gods are the film critics, they'll do anything for
a seat in the heavens of a television studio, providing
there's a camera with a red light on pointing toward
them."

"You're not far wrong, if a little tough. And the
filmmakers themselves? Have you spoken to any?"

"Not many. But I'm banking on the publicity
angle. Anything to sell the product. And, with any
luck, we could have some pretty entertaining debates
on our hands."

"Not to mention fisticuffs," Bill remarked.

"My thoughts exactly. But what about the spin-
offs I outlined in the document? The opportunities for
new film-makers, writers and the like? Did they say
anything about that?"

"A few noises were made, but I think they want
to see how the program itself does first."

"And the awards?"

"Yes, the awards. They liked that. Gives them a chance to be involved in the arts, and providing the series does take off, unless I'm greatly mistaken, the awards will soon follow."

Jenneen was smiling all over her face. "This is great news, Bill," she said. "Thanks."

"Don't mention it. I wouldn't mind having a go at something like that myself. I trust you're not forgetting me?"

"As if I would," she said. "It's the reason I gave it to you in the first place. I was hoping, should anything come of it, that you might like to edit it."

"That sounds distinctly like a job offer to me," he grinned.

"It is."

"You're nothing if not an upstart. I accept, if it goes ahead. Now, what about some lunch? We can discuss it in greater detail. I'm starving."

"You paying?"

"I'm paying," he agreed, reluctantly.

"Then you're on. I'll get my bag."

Bill watched her walk from the office, and sat back in his chair. He hoped that he was doing the right thing. He didn't want to take too many chances with this one. The idea was good. The best he'd seen for ages. The last thing he wanted to do was a double deal on Jenneen, but the way things had been going over the last six months or so made him nervous. These last weeks she had seemed more relaxed, but there was still something bothering her, he knew it. And he knew too that it was extremely unlikely that she would ever tell him what it was. Well, he just had to hope that now she had her own project to work on, she would go back to being her old reliable self. Although the chaps upstairs had been impressed with the idea, they had been less impressed when they had discovered whose it was. They were depending on Bill now to make sure that it worked. And, in turn, Bill was depending on Jenneen.

He would just have to pray that she didn't let him down.

When Jenneen arrived home that evening she threw down her bag and hung her coat on the stand in the hallway. This was the best she'd felt in so long, that she realized she had almost forgotten what it was like to be happy. She was eager to get on with her project, there was plenty to do, and she was determined she wasn't going to let Bill down. She could kiss him for doing what he'd done, and not for the first time she wondered what she would have done without him.

As she walked in from the hall she was so engrossed in the evening paper, searching for film reviews, that she didn't notice Vicky, sitting on the settee in the lounge.

"Hello."

Jenneen jumped, and almost dropped the paper. "Vicky! What are you doing here?"

"The lady upstairs let me in. I think she felt sorry for me, sitting out on the landing."

"But you didn't say you were coming round tonight," said Jenneen, her eyes darting instinctively to the calendar in case she had forgotten. "Not that I'm not pleased to see you," she added quickly.

"I had some things to do in the shop in Kensington, so I thought I'd call round, you know, on the off-chance."

"Have you been waiting long?"

"Well," said Vicky, "as a matter of fact I have. Not that I intended to, but something happened, so I thought I'd wait."

"Nothing serious, I hope. Look, let me get you a drink, then you can tell me all about it." She walked over to the sideboard, and poured them both a Scotch and soda. "No one's upset you have they?"

"No, it's nothing like that. Thanks," and she took the drink from Jenneen.

"Then what?"

"Actually, it's not to do with me at all. It's to do with you."

"With me?" said Jenneen, swallowing her drink.

"Yes. When I arrived earlier there was somebody else waiting here for you."

Jenneen paled. It took no great intelligence to work out who it had been, even without the look on Vicky's face.

"I recognized him immediately," said Vicky.

"Where is he now?"

"He left when I said that I'd come to see you."

"Doesn't sound like Matthew, to give up so easily."

"I told him that you were expecting several others as well. It seemed to put him off."

"Thanks," said Jenneen. "But he was here only last night. Why has he come again?"

"That, only he can tell you. Does he come round often then?"

"I'm afraid so. Too bloody often."

"So it's all still going on then?"

Jenneen nodded.

"You're going to have to do something about it, Jenn. You can't carry on like this, you know."

"If only it were that easy. He'll never go away, I know he won't."

"Does he threaten you?"

"Threaten me!" Jenneen cried. "Are you kidding? He does nothing else but threaten me."

"No, I meant violently."

"I'd call it violently, yes," Jenneen answered. "But if you mean physically, then the answer is no, not usually."

"Not usually? You mean he has?"

"Sometimes, in the past. But I've realized now that if I just give in gracefully and hand over the money, then he goes fairly quickly. And now he's living with that little tart Maggie, I assume he has his meals cooked for him there, so he doesn't expect me to do it any more. Did he say anything to you?"

"Not really. We've met before, actually, but I don't know if he remembered. It's because of that that I waited around. There's something I think you should know, about me I mean."

"Oh blast!" Jenneen said, as the telephone began to ring. "Won't be a minute."

It was Ashley calling to tell her that there would be a Barnes Conference the following evening, if she could make it, she had some pretty important news.

"I'm intrigued," Jenneen laughed. "Yes, I'll be there. See you," and she rang off. "Sorry," she said, turning back to Vicky. "Where were we? Oh yes, you were saying you didn't know if Matthew remembered you. Well, you're lucky if he didn't. I only wish he'd forget me."

The telephone interruption had robbed Vicky of her confidence; she decided not to say what she had intended. "Well, he's not going to," she said. "Not as long as you keep giving in to him."

"I don't see any alternative."

"You can go to the police."

Jenneen looked shocked. "Now you really are kidding me. I can't afford to have my name splashed across the headlines like that. No one can. And don't underestimate him, he's perfectly capable of doing it. In fact it wouldn't even surprise me if one of these days he did it, just for the sheer hell of it. He's a cunning, deceitful, sly little toad, is Matthew Bordsleigh, with all the charm of Genghis Khan, though few ever get to see that far. No, the last thing I'm going to do is tell the police, that'll be playing straight into his hands."

"I assume he's beyond reasoning with?"

"You assume correctly."

"But you can't go on like this, Jenneen. You'll have

no life to call your own. No money, no freedom, no peace of mind. You've got to get rid of him."

"Short of murder, nothing else springs to mind."

Vicky laughed. "Well, he'd deserve it, but I suppose that's no answer. No, we'll have to think of something. Somehow he's got to be stopped. The problem is, how?"

"There's no point in even talking about it. Believe me, if there was a way out of this, I'd have found it by now. I almost did, until you stopped me. No, Matthew Bordsleigh will be a leech on the Jenneen Grey coffers, until he decides otherwise. And I'm just going to have to accept it."

"Why don't you let me talk to him?"

"He won't listen, and besides I'd rather that you didn't get involved. He's a very nasty character, capable of almost anything."

"It's funny, but when I saw him earlier, I thought how nice he looked. Attractive, with a certain sort of style, a ready smile. It's difficult to believe that he's a liar, a cheat, and a blackmailer."

"I can assure you he is," said Jenneen. "And there's nothing more deceiving than looks. Especially his, and I should know."

"Well, I'm not going to let it rest there. There must be something we can do, I'll just have to think of it."

Jenneen looked worried. "Look, I've never discussed this with anyone, not even my closest friends. No one else knows."

Vicky smiled. "Don't worry, it'll be our secret, if that's what you want. Now, any more Scotch?"

"Sure," said Jenneen, getting up. As she poured the drinks she was beginning to regret ever having told Vicky anything. She thought back to the day that Vicky had saved her life, and wondered sadly if she would ever reach that pitch again. But that was a silly thing to think. Weren't things looking up now? Everything had been sorted with Kate, and she was getting

her own program idea off the ground, with the bless-
ings of the company, and under the auspices of Bill.

"I've got something to celebrate," she said, turning
back to Vicky.

"That makes a change," was Vicky's dry reply.

Jenneen laughed, and fell back into the chair.
Vicky was delighted with her news and suggested that
they go out to eat, on her.

"Lunch and dinner? I am doing well today," Jenneen remarked. "I'll go and change, I can't go like this,
I look a mess."

"You look fine to me," said Vicky, arching an eyebrow. "In fact, don't I recognize that dress from somewhere?"

"Indeed you do. But it's a bit crumpled, I've had
it on all day. No offense meant."

"None taken."

Jenneen put her Scotch on the table, and got up
to leave the room.

"Jenn."

Jenneen turned back, alerted by the serious note
in Vicky's voice.

"Look, Jenn, I'm sorry. I shouldn't have poked my
nose in. It's none of my business, and I'm sorry, I was
only trying to help."

"Oh Vicky," said Jenneen, sitting down again. "I
know you were."

"Well, I hope you believe me when I say that it
will go no further. If any of this ever gets out, then I
can promise you, it won't have come from me. But I'm
glad you told me. As I said before, it doesn't do any
good to bottle these things up. But it's your life, and
you must handle things your way. I won't mention it
again, I promise."

"Thanks," said Jenneen. "And I'm sorry if I
seemed a bit off."

"You weren't. Now, you go and change. I'm starving, and I want to hear all about this program idea of
yours."

TWENTY-FIVE

I‍T HAD ALL HAPPENED SO QUICKLY ASHLEY COULD HARDLY BE-
lieve that it was only four weeks since she had asked
Julian to arrange it for her. And now she was here, in
New York, in Manhattan, and she had never felt so
alive. She longed to throw out her arms and spin round
and round with the sheer excitement of it all. Already
she adored the exhilaration of the place. Everything
was so fast, so electrifying, and she, Ashley Mayne,
was a part of it. She was no mere tourist, stopping over
on a quick week's holiday—or vacation—she was a
real, *bona fide* citizen of New York. At least, she would
be once she had found herself somewhere to live.

In the meantime she was staying in a small, rather
English hotel over on the East side, where the people
fussed over her and "just loved her cute English accent."

She had thought that she would be lonely at first
and, in truth, if she had allowed herself the time, she
probably would have been. She had had five days free
before she started work on Madison Avenue, and had
crammed as much into those five days as was humanly
possible—a bus tour of the city, visits to museums, art
galleries and all the tourist sites. The place that gave
her the greatest thrill of all was, without a doubt, Fifth
Avenue. All those glorious shops—stores—displaying
a myriad of riches, from diamonds to furs, and Cartier

to Tiffany. She had already opened an account at Saks, and was now toying with the idea of opening another at Tiffany. Not that she could afford to use it, but what the hell, wouldn't the others be impressed!

She had called home a couple of times, but her mother was so worried about the expense of the trans-Atlantic connection that she always hurried her off the line. Jenneen had phoned twice, and Ellamarie and Bob had called her once too. She had been especially pleased to hear from Ellamarie; she hadn't seemed herself at all in the weeks leading up to Ashley's departure, and Ashley had wondered if it had had anything to do with Bob. But Ellamarie had sounded better when she'd rung, and Bob had been with her, wanting to speak too. Hopefully, whatever it was that had been wrong between them, had been sorted now. She had not only received a phone call from Kate, there had been a bottle of champagne and some flowers waiting for her at her hotel when she'd arrived. The card had read: "With all my love, Kate. And mine too, Nick." Nick's addition had made Ashley smile, and she had had to admit to a pang of homesickness at that moment. But really, her only sadness was that they weren't all here to share her new life with her.

On the Friday morning after she'd arrived she called in at the IBM building on Madison Avenue where Frazier, Nelmes had their offices. She received a friendly welcome from a smart and surprisingly middle-aged woman, called Jan, who was to be her secretary. When Jan showed her into her office, Ashley tried very hard not to look as overwhelmed as she felt. It was almost as big as the entire Art Department at Frazier, Nelmes back in London, with a desk of such monumental proportions that she felt faintly ridiculous sitting behind it. At the other end of the room was a small alcove where two leather sofas flanked a marble-topped coffee table. Jan referred to this area as a casual, where less formal meetings could be held, and Ashley noticed a drinks cabinet built into the wall, which, she found when she opened it, was stocked with everything she could imagine, and more.

Later, after Jan had shown her round and introduced her to the heads of every department, she took her along to Conrad's office, where she introduced Ashley to Candice, Conrad's secretary. Candice was no surprise. She was exactly how Ashley imagined Conrad's secretary would be. Chic, sophisticated, and very glamorous. Ashley liked her immediately, and the feeling appeared to be mutual. Candice told her that Conrad was away right now and wouldn't be back until the end of the month. He was cruising the Caribbean with clients—one of the more enviable functions of the Chairman.

Ashley was secretly relieved that he wasn't there; she did not relish their inevitable meeting. She was sure that he was deeply resentful of her being foisted upon him by Julian, and was in no doubt that he had probably made the telephone lines to London curl with his opinion of the situation. Still, she would deal with him when the time came.

When she returned on Monday morning, fresh and ready to go at eight-thirty, she found that everything had been set up for her. She was quietly impressed by the efficiency of her department, and most of all of Jan. At ten o'clock she held a meeting in her "casual" of all the Account Execs who could make it, and was pleasantly surprised by their manner toward her. She had expected a certain amount of resentment, hostility even, but she only received friendship, and offers of help; she knew they were all going to get along.

At lunchtime Candice took her to a restaurant called Prima Donna where she proceeded to fill Ashley in on everyone at the agency. Ashley didn't ask anything about Conrad, and if Candice mentioned him at all it was with a good deal of affection. Ashley was more surprised by that than perhaps anything else so far. She could imagine a lot of feelings one might have toward Conrad Frazier, but affection was certainly not one of them. Still, what Candice felt about Conrad was none of her business; she was here to do a job, and start a new life, and that's what she aimed to do.

The first couple of weeks flew by, leaving her with hardly a minute to herself. There were so many meetings. She had heard how the Americans liked to meet, but this was beyond anything she had expected. The first ones of the day started at breakfast, around eight in the morning, and continued on and off all day, sometimes until well past midnight, in some club or restaurant.

She found the clients to be a great deal less awkward than those she had come across in England, but in being less awkward, they were far more demanding. Everything had to be done yesterday, and if not yesterday, then last week. It was all go. Commercials were being shot every day; billboards and posters were going up and down all over town; newspapers and magazines were continuously bombarded for the purchase of space, and the Art Department churned out their work with such speed and efficiency that Ashley almost blushed to think of its small counterpart in London. These people certainly knew how to work. And they did, solidly, until the job was done.

All she had to do now was find somewhere to live, but that wasn't an immediate problem, luckily. Jan helped out as much as she could, and every day she searched the real estate pages to see if she could find something suitable. Ashley was happy to put herself into Jan's capable hands, as she had no idea where was acceptable for a woman in her position to live. She tried not to shudder every time Jan circled something; it was even more expensive than London. What she kept forgetting was that she now had the salary to afford it.

The end of the month soon came round, and before she knew it Conrad was back. She wanted to get their first meeting over with as quickly as possible, and had expected him to summon her almost immediately, but she was disappointed. He closeted himself with the Financial Director and President for the best part of the week, and then disappeared again.

This made Ashley even more nervous about seeing him than she already was. To have ignored her so blatantly must mean that he was still resentful of her being thrust upon him. Oh well, let him stew in it. She was here now, and he would just have to lump it. She wished her emotions matched her sentiments.

Halfway through her fifth week Conrad finally called her in. She was surprised when the call came from Candice, she hadn't even known he was in his office. Luckily things were marginally less hectic than they had been up to now, and she felt as able to cope with it as she supposed she would ever be.

Candice was sitting at her desk speaking into the telephone when Ashley let herself into the Chairman's suite. She looked up and waved Ashley on through, mouthing the words "he's waiting."

Ashley knocked on the door and waited. When he didn't answer she pushed the door open and looked inside. He was on the telephone and glanced up as she put her head round. His eyes moved to the seat at the other side of his desk, so she went in and closed the door behind her. She walked over to the window and looked out at the tiny streets in the distance below.

Whoever Conrad was speaking to, it was not a business call, and she tried not to listen. At last he put the phone down and swung round in his chair to face her.

Immediately she felt like slapping his face. He had that aggravating half-smile on his face and his eyes were quite openly assessing her. It was already more than plain to her that they were going to get along no better now than they ever had.

"So," he drawled, sounding more American than

she had noticed before, "you've come to join us, Ashton."

Her nostrils flared to capacity. "Ley," she snapped.

"Leigh?" He looked down at a sheet of paper in front of him. "I thought your name was Mayne."

"It is. And my other name is Ashley."

"I apologize," he said. "Come and sit down, I'd like to have a talk."

At first she made to sit in the chair at the other side of his desk, but he had got to his feet, and was strolling across to the casual at the far end of his office. She followed him over and sat down facing him. Candice came in with some coffee, and as she put it down on the table she winked at Ashley.

Conrad poured the coffee. "Didn't see you at the wedding," he said, as he handed her a cup.

She took it, and smiled sweetly at him. "I wasn't there," she said, refusing to be baited.

"So, how are you settling in?"

"Very well," she answered, relieved that he'd changed the subject. "Everyone's been marvelous, and very helpful. I'm learning the ropes far quicker than I imagined I might."

"Good. They're a pretty good bunch. High turnover, of course, not like in London."

"Most London agencies do have a high turnover."

"Ah, but not Frazier, Nelmes."

"No. Not Frazier, Nelmes. Julian seems to instill a sense of loyalty in his bunch, as you call them."

"But haven't you flown the nest?"

"I'm still with the same agency."

"Yes, indeed you are. Incidentally, my congratulations on your speedy promotion."

Ashley flushed, and as she couldn't think of a suitable answer, she said nothing.

"Anyway," Conrad went on, "Julian assures me that I have a gem in you, and so I suppose I have to believe him."

"You'd better see how I do, before you start believing Julian."

"Oh, I already know how you're doing," he said. "I might not have been here, but I've had a close eye on you. And, you'll be pleased to hear, I'm impressed with what I've heard so far. I hope you can keep it up."

God, this man was so infuriating; she could only hope that contact with him would be limited.

"Have you found anywhere to live yet?"

"So the eye isn't that close then?"

He lifted a heavy eyebrow, but didn't answer.

"No," she said, feeling herself beginning to blush. "No, I haven't found anywhere yet. Jan is helping me look."

"Where are you staying?"

"In a hotel."

He nodded, and with the niceties over, went on to tell her more about the agency and the monthly progress meetings that he held in the boardroom. Ashley listened, and found herself more than once caught by his penetrating eyes. And every time she did, she felt the color rush to her cheeks. By the time Candice knocked on the door, half an hour later, Ashley was so relieved she let go an audible sigh and knocked her cup over in the saucer. Luckily it was empty. Conrad glanced at her, and she saw that he was amused.

Candice said that Gavin Berkley, the Financial Director, was outside. "Shall I ask him to wait?"

"No," Conrad answered, getting to his feet. "I've finished here. Ask him to come in."

Ashley stood up. Apparently she was dismissed.

"I'm sure we'll run into one another again soon," he said, walking with her to the door, "but I just wanted to say hello, welcome you to New York."

"Thank you," she said, surprised. He sounded as though he meant it.

He reached out for the door handle. "How about

your social life?" he asked. "Are you getting about much?"

"Enough, thank you."

The door opened and Gavin Berkley came in, followed by Candice.

The four of them stood in a cluster at the door. Conrad pulled it wider so that Ashley could get through.

"I'll have Candice draw you up a list of good swimming pools," he said, looking at her with a perfectly straight face. "From what I seem to remember, you have something of a liking for water sports."

Ashley gasped, and felt her face flood with color. She was aware of Candice and Gavin watching her curiously, but as there was nothing she could say, she attempted a quick smile and swept out of the office.

Without turning on the lights, Ellamarie stomped up the stairs to her flat and threw open the door. She slammed it behind her, then walked into the kitchen and dumped the flowers she was carrying into the sink. Then she went to pour herself a very large brandy. She was furious. Absolutely hopping mad.

Tonight had been the last night of *Twelfth Night* and everyone was going out for dinner. Everyone, that was, except her and Bob. And where he was now she had no idea, which was probably just as well for him, given the rage she was in.

He had promised that he would be back in time to pick her up after the show. He had had to be at the Colisseum tonight, and then he was meeting Adrian Cowley about the *Queen of Cornwall*, though he hadn't told her where, and she hadn't thought it necessary to ask. He had never let her down before. Maureen Woodley, with a nasty little smirk on her face, said that she'd seen him directly after the performance was over, but where he was now, she was sorry, but she really had no idea. Ellamarie then checked with Bob's secretary, but she confirmed that Bob hadn't any other meetings planned for later that night. If Ellamarie had been less angry she might have noticed the secretary's discomfort.

But if he went back to the theater as Maureen had said, then where was he now? And why hadn't he waited for her? It wasn't as if they'd had a fight earlier, in fact it had been quite to the contrary. They had spent the best part of the afternoon in bed together.

She had waited by the Stage Door for over half an hour, until Nick, who waited with her, said that he really must go. He had to go and pick up Kate, who was staying the night at her flat in South Kensington.

Ellamarie hadn't minded him going. She was delighted that Kate had agreed to a night out at long last; it would do her the power of good. But that in itself made her more angry. She had wanted to see Kate. But when Bob really didn't look like he was going to show, Ellamarie knew that the evening was ruined for her, so she had jumped into a cab, and come straight home.

She picked up the phone and rang his mews house. There was no reply, not that she had really expected one, so she slammed the receiver down again. There was no point in going to bed, she wouldn't be able to sleep. And there was no point in watching TV, she wouldn't be able to concentrate. And she wouldn't be able to read either. So she poured herself another drink.

For almost two hours she sat there, getting more and more drunk and, as her anger began to subside, more and more upset. He could at least call, let her know that he was all right, but he didn't even bother to do that. Finally she gave up and went to bed.

It was past two o'clock in the morning when a knock on the door finally penetrated her dreams. She reached out to wake Bob. As her hand brushed over the empty pillow she opened her eyes. With a wave of annoyance she dragged herself from the bed and threw on a wrap. She turned on the light and looked at the clock. There was another knock on the door, more impatient this time, and she called out that she was coming.

She didn't bother to turn the light on in the hall, she could see well enough from the light in her room.

There was another knock.

"All right, all right," she grumbled. "I'm coming."

She pulled open the door. "I was asl . . ." She barely glimpsed the figure in the doorway before she was thrown violently against the wall. She opened her mouth to scream, but a hand was clasped firmly over it. Then she heard the door slam, and she was being pushed back toward her room, prodded and poked viciously from behind. With a violent shove she was thrown across the bed. She managed to turn herself round, and look at whoever it was who had forced their way in. Her eyes began to bulge with terror.

He closed the door silently behind him, and she felt that behind his woollen mask he was smiling. She knew from the way he was holding himself what was about to happen.

As he started toward her she recoiled back against the bed. "Wh-what do you want?"

"Hello, Ellamarie."

Oh God, how did he know her name?

He was still walking toward her, very slowly, and suddenly she felt some strength seep back into her body. She twisted herself from the bed, and onto the floor at the other side. He seemed unperturbed, and continued toward her, smooth, milk-white hands dangling at his sides. He reached out to touch her hair. She flinched before he had even touched her and drew away. "No, please. Who are you? What do you want?"

"I want you, Ellamarie." His voice was like silk. "I thought you would know that."

"How do you know my name?"

He was standing over her, the toes of his trainer shoes only inches from her knees. She pressed her back against the wall and tried to pull herself up from the floor. He laughed quietly and pushed her back down again. She looked up and her hand flew to her throat as an overwhelming surge of fear almost choked her. He looked grotesque peering down from the shadowed height, the lamp beneath his face. The lamp! Her eyes flew to the dressing table beside her, and without thinking she grabbed at the lamp. But he was too quick for her, and chopped his hand viciously against her arm.

"That wasn't very nice, was it?" he said.

She barely heard him, the pounding of her heart was drowning all other sound. She drew back again, pressing herself into the corner and watching, mesmerised, as his knees moved closer to her face. As she lashed out he caught her by the wrist and twisted her arm painfully.

"Get up," he said.

She lifted her eyes, her whole face quivering with terror. Slowly she shook her head.

"I said, get up." The tone of his voice told her that she would be wise to do as he said. She struggled to her feet, never taking her eyes from the terrible mask. She held onto the dressing table.

"There," he said softly, pointing to the bed.

She sobbed and clutched at the neck of her robe. "No."

She followed his hand as it sank into his pocket. When he brought it out again he was holding a knife. She tried to scream, but nothing would come. She fell back against the wall, knocking everything from her dressing table and sending it crashing to the floor.

She began to cry. "Please! Please!" she begged. "Don't hurt me. Please don't touch me."

"I don't want to hurt you," he said, sounding surprised that she could even think such a thing. "Just get onto the bed."

She stayed where she was, too terrified to move.

He pressed a button at the side of the knife and the blade flicked toward her. He held the cold steel against her throat. "I said, onto the bed."

She edged round him and toward the bed. Maybe if she just did as he said, he wouldn't hurt her. But oh God, would he kill her afterward? Would he just kill her anyway?

She perched on the edge of the bed. Still holding the knife over her, he pushed her back onto the pillows. He leaned forward and ran his hand across her face and down over her neck. She turned her head away, and immediately realized her mistake. It made him angry. He pushed the knife up against her throat again, and she screwed up her eyes. She could feel the cold blade against her skin, and she waited, paralyzed by terror, for him to plunge it into her neck. And then it was gone. She felt him move closer to her, and winced as his foul breath penetrated through the mask. She felt her wrap fall loose; he had cut the belt with his knife.

She began to whimper as he feasted his eyes on her nearly naked body. And then he was on the bed beside her, with the knife back at her throat. He slipped an arm round her, and tried to pull her close.

"I don't want to hurt you, Ellamarie," he murmured. "I want to be nice to you. And I want you to be nice to me. Tell me what turns you on."

She shook her head. "Nothing! Please, nothing!"

"But something must turn you on. How about this?" and he ran a hand over her thighs. "Do you like that? Is that nice?"

"No! No! Yes!" she shrieked, as he pressed the knife against her throat once more.

"Do you want to know what turns me on?"

She didn't answer.

"You do? Then give me your hand."

She tried to push her hands under her body, but he wrenched one of them free, and pushed her balled fist into his groin. "Do you feel that?" he said. "Answer me? Do you feel that?"

"Yes!"

"It's ready for you, Ellamarie. Ready, just for you. And you're going to do everything it wants you to, aren't you?" He ran the blade down over her breast, leaving a thin line of blood in its wake. "Aren't you?"

"Yes," she sobbed. "Yes."

He drew back his hand and hit her face. She screamed out, but he caught her jaw between his fingers. "Shut up!" he hissed. "Now, pull down my zip," and he thrust his groin toward her.

Her fingers were shaking so badly that she could hardly take hold of the zipper. He became impatient and hit her again. Then he grabbed the zip himself, and dragged his jeans down over his hips.

He was like a dead weight on top of her. She lay beneath him, every muscle in her body tensed. He wriggled around, breathing into her face and forcing her legs apart with his own.

The violation and degradation that followed was complete, and though he didn't use the knife, he might just as well have done. His sexual appetite was vile, violent and insatiable; again and again he ravished her, hissing vulgar words into her ear. Not even at the height of his salacity did he lose control.

Tears streamed silently from her eyes, as she stared unseeingly at his discarded jeans, lying in a heap on the floor. She could taste the blood on her lips as her teeth sank into them. His perversion knew no bounds, and as he grabbed her about the waist and turned her over, she heard herself muttering insanely. And then she screamed. The pain was so intense she almost passed out, but he was determined she should know the full extent of his lust, and gripped her hair in his hands while he pounded his loathsome body into her.

And then it was over. He fell blubbering onto the pillow beside her, perspiration running from under his

mask. She lay still, aware only of the knife that was
now lying on the floor beside the bed. If she could only
reach it, she could kill him. He was still panting, basking in the waves of satiated lust. It was her only chance.
And then, to her horror, as she slowly began to move
her hand, he reached out and took her in his arms. He
forced her face round to his and, lifting the mask over
his mouth, he tried to kiss her. She sank her teeth into
his bottom lip. He drew back and glared at her. It was
then that she first really noticed his eyes, staring down
at her through the slits of the woollen mask. Her heart
tightened as the cold fear of recognition hit her. Those
pale, cold eyes that had watched her across a crowded
room. Those hideous, light gray eyes that had studied
her every move. The Adonis at Robert Blackwell's
party. Those eyes would live with her for the rest of
her life.

He heaved himself from the bed and looked down
at her. She fought against the bile that rose in her
throat. As he stopped to pick up his clothes, a sharp
pain shot through her arm, but she didn't look to see
what it was. She was hypnotized by his eyes and beyond caring now. All she wanted to do was die.

"I told you I would wait," he said, "and I got tired
of waiting."

She closed her eyes and listened as he dressed himself. When there was only silence she opened them
again and peered around the room. She heard the front
door slam. He had gone.

Slowly, shaking all over, she lifted herself carefully from the bed. She hurt so badly it was difficult
to move. She saw that there was blood on her arm, and
realized that he must have cut her with the knife. Then
she saw the blood on her thighs, and on the sheets. She
tried to lift the sheets from the bed, but her arms were
heavy and bruised. Tears still trickled from her eyes;
she felt like a hunted and trapped animal that had lost

its final bid for life, exhausted, and only able to whimper now.

She managed to drag herself into the bathroom. She turned on the hot tap and filled the tub with scalding water.

The pain was almost unbearable as she lowered her battered body into the steam, but it was the only way. She picked up the nail brush and rubbed soap into it. Then slowly, methodically, she began to scrub her body. But no matter how hard she scrubbed, the feel of his hands would not go away. Her defilement was inside her, as well as outside, and she was afraid she might never be clean again.

She pulled herself from the tub, and wrapped a towel round her. She lowered her eyes from the mirror, unable to look at herself, as she opened the cupboard above the basin. She took down the bottle of aspirin. Then she went to the kitchen and filled a glass with water. It was painful to walk, and her progress was slow. Finally she reached the settee in the lounge and eased herself down onto the cushions.

Her mouth was dry so she swallowed some water. Then she placed two aspirin on the end of her tongue and drank some more. Then two more, and she drank again . . .

The shrill sound of the phone woke her. Ellamarie opened her eyes and looked around. She wasn't curious as to why she was in the lounge. Not for one minute, even while she was asleep, had she forgotten what had happened, what he had done to her. In the cold light of day, it was worse than a nightmare.

The phone carried on ringing, and she rolled off the settee, onto the floor. She couldn't stand, her legs were stiff and the pain was still too great, so she crawled over to the telephone and picked it up.

"Ellamarie?" It was Bob.

She didn't answer.

"Ellamarie? Are you there?"

"Yes," she croaked.

"Are you all right?" He had expected her to be mad at him, and to be raving down the phone. But she sounded half asleep, and he sensed straightaway that something was wrong.

"Yes."

"You don't sound it."

She didn't answer.

"Are you still there?"

"Where were you?" she said, feeling the tears begin again. "Where were you?"

"I can explain. I'll come right over."

"No! No. Don't come now."

"What? What's going on over there? Are you all right?"

"Come later. Don't come now," and she hung up.

She let herself fall back onto the floor, and gazed up at the room around her. Flowers! So many flowers! Flowers from the rapist—the sodomite.

There were aspirin on the floor beside the settee, and an overturned glass beside them. She must have passed out before she'd been able to take enough of them, else she'd be dead now, and not having to suffer this terrifying, degrading memory.

From somewhere she managed to find a morsel of energy, and with difficulty pulled herself to her feet. The towel that was wrapped round her body fell to the floor, and she started to panic. She must cover herself. She was filthy, unclean, she must keep herself covered.

She rolled up some newspapers, put them in the hearth and lit them. One by one, she threw the flowers into the blaze. Then she went into her bedroom. The sight of her bed made her shrink back in terror. But she forced herself to take the sheets from it. She carried them into the sitting room, pulled open a drawer, and took out a pair of scissors. Slowly, laboriously, she cut the sheets to shreds. When that was done she put them on top of the fire, and then sat and watched them burn.

It did cross her mind to call the police, but what use would that do? He had done it now. He had violated her body, it was done. What good would the police do? Oh yes, they might stop him doing it again, if they caught him. But she didn't know who he was, not really. And she didn't want to find out, not ever. And what if it should get out? Did she really want people coming to the theater or the cinema to see "that actress who was raped"? People would look at her differently if they knew. She was unclean, tarnished. She had been raped.

Bob came straight round. She was in the tub again when he arrived. But he couldn't get in. The chain was on the door, and she wouldn't let him in. She made him go away, and promise not to come back until later. The way she felt now, she didn't ever want to see another man again as long as she lived. The very thought of one even coming near her made her skin crawl. She had to think. She must make her mind work. But it wouldn't so she gave up.

When Bob came back again he found the chain was off the door. The flat was so quiet he half suspected that she had gone out. But she was sitting beside the fire, staring into the ashes; she didn't even look up as he came into the room.

"Hello," he said, standing in the doorway.

She didn't answer.

He looked around the room, noticing that something was different. Then he realized that all the flowers had gone. He looked at her again, but she was staring into the middle distance and he could sense the tension in her body. "I can explain," he said, starting toward her.

"Can you?" she said, not looking up.

"The meeting went on longer than I expected."

"Did it?"

He knew that she didn't believe him. His face tightened, and he felt angry with himself. He should have known that we would have to tell her the truth. She wasn't stupid. She would know that if the meeting really had gone on, then he would have called her, and come home later. But he had never seen her like this before, and he was afraid of telling her what had really happened.

He went to sit in the chair opposite her, and she was glad that he hadn't tried to touch her. She didn't know how she would react. He leaned forward, resting his elbows on his knees, and tried to look into her face, but her hair was in the way, and she wouldn't look up. "I suppose I had better come clean."

"If you like."

"My wife was at the theater last night. I'm sorry," he rushed on, "I had no idea she was coming. She was there when I got back from the meeting with Adrian, so I had to take her away, before you came out of your dressing room."

He waited for her to say something, but she didn't. He watched her, and he wanted to reach out and touch her, but there was something about her that made him hold back.

"I've never seen your wife," she said eventually.

"No."

"What's she like?"

Bob didn't answer. He didn't know what to say. He wished she would get angry, shout at him, throw something at him even, anything would be better than this.

"I'm sorry," he said again. "Really, I'm sorry. I should have rung, I know I should, and I'm sorry. What else can I say?"

"It doesn't matter now."

He fell onto his knees beside her, and tried to take her hands.

She snatched them away. "Don't touch me!" The hatred and fear in her voice made him pull back. As she leapt to her feet, he saw the bruising on her face. "Don't touch me!" she cried. "Not ever again," and she ran out of the room.

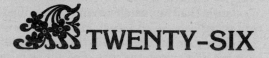

TWENTY-SIX

FOUR WEEKS LATER, AND STILL ELLAMARIE WAS UNABLE TO tell anyone what had happened. Instead she withdrew further and deeper into herself so that no matter how hard they tried, neither Jenneen nor Kate could get through to her. Two days after she had run out on him, Bob had flown to Rome to have talks with an Italian film company about the *Queen of Cornwall.* The meetings were taking longer than he had expected, and he still wasn't sure when he'd be back. His calls to Ellamarie were frequent, though brief—even at that long distance he could feel her withdrawing from him. But for the moment there was nothing else he could do. She had refused to fly out and join him.

Kate had rung Ashley, in the hope that she could reach Ellamarie, for some reason Ashley was the one Ellamarie had always seemed to listen to. But even Ashley had had no success; it wasn't easy on a long-distance telephone call, and Kate knew that it had been a vain hope anyway.

Ashley worried about it for days after, but then she had to push it from her mind and concentrate on what she was doing. Conrad Frazier was a hard task-master.

After yet another meeting with him she returned to her office in a blazing temper. He seemed hell bent on making her life as difficult as possible and each time she saw him she ended up leaving his office in a rage, which was only fueled by his undisguised amusement that he had managed to rattle her yet again. And no matter how hard she tried she could not stop herself rising to the bait.

Jan looked up as she stormed in. "Didn't go too well, huh?"

Ashley looked at her, but she was still too angry to speak. The telephone rang on Jan's desk, and Ashley turned away and swept into her office. She picked up the press proofs that had been left on her desk while she was away, and started to flick through them. It was difficult to concentrate, and when, several minutes later, the buzzer sounded on her phone, she was relieved to have an excuse to put them down again. Jan announced that there was a call for her from London.

Ashley looked at her watch. It would be almost ten at night in London now. "Put them on."

"Ash?" The voice at the other end sounded a long way away.

"Is that you, Ellamarie?"

"Yes," came the reply. "It's me."

"Oh Ellamarie, I'm sorry I haven't rung for so long, things have been so chaotic here. But how are you now? Are you better?"

"I'm OK. How are you?"

"Well, since you ask," said Ashley, "right now, I'm bloody livid. I've just had yet another encounter with Conrad Frazier."

"What happened?"

"I'll tell you some other time. But tell me about you. You sure you're all right? How's Bob? Is he back yet?"

"No, not yet."

Jan popped her head round the door, and Ashley looked up. "Hang on a mo," she said into the phone.

"You've been summoned again," said her secretary. "He wants you to join the meeting."

"He would," Ashley snapped. "Ok, I'll be right there," and she turned back to the phone.

"He said now," said Jan, looking apologetic.

Ashley rolled her eyes. "All right."

Jan closed the door again.

"I'm sorry, Ellamarie," said Ashley, "I'm going to have to ring off. Can I call you again later?"

"If you like."

Ashley was disturbed by the tone of Ellamarie's voice. "Look, this meeting shouldn't take too long, I'll call you in an hour, OK?"

"Sure."

"Where's Kate? Or Jenneen? Can you call them in the meantime?"

"No, it's all right, I'm fine. Honest." She hesitated. "Oh, Ash, I miss you so badly," and Ashley could tell that she was crying.

"Ellamarie, what is it? Please, tell me what's wrong."

"Ash, I've just got to speak to someone. Something terrible happened, and now . . ."

"What is it? Tell me. Surely it can't be that bad."

"It is," said Ellamarie. "Oh, it is."

"Then what is it?" Jan came back in again, and Ashley looked at her pleadingly, to go away. Jan shrugged, and shook her head. Conrad didn't like to be kept waiting.

Ellamarie was sobbing into the phone, and Ashley felt utterly helpless. "Look," she said. "I'm really sorry, Ellamarie, but I'm going to have to go. I'll call you the minute I can and we'll have a long chat."

"OK."

"Will you be there all night now?"

"Yes. I'm not going anywhere."

"I'll call as soon as I'm free," said Ashley, and she put the phone down.

Jan came in and thrust a set of files into her hands. "I think you'll need these."

Ashley didn't even say thank you. Her mind was back in London, wondering what on earth it was that had so upset Ellamarie. She scribbled down Kate's and Jenneen's telephone numbers and told Jan to get hold of them and tell them to ring Ellamarie. Then, riddled with guilt that she had had to desert her friend when she had finally decided she could talk to someone, she went to join Conrad in his office, burning with resentment.

After she put the phone down to Ashley, Ellamarie sat on the floor staring into space, trying not to think. It seemed hard to believe that a whole month had passed since that terrible night, when the man with the pale eyes had forced his way into her apartment; the pain, the humiliation, the sheer degradation lived with her constantly. It seemed that everything she did was done in a dream, that any moment she would wake up, and he would be there again, staring down into her face, with those hateful eyes, pressing a knife to her throat. Now, every man she saw reminded her of him, and she was becoming afraid to go out. If there was a knock on the door she would begin to shake, uncontrollably, and never, not even in daylight, would she answer it.

She had told no one, not even Kate or Jenneen. Tonight she would have told Ashley, but it was too late now, the moment had passed.

She was glad Bob wasn't there. She hated her body, and never looked at it. It was as if it no longer belonged to her; instead it belonged to the rapist. He had taken it and violated it, and by forcing himself on her he had stolen everything from her. Sometimes her skin burned with the memory of his vile hands upon her body, and it was at these times that she would break down, falling to the floor, and praying to God to release her from the torment of memory.

Pangs of hunger were gnawing at her insides, but she couldn't eat. She lifted her arm and pulled back her sleeve to stare at the faint scar left by the wound of his knife. It was all so horrible, and so unfair. Why did it have to happen then? Why did it have to happen at all? But then. Of all the times, why then? How was she ever to know the truth?

She pulled down her sleeve, and wrapped her arms round her knees. Suddenly she froze as she heard a noise out in the hall. The front door was closing, and then she heard a strange voice, and realized that it was hers, whimpering and sobbing. The door in front of her opened. It was Bob. She fell back against the chair behind her, burying her face in her knees. Bob crossed the room quickly, and tried to take her in his arms.

"No, no," she whispered, her voice hoarse. He struggled to keep hold of her, begging her to tell him what was wrong, but as he saw her begin to panic he let her go.

He looked down at her, feeling as helpless as he had done at the other end of the telephone. Finally he turned and walked over to the window. It was dark outside, so he pulled the curtains. He had been tempted not to come tonight. He was tired, his flight back from Rome had been delayed and Ellamarie hadn't been at the airport to meet him. In truth, he hadn't really been surprised when she wasn't there, but he'd been angry. He had hoped that by the time he got back to London she might have forgiven him for letting her down that night, but things were as bad now as before he'd left. He turned back to look at her. She was crying, and with her arms wrapped about her knees, she looked as if she was trying to protect herself. Her hair was a tangled mess, her fingers dirty. He noticed that she was thinner, and found himself wondering if she had stopped eating. Suddenly he was afraid. He was losing her, and he didn't know how to stop it.

He took a step toward her then stopped as he saw her draw back. For a moment his frustration made him angry again. What the hell did he have to do to get through to her? Perhaps he should leave, after all, there seemed no point in staying. She didn't want him here. But something deep inside told him that despite everything, she needed him. And when you loved someone as much as he loved her, you couldn't just walk out and leave them.

Quietly he crossed the room, and sat down on the floor beside her. She didn't move, but he could hear the tiny sobs catching in her throat. They sat, side by side, saying nothing, for a long time, until finally, very gently, he reached up and put his arm round her shoulders. Immediately he felt her stiffen, and he could tell she was holding her breath. He pulled the damp hair away from her face, but she didn't turn to look at him. But neither did she pull away, which is what he had expected.

The time passed, and still they sat there, saying nothing. He thought she had stopped crying. She was very still, and he could feel the tension in her body. He dared not move any closer for fear that she might push him away.

The phone rang several times, but she made no move to answer it, so neither did he. And then finally, when the clock had turned midnight, he started to get up, trying to pull her with him. She resisted, so he let her go. If he made some coffee, perhaps they could talk. A silly supposition, but he had to tell himself something.

He looked down at her. She was staring into the open hearth, her eyes inscrutable, her face white and drawn. He started to walk from the room.

"Bob," she whispered.

He turned back, but she was still staring into the

fireplace, and he wondered if he had only imagined her voice. Then she said his name again. He went back to her, and this time she looked up at him, and the despair and agony in her eyes moved him like he had never been moved before in his life.

"Bob," she said, and her face crumpled as she clutched him, burying her face in his legs, her body heaving with the abnormal strength of the sobs that shuddered through it.

Quickly he pulled her arms away, and knelt on the floor in front of her. He took her face in his hands, and very gently laid it on his shoulder. Then he held her tightly while she cried and cried, as if she would never stop. Gradually her arms began to go round him, until she was clinging to him so tightly he could barely breathe, and over and over again she said his name.

It was a long time before she was calm again. Then very gently he laid her on the settee. Her hands were like ice, and her whole body was shaking. He sat down beside her and taking her hands between his tried to warm them. She caught his hands to her face, and began to kiss them, with a desperation he had never witnessed in her before.

"Oh Bob, Bob, Bob. Don't ever leave. Please, don't ever leave me." She looked into his face. "Say it, please say it. Say you will never leave me."

"Oh my darling," he said, his voice catching in his throat. "Of course I will never leave you. Never. Not for a minute," and he held her in his arms, and rocked her like a baby.

"I'm sorry," she said, over and over. "I'm sorry. But please don't leave me."

"Sssh. I'm here now. I'm here."

She looked up into his face, and began to fumble with the collar of his shirt. "You do love me, don't you, Bob? Please say that you love me. Please."

"Darling, you know I do."

"Say it. Please say that you love me."

"I love you," he breathed. "Oh my darling, I love you."

She choked, burying her face in his neck again. "Please hold me. Hold me close."

He pulled her over so that she was almost sitting on him, and held her in his arms, gently kissing her hair. "I'm sorry I hurt you. I never wanted to hurt you. I'll never do it again, I swear."

"No," she said, her voice muffled. "No."

"No. I'll never do it again."

She pulled away, and looked into his face. Slowly at first, she began to shake her head, and then faster and faster. He caught her by the shoulders, and tried to steady her.

"You don't understand," she cried. "You don't know. It's not your fault. It's not you, Bob, it's me. It's me!"

"No. You've done nothing wrong. It was all my fault, and I'm sorry, my darling, I'm so very sorry," and he tried to take her in his arms again.

"Please, please listen to me. Nothing is your fault. Nothing. You must understand, it's me."

He looked at her, and realized that she was trying to tell him something. He reached up and stroked the hair from her face. "What is it? Tell me."

Her face began to tremble again, and he thought she was going to cry, but she didn't. Suddenly her breathing became labored, and she was fighting to gain her breath. It frightened him, and he sat her up, holding onto her. "What is it? Ellamarie, what is it?"

"Oh Bob," she gasped, "Bob. It's so awful. I can't talk about it. I can't say it," and her shoulders began to heave with the effort of catching her breath.

"Calm down, take it slowly. Take a deep breath," and he took deep breaths, trying to force her to do the same. She watched his face, and fought to steady herself, until she was a little calmer. Then she took his hand, and curled her fingers round his. She opened her mouth to speak, but he pressed his fingers against it.

"Don't say anything. Not until you're ready. It doesn't matter, I'm here, you'll be all right."

She pushed his hand away from her face, and shook her head. "I have to tell you. I have to tell you now. Please, promise me you will listen."

He nodded, and took both of her hands in his.

She looked up into his face, and tried to smile, but couldn't. Any minute now she would see him turn away from her in disgust, and she didn't know if she could bear it. His eyes were gentle, full of understanding, and she wondered how they would look after she told him. It was tearing her apart inside.

She swallowed hard, then took a deep breath. But she shook her head and looked away, she couldn't say it.

"It's all right, darling, it's all right."

"It was so terrible. I was so afraid."

"Why? What was?" he said, trying to soothe her with his voice. "Come on, take it slowly now."

"I can't, I can't."

"Then it doesn't matter," he said, trying to turn her to face him.

"I was raped!" she cried. "Bob, I was raped! Raped! Do you understand? Raped! Raped! Rape . . ."

"Stop it. Stop," and he caught her roughly in his arms. He pressed her face into his shoulder, not wanting her to see the look on his own. He gazed around the room, trying to take in what she had said and rocking her back and forth, trying not to choke on the murderous rage that was creeping in a strangling grip to his throat.

"When did it happen?" he eventually managed to ask her. "Tell me, when did it happen?"

"The night your wife came to the theater," she sobbed. "I was here on my own, and I thought it was you. I thought you'd forgotten your key. I let him in.

The door . . . I opened, and then I fell, and he had a knife, and I begged him. So dirty, so . . . Oh Bob, it was so terrible. Don't leave me, please don't leave me."

He squeezed her tight. "Sssh," he whispered, "I'm not going anywhere. I'll never leave you again. If I hadn't left you that night then this would never have happened. Oh Ellamarie, my darling, my love. What have I done to you? What have you been going through? Oh my darling, I'm sorry. I'm sorry."

"Just hold me, and don't ever let me go. Tell me you still love me, even now. Please, still love me."

"Oh darling, of course I still love you. Don't ever doubt it. I'll always love you."

"You won't," she cried, pulling away from him. "No, you won't. You can't."

"Don't be silly." He tried to pull her back into his arms. "Of course I will."

"You won't," she said. "You can't. I'm pregnant, Bob! Do you hear me? I'm pregnant!"

They sat up all that long night, holding one another, sometimes crying, sometimes talking, but neither of them slept. Together they tried to find an answer to the turmoil, and that night brought them closer than they had ever been before.

Day was breaking when finally Bob plucked up the courage to ask her the question he had been wanting to ask all night.

"Have you considered an abortion?" he said, very tentatively, remembering only too well what Kate had been through, and knowing that it would be uppermost in Ellamarie's mind too. "I don't know if it's the answer, but have you thought about it?"

She nodded. "Yes, I've thought about it." She looked down into her lap, and clutched her hands together tightly.

"Well?"

"I would, if I could be sure that the baby wasn't yours."

"But . . ."

"I know, I know," she said. "But I did a really silly thing. When Kate got pregnant I thought that, even though it wasn't the answer for her, that it might be for us. So I stopped taking the pill. Oh Bob, I know I shouldn't have done it, not without talking to you about it first, but I was afraid you would say no. And then I thought that if I was having a baby, that it would help you to make up your mind what you wanted to do. I only did it because I love you so much, and I couldn't bear to ever think of losing you, and I thought that perhaps it would make you love me more, and that you would leave your wife, and come to me. I know how that must sound, but I just had to do something. Things were so good between us, and I wanted you to know how much I cared—how much I really cared, and how much I wanted you. And now everything is a mess, and it's all my fault. But you see, because there is a chance that it might be your child, well, you must see . . ."

He took her face between his hands, and then, for the first time in over two months, he kissed her. Her lips were soft and warm beneath his, and the feeling of being close to her again was something he knew he never wanted to lose.

Finally he pulled away from her and looked into her eyes.

"I love you so much," she whispered. "And truly, I do think it's your baby. Truly I do Somehow I just know it."

"Of course it is," he said, "and we mustn't ever doubt it."

She lifted her mouth for him to kiss her again, and for the thousandth time she tried to tell herself that it really was his child she was carrying.

He cupped her face in his hands. "How about some

breakfast?" he smiled. Even if it was only a few minutes, he needed some time alone to think.

She nodded.

He told her to stay where she was, with her feet up, and try to rest. Later, he insisted, she would have to go to bed, and sleep, for the rest of the day.

She waited while he was in the kitchen, and although she was smiling, there was still trepidation in her heart. That he loved her, that he truly loved her, she was now in no doubt. But the baby, was it his? Please God, it had to be. But would he always look at it and wonder? Would he ever be able to truly accept it, like he had said he would? And what if, when it was born, it had those hideous pale eyes. Oh please God, no. She could never bear to live with those pale eyes, looking at her, watching her, every day. But she wouldn't have to. It was Bob's child she was carrying. Hers and Bob's, and it would have the beautiful sapphire blue eyes that belonged to him.

But what was he going to do? Would he really leave his wife? With a doubt as great as this in his heart, would he be able to leave his wife and come to her?

And suddenly she knew she couldn't let him. She couldn't do this to him.

He brought the breakfast in, and looking at him her heart contracted with love. There were dark shadows under his eyes, and the silver lines in his beard stood out more strongly than she had noticed before. When he looked at her he smiled, and she thought how very handsome he was when he smiled. And she thought, too, of how she was going to miss him. She was going to miss him so badly that she didn't know if she could bear it.

He put the tray on the table, and then pulled up a chair for her to sit down. "Every bit," he said. "Nothing left on the plate."

She stood up, but she didn't go to the table. Instead she walked to the window and pulled back the curtains.

When she turned back she saw that he was watching her, and she wondered what was going through his mind. She turned her head away, unable to meet his eyes.

"What is it?"

She tried to look up, but she couldn't. "Will you sit down? Please. There's something I want to say."

He pulled up a chair and sat beside the table.

She walked across the room and taking his hands she knelt at his feet. She saw the look of confusion in his eyes, and all she knew was that she didn't want to cause him any more pain.

She looked down at their hands. "Bob, I'm going to let you go."

"What do you mean?" he said, tilting her chin to make her look at him.

"I mean that I can't do it to you. I love you too much. And now that I know how much you love me, I just can't hurt you like this. You must go, Bob, we can't live a lie. You'll only end up hating me, and I just couldn't bear that."

He looked deep into her eyes. "Ellamarie, I could never hate you. I love you too much."

She tried to smile. "Not now, I know, but you will. You will feel trapped and resent me for it, and you'll be right to."

"Stop talking like that. I swore I would never leave you, and I meant it. I will never leave you again."

"I don't want you to go, you know I don't. But you must. In a day or two you'll see things more clearly, and you will know that I'm right. I promise you." Her mouth was quivering, but she was determined to hold onto the tears.

He ran his thumb across her lips and tried to pull her up, but she resisted. "No, Bob," she said. "No."

Suddenly his face was angry. "Stop pushing me away. I love you, can't you accept that? I love you and I am not going anywhere, no matter what you say."

She got up and walked across the room. "Please, don't argue any more."

And then he was beside her, turning her to look at him. "There's only one thing left to say, I want to marry you."

Her eyes rounded.

"Will you marry me?"

"But . . ."

"Yes or no."

She looked into his face for a long time, and he watched her eyes, searching to find the right way. And then at long last she began to smile, and he smiled too.

"Does that mean yes?"

"Yes," she whispered. "If you're sure, then yes, it means yes."

"I've never been more sure of anything," he said, and pulled her into his arms.

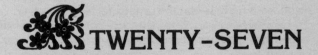 TWENTY-SEVEN

WITH A FILM EDITOR EITHER SIDE OF HER, JENNEEN TOOK the stairs two at a time. They laughed as they reached the top and stopped to catch their breath.

"What brings you here so late in the evening?" Richard puffed.

"Just wanted to pick up a few things," Jenneen answered.

"Bar's still open," said Gary. "Tell you what, I'll let you buy me a drink."

"Thanks for the honor."

"I'll buy," said Richard.

"Sorry, too much to do."

"You know what hard work did to Jack," said Gary.

"And I'm even duller," she said. "But seriously, I can't tonight. If you're around tomorrow lunchtime, I'll buy you both one then, does that suit?"

"Well, I suppose it'll have to do," said Gary. "Give us a kiss then before you go."

"Tomorrow," and she started to walk away.

Suddenly she was swept off her feet and they were carrying her toward the bar on their shoulders.

"Put me down," she laughed, but they walked right on into the bar, and dumped her in front of the counter.

"Two pints and a gin and tonic for the lady," said Richard.

"Honestly," said Jenneen. "Don't you ever take no for an answer? Just a quick one then, and I'll have to go."

As she looked around to see who was in there she noticed Stephen Sommers sitting in the corner with several researchers from the *Afternoon Program.* As their eyes met he gave her a sour look.

"See your fan club's in tonight," Gary remarked, as Jenneen turned back to the bar.

"He's bloody furious about your new program, you know," said Richard, perching on a stool beside her.

"You mean he knows about it?"

"Doesn't everyone?"

"Silly question. What did he say?"

"I'd rather not repeat it," said Richard, "but I'd watch him if I were you, he's got it in for you."

"Well, that's nothing new," said Jenneen. "Stephen Sommers has got it in for anyone female who has the audacity to be above the rank of secretary."

"True," said Gary.

They watched Stephen as he stuffed his cigarettes into his pocket, and left the bar. Jenneen shrugged, and raised her glass to the closed door.

When she had finished her drink Jenneen insisted that she really must go now. She went back along the corridor to the production office. The lights were still on when she got there, and looking at her watch she guessed that the late-night news team were probably using it for the last bulletin of the day, as it was nearer the presentation studio than their own.

Sure enough, as she rounded the filing cabinets, she saw a couple of journalists banging away on typewriters, and a secretary busy photocopying the scripts. She said hello to one of the journalists as he rushed out of the office, then walked on round the row of filing cabinets toward her desk. Suddenly she stopped. Someone she had not expected to see was Stephen Sommers.

Normally she would have ignored him, and not even bothered to wonder what he was doing there. But he was standing beside her desk, reading something that he had quite clearly taken from the drawer; he had left it open.

Luckily no one had noticed her come in, so she drew back behind the filing cabinets, and watched him for several minutes. It soon became evident from the way he was rummaging through the desk that he was looking for something in particular, and she wondered what it could be.

She didn't have to wait long. From the bottom drawer, where she kept everything to do with her new series, he pulled out the small buff file that she had come back for. Quickly he flicked through it, barely giving himself time to read it. Obviously satisfied that this was what he was looking for, he walked over to the photocopier, duplicated the whole file, then replaced the original in the drawer.

She continued to watch as he tucked his copy inside his jacket, and started to walk toward her. Quickly she stepped back into Bill's office behind her, and hid behind the door until he had passed.

When she was satisfied that he had gone, she walked over to her desk, and took out the file from the bottom drawer. What possible use could that file be to him? OK, she had never discussed the project in the office, but there was nothing to hide. The company had given the go-ahead for the pilot, and he only had to read the studio schedules to see that it was down for recording in two weeks' time.

She shrugged. Well, if he was so fascinated by her and what she was doing, then good luck to him. Just to know what the idea was would do him no good that she could see, unless it was merely to satisfy his curiosity.

But in the following week or so, she couldn't shake it from her mind. She had a nagging feeling that there was perhaps more to this than she realized.

Nick was quite taken aback when Kate threw open the door. Her face was covered in smiles, and she was almost jumping up and down with excitement.

"Have you heard?" she said, pulling him inside. "Have you heard?"

"Heard what?"

"About Ellamarie and Bob?"

"What about Ellamarie and Bob."

"They're getting married."

"They're what!" Nick gasped.

"Getting married."

"But how? I mean when? I mean, well, how can they?"

"I don't know," said Kate, "but they are. Isn't it simply marvelous! Come on, I've got some champagne. Let's celebrate!" and she skipped off into the kitchen.

Nick laughed. "You've got champagne? But it's them who are getting married."

"What difference does that make? We can still celebrate, can't we?"

He shrugged. "Sure, why not?"

"Will you pop the cork?"

He took the bottle from her, and she stood at the ready with two glasses. He filled them up, and they drank a toast to Ellamarie and Bob.

"Mmm, good stuff," he said. "And now, how about a toast to you?"

"To me?"

"Yes. I've been reading the first chapters of your book today, and I think we've got something to celebrate."

"Do you really? Did you like it? Be honest with me, Nick, did you really like it?"

"Yes, I did. Don't look so surprised, it's good."

"But were there any bits you didn't like? You can be brutally honest, I won't mind."

He opened his mouth to speak.

"Well, not too brutal," she said.

He smiled. "There is one thing I'm unsure of."

"Oh," said Kate, unable to hide her disappointment. "What's that?"

"Exactly when it's supposed to be taking place."

"In the seventies," she said, as if it were obvious.

"But you haven't said that."

"Do I need to?"

"Well, I'm no expert, but I'd have thought so, yes."

"I'll look at it," she said. "Come on, let's go and sit down."

He followed her into the lounge, and took up his usual chair beside the fire. July it might be, but there was still no real sign of summer yet; in fact it was damned cold outside tonight.

"So," he said. "Has Bob told his wife yet?"

"I presume so. I didn't ask. It was just so good to hear Ellamarie back in spirits again."

"Mmm," Nick sipped his champagne. "Did you ever find out what it was, you know, why she was like she was?"

"No, she didn't say. But whatever it was, well, I don't suppose it matters now really, does it? As long as she's all right now. I mean, we all get down sometimes, even Ellamarie."

"I suppose we do."

"Did you find out today when the real reading for the *Queen of Cornwall* is happening?"

"Nope," said Nick. "Couldn't get hold of Bob. Don't know why I didn't think to try Ellamarie's. Still, under the circumstances it's probably just as well I didn't. When did they decide?"

"Yesterday, she called me this morning."

"Have you ever met his wife?"

"No, never. Have you?"

"No, I haven't actually met her, but I've seen her."

"Really?" said Kate. "What's she like?"

"Well, it was quite some time ago now, and I didn't get a very good look, but from what I saw I'd say she's probably about the same age as Bob, and about the same height. She's dark, and rather more glamorous than I'd have expected."

"I always imagined, from the things Ellamarie's told me, that she would be sort of quite mousey and plain."

"I must admit I thought she would be too, but she's certainly not plain. But I only caught a glimpse."

At that moment the phone rang, and Kate got up to answer it. From the warmth in her voice Nick guessed that it was her father on the other end, so he went back to the kitchen to fetch the champagne. When he came back again she was still on the phone, so he sat down, feeling uncomfortable. He always hated it when people were on the phone and he was a visitor in their home. It made him feel like he was eavesdropping.

Kate seemed to sense it, and said: "I'll have to go now, Daddy, I've got a friend here."

Nick felt a twinge of annoyance that she hadn't said who.

"Well, before you ring off," said her father, "tell me, how's the book coming along. Well?"

"Yes, it's coming along fine I think," and she winked at Nick.

"Jenneen's with you, is she?"

"No, she's coming around later. Nick's here at the moment."

She heard her father sigh on the other end. "Is he still pestering you?"

Kate turned the phone into the wall. "Not at all."

"Darling, he's an actor, for goodness' sake. What on earth do you see in him?"

"It's not like that," she answered, trying to keep her voice low, thankful that Nick couldn't hear what her father was saying.

"Well, I'm glad to hear it. So why don't you tell him straight that you don't want to see him again. He's always round there these days, it must be driving you mad."

"It's not, and I won't."

"Don't be angry. I'm only trying to make you see sense. All you need right now is to get on with your novel, and you'll never do it with him hanging round you."

"Look, I'll call you later."

"I'm going out," said her father. "Call me in the morning. And try and get rid of that moron."

"No!" she said. "I won't, and don't say things like that again."

"You're not falling for him, are you?"

"No. Yes, actually, I am."

"I thought you might have learned your lesson by now, Katherine."

"What do you mean?"

"Darling, I'm only trying to save you from being hurt again. We don't want a repeat of the Joel Martin affair, now do we?"

Kate flushed. "Don't ever mention that again. I don't ever want to talk about it, and I don't ever want you to talk about it either. And what's more, I'll do as I please, so stop interfering. I'll call you tomorrow," and she hung up.

"I'm sorry about that," she said to Nick, "but sometimes fathers can be so blasted infuriating."

"I won't ask what it was all about, I think I can guess. But tell me, who's coming round later?"

Kate frowned.

"You said on the phone that she'll be coming round later."

"Oh, yes. Jenneen. She's calling in for a drink, and perhaps something to eat. She wants me to look over the first draft script that she's done for her new series."

"Oh no, does that mean takeaways again?"

" 'Fraid so. But cheer up, I'll cook you a nice dinner on Saturday night. How does that sound?"

He raised his glass to her.

"I've got another treat. I've been to Cliveden House today, researching for the series of articles I'm doing on stately homes that don't belong to the National Trust."

"But I thought Cliveden did belong to the National Trust," said Nick.

"They've leased it to Blakeney Hotels, don't you remember? I told you, it's a hotel now. Just wait till you see it."

"Oh, I'm going to see it, am I? When?"

"Sunday. We're going down for the day. I fell in love with it when I was there today, and I know you will too. So we'll make a whole day of it next Sunday.

Let's just hope the weather cheers up. Ah, that'll be Jenneen," she said, as the buzzer on the intercom sounded.

Jenneen came in, carrying more champagne, and laughed when she saw the half full one on the coffee table. "Looks like we all had the same idea." She took the glass that Nick was offering her. "Well, here's to the happy couple. Have you seen either of them yet?"

Kate shook her head, and put down her glass. "No. Have you?"

"No, but being love's young dream, I don't suppose they really want to see anyone just yet. Has he told his wife, do you know?"

"Don't think he's had a chance yet," said Kate.

"Wonder how she'll take it."

"Well, I don't think they're very close, are they? Haven't been for some time. Probably won't come as a surprise. Might even come as a relief."

"I wouldn't go quite that far," said Nick. "Breaking up is never easy, even if you don't love someone any more."

"No, I suppose it's not," said Kate. "Well, why don't we drink to Linda as well. That she can find happiness too."

So they drank Linda's health, and then settled down to go over Jenneen's script.

About eight o'clock Nick went out for Chinese, and by nine-thirty they were well fed and quite merry.

"So," said Jenneen, leaning back in her chair, and closing the script. "You think it's good?"

"Excellent," said Kate. "Just those few alterations, and check on whether or not you can actually mention those couple of things in the closing link, and you're home and dry. It's a winner!"

"What do you think, Nick?"

"Same as Kate. There are several critics, not to mention directors, I'd like to see in the hot seat. What time of night will it be going out?"

Jenneen shrugged. "It doesn't have a slot yet. But it will be quite late, I think. Around elevenish."

"Shame," said Nick. "Still, once it's been running a while, they might give it an earlier slot."

"Might," said Jenneen, "one can only hope."

The phone rang and Jenneen looked at her watch. "Great! That's probably Ashley. I left a message with her service, telling her to ring us here tonight."

"Hello," she said, lifting the receiver. "Hello," she said again. She waited, but there was no reply. She looked at the others and shrugged. "No one there." The line crackled. "Hello," she shouted. "Ashley, is that you?" Still there was no answer. She put the phone down. "Probably a bad connection."

After a couple of minutes the phone rang again, and this time Kate answered it. "Hello, Ash!"

"Hello," said a muffled voice, quite clearly not Ashley's.

"Hello? Who is it?"

"Kate," said the voice. "Hello, Kate."

Kate frowned, and some of the color left her face. She turned to look at Nick.

Quickly he jumped to his feet. "Is it him again?"

"Who?" said Jenneen, bewildered.

"I think so," Kate whispered, handing Nick the receiver.

Nick put the phone to his ear and listened. A few seconds later the line went dead, but he heard all he needed to hear. He could feel both Kate's and Jenneen's eyes on him, waiting for him to speak. He turned away, closing his eyes against the feeling of nausea the voice had left him with.

Kate's face was taut. "It was him, wasn't it?"

"Who?" said Jenneen.

Nick looked round.

"What did he say?"

"What's going on?" said Jenneen. "Who is it?"

Nick looked at her, then avoiding Kate's eyes he started to leave the room. "I'll get some more wine," he said.

TWENTY-EIGHT

"So," said Conrad, leaning back in his chair and indicating that he was bringing the meeting to a close, "I want every effort put into this. As you already know, it's an account that used to belong to this shop, and I want it back again. I've every confidence in you, but it's going to be a tough one. Practically every other agency in town will be making a pitch, so it's up to you to make sure it comes our way. I want round-the-clock effort, no excuses, and every ounce of talent in your pretty little heads working toward it. You don't need me to tell you how many millions are at stake, and I want them." He looked at Ashley. "Candice will give you the available figures as you leave," Ashley nodded and Conrad continued: "They will impress upon you how serious I am about getting Mercer Burgess Insurance back at Frazier, Nelmes, if I haven't done so sufficiently already. As soon as anyone feels they're onto something, and I expect that to be within the next forty-eight hours, then bring it to me. I shall be taking a personal interest in this one, and if I'm not here, then Candice will know where to reach me. So as I said, it's up to you now, go to it!" and he smiled.

Bill Fownest, the President of Frazier, Nelmes,

New York, stood up and catching Ashley's eye winked at her. He loved it when the agency was involved in a pitch of this stature. It made his blood race, and gave him a greater high than anything else—with perhaps one, maybe two exceptions. He watched Ashley as she gathered up her papers. If he wasn't greatly mistaken then she was already accumulating and discarding ideas in that brain of hers, and he'd wager she was looking forward to this as much as he was. He had heard how it was largely down to her that Frazier, Nelmes in London had clinched the lucrative Newslink account, and he was interested to see what she would come up with this time. She had a good creative team under her here in New York, and in the short time she had been here she had already earned a healthy respect from them, and, indeed, the twenty or so other Exec VPs in the company. Shame she didn't get along so well with Conrad, but it didn't seem to bother her any, so what the hell.

"Ashley!" Conrad was standing behind his desk.

She stopped at the door and turned back. So did a couple of the others, though from the look on Conrad's face they could see that whatever he had to say to Ashley, it was no concern of theirs. Quickly they left the room.

Conrad picked up his pen and began to write something on he pad in front of him. He looked up, and again she had that feeling that he was sizing her up.

"This is the biggest challenge you have had since you've been in New York," he began, "so I thought you might be wondering why I have assigned this particular pitch to you."

Like hell she was wondering, hadn't she been busting a gut, as Jan put it, to try and make sure this one came her way? She waited for him to go on.

"I don't want to have to spell it out," he said, and she wished his face was a little less grim. "I think you are already well aware of the importance of winning, and although your track record in London speaks for itself, I want you to remember that you're in New York now, where standards are high, and those that don't rise to them go. We can't afford to lose this one and it would be as well for you if we didn't."

She looked into his face, dark and serious, watching her with his eyebrows half raised, almost as if he had asked her a question. She understood exactly what he was saying, and hated him for it. "I think you've made yourself perfectly clear, Conrad."

His eyes were piercing as he looked back at her. "Yes, I hope I have," and he picked up the telephone.

"Is that all?"

"For now."

She turned to go.

"Oh, one thing," he said, as she was opening the door, "I'll pick you up at seven tonight. We're going to the opera."

She opened her mouth to speak.

"That's all. Just be sure you're ready on time. Candice, get Bill Fownest back in here will you?" he added into the phone.

Jan was waiting for her when she returned to her own office. "Anything you need before I go?"

Ashley shook her head. "Apart from a brilliant idea, no."

"Can't help you there, I'm afraid," Jan laughed as she began to pack away her things. "I take it we were right, it was Mercer Burgess?"

"Yes, Mercer Burgess. And, if I'm not greatly mistaken, my career."

"Excuse me?" said Jan, stopping what she was doing.

Ashley looked up, surprised to find that she had voiced her thoughts aloud. "Oh, nothing," she said, "nothing. Did you remember to send the date plan to Jill Robertson?"

"Done. Oh, and I've been down to Research and picked up the old Mercer Burgess files from the last time we ran their campaign, and I got them to dig out anything else they had on insurance. And Maggie brought in the feasibility study you asked for. They're all on your desk."

"How would I manage without you?" Ashley smiled. "Now off you go, or you'll be late."

"Thanks," said Jan, with evident relief.

"Have a good time," Ashley added. Jan's son was opening on Broadway tonight. Only a small part in the chorus of *Cats,* but nevertheless, it was Broadway, and it was *Cats.*

Ashley walked into her own office. It was five-thirty now, time enough to get a good three hours in before she went home. She picked up the old Mercer Burgess files and started to flick through them. But Conrad's words kept ringing in her head, she couldn't get them out of her mind. She knew she had understood him correctly, but still she didn't want to believe that her future here in New York was now hanging on whether or not she clinched the Mercer Burgess account. If she failed, then Conrad would send her back to London. But that was preposterous, he couldn't do it. She gave a dry laugh. Oh yes, he could do it, and what's more he would. It made her uncomfortable, knowing that he disliked her presence here so intensely, and she resented his holding a Sword of Damocles over her head. But she was getting to know him a little better now, and one thing she had quickly realized was that Conrad Frazier liked to make his own decisions, he did not take kindly to having them made for him. And in this instance it had been her who had made the decision to join his agency in New York, not him. And now he was telling her that either she proved herself, or she was out.

But then he had invited her to the opera. Obviously it wasn't enough for him to push and bully her around during the day, he was now laying claim to her private life too. Well, he could just damn well go to hell! If he wanted to go to the opera, he would be going alone.

She opened a drawer to take out her notebook. As she took it out a card fell to the floor and she stopped to pick it up.

Her face softened as she read it. It was from Julian, wishing her good luck in her new life. It had been a generous gesture on his part, and she hoped that he would find in the end that he had made the right decision in marrying Blanche. These past two months in New York had already confirmed to her that she had done the right thing in coming.

She put the card on her desk, and stared at it. Julian. Conrad. Julian and Conrad. They were so different. Conrad was ruthless where Julian was considerate, and she was uneasy at having to pit her wits against him, or more correctly in this instance, for him, in order to survive.

He was an irritatingly confusing person, she decided, and an extremely dislikable one too. But during the meeting earlier, she had found herself watching him with interest, and had once or twice been guilty of a lapse of concentration. Despite her feelings toward him, she couldn't help wondering what he was *really* like—as a man. She was only too aware of what he was like as an employer, though grudgingly she had to admit that she did respect him. But what did he do when he wasn't Conrad Frazier, Chairman of Frazier, Nelmes, New York? Without a doubt he must be one of the more eligible men in town, though she had never heard mention of a woman. And he was extremely good-looking, too good-looking in fact, Ashley thought. He knew it of course, and more than once she had seen him play on it where the wives of clients were concerned. But somehow, she sensed, behind his charm he was either bored or irritated by these women, almost as if he saw it as a weakness in them that they could be so easily flattered.

Abruptly she pulled herself together. There was nothing to be gained from pondering over Conrad Frazier. She looked down at the files in front of her and felt a pang of nerves. For this campaign she would be pitting her brains against those of the most successful commercial people in the world. But everybody had to start somewhere, and she was only just beginning. Her ideas would be newer, fresher, and more ambitious. She would start by calling up Arthur Fellowman, the President of Mercer Burgess. She would have to persuade him into increasing his budget to at least twice what it already was. It was only a seed of an idea that she had been working on so far, but already it was beginning to grow, and by the time she left tonight she should have something that would convince him that he would be doing the right thing in considering the astronomical budget she needed for the high profile campaign she wanted to run.

She picked up her pen and began to write, a tiny smile of defiance on her lips. If anyone was going to decide whether or not she stayed in New York, it would be her, and Conrad Frazier and his veiled threats could go to hell.

At six-thirty she stopped writing and looked at her watch. She felt a strange stirring sensation creep through her bones. It was giving her pleasure to think of standing up Conrad Frazier. He'd be furious, and the very idea of making Conrad Frazier furious gave her an extremely smug feeling of satisfaction. She'd wanted to get her own back on him for so many things, and for so long; and now at last was her opportunity. It would teach him a lesson. Next time he wanted to ask her on a date perhaps he would make an attempt to be a little more civil in the asking. Her only regret was that she would not be there to see the look on his face when he found she wasn't at home. She shrugged, and then picking up her pen carried on with what she had been doing.

It was ten minutes past seven when the door of her office flew open and Conrad stalked across the room to her desk. His eyes were blazing and his face was dark with rage. Ashley felt herself shrink back.

"What the hell are you doing here?"

"I'm getting . . ."

"I don't give a damn what you're doing here!" he continued, through clenched teeth. "When I tell you to be ready at seven, I expect you to be there. Just what the hell do you think you're playing at? This isn't a game, you know. And I won't have one of my staff trying to make a fool out of me. Now get to your feet," and he caught her by the arm, and pulled her out of her chair.

Her notebook and pen fell to the floor, and so did the card. She bent to pick them up, but the card had floated to his feet and before she could reach out for it, he picked it up. It had fallen open, and he couldn't have failed to recognize the handwriting inside. As he handed it to her she didn't miss the look of scorn that shot through his eyes. She looked away again.

"Get your things."

"Now just a minute . . ."

"Shut up," he snapped, swinging round to face her. "Get whatever you need, you'll have to go as you are," and he started to walk toward the door.

"I'm not going anywhere, with you or with anyone else. If you want me to go to the opera with you then you can damn well ask with a civil tongue in your head. But don't bother, I'll save you the trouble. The answer is no! I don't want to go to the opera. And I won't have anyone pushing me around like this, least of all you!"

He turned back to her, and to her astonishment and fury she could see that though the anger had not disappeared entirely from his eyes, he was laughing.

"Nice show," he said. "But you flatter yourself. I

am taking clients to the opera tonight. Clients of yours, actually, that you should get to know." He looked at his watch. "I've got a taxi waiting downstairs, you've got two minutes," and he stalked out of the room.

Ashley was glad that he didn't look back. She was smarting with humiliation. Still, there was nothing for it but to pick up her bag and follow him down to the street.

The door of the taxi was open so she slipped in beside him, and kept her face averted. This was the most ridiculous position to be in and she had brought it upon herself. She didn't even know who the clients were. She wasn't going to ask. Let him tell her. And her hair was a mess, she wasn't dressed for the opera, and she wanted to freshen her makeup. Damn him! Damn him!

"Ashley," he said, interrupting her silent onslaught.

She turned to glare at him.

"Shut up!" he said, quite calmly.

She gasped. "But I haven't said anything."

"You don't have to. Now calm down. If anyone should be angry around here it's me. And I am, but I'm managing to keep myself under control. Try and do the same."

Ashley sat looking straight ahead, her mouth opening and closing like a flustered goldfish, unable to think of a thing to say.

Neither of them spoke again until they arrived at Lincoln Center. Conrad paid the fare, then turned and strode purposefully through the crowds, toward the Metropolitan Opera House. Ashley had to all but run to keep up with him.

They met up with Mr. and Mrs. Halworth, of Halworth Foods, in the lobby, and Ashley didn't miss the sweeping look Mrs. Halworth gave her inappropriate dress. Ashley tried to smile, and felt even more foolish.

She suffered, rather than enjoyed, *Russalka*, an

opera that had never been a favourite of hers, and she was glad when it was over.

Now what? She didn't have to wait long to find out. A black limousine which looked as though it had spent many tortuous hours on a rack was waiting for them outside, and they were swept off into the hot, sticky night, to the Twenty-One Club.

Ashley tried hard throughout dinner to make polite conversation with Mrs. Halworth, but it was plain to see that Mrs. Halworth was only interested in Conrad. And, if Ashley wasn't greatly mistaken, her interest would need little persuasion to extend beyond the restrictions of a business dinner. Ashley eyed her with distaste.

During the course of the dinner she noticed several women looking in Conrad's direction, and every now and again he would lift an eyebrow in acknowledgment of their looks. She wondered if he knew them, and felt inexplicably annoyed with him.

She wasn't too sure when it was that she first began to realize that Mr. Halworth assumed she was Conrad's wife, and when she did she found it so incredible it left her speechless. Surely Conrad must have told him who she was. But the introductions had been so brief that she had to struggle to try and remember exactly what it was Conrad had said. To her annoyance she couldn't. But why didn't Conrad put him right? Maybe he hadn't noticed. She glanced at him from the corner of her eye, but his face told her nothing. She looked back to Mr. Halworth who winked at her. She felt herself blush, then realized, with horror, that he probably thought that she and Conrad had had some kind of domestic fight before they'd come out this evening. She had to admit that he had good cause to think it, it was exactly how they were behaving.

With relief Ashley saw the coffee being brought. She couldn't wait to get home now.

Mr. Halworth ordered brandy, which Ashley refused and the others accepted, then he sat back in his seat and openly regarded both her and Conrad.

Ashley lowered her eyes under such severe scrutiny, and began to twist the wedding ring she still wore on her third finger. But her head soon snapped up again when Mr. Halworth said: "I had heard you were getting married, Conrad. Didn't know you'd already gone and done it. When was the big day?" He didn't add that he had thought that Conrad was marrying one of America's most celebrated models, Candida Rayne.

Ashley turned to Conrad, expecting him to lose no time in putting Mr. Halworth straight. But his dark eyes were dancing, and it was quite plain to see that he was going to say nothing. His smile widened a fraction as he saw her eyes narrow. He lifted the brandy to his mouth, and she thought she saw him salute her with it. Right, she thought, he's asked for it this time.

She turned away from him, aware of Mrs. Halworth's curious eyes upon her. Throwing Mr. Halworth a dazzling smile she said: "Just a couple of weeks ago, actually." She didn't look at Conrad, but in a conspiratorial manner she leaned toward the older man. "I'll let you into a little secret," she whispered, trying to hide a smile as Mrs. Halworth leaned forward so that she could hear. "We're expecting our first baby at Christmas."

Conrad choked, and sat up abruptly as he spilled brandy over his shirt front. Ashley threw him an indulgent smile, and said, "Oh darling, you really should be more careful," and she leaned over and began to mop him up. "Get out of that one," she hissed in his ear.

Mr. Halworth was laughing, and calling for the waiter to bring more brandy. "Why didn't you say something earlier?" he cried. "We could have cracked open the champagne."

"You've been married a couple of weeks, you say," said Mrs. Halworth, who, just as Ashley had intended, had taken no time at all in working out the dates. "How very, nice."

Ashley took Conrad's arm. "Oh, it is, isn't it, Connie darling?" and she had the immense satisfaction of feeling him tense.

"Tell me," said Mrs. Halworth to Ashley, "will you be giving up your job? When the baby arrives."

"Oh I'm sure I will. In fact, Connie insists, don't you, darling?"

"How sweet!" said Mrs. Halworth. She turned to her husband. "Don't you think it's sweet?"

"Sure do," he said, beaming all over his face.

"Excuse me," said Mrs. Halworth. "I think I need the ladies' room."

Conrad and Mr. Halworth both got to their feet as Mrs. Halworth stood up.

Ashley was steeling herself, waiting for some sort of reaction from Conrad. She allowed herself a quick look in his direction, but his face was inscrutable as he reached for his brandy. "I'll have my secretary call yours tomorrow," he said to Mr. Halworth, "I'd like to get a meeting in before the end of the month. When do you go away?"

Mr. Halworth chuckled at the abruptness of the change of subject and turned away from Ashley. "Mid-October. Sure, that'll be fine. By the end of the month. Have you contacted anyone else yet?"

"Not yet, but I will. We've got a match at the weekend."

"Yeah, sorry I can't make it. You playing?"

"Yes."

It was some time before Ashley realized that they were discussing polo.

Mrs. Halworth came back, and Conrad said that it was about time they were leaving. He handed Ashley her bag, and avoided her eyes. She was beginning to feel a little nervous.

When they were outside, Mr. Halworth tried to insist that they ride home in the limousine, but Conrad was firm. "We don't have far to go," and added without a glance in Ashley's direction, "Ashley enjoys the night air."

They waved the Halworths off, and when the limousine had turned the corner, Conrad hailed a taxi.

He waited for it to draw alongside, then pulling open the door he turned to let her in. But she was gone. He looked around, and saw her marching off down the street.

"Wait here," he told the driver, and leaving the door open, he went after her.

"Let go of me," she said, as he caught her by the arm.

"Don't be childish," he snapped. "And in case you hadn't noticed, you're walking in the wrong direction."

She turned to face him, her eyes flashing. "I fail to see what it has to do with you which direction I walk in. Now let me go."

"Get into the taxi," he growled. "I want to speak to you."

"I won't! I'll call my own taxi."

His voice was dangerously low. "Get into the taxi, or I'll pick you up and put you in it."

"Stop behaving like a second-rate movie star," she seethed. "If I . . ."

Before she could say another word, he had lifted her from the ground and was marching back to the taxi. He dumped her inside and climbed in beside her. The driver chuckled, and drove off.

"Madison and Seventy-fifth, the Montclair," said Conrad, then sat back in his seat and looked out of the window.

"That's where I live," said Ashley.

"You want to go home, don't you?" he barked.

They said no more until they reached her apartment block. He got out of the taxi and walked round to open the door for her. She could see that he was still furious.

"I think you got the meaning of what I was saying in my office earlier," he said, as she started to get out, "so maybe you'd better wake up to the fact that you're in the real world now. And while you're about it, you can start thinking of an explanation for your inexcusable manners toward the Halworths this evening." He got back into the taxi. "I will see you in my office tomorrow afternoon, by which time I will expect you to have rung Halworth and apologized for the lies you told this evening. Good night!"

She had no opportunity to reply, he had pulled the door closed. The taxi drove off, and she stood in the street, watching it, until it had disappeared.

Suddenly she began to cry with rage. Of all the stupid, idiotic and senseless things to have done. Instead of getting her own back, she had only succeeded in making a complete fool of herself, and throwing her position into even greater jeopardy than it already was.

She turned to her door, and for the first time since she had been in New York, she felt truly homesick.

The following morning Ashley called Mr. Halworth at his office on Lexington and made her apologies. She had been up most of the night thinking about what she could say. In the end she had decided that there was nothing for it but to come clean and own up to her petty attempt at revenge.

Mr. Halworth laughed loudly when she finished her explanation, and told her that he guessed Conrad had had it coming to him, and that he was only sorry for her sake, that her boss had had the last word.

By the time their conversation was at an end, Ashley and Mr. Halworth were firm friends, and he invited her to join him for lunch the following week. That would certainly be one in the eye for Conrad. But Mr. Halworth's parting words were disconcerting.

"Just one thing before you go," he chuckled, "if you two really do decide to tie the knot, don't forget to invite me to the wedding," and he hung up before she had time to answer.

She was sorely tempted to ring him back and put him straight, but she didn't.

The rest of the day was taken up with planning meetings for the Mercer Burgess campaign. The rest of her team entered wholeheartedly into her scheme, though there were one or two who were a little hesitant about the size of it. She didn't worry too much about that; once she had persuaded the President of Mercer Burgess that she was right, she knew she would have everyone behind her. Arthur Fellowman agreed to see her later that afternoon, so she had to get to work on the formula she wanted to propose. She made no attempt to see Conrad and he didn't send for her. She saw him as he was leaving the building at about three o'clock, but thankfully he didn't see her.

There was no doubt that Arthur Fellowman was impressed by her proposals. He called in his marketing people and the meeting went on much longer than she had anticipated, breaking up at six-thirty with an agreement to call Ashley the following morning. Meanwhile, Arthur told her to go ahead with the idea, in theory, and see what else she could come up with.

Her team were already doing that. It had shaken her confidence a little when Arthur told her as she was leaving that they had already seen someone from another agency that morning, though he wouldn't name names. And that what they were proposing was also extremely attractive, and not half so costly.

"I just want to make you aware of it," he said as they walked together to the elevator, "because a budget the size you are asking for, not to mention what you're asking us to give over and above that, is not going to be easy to get through the board."

She had thanked him for being honest with her.

"Our board is no different to any other," he said. "Never want to part with any money, but when they do, the less the better. But for what it's worth, I think your idea could be a winner, provided the casting is right. Though, sadly for you, so could the other one. And no doubt there will be many more coming my way in the next few days. But anyway, best of luck, eh?"

She fought against being disheartened as she went back to Frazier, Nelmes. Her idea would be the best, it had to be. But the best always costs more, and Mercer Burgess would just have to be persuaded round to seeing it that way.

By seven-thirty there was very little more she could do at the office. She had agreed to go to the cinema with Candice, and she welcomed the distraction. She still needed to see the producer, but Gemma was out on a recent already, searching the downtown areas for possible locations. Jan told her that Gemma would be back around ten, so with the art directors and copy writers assuring her that they were quite capable of making their own coffee and giving one another moral support she left with Candice, saying she would be back after the film.

"You know, one of these days," Candice said, as they paid for their tickets for *Mona Lisa*, "I'm going to get over to London."

"Yes, you must, you'll love it," said Ashley. "But let me know when you do, I've some very good friends there who will be only too glad to take care of you, show you around."

"You're on." Candice looked up at the clock on the wall. "Why don't we have a drink before we go in, we're early yet."

Ashley ordered two glasses of wine from the bar, and they sat down at a corner table.

"What time are your folks arriving tomorrow?"

"Oh God, I'd almost forgotten," said Ashley. "What a time to arrive."

Candice chuckled in sympathy. "Are they bringing your little boy with them?"

"Are you kidding?" said Ashley. "Alex wouldn't miss an adventure to New York!"

Candice laughed. "I wish you could see your face right now," she said, a little wistfully.

"Why?"

"Because you have the look of a woman in love."

"I seem to remember someone else saying that to me once," said Ashley, "about Alex. I can't wait to see him. He'll be eight next week, while he's here, so I've got to think of something special for him to do."

"And do I get to meet him at all?"

"Of course. He's determined to come into the office one day, but I'd better make it a day when Conrad's not about. Don't think he'd approve, somehow. But you must come to dinner one night as well, and meet my parents."

"Thanks," said Candice, and she picked up her wine. "How's the research coming along for Mercer Burgess?"

"Not so bad. It won't be easy, but I think we're in with a chance."

"Anything for Conrad yet?"

"No."

"That sounded rather final."

"I don't think I've got anything he'd be particularly interested in yet."

Candice laughed to herself, and watched Ashley's face. "You sure as hell don't like him much, do you?"

"No."

"But why?"

"If you've got an hour, I'll tell you," said Ashley. "Pity really."

"What's a pity?"

"That you don't like him."

"Well, the feeling's mutual, in case you hadn't noticed."

Candice merely smiled at that.

"Are you, you know, seeing him?" said Ashley, and immediately blushed. She was becoming quite American with her direct questions, but they still embarrassed her.

"Me! Good God, no."

"But I thought . . ."

"You thought that I was crazy about him?"

"Well, yes."

"I was, once. A long time ago. But he's never really been interested in me. Now, well, I just love him for being him."

Ashley shook her head. "It's beyond me how anyone can love him, just for being him."

Candice chuckled. "He's not so bad, you know."

"That's a matter of opinion," Ashley retorted, and picked up her wine. "I saw him leaving early this afternoon."

"Went to pick up his sister and her kids to bring them to town for the week. Her husband's gone away and she fancied doing a bit of shopping."

"Oh?"

They both looked up as a crowd of teenagers came into the bar, laughing and falling over one another.

"Oh no," Candice groaned. "I hope they're not going to be sitting anywhere near us."

"Does Conrad have a girlfriend?"

Candice looked at her, and grinned. "You're mighty interested in Conrad Frazier, for someone who can't stand the sight of him."

"Not really. I only wondered."

Candice pondered the question for a minute or two. "Does Conrad have a girlfriend?" she repeated, finally, and looked at Ashley again.

"You're making it all sound very mysterious," said Ashley, beginning to regret asking.

"Well, it is mysterious. In a way."

"Well, surely either he does or he doesn't."

"Let's just say, he has someone in mind."

"Anyone I know?"

Candice nodded, but didn't enlarge.

"Well?" Ashley persisted, "Are you going to tell me?" She didn't know what she was getting so agitated about. What possible difference did it make to her if Conrad had someone in mind or not? But she had to admit, she was intrigued to find out the identity of the victim.

"You mean you really don't know?"

"Of course not. I wouldn't be asking if I did."

"He's never told you?"

"Me! I'd be the last person he'd confide something like that in."

Candice laughed. "I wouldn't be too sure."

Ashley didn't feel particularly comfortable with Candice's rather odd reply, nor with the way she kept laughing. "Look," she said, "I'm sorry I asked, and as I'm not really all that interested, shall we change the subject?"

"If you like."

Ashley picked up her glass again and, surprising herself, accepted the cigarette Candice offered her. She only ever smoked when she was worried about something, or nervous.

"Where does he live?" she asked, puffing on the cigarette in a very amateurish way.

Candice gave a shout of laughter. "Ashley! You sure are the limit. He lives about three blocks from you, if you must know. And, in case you didn't already know, it was him who found your apartment."

"Conrad? But Jan never said."

"I think she was told not to. Let's face it, if you'd known, you might have refused."

"I wouldn't," said Ashley, her face a picture of indignation. "But why would he do that?"

Candice shook her head. "Ashley, Conrad Frazier is in love with you. Don't tell me you didn't know."

Ashley dropped her cigarette into her lap. She jumped up and knocked over the wine.

"You're mad!" she said, when order was finally restored.

Candice was obviously enjoying herself immensely. "You mean you really didn't know?"

"Of course I didn't," said Ashley. "It's not true."

"Well, I won't argue with you. But take it from me, he's absolutely crazy about you. No doubt he'll get around to telling you himself one of these days. I must say, though, it's not like Conrad to wait this long."

"I don't want to talk about him any more," said Ashley. "It's absurd. The whole thing is utter nonsense. I don't mean to be rude, Candice, but you've either got it all terribly wrong, or you've taken leave of your senses."

Candice shrugged. "Have it your way. But remember, I know Conrad, and you'll see if I'm not right." She looked up at the clock. "Come on, time we were going in."

Ashley followed her down the steps to the auditorium, her mind in complete turmoil. How was she ever going to concentrate on the film now?

In fact, it was less difficult than she imagined. It was so good to see her beloved London up there on the screen, even if *Mona Lisa* did major on the sleazier side. But she soon became immersed in the story, and if Conrad Frazier crept into her thoughts at all during those couple of hours, she hurriedly pushed him away again. The whole thing was quite unthinkable.

When they left, Candice suggested that they grab a bite to eat somewhere. Ashley didn't really feel hungry, but she agreed to go, to keep Candice company. They didn't stay long over their food, Ashley wanted to get back to the office. And she had plenty to do at home, before her parents arrived tomorrow.

There wasn't much sleep for her that night. Every

time she closed her eyes she could see the face of Conrad Frazier looking down at her, and she couldn't stop her ears ringing with the words, first of Mr. Halworth, then of Candice.

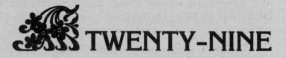

TWENTY-NINE

"**W**HAT'S THIS?" SAID VICKY, STANDING AT THE DOOR AND laughing. "Taking naps in the afternoon now, are we?"

Jenneen smiled, nervously. "I had a bit of a headache," she said, running her fingers through her tousled hair.

"Well, aren't you going to invite me in?"

Jenneen glanced quickly over her shoulder before she opened the door wider. "Yes, of course."

Vicky gave her a strange look. "I've brought along some things I thought might be suitable for tomorrow."

Jenneen cast a look back at the bedroom, then followed her into the lounge.

"Tomorrow?"

"Tomorrow. Don't tell me you've forgotten."

Jenneen shook her head. "Sorry. No, of course I haven't forgotten. The pilot program." She closed the door behind her.

"You look awful," said Vicky. "Still, I suppose it's nerves. Have you got any makeup remover? Best not try these on with all that makeup over your face."

Jenneen put her hands to her cheeks. She had remembered to take off the wig before she'd answered the door, but she had forgotten about the makeup. "Sure," she said. "I'll go and get some. Wait here."

"I remembered what you said," Vicky called after her, as she sat down by the table. "No blues, no whites, no stripes, no checks."

Jenneen didn't answer, so Vicky merely shrugged, and assumed she hadn't heard her. She started to unpack the dresses. Jenneen had mentioned something about strobing on camera, and then some queer word, Ultimatte or something, that ruled out certain colors or patterns. She had brought along an assortment of what she thought would be the best. Personally she rather liked the cream shirt dress, or the lime Calvin Klein suit, but she wasn't sure that Jenneen would be so keen. She laid them all out neatly on the table.

She had just finished when Jenneen came back into the room. Vicky was pleased to see her looking marginally better now. Heavy makeup really didn't suit Jenneen. Vicky assumed that that was what everyone who appeared in front of cameras wore. But Jenneen had not been into work at all today; maybe she had been experimenting.

One by one Jenneen tried on everything Vicky had brought round, but she insisted that Vicky wait in the lounge while she went to look in the mirror. She was behaving very strangely, but when Vicky asked her if she was all right she only said that she still had a touch of the headache.

Finally, after she had decided on the cream shirt dress, Jenneen asked Vicky to go. "I think I'll go back to bed for a while," she said. "It's the only cure, I find, for a headache."

"You're probably right. Mind if I use the bathroom before I go?"

"Sure," said Jenneen, but Vicky could tell that she didn't really want her to. And when Vicky went into the bathroom, she found the reason why.

Jenneen must have forgotten that she had left it

lying on the shelf at the side of the bath, and Vicky noticed it straightaway. She sighed, sadly, and picked up the dark, curly wig. Jenneen had never mentioned Mrs. Green again, since the night she had stayed at Vicky's flat, and Vicky had thought that perhaps Jenneen no longer felt the need to satisfy her alter ego. But this wig, and the heavy makeup Jenneen had been wearing, confirmed that Vicky had been wrong. Jenneen obviously still needed help.

She put the wig back where she had found it, and went into the lounge. Jenneen was wrapped in her robe again; she didn't look up as Vicky came into the room.

"Jenn," said Vicky, very gently.

"Mmm?"

"Are you sure everything's all right?"

"Course I'm sure," said Jenneen, forcing a smile onto her face. "Now, here you are, I've put everything back under the plastic. Is it all right if I write you a check for the one I'm taking?"

Vicky nodded. She could see that there was no point in pressing the matter, so she decided to let it go. At least, for the time being. She waited while Jenneen filled out the check, then taking it from her, she dropped a light kiss on her cheek, and left.

Jenneen leaned against the door for several minutes after Vicky had gone, quaking at her narrow escape. She had forgotten that Vicky was coming this afternoon. But Mrs. Green had no interest in the everyday life of Jenneen Grey. When Mrs. Green craved attention, Jenneen Grey no longer existed.

Jenneen looked over at her bedroom door, and felt her temper beginning to rise. She walked across the hall, and threw open the door. Her lip curled in disgust to see him sitting there, in her bed. What the hell had got into her, bringing him here?

The man in the bed looked over at her and grinned. "Got an ashtray, love?" he asked, blowing a cloud of smoke into the air.

"Get out of that bed!"

He looked surprised, but made no move.

"Did you hear me? I said get out of that bed! Now!"

"Aw, come on, love," he said, "it's still early."

"I don't care what the bloody time is, just get out!" She stormed over to the bed and threw back the covers. She turned her back on his nudity and, grabbing his trousers from the chair, threw them at him.

"What's all this about?" he grumbled, getting to his feet. "I didn't ask to come here, you know."

"Don't say another word. Just get out as fast as you can," and she left the room.

Several minutes later the man appeared in the doorway of the lounge. Jenneen looked up at him, then closed her eyes in dismay. How could she have done it?

"Off now then," said the man. She didn't answer. She didn't even know his name.

"Nice knowing you," he said, quite pleasantly, and left.

Jenneen began to pound her hands against the settee. Why? Why? Why did she do it? He was revolting. He had smelt of beer and tobacco, and he had burped almost continuously throughout their short encounter. And to have brought him here. She must be going out of her mind. What if Vicky had opened the bedroom door? What would she have said if she'd seen that caricature of Desperate Dan lying there in the bed, perfectly at home? Jenneen shuddered to think of it.

Earlier, without even really thinking about it, she had put on her disguise and gone out. She hadn't even planned to put on the wig or makeup, it had just happened. And then she had got into her car, drove down to Reading, parked, and hitched a lift back to London.

The truck driver had been very friendly and chatty, and was quite clearly glad of the company. He had looked at Jenneen in surprise when she had offered to pay him for the journey, and had shaken his head.

"No," he had said. "No. Was nice to have you along."

She felt sick now, as she remembered the expression on his face when she had explained a little more graphically what sort of payment she had in mind. But even then he had said, "Aw no, there's no need for that." But she had insisted. She had bloody well insisted.

She jumped to her feet and paced up and down the room. Mrs. Green and Matthew Bordsleigh. She would never be rid of either of them. They both had a suffocating grip on her now, and neither of them were ever going to let go. She wondered how much longer she could carry on without anyone finding out. But it didn't matter really, did it? She was cheap, and no good, and she deserved no less. There was really little point in even going to have a bath to try and wash away the memory of the lorry driver. She would probably only go out again later, and find someone else.

From time to time she considered the health risks, but even that didn't seem to stop her.

She stopped in front of the mirror and looked at her reflection. "Ugh!" she spat at it. "Vile! Ugly! Miserable!" and she turned away in disgust.

She heard a car pull up outside, and went to look out of the window. All she needed now was Matthew to come along, and the day would be complete. But it wasn't him, it was only her neighbor, back from shopping.

She walked into her bedroom and began to pick up Mrs. Green's makeup that she had left lying around. She found the case under the bed, and dumped it all inside. Then she looked around for the wig. She couldn't find the damn thing anywhere. She pulled back the bedcovers, wondering if it had slipped off, but it wasn't there.

And then she remembered. Her heart skipped a beat. When Vicky had knocked on the door and called out, Jenneen had rushed out of bed and into the bathroom, where she had torn off the wig and, casting it to one side, had run to open the door. And Vicky had gone into the bathroom when she had been here. She had probably seen it. And more than likely she had guessed what had been going on.

Jenneen closed her eyes and sat on the edge of the bed. Of course Vicky had guessed. Hadn't she been trying to say something before she left? Maybe she'd even seen that repulsive lump, lying in bed, smoking his roll-up.

Despite the warm evening, Jenneen began to shiver. It was one thing for Vicky to know about Mrs. Green, but quite another for her to have seen the victim. What must she think? She would change her mind about everything now. Who in their right mind would want to have someone like Jenneen Grey for a friend? And with the overwhelming hatred she had of herself, she threw herself onto the bed and screamed through tears of rage. She never wanted to see Vicky again. She hated her for knowing.

"Nick!" Kate cried into the phone. "At last! I've been ringing you all day."

"I've been with Adrian. Just got back."

"Adrian?"

"Adrian Cowley, the producer of the *Queen of Cornwall.*"

"Oh God, yes, of course. How did it go?"

"Pretty well. Looks like we might have to go to New York in a couple of weeks. They've got American backing for the film now, and for some reason Adrian wants me to go over there with him. I think it's something to do with Bob not being able to fly out straightaway, or something."

"How long will you be gone?"

"Only a week, I think. Maybe two."

"Oh," said Kate. "Quite a long time."

"Does that mean you'll miss me?"

"Stop fishing for compliments," she answered. "Actually I've rung about tomorrow."

"Yes. What about tomorrow?"

"Well, you know we were going to Cliveden House?"

"Mmm."

"Well, I'm afraid we can't now."

"Oh?"

"It's Daddy," she explained. "He's got terribly upset because I haven't been down there these past couple of weeks, so I feel I ought to go and see him tomorrow."

"I see. And tonight?"

"I'm cooking your favorite. Sardines on toast."

"Sardines on toast! I hate sardines."

"Only a joke," she said. "No, it's a surprise. I'm not telling you till you get here."

"Shall I bring some wine?"

"Lots."

"I don't want you getting out of hand," he remarked.

"Don't be a spoilsport. What time will you be round?"

"Seven-thirty?"

"Great. See you then. And Nick . . ."

"Yes?"

"You're not too disappointed about tomorrow, are you?"

"Very."

"Really?"

"Yes. I was looking forward to it."

"Well, I did wonder if you could keep the day free on Friday. I could ring them and ask if we can go along then instead. Yes, Mrs. Adams, I'm coming," she called in response to the knock on the door. "How does that sound?"

"I'll have to check my social calendar," he quipped. "See you at seven-thirty," and they hung up.

Nick tried to shake off his feelings of ambivalence about Kate's dependence on her father. On more than one occasion he had attempted to talk to her about it, but she always refused to discuss it, treating it as if he were making a fuss over nothing.

But maybe there was something he could do about it, and who knows, with the way things were going lately, he might even try. He walked into the bathroom of his bachelor flat in Holland Park, and turned on the light. Catching sight of his reflection in the mirror on the opposite wall he threw himself a complacent grin, and winked. Yes, maybe the time was approaching, at long last. He wondered what she would say, and then he smiled again.

"Will you hurry up," said Bob, turning back and taking Ellamarie by the arm.

"In case you hadn't noticed," said Ellamarie, raising her voice over the din of the traffic, "I'm trying to drop a hint."

Bob's eyes were twinkling, but he said nothing and turned to walk on.

"OK, I know, taking hints was never a strong point with you," she remarked, walking after him.

"Ellamarie, we have been up and down Bond Street at least three times, and now you've dragged me down to Knightsbridge. If you want an engagement ring, couldn't you at least pick somewhere a little less expensive?"

"So you had noticed!"

"Well, as we've stopped at every jeweler's we've passed so far, I'd be some kind of an idiot if I hadn't noticed, wouldn't I?"

"So? Can I have one?"

He looked at her.

"Please!"

They were blocking the pavement, and he moved to let some people go by, but she didn't miss the look on his face before he turned away. The sparkle had seemed to disappear from his eyes. Her face fell. He was going to say no.

"Don't you think we're just a little premature?" he said, turning back to her. He put his arm round her shoulders and tried steering her through the crowds. "I mean, I haven't even told my wife yet."

"But you'll be telling her at the weekend," Ellamarie pointed out. "It'll probably need adjusting, so if we order it now it should be ready without us being premature."

The crowd suddenly thickened again and Bob pushed her in front of him to go through. He almost laughed to see the way she was walking. She didn't even show yet, not even when she was naked, yet she was wearing a smock, and was practically waddling instead of walking. He caught up with her again, and she turned to look at him. Her eyes were pleading, and she was pouting. "All right," he relented, "if it makes you happy. Have you seen anything you like?"

"Oh Bob!" she cried, and flung her arms round his neck. "We're getting engaged," she said to a man in a bowler hat as he pushed past them. The man nodded, and smiled, and Bob felt very embarrassed.

"Not so loud," he said.

"But I want the whole world to know."

"Wait until next week. If anyone recognizes me, it'll be all over the press, and I don't want my wife finding out like that."

Ellamarie sighed. "No, I suppose not. But what about the people in the jewellers? They might recognize you."

"Precisely," said Bob, who hadn't actually thought

of that. "All the more reason to shop for one next week. What do you say?"

She seemed reluctant.

"It does make sense," he said.

"Do you promise? Next week?"

"I promise. Now, didn't you say you wanted to go to Harrods before we went home?"

She nodded, and took hold of his hand. Sometimes she was like a child, he thought, only happy when she got her own way. But he loved her, for better or for worse, and in truth he loved the worse every bit as much as the better.

He hadn't allowed himself to consider what he was going to say to Linda. He was putting it off, and even now his heart contracted to think of the pain he was going to cause her.

Matthew ambled across the room, and helped himself to a Scotch. Jenneen remained standing at the door, watching him.

"So," he said, taking his Scotch across to the settee and making himself at home, "how did the pilot go?"

Her eyes narrowed, and he smiled.

"What do you know about it?" she said.

"Oh, you'd be surprised what I know. Today, wasn't it?"

Jenneen regarded him coldly. It didn't take long to work it out. "I didn't realize you knew Stephen Sommers," she said. "But of course, it's a close-knit community in the world of drug addicts and alcoholics, isn't it?"

He grinned. "Aren't you going to have a drink?" he waved his glass toward her bar.

"How did you get him to tell you?"

He shrugged and slurped at the whiskey.

"Don't tell me you paid him for the information?"

"I might have."

"With the money I gave you?" She smiled bitterly at the irony of the situation.

"Well," he said, "it was today, wasn't it?"

"Why bother to ask when you already know the answer?"

"And?"

"And what?"

"And, how did it go?"

"All right."

"All right. Is that all?"

"I don't want to discuss it with you, Matthew. It's none of your damned business, so just tell me what you want, and go."

"None of my business?" He leaned back and lifted his feet onto the coffee table.

"No. So get on with it. How much do you want? Or should I say how much does Stephen want?"

He took a large mouthful of Scotch. "Nothing," and he grinned as he saw the look on her face turn from surprise to suspicion.

"Then exactly why are you here?"

"That's just what I'm about to tell you," he answered. "Why don't you come and sit down?"

"I'm perfectly all right where I am, thank you," she said, leaning against the door. "And stop playing host in my flat."

"Jenneen," he drawled, "just in case you had forgotten, I can do precisely what I like in your flat."

She folded her arms. "Get on with it. What do you want?"

He got up, and she waited while he went to refill his glass. "I want a part in your program," he said simply, turning to face her.

"You what!" she gasped.

"I want a part in your program."

"You're crazy."

His face hardened.

"It's a magazine show, Matthew, not a drama. There's nothing in it for you."

"You're looking for a reporter, aren't you?"

"A reporter, yes. Not an actor."

"Around the sets of movies being shot in England?"

She looked at his face, bloated and ugly, and realisation began to dawn.

"Could find myself a couple of good parts that way," he said, confirming her fears. And he went to sit down again.

"But we're looking for someone who knows the business," she said.

"I'm an actor, don't you think I know the business?"

"Yes, as an actor. But you're not a journalist. How can you write scripts, or do pieces to camera? Oh, for God's sake, I don't even know why I'm having this conversation, it's too ridiculous for words."

"I can do it."

"You can't!"

"Oh yes I can," he said. "And what's more, you're going to see to it that I do."

"Forget it," she snapped. "You're not right for it, you can't do it, and what's more you're not bloody well going to do it. So get it out of your head right now."

"Jenneen," he said, crossing one leg over the other, "I want that job. If I don't get it, starting the same day as you, then you won't be starting either."

She felt the muscles in her face begin to freeze. "You can't ruin this for me, Matthew, you can't. I've worked hard for this, it's what I've always wanted. Can't you leave me alone? I give you money, isn't that enough?"

"Nope," he said. "I've decided I want more."

"But I've got no more to give." She looked at him, and felt a violent hatred erupting inside. "You sadistic bastard!" she hissed. "You're ruining my life, and you're fucking well enjoying it!"

"That's right," he said, and this time his voice was tinged with anger.

Suddenly the strain of the last few days took hold of her, and she felt her control slipping away. "You fucking son of a bitch!" she yelled. "Get out of here! And don't ever show your ugly face here again. Go on, get out! Get out of my life. The very sight of you makes me sick, sitting there throwing back the whiskey like some fucking moronic distillery. You're a waste of space, Matthew. Why don't you do us all a favour and take the bottle with you and drink yourself to death."

He leapt up from his chair and threw his glass to the floor. "Don't you speak to me like that, you bitch!" he snarled. "Not a little tramp like you." He caught her by the hair and yanked her round to face him.

"Let go of me!"

"Shut your mouth!" he yelled, and slapped her hard across the face.

She gasped, and then lashed out with her fists, but he was too strong for her. "Stop it! Stop!" she cried, but he was pulling her across the room, tearing at her hair.

He threw her against the wall. "Now just you see to it that I get that job. And I'm telling you now, I will want an answer the next time I'm round. And it'd better be the right one."

"It's not my decision. I don't have that sort of power." She could hardly get the words out, he was squeezing her jaw so tightly.

"I don't think you're hearing me," he said, lifting his hand ready to strike another blow. "If I don't do this program, then you don't either. Get it? Now, it's up to you."

She looked at the threatening hand, and then back into his face. He was glowering down at her, his hair falling across his bloodshot eyes, saliva dripping from his mouth. She pulled back her head as far as she could, and spat into his face.

The blow to her head was agonizing, and she fell to the floor. He was standing over her, and suddenly she felt a searing pain in her side. And another, and another. He was kicking her with a reckless and insane violence, as though he meant to carry on until he killed her. She tried to get away, but he came after her, pushing her back to the floor. And all the time he called her the names she had called herself, and taunted her with the sinister truth of her life.

Finally she managed to crawl under the table, where he could no longer reach her. Curling herself into a ball, she waited to see what he would do. She could hear him breathing, and watched his legs as he stood there for an instant, then went back to the small bar she kept on the sideboard. She could taste the blood in her mouth; she held on tightly to her body, shivering and shaking, trying to hold her battered self together. He turned round, and took a step toward the table. She held her breath.

"Get out from there, bitch!"

She didn't move.

"I said get out," he yelled, and she saw the contents of her bar go crashing to the floor.

Still she didn't move.

He picked up a chair and threw it across the room. Then, getting to his knees, he looked under the table. She forced herself back, wincing with pain, but he reached out and grabbed her. "That's it," he said, pulling her toward him. "Suffer, you bitch. Suffer!"

"Stop it, Matthew. Please," she begged. "No more."

"I said suffer," he yelled, and banged her head against the floor.

"Stop! Stop!" she screamed.

He threw her backward, and got to his feet. "Get up."

She looked up at him, terror making her eyes bulge from her head.

"Get up!" he yelled.

Never taking her eyes from him, she reached out for the edge of the table, and began to pull herself to her feet. She was sobbing quietly, as much with pain as fear. Finally she managed to drag herself up, gasping at the pain in her side, and fell back into a chair.

"Please," she said, as he started to come toward her. "Please, don't hit me again."

He stood over her, very drunk now, and she cowered away. Then he took her by the throat again, and forced her face up to his.

"The job," he snarled.

She nodded.

He let her go, and swilled another mouthful of whiskey from the bottle he was holding. She watched him, mesmerised. Suddenly she heard herself speaking, and her voice seemed to echo through her ears. "Why, Matthew?" she was saying. "Why?"

He slammed the bottle on the table beside her, making her jump, and stuck his face into hers.

"Why?" he said, showering her face with saliva. "Why? I'll tell you why. Because I was fucking stupid enough to fall in love with you, that's why! And all you've ever done is shove it right back in my face. You! The whore! The slut! I loved you and you're no fucking good, Jenneen. And now you're going to pay for all the misery. And if you don't deliver, you whore, then you're dead! Do you hear me? You're fucking dead!"

She stared into his face. He was sick in the head, and not once did she doubt his threat of death. From the look in his eyes now she knew he was capable of anything.

He let her go, and walked to the door, taking the nearly empty bottle with him. "I'll be back," he said, "and soon. You know what I want, and you know what

I'm prepared to do if I don't get it. Think on it." He turned and went out of the room.

She waited until she heard him leave, then tried to pull herself to her feet. But the pain was excruciating, and she fell to her knees, groaning.

As she pulled her car to a stop outside, Vicky looked up and saw Matthew staggering out of the building. From the look on his face she could tell that yet another unsavoury scene had taken place upstairs. She waited for him to weave his way off down the street, then hurried inside.

She found the door open so she let herself in and called out. There was no reply, so she closed the door behind her, and went in search of Jenneen. At first she could hardly take in the wreckage of the room, and then she saw Jenneen lying on the floor, her frail body wracked with sobs, blood all over her face. Vicky dropped her bag and ran over to her.

"Oh, Vicky! Vicky!" Jenneen sobbed. "He kept hitting me, and kicking me, and now he wants me to help him, and I have to help him. If I don't, he says he'll kill me, and I know he means it. Oh, God, what does it take to make him stop?"

"It's all right," said Vicky, trying to keep her voice calm. "It's all right. Come on, let's try and get you onto the sofa."

She laid Jenneen back against the cushions then ran into the bathroom to get hot water and cotton wool. When she came back again Jenneen was trying to get up. Gently she pushed her back down, and started to bathe her face.

"Don't move," she said. "Don't try to move."

"He said he'd kill me," Jenneen cried, verging on hysteria and trying to sit up again.

"Sssh," said Vicky. "Sssh. Lie back now."

Jenneen caught Vicky's hand as she lifted it to her face, and held it to her. "He wants my program. He said

I've got to give it to him. He wants my program. What am I going to do?''

"Sssh," Vicky soothed. "Sssh!"

Jenneen let her head fall back, and allowed Vicky to bathe her face. Her hands were soft and kind, and after a while the trembling in her limbs began to subside.

"I want my mother," said Jenneen, looking up into Vicky's face, with pathetic eyes, and she giggled.

Vicky smiled. "I know," she said. "I know. You need a rest, my darling. You so badly need a rest."

"Yes, I want to sleep. I want to go away. Please, help me to get away from him."

"I will," said Vicky.

"Will you ring my mother, get her to come and fetch me? Please!"

"Of course. Where's her number?"

"She's not on the phone," said Jenneen, and began to cry again.

"Oh my poor, poor darling."

Jenneen clung to her, and sobbed into her shoulder. "What am I going to do?" she pleaded. "Tell me, please, what am I going to do?"

"You're going to get right away from everything, where no one can hurt you any more, and where people care for you and want to help you."

Jenneen's face was panic-stricken. "You're going to send me away," she cried. "I won't go. Don't send me away. Please, don't send me away. I'm not mad! I'll get better. I couldn't bear it," and her face crumpled again.

Vicky hugged her. "Don't be silly," she said. "No one's going to send you away. Just tell me what your commitments are for the week, and we'll work everything out from there."

Jenneen pulled away, and looked up into Vicky's face. Vicky smiled. She had never seen a woman look more like a child. "I've got to edit," said Jenneen, "but

I'll be free by Friday, and for the weekend. Can we go away somewhere? Will you come with me?"

"Of course I will. Why don't we go down and spend the weekend at my parents' house in Wiltshire? We can go for lots of long walks, and talk, if you feel up to it. But most of all, we'll take you away from London. Is that what you want?"

Jenneen nodded. "Yes, I want to get away from London."

"Then that's what we'll do," said Vicky. "I'll ring my parents tomorrow and let them know. Now, off to bed with you. Try and get some sleep. It's OK," she added, when she saw the look on Jenneen's face. "I'll be here. I won't leave you. I'll sleep on the sofa. If you want anything, then all you have to do is call out. Is that OK?"

Jenneen smiled weakly, and nodded. "You're uncanny, you know."

"Uncanny?"

"Yes. This is the second time in my life that you've turned up when you're least expected, and most needed."

Vicky's eyes were gentle, and she smiled. "Isn't that how it should be with friends?"

Jenneen looked back at her. "Yes," she nodded. "Yes, I suppose it should."

THIRTY

Ashley SWEPT OUT OF HER OFFICE CARRYING THE LATEST composite artwork for the Mercer Burgess pitch, and started to make for the Art Department. Along with the rest of her team she had worked through the night for the last two nights, grabbing sleep when she could, and knew she should have been exhausted. But things were going well, even better than she had dared hope, and she was buzzing. When Arthur Fellowman had rang her as he'd promised he would, he had been a great deal more encouraging about her ideas than he had when she had left him after their first meeting. She felt that he was on her side, and would do all that he could to push it through the board. If only she could reduce the cost a little, then she really would be in with a chance.

She was at the end of the corridor before she remembered that she had meant to speak to Jan before she left. She turned back.

Jan was just putting the phone down as she walked in. "Oh, you're back," she said. "That was . . ."

But Ashley wasn't listening. "I need to speak to Arthur Fellowman sometime this morning. Get onto his secretary and find out his movements. And can you take the blue file I've left on my desk and have the entire thing copied. Make that two copies. And ring Walter and ask him if he's got the changes I asked for yet. And then ring Media and ask them to send up the latest

TV figures we asked for yesterday, and if necessary go down and fetch them. Oh yes, and I'm still waiting for the provisional cast list from Gemma, that's very important, then ring Candice and make an appointment with Conrad, we're going to knock him off his feet." She grinned, and Jan laughed.

"Bill is on his . . ." Jan started to say, but Ashley had already gone out of the door.

"Is there a fire?" said Bill Fownest, catching her by the arms before she careered into him.

Ashley laughed. "Sorry, I was in a bit of a hurry, that's all. Want to get this to Conrad before lunch."

"Just what I've come to see. May I?" Bill asked, looking down at the designs.

"Sure," said Ashley. "Don't see any reason not to impress the hell out of you."

Bill laughed, and took the artwork from her. "Mmm," he said, looking it over, "interesting. I'll look forward to seeing the complete thing."

"You will, soon enough, and if you wait till tomorrow you can see it lifted from the paper and presented in all its celluloid glory," said Ashley, taking them back.

"Have you shown Conrad anything at all yet?"

"Not a thing," she answered, sounding a great deal more nonchalant than she felt.

Bill seemed surprised. "Something on that scale, and you haven't even mentioned it to him? I mean, you've sure deviated from the Mercer Burgess brief."

She shrugged. "It was the only way, I found."

"Does Arthur Fellowman know?"

"Yes."

"You've talked to him?"

"Sure."

"But not to Conrad?"

"No."

"I'd like to be around when he finds out about that."

They started along the corridor together. "He's not easy to please is he? Conrad, I mean."

"Not always."

"I'm going to win this one, you know, Bill."

"I know."

She laughed. "So you do have confidence. Thanks," she said.

"Don't thank me, thank Conrad."

"Conrad? What do you mean?"

"Just what I said. Thank Conrad. He's seen to it that you'll win."

"He's what! How?"

"He just has."

"Do you mean he knows about all of this already then?" she asked, lifting the artwork in her arms.

"Not as far as I know."

"Then what are you talking about?"

They reached the elevator and Bill pressed the button. "Would I be correct in thinking that there might be certain, shall we say, conditions attached to this campaign? As far as you're concerned, thát is."

Ashley looked at him in surprise. "You know about that?"

Bill nodded.

"Conrad told you?"

He nodded again.

"I still don't think I'm following you. How does that mean that Conrad has seen to it that I win the account?"

"Bill!"

Bill and Ashley looked round, and saw Conrad walking toward them. His face was like a thundercloud. Ashley hadn't seen him at all since the disastrous episode at the Twenty-One Club; she had gone out of her way to avoid him.

"Conrad," said Bill.

"Last month's figures, I want to go over them with you. If you can spare the time."

Bill removed his hand from Ashley's arm. "I'll come now."

Conrad turned on his heel, and walked off down the corridor. Ashley looked at Bill, and pulled a face. Bill winked, then went in pursuit.

Impatiently, she pressed the button for the elevator again, relieved that Conrad had chosen to ignore her. But an hour later, as she returned from the Art Department, she was still mulling over what Bill had said. And try as she might, she could make no sense of it.

It was lunchtime, and Ashley was sitting back drinking a well-earned cup of coffee and relaxing. She looked up as the door opened, surprised that whoever it was hadn't knocked, and even more surprised when she saw Conrad.

He walked across to her desk and dropped a file in front of her. "Just what the hell do you call this?"

She reached out and picked up the file.

"Well?"

Ashley opened it. Her face was set, and her hand shook slightly as she took out the contents.

"Let me tell you," said Conrad, planting his hands on the edge of her desk, "if that's an illustration of the campaign you are planning for Mercer Burgess, then you can just forget it! Now! Before you waste any more money, time, or talent. I've seen raunchier campaigns for church services."

Ashley flinched, and put the file back on her desk. Then, with eyes as cold as ice, she looked at him.

"You're not in London now," Conrad went on. "This is New York. New York, where you have to be better than tomorrow's ideas, sharper than the rest of them out there, and original! That," he spat, pointing at the file, "is not! And if that is an illustration of what you have to offer to this agency, then you can just book your ticket for the next plane back to London. Now!"

Ashley got to her feet. "That," she said calmly,

picking up the file and waving it in his face—is not mine! It belongs to J.S. & A."

"Then what the hell was it doing on my desk?"

"I haven't the faintest idea," she answered. "Maybe Jan picked up the wrong file and brought it to you. "This," she said, picking up another file, "is mine," and she thrust it at him.

He took it from her, but didn't look at it. "Just how the hell did a J.S. & A. file come into your possession?"

"Into my possession!" she said, her voice rising. "It's you who's got the file. I've never seen it before."

"I don't like this sort of underhanded affair," said Conrad, his voice dangerously quiet. "If we win this contract, we win it fair and square. I don't want any of this amateur espionage going on, not in my agency! So you'd better talk to whoever got hold of this file in the first place, and have them take it back to J.S. & A. And then you can send whoever it is to me."

"You're talking as if I know who it is," said Ashley, beginning to bristle again. "You know your staff better than I do, why don't you find the culprit?"

"I asked you to do something, and I expect it to be done. I'll expect a full report by tomorrow morning. Now, this," he said, opening her file, "let's hope it's an improvement on what I've already seen," and he sat down in the chair opposite her desk.

She was surprised. She had expected him to take it away and read it in the privacy of his own office before speaking to her.

"Perhaps you'd like to talk me through it," he said, looking up at her. "And sit down."

She sat down. "Well," she began, not feeling the slightest bit inclined to talk it over with him at the moment, "as you can see, it is based on an offer of further insurance in return for taking up an initial policy."

"Go on," he said, sorting through the pages.

"The main aim is to attract the average person, mainly the young. At present Mercer Burgess has rather a stodgy image, so by aiming for the young, up-wardly mobile set, it should give the company a more upmarket and desirable image. The idea is that if you take out, for example, a household policy, then Mercer Burgess will offer a discount on a motoring policy. If you take out both, then they will insure up to, say, $3,000 worth of luxury goods for free, for one year, known as a Luxsure policy, which will enable the not-so-well-off to identify with the wealthy. And the media approach will be done, in the main, through the luxury items, hi-fi's, computers, etc., with animated graphics as well as a star cast. The provisional cast list is there. There's a study on positioning at the back, and a look at the possibility of adopting a direct mail scheme, coupled with policy forms being printed in newspapers and magazines. The scripts could be better, Walter is still working on them, but I believe that the essence of what we are trying to say is already there."

Conrad continued looking through the file and art-work, then put them on the desk in front of him.

"And that's it?"

"Well, in a nutshell, yes."

"Are you out of your mind?"

"What!" she gasped.

"I asked if you have taken leave of your senses?"

"That," she said, picking up the file, and waving it at him, "is good! And you know it!"

"It is not what you were asked for. I thought I had made myself perfectly clear. I want to win this account, and I was relying on you to do it. I was a fool. You can't just plan a presentation because you think it's good, and ignore the cost."

"I haven't ignored the cost. I've discussed it with Arthur Fellowman. He knows all about it."

Conrad looked incredulous. "You mean to say you have discussed it with Arthur Fellowman, and not with me? What the hell has gotten into you?"

"A campaign. A bloody campaign. You said you

wanted to win. You as good as threatened me with what would happen if I didn't, so I've gone all out to get it."

"You have deliberately gone out of your way to make a fool of me . . ."

"You are making a fool of yourself. You know that pitch could win. You know damn well it's good. But you're sitting on your pride because I went to Arthur Fellowman without telling you first. Well, why don't you ask me what he said, instead of sitting there shouting at me?"

Conrad eyed her with hostility. "Well? What did he say?"

"He likes it. He's going to talk to his board, try and increase the budget."

"Triple it, you mean."

"OK, triple it."

"Has Fellowman offered you a job?"

"What do you mean?"

"Well, it seems to me, looking at this, that you have turned the entire Marketing Department of Mercer, Burgess on its head."

"As I said, he likes it."

Suddenly Conrad began to smile. This threw her off-balance even more than his anger. "I have to hand it to you, Ashley," he said, "you've got guts. You mean you actually took this proposal to him, and asked him to triple his budget?"

"Yes."

"And he's agreed to try. Has he talked to David Burgess?"

"I don't know," said Ashley.

"He can't have, yet. If he had, the old man would dhave been on the phone to me by now." He picked the file up again, and opened it.

"So, do you approve?"

"No," he said, and he sounded angry again. "I certainly do not approve. I told you I was taking a personal interest in this, and you ignored it. In future, should we win this one, you will carry out my instructions. Is that understood?"

"Yes," she said. "But you still haven't told me what you really think."

"I think that if you were allowed to carry on like this, you would be in grave danger of dragging this company to its knees."

Ashley's eyes dropped to her hands in front of her. He seemed to have already made up his mind that, success or no success, she would not be staying at Frazier, Nelmes.

He was getting to his feet, so she stood up as well. "I'm taking this with me," he said. "And you make sure that you get that J.S. & A. file back to where it belongs. Then start saying your prayers that it hasn't been missed. But it's probably already too late." He turned to go, and just as he reached the door, it opened. Jan walked in—with Alex.

Ashley sat down, and closed her eyes. What the hell was Conrad going to say about this? He was in such a vile mood, he probably wouldn't even wait for Alex to go before he started shouting again.

"Oh, Mr. Frazier," said Jan, coloring to the roots of her hair and throwing an apologetic look toward Ashley. "I didn't know you were in here, excuse me."

"Obviously not," he said, glaring at her, then he lowered his eyes to the frightened gaze of the little boy standing beside her. Ashley's heart went out to her son. It wasn't often that anything frightened Alex, but Conrad's anger was so thick in the air, and his face so black, even Alex had not failed to notice it. And Conrad, standing over six feet high, would appear so daunting to someone as small as Alex.

Then, to her complete astonishment, Conrad's face softened, and he held out his hand toward Alex.

"Hello there, little fella," he said. "Haven't we met before?"

Alex looked at his mother, who barely managed to nod, then turned his eyes back to Conrad's, and tentatively took his hand.

"Isn't your name Alex?" said Conrad.

Alex nodded, but still he didn't speak.

Conrad looked at Ashley. "I didn't know your family were here." He turned back to Alex. "How long are you here for, son?"

"Three weeks," Alex answered, in a little voice.

Conrad lowered himself to Alex's height, and smiled into his face. "What do you say to coming to a ball game with me tomorrow?"

If it hadn't been for her own shock, Ashley might have burst out laughing at the look that shot to her secretary's face.

Alex's eyes were round. "A ball game? What sort of ball game?"

"Baseball," said Conrad. "I'm taking my nephews tomorrow. They're about your age. Why don't you come along too? That's of course," he added, turning to Ashley, "if your mother will allow it."

Alex looked at her. "Can I, Mum?"

Ashley had to struggle to find her voice. "W-would you like to?" she finally managed to ask.

"Would I?" Alex gasped, and looked back at Conrad as if he were a god.

Conrad smiled at him and stood up again.

"Then of course you can go," said Ashley, hardly able to take any of it in. "That's if Mr. Frazier is sure."

"Mr. Frazier is sure," said Conrad. "And as a special treat, you can call me Conrad, just like my irreverent nephews."

"Cor, thanks," said Alex, glowing with pleasure. "Can Grandad come too?"

"He sure can," said Conrad. He turned for the door. "Well," he said to Jan, "what are you waiting for? Get on the phone and fix the extra tickets," and before she could answer he had gone.

Jan and Ashley stared after him.

Ashley was the first to pull herself together. "You'll catch flies any minute," she said to Jan, whose mouth was gaping open.

Jan turned to her. "I don't believe it," she said, shaking her head. "I just don't believe it."

The phone rang, and taking Alex with her, Jan went to answer it.

Ashley closed the door and went back to her desk. She simply didn't know what to make of it. One minute he was shouting and raving at her, and the next he was inviting her son to a ball game.

Jan buzzed through. "Bill Fownest just called," she said, through the intercom. "He asked could you go along to his office."

"Did he say what it was about?"

"Seems Reeds wants to relaunch their series of Winter Love novels. I've sent down to Julia Peterson's office for the files. She handled them last time."

"Thanks," said Ashley. "Be right out."

When she returned to her office later, she found Alex enveloped in the chair behind her desk, picking up the telephones and playing with them. She laughed at his little face, barely peeping over the edge of the desk. Obviously, in his lone attempt at adjusting the height of the chair, he had only succeeded in lowering it.

"Grandma will be here any minute, young man," she said. "Have you got everything?"

"Sure have."

She raised her eyebrows. "Very American."

"Sure am," he answered, making her laugh.

"What have you got there?" she asked, watching him pick up what looked to be a rather heavy bag.

"Conrad gave it to me."

"Conrad?"

"Sure, he came back just now."

"What is it?"

"It's for baseball," Alex answered, emptying the bag out on the floor. "A hat, a shirt, a bat and a ball. They're American."

"Well, it looks like you've got some growing to do before you'll fit into this," Ashley remarked, holding the shirt up.

"Doesn't matter," said Alex. "Conrad said that everyone wears them big."

"Oh, I see. And what are those there?"

"Photos of the players. That's the most famous one, but I can't remember his name. Conrad said he's really mean."

Ashley gave a wry smile and took the picture from him.

"Conrad said that after the game tomorrow, we could go to the park, and he would teach me to play."

"Did he?" said Ashley, unable to hide her surprise.

Alex nodded. "He said that his nephews play it all the time, and that I should learn too, if I was going to live in New York."

Ashley looked at her son in amazement, but she didn't comment. More than anything else in the world, she wanted Ale to live with her here, but she hadn't plucked up the courage to tell her parents yet.

"You seem to quite like Conrad."

"He's great!" said Alex. "Can we take him to Long Island with us at the weekend? I think he'd like to come."

Ashley laughed. "I don't think so. I'm sure he has plans of his own."

"He hasn't," said Alex. "I asked him. He said he was going anyway, and that he might see us there."

"Long Island is a very big place. I don't expect we will."

"But he said that we might. He said he's got horses there, and that I could have a ride on one of them."

This was getting to be just a little too much for her.

"Tell me, darling, just what else did Conrad have to say?"

"Quite a lot, as a matter of fact," said Conrad.

Ashley spun round and saw him standing at the door. "I'm sorry," she said, blushing, "I didn't realize you were there. You've really been very kind. You shouldn't have gone to all this trouble, you know. Did you say thank you, Alex?"

"Thank you," said Alex, obediently, and threw his ball up in the air.

Ashley gasped, and grabbed it from him. "Later," she said.

She looked curiously at Conrad as she saw him wink at Alex, and then abruptly his expression reverted to a scowl.

"Thursday evening," he said, "Warners are holding their annual ball and, as usual, they have invited some of us along. I'd like you to be there. Bill Fownest will be there too, with his wife." Ashley didn't miss the emphasis Conrad had placed on the word wife, and she flushed. "I take it you're free."

"I don't suppose it would make much difference if I wasn't."

"No," he said, and left.

"Well," Ashley sighed, turning to put an arm round Alex. "That is one strange man. He might like you, darling, but he certainly doesn't seem to like me very much. I wonder what one has to do to please him." She smiled at Alex's upturned face. "But that would never do, would it?" she laughed, and not understanding in the least what his mother was talking about, Alex laughed too.

THIRTY-ONE

THURSDAY EVENING AT SEVEN-THIRTY PROMPT CONRAD arrived at the Montclair building on East Seventy-fifth Street. The doorman announced him, then pressed for the elevator to take him up to Ashley's apartment. Ashley's mother was already waiting at the door, and surprised Conrad with the warmth of her greeting. She couldn't help but admire how handsome he looked in his black dinner jacket and white starched evening shirt. Seeing him standing there she could now understand what all the fuss was about. Alex had talked of practically no one else since they had gone to the ball game on Wednesday, and even her husband had said more than he usually did after meeting someone for the first time. Ashley, on the other hand, was coolness itself when it came to talking about him. So much so, that Mrs. Lakeman had smiled to herself on several occasions, but had refrained from making any comment.

"My husband's through here," she said, leading the way across the hall. "Ashley will be right out."

"Thank you," said Conrad.

"Conrad," said Mr. Lakeman, as he came into the room. "Good to see you again. Will you have a drink?"

"Mr. Lakeman," said Conrad, shaking him by the hand. "Scotch, please."

"Do sit down," said Mrs. Lakeman, hurriedly

clearing the chair of the discarded Bergdorf Goodman bags that Ashley had left there.

"Thank you." Conrad looked across the room, taking it all in, and particularly admiring her taste in art. "No Alex," he remarked, as Mrs. Lakeman took a sherry from her husband and settled in the chair opposite.

He didn't miss the quick look Mrs. Lakeman threw her husband.

"He's gone to the cinema," she said.

"Oh? Don't tell me he's made even more friends."

"Uh, no, not exactly."

"Thank you," said Conrad, taking his drink from Mr. Lakeman.

"Actually," Mrs. Lakeman continued, "he's gone out with his father."

Conrad raised an eyebrow. "I had no idea that Ashley's husband was in town."

"He arrived this morning," said Mr. Lakeman, "a little unexpectedly."

"Well, I'm sure both Alex and Ashley are delighted," said Conrad, but Mrs. Lakeman didn't miss the strain in his voice.

"Well, Alex certainly was," she said. "But I think surprised would be a better way to describe Ashley. Ah, here she comes."

"Good evening, Conrad," said Ashley, standing in the doorway.

Conrad stood up, and she was pleased to see his eyes widen as he looked at her. The last-minute trip to Fifth Avenue had been worthwhile.

"You look beautiful, dear," said her mother. "Doesn't she look lovely, Dad?"

Ashley blushed.

"She certainly does," said her father, beaming at her in the way that proud fathers do.

Ashley looked at Conrad, and immediately looked away again. He was smiling the smile she hated so much. Funny though, how it didn't seem to bother her quite so much of late. Probably she was just getting used to it.

"Have you seen my bag, Mum?"

"Yes, it's here, dear," and her mother picked it up from the table.

Ashley took it. "Shall we go?"

"By all means," Conrad said.

They walked downstairs, and got into his car. As he switched on the engine, the stereo came softly to life, and Ashley settled back to listen. Conrad steered the car out into the street, and then threw a look across at her, but her eyes were closed, and she didn't see. He smiled, and turned the car onto Park Avenue.

"I spoke to David Burgess today."

Ashley's eyes flew open. "Well? What did he say?"

Conrad smiled, and pulled out round a double parked taxi. "As a matter of fact, quite a lot."

"And does he like it?"

"I wasn't sure at first, he was too busy tearing me off a strip for the sheer audacity of it."

"Oh," said Ashley.

"But you can relax, he likes it."

"But that's terrific. Does that mean we've got the account?"

"Not yet."

"When will we know?"

Conrad smiled. "You'll know soon enough," and that seemed to be all he was going to say on the matter.

She wanted to ask him if that meant that she would be staying at Frazier, Nelmes, but she didn't, she was too afraid of the answer. They didn't speak much after that, and in no time at all they were at the Pierre.

Conrad sent someone to find their table. Ashley waited beside him, looking around to see if she recognized anyone. She wished that Kate was there, she was always good at spotting the rich and famous.

Conrad watched her for a moment, until she turned to him and caught him looking. She blushed, and he smiled.

"You do, you know," he said.

"Do what?"

"Look very beautiful tonight," and he smiled again to see the look that came over her face.

The waiter returned, and showed them through the crowd to their table. Bill Fownest and his wife were already there, and Ashley was surprised to see Ron Fairchild and Cole Wallace, two other Account VPs from Frazier, Nelmes, sitting at the table with them.

The men stood up as Conrad and Ashley approached, and Ashley greeted them all warmly. Bill introduced her to his wife, an attractive woman in her late thirties. Ashley liked her on sight, just as she had her husband.

Later, after the tables had been cleared of dinner, a band began to play, and the Chairman of Warners took the floor first with his wife. Others were quick to follow, and Ashley accepted immediately when Bill asked her to dance.

"Doesn't everyone look wonderful," she remarked, as they pushed rather than danced their way round the floor.

"Mmm, don't they just," said Bill, looking down at her, and she laughed.

"Your wife seems very nice. How long have you been married?"

"A couple of years. You?"

"Me? I'm not married any more."

"But you still wear the ring."

"I know," she said, looking at her left hand. "I don't know why. Maybe I should move it over onto my other hand."

"How long have you been divorced?"

"A couple of years," she said, and he smiled.

They could hardly be supposed to be dancing, they

were stopping so frequently. Bill knew just about everyone, and introduced her to them all. She protested, laughing that she would never remember so many names, and begged him not to introduce her to anyone again, at least for the next two minutes.

He obliged, and devoted his attention to her.

"You haven't told me yet what Conrad thought of your Mercer Burgess pitch."

She grimaced. "Ah, well, that's not easy. I think he liked it, but I'm not sure. Has he said anything to you about it?"

Bill nodded.

"He has? Well, aren't you going to tell me what he said?"

"No."

"No? No, just like that."

"No," he chuckled, "just like that."

"Oh."

"You'll know soon enough," he said, repeating what Conrad had said earlier, and she had to be satisfied. At that moment they came across his wife, dancing with Cole Wallace, and exchanged partners.

Ashley didn't know Cole too well, but he seemed pleasant enough. And he danced well.

"So," he said, twirling her round, "how are you liking us, here in New York?"

She smiled. "I'm liking you just fine. In fact, given the chance, I think I might grow to love it here."

He raised his eyebrows, and chuckled. "Don't you miss London?"

"Terribly, but it will always be there. I can always go back, if I want to."

"But right now, you don't want to?"

"No, I'm staying right here. Apart from anything else, I've got a major account to win."

"Do you think you will?"

"Of course," she answered. "Don't you?"

"Of course," he said.

She looked across the room, and through the crowd she saw Conrad talking to some strangers.

"The President of Warners," said Cole, following her eyes.

A rather drunken couple fell against them, and Cole caught her about the waist. She laughed, and gracefully accepted the rather slurred apologies.

"I think it's time we sat down again now," she said, and Cole walked her back to the table.

Conrad didn't come back, so when Bill asked her to dance again, she accepted, feeling annoyed with Conrad that he was ignoring them all.

"I was wondering," she said to Bill.

He lifted his hand. "I'm saying no more about Mercer Burgess."

"No, it wasn't about them. But I'm determined to get it out of you one way or another. No, I was wondering why Ron and Cole came alone."

"Ah, the answer to that is simple. Warners always reserve Frazier, Nelmes a table for six, and Conrad decides who the six are to be. He generally invites the Account VPs in charge of the account. You, Cole and Ron, I believe."

"Oh," said Ashley, "so I shouldn't feel honored then?"

He chuckled. "Sorry, but this is quite usual."

"And there was me thinking that Conrad had done something nice for me, for once," and despite herself, she felt disappointed.

Bill looked at her. "Didn't he?"

Ashley looked at him curiously. "No."

"But didn't he call for you, and bring you here?"

Ashley nodded.

"Then, I suppose you could say that Conrad did do something nice for you, for once. After all, he didn't call for Ron, or Cole."

She laughed. "Point taken."

They were held up for a moment by the volume of people.

"Tell me," she said, when they were able to move on again, "who did Conrad call for last year?" The question was out almost before she could stop herself, and seeing the look on Bill's face, she could have bitten out her tongue. It seemed that everyone looked at her that way these days whenever she mentioned Conrad's name, even her mother.

There was a slight commotion at the door, and Bill looked past her shoulder to see what was going on. She saw him grin.

"Right on cue," he said. "Don't look now but the answer to your question has just walked in through the door."

Ashley looked, and immediately regretted it. Being shown to a table was one of the most beautiful women she had ever seen. She moved across the room with the elegance of a swan over water, and her bright eyes laughed as she stopped once or twice to exchange greetings with someone she knew. Virtually all heads at that side of the room were turned in her direction, and though she must have known it, she seemed unaffected. She had arrived with an escort of three men, and Ashley watched as they sat down at a table, not too far from theirs. Waiters rushed back and forth, bringing champagne and glasses, and small trays of delicacies. The woman dipped her long fingers into them, and put them into her mouth in the most outrageously flirtatious manner.

Ashley turned back to Bill. "Conrad brought her last year?"

Bill nodded.

"Who is she? She's beautiful."

"Candida Rayne. Top model and granddaughter of David Burgess of Mercer Burgess fame."

"Oh," said Ashley. "I see."

"I don't think you do."

"Does he still see her?"

"From time to time, I think."

"Would that account for Conrad's personal involvement in the campaign?"

"Yes."

Ashley looked away, and back to Candida.

"And yours," Bill added.

"Mine?"

"All I'm saying is that when Conrad wants something, he knows how to get it. His methods may be a little convoluted at times, not to mention devious, but they seldom fail. And now, as we seem to have stopped dancing, shall we sit down?"

Ashley followed him back to the table completely baffled as to what was going on. But Bill would not be drawn any further on the subject, so she had to try and puzzle it out for herself. She didn't know where to begin.

Conrad was still talking to the President of Warners when they returned. He was standing very close to where Candida Rayne was sitting.

Ashley turned to the bottle of champagne on the table, and picked it up. She had so wanted to enjoy this evening, but now everything seemed to have fallen flat. Perhaps a little more champagne would lift the sudden dip in her mood.

Bill's wife, who had been dancing with Ron, came back to sit down too, and Cole, who had disappeared for a while, ambled up to them looking very down in the mouth because his devastating charms had failed to work on the starlet of his choice. Bill slapped him on the back and told him to try again later when she'd had more to drink.

Ashley watched Conrad as he extricated himself from the group around the President, and went over to speak to someone else. But it wasn't long before he came back to their table again. He seemed to be in an extraordinarily good mood this evening, and Ashley thought that perhaps she could see, at last, why everyone else at Frazier, Nelmes had such a liking for him. This was a side of him she had never seen before.

Cole was sitting beside her; he kept her glass topped up, and not once did she object. She danced with him again, several times, and with Ron too, but Conrad didn't ask.

It was much later, when Ron was in the middle of one of his mind-stretching stories, that Ashley found herself watching Conrad's face, and actually liking what she saw. Of course, he was extremely handsome, that she had never denied. But seeing him laugh was something new to her, and she liked it. Like so many men who smile infrequently, the impact of the smile when it did come was much greater than expected. But now he wasn't smiling; in fact, he wasn't even listening. His face was serious, and he was looking across the room at something else.

Ashley followed his gaze, and when she saw who he was looking at her heart skipped a beat. Candida was surrounded by men, quite clearly having a thoroughly good time. She tossed back her mane of blonde hair, and her eyes sparkled into those of her companions. God, men could be so hateful at times, fawning around a beautiful woman like she was some Greek goddess, hanging onto her every word. Why didn't they just peel her some grapes and be done with it?

She looked again at Conrad, and saw that he was still watching Candida. Ashley turned away, moving herself so that her back was half turned to Conrad, and took Cole by the hand. He seemed surprised, but pleased, and with his other hand he stroked her fingers.

"You having a good time?"

She nodded, and hoped that her smile reached her eyes.

She didn't actually like Cole stroking her fingers, so she excused herself, saying that she must find the ladies' room.

When she returned, pushing her way through a cluster of people who were standing near their table, Ashley suddenly came to a stop. Sitting down in the chair she had vacated was Candida Rayne. Ashley looked around in panic, trying to think of somewhere else she could go, not wanting to return to the table. She was forcibly struck by an eerie sense of *déjà vu*, when almost a year ago now, she had returned from the ladies' room at the Ritz and found Julian at her table, with Blanche. But that was completely different. Her feelings then were not what she was experiencing now. At least, that was what she was trying to tell herself. But what could she do? Bill was looking at her, so she just had to go and sit down. But there was nowhere for her to sit. Surely one of the men would get up. But she didn't want to sit down at the table while Conrad was talking to Candida. And he was laughing. Candida was making him laugh, and Ashley felt a pang that she had never made him laugh like that. Not that she had ever tried. Was it really necessary for Conrad to look so deeply into Candida's enormous green eyes? And why, when they were sitting at a table, did he have to hold her hand? Ashley was suddenly aware that her own hands were shaking, and she clasped them together to steady them. She realized, with horror, that she was jealous.

"Dance?" said a voice in her ear. Ashley turned, and found a complete stranger standing behind her.

"Please," she nodded.

He put his arms round her, and began to sway her gently in time with the music.

She nodded and smiled mechanically in response to his Yuppie small talk, but almost wished that she knew him well enough to ask him to take her home. Her eyes kept straying back to their table; Candida looked like she was settled for the rest of the evening. Ashley watched as Conrad poured champagne into her glass again, and then lifted his own, to drink an intimate toast with her.

"Something the matter?"

Ashley looked at her partner.

"Relax," he said. "You're too stiff."

"Sorry." She moved her arms further round his neck.

"That's more like it," he said.

She laughed, and despite the way she was feeling, she started to flirt with him. She was determined, as long as Candida sat in her chair, that she would not return to the table. If need be, she would remain dancing for the rest of the evening. And her partner wasn't so bad. Actually, he was rather good-looking. If Conrad wanted to take Candida home, Ashley was sure she wouldn't have to take a taxi.

The music became even slower, and the man pulled her very close. Ashley didn't object, and rested her head on his shoulder.

"No, no," he said, lifting her head. "Not like that. Let me look at your eyes."

Ashley looked into his face, and she could feel his hands sliding down her back. She did nothing to stop him. Catching sight of Conrad, who was now on the dance floor with Candida, she pushed herself even closer to her partner and pulled his head down to hers. His response was everything she could have wanted.

Then suddenly she felt her shoulder being grabbed from behind, and before she knew what was happening, Conrad was holding her in his arms.

The other man began to protest.

"Sorry, chum," said Conrad. "My wife has reserved this one for me."

Ashley gasped, and then giggled as the man turned away, clearly embarrassed, and not a little angry.

She turned back to Conrad. "Don't you ever ask for a dance?"

"Sometimes," he said.

"As I remember, you interrupted me once before at a party, when I was quite happy elsewhere."

"And as I remember, you slapped my face."

She giggled. "So I did."

He was smiling as he said, "I trust you're not thinking of doing it again," and she felt his hand move across her back, and pull her closer.

"Can I butt in?" said Cole, coming up behind them.

Ashley looked at him in dismay.

"No," said Conrad.

She laughed. "You seem to be rather adept at making my decisions for me."

He lifted an eyebrow, and gave a lazy smile. "You're a better dancer now than when I last had the pleasure."

There were fewer dancers on the floor than before, and they were able to dance unmolested, and uninterrupted. He watched her as her eyes began to scan the room.

"Are you looking for someone in particular?"

Her eyes darted back to his. "No," she said. "No, at least, well, uh, I was just thinking . . . where's Candida? Won't she mind? You dancing with me for so long."

Conrad looked at her, surprised that she knew about Candida. "Should she?"

Ashley shrugged, and wished she could stop the blood that was rushing to her cheeks. "Well, isn't she . . ."

"Isn't she what?"

"Well, aren't you, well, seeing her?"

"I was."

She felt unaccountably pleased at the past tense.

"Would it matter if I was?" he asked.

"Matter? In heaven's name, no."

"I believe your husband's in town," he said, after a minute or two.

Ashley nodded. "My ex-husband," she corrected him. "Why? Does it matter?"

He grinned. "Yes."

She looked away, flustered.

"I said yes."

"I know," she said. "I heard."

"So aren't you going to ask why it matters?"

"I don't know if I should."

"Why? Are you afraid of the answer?"

She felt her heart beginning to pound, and she wondered if he could feel it too. But he only chuckled when she didn't say anything.

After several dances he took her back to the table. The others were still on the floor, so they sat down and Conrad poured the remainder of the champagne into their glasses.

"To a successful presentation," he said, and touched her glass with his own. "I'd like you to meet David Burgess."

"Of Mercer Burgess?"

"The same. I've organized a meeting for Tuesday morning. I think you should look on it as a final, and perhaps the most important stage of the review. It will be the meeting that will decide what is to happen, in perhaps more ways than one."

She looked at him, and despite the impassive look on his face, she knew what he meant. She wanted to ask him why it was so important that she won this particular account. Why, when she was doing so well anyway, was he holding this one over her? She was beginning to feel that somewhere there was a grand scheme going on way above her head, and that she was a mere pawn in a much bigger game than anyone was letting on. Bill knew about it, of that she was sure, and obviously so did Conrad. But it was pointless her asking, neither of them would admit to anything.

She looked at Conrad again. His light-hearted mood of only moments ago had vanished, and again he was the cold and unapproachable Conrad she had always known. She tried desperately to think of a way to get them back on an easy footing, but it was no good, her own spirits were sinking fast. She felt miserable, sitting here with him, no one to interrupt them, unable to think of anything to say, or do.

She watched the deliberate movements of his hands as he picked up his glass, and then as he lit a cigar. From the corner of her eye she watched his face as, seemingly deep in thought, he looked out across the dance floor. Was he looking for Candida? Was he jealous because perhaps she was dancing with someone else?

Ashley turned away from him. She wanted the ball to end now, she wanted to go home, and think. She had had far too much champagne.

At last, Conrad's car was brought round to the front of the hotel and René, the doorman, opened the door for Ashley to get in. She wanted to say that she would get a taxi, but she was afraid it would sound rude. At least, that's what she told herself.

To her relief, Conrad drove in silence, and she made no attempt at conversation either. Five minutes later he was pulling the car to a stop outside her apartment block. He switched off the engine, and turned to look at her.

She smiled at him, a little uneasily. "Thank you for a lovely evening."

He inclined his head, and slipped his arm along the back of the seat.

"I suppose I should be going in now," she said, making no attempt to do so.

"Yes, I suppose you should."

"Well, good night then."

"Good night."

She looked at him, and saw him smile in the darkness. She felt her heart begin to race again, like it had earlier, when he held her so close on the dance floor.

"Well," she said, "thank you again. I really had a wonderful time."

He was still watching her. She leaned forward to take her bag from the dash, and as she sat back again he caught her hand in his, and pulled her round to face him. Slowly, so slowly, he bent his head to hers, and kissed her on the mouth. Unable, not wanting, to stop herself, she wrapped her arms about his neck, and kissed him back.

Finally he let her go, and reached up and touched her face. She felt embarrassed, and didn't know what to say. And he smiled at her confusion.

"I think you'd better go in," he said, handing her her bag, "before we both do something we might regret."

She took it from him, and without speaking got out of the car. When she turned back he was no longer looking at her, and it took every ounce of willpower she had to turn and walk away.

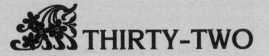 THIRTY-TWO

CATCHING A BRIEF GLIMPSE OF KATE AS SHE RUSHED through the outer office, Margaret Stanley, Features Editor of *Gracious Living* magazine, leapt to her feet and ran to the door.

"Kate! Kate!"

Kate was already at the door and she groaned as she heard Margaret's voice. She had hoped to escape without actually seeing the editor. She looked quickly at her watch and tried not to groan again. Nick would probably already be outside waiting for her by now. Still, she had no choice so she forced up the corners of her mouth and turned back again.

"Margaret," she beamed. "I thought you weren't in today."

"Really?" said Margaret. "Who on earth told you that?" She looked a little perplexed. Then her face brightened again. "Still, anyway, it doesn't matter. Helen tells me you're off to Cliveden again today."

Kate threw a look at Margaret's secretary who was sitting at her desk by the window, making herself suddenly very busy with the telephone and a notepad.

"I just wanted to let you know that I was quite impressed with your article so I am sending a photographer down."

"But I gave you all their bumph," said Kate.

"Yes, but I want some shots of the staff. And perhaps you having tea, or walking beside the swimming pool or around the grounds."

"Me!" said Kate. "Since when have I started to feature in my own articles?"

"Since now," said Margaret, a little loftily. "I particularly liked your bit about feeling the presence of the past. You know, surrounded by people, even in an empty room, and their escorting you through time. So, as I said, I've sent a photographer to meet you there."

"But I'm not working for the magazine today."

"You are now," Margaret grinned, but as usual the smile didn't get quite as far as her eyes.

"But I'm taking someone with me."

"That won't matter, surely?"

"Actually, it will."

"Oh, don't be silly. It won't take long, you'll be finished by lunchtime and then you can have the rest of the day to yourself."

"We won't get there until lunchtime," Kate pointed out, not bothering to disguise her annoyance.

"You won't if you continue to hang around here."

Kate glared at Margaret for a moment, but knew there was no point in arguing. "Who's the photographer?"

"Jillian. Jillian Jones."

"Oh no!" Kate groaned.

Margaret's eyebrows lifted so high, they succeeded in pulling her head backward and adding another chin to the two she already had. "She's the best, Katherine, I thought you would have been pleased. Besides, I thought you two got along well together."

"We do, normally. But did you really have to send her today?"

" 'Fraid so," said Margaret. "She's already on her way, so off you go, dear. Have a good time," and before Kate could protest further Margaret disappeared back into her office.

"Off you go, dear. Have a good time," Kate mimicked. "Why doesn't someone write her another script?"

Helen giggled. "Sorry," she said. "But when she asked me where you were today I thought that if I said you were spending the day at Cliveden *with a friend*, I'd be getting you off the hook. I had no idea. Sorry."

"Not your fault."

"If you don't mind," said Helen, tearing a piece of paper from the pad in front of her, "would you give this message to Jillian. Someone called just after she'd left."

Kate took the scrap of paper and shoved it into her pocket. "Jillian. Bloody Jillian. Of all people, it had to be her."

"But I thought you liked her. You two are always talking about the good times you have when you're out together."

"When it's just the two of us, yes, but not today."

Helen rested her chin on her hands and looked interested. "Not today? And can one ask, why in particular not today? Not hiding something from us, are you, Kate? Or should I say someone?"

Kate grinned and walked over to Helen's desk. She leaned forward and tapped her finger on Helen's nose as she spoke. "As a matter of fact, I am. I had high hopes for today, until now."

"Going to tell me who he is?"

"Nope!"

"Go on. Jillian will tell us anyway."

"I know," said Kate. "That's partly why I'm so bloody annoyed about it. But only partly."

"And the other part?"

"Is the biggest part. Jillian herself!"

"But what's the matter with Jillian?"

"Nothing—that's the matter with Jillian. She's beautiful. And tall and blonde, and slim and kind and sexy and irresistible and . . . Shall I go on?"

"I think you've made your point," Helen laughed. "Someone special then, this, uh, friend?"

Kate looked at her watch again. "Talk to you later, and tell Margaret I'm claiming expenses for the day. The whole day!" and she ran out of the office.

Helen shook her head, and went back to what she was doing. Libel, journalists, expenses and Margaret Stanley, they were the bane of her life.

"I'm afraid we're going to have company," Kate said, looking straight ahead. "At least for part of the day anyway." They were speeding along the motorway, toward Taplow.

Nick looked over at her, his eyes wary. "Don't tell me you've invited your father."

Kate turned to face him. "No," she said, surprised at his tone of voice. "No, I haven't as a matter of fact. Why? Would it matter if I had?"

"No," he said. And then: "Yes, actually. Yes, it would."

"Why?"

"What do you mean why?"

"What I said."

"Because it would."

"Why?"

"It doesn't matter," said Nick. "Who have you invited, then? If it's not your father?"

Kate looked out of the window again. "Actually, I haven't invited anyone. She's been thrust upon us. Margaret has decided to send a photographer down so I'll have to spend some time with her."

"Oh."

"Do you mind?"

"No."

"As long as it's not my father?"

"Yes."

"I see."

"You don't."

"Then explain."

Nick glanced up at the rear view mirror and then indicated to pull out into the fast lane. "All right, I'll explain. I didn't want your father to come because I thought we were spending the day together. Just the two of us. Does that explanation satisfy you?"

"Yes."

"Good."

"But we won't be just the two of us now anyway."

"The photographer. How quickly can we get rid of him?"

"Her."

"Her."

Kate shrugged. "It shouldn't take too long."

"What you mean is, it *won't* take too long."

Kate grinned. "Oooh, I love it when you're masterful. Particularly when you haven't shaved."

Nick threw her a look and maneuvered the car back into the center lane.

They were passing Heathrow Airport.

"Look!"

Nick hit the brakes, and tried to pull over. But then he saw what she was pointing at, and carried on.

"Concorde!" He shook his head. "I should have known."

"Sorry," she said, a little red in the face. "Funny, isn't it. I don't know how long it's been flying now, but I still get excited when I see it."

"You and several million others," said Nick, slowing down for the plane spotters in front.

"But you must admit, it is quite something. Actually seeing Concorde reminds me. I had a telephone call from Ashley this morning."

"How is she?"

"Oh she's fine, or at least she says she is. But you know I couldn't help thinking that there was something on her mind. For one thing, it was seven o'clock when she called, which means it must have been the early hours of the morning in New York."

"Perhaps she wanted to take advantage of the cheap rate."

"Mmm, maybe."

"Well," he prompted, "what did she say?"

"That's just it, nothing really. She asked how I was, and she asked about you too."

"Me?"

"Yes, why not?"

His smile was thoughtful. "What did you say?"

"I said that you were awfully well, and that you might be going to New York in a couple of weeks' time. By the way, she said you must stay with her, unless of course you have other plans." She looked at him, waiting for his answer.

Nick just grinned.

"Anyway," Kate went on, "I asked how she was, and she said she had just come in from some ball or something. It sounded frightfully grand. And when I

asked who she had gone with she changed the subject.
Then I asked how work was going, you know she's
right in the thick of this crucial presentation, but she
didn't seem to want to talk about that much either. And
then I asked her about Conrad, and she almost bit my
head off."

"Those two never did see eye to eye, as I remember."

"No," said Kate, thoughtfully. "No, they didn't,
did they? Anyway, she obviously didn't want to talk
about him. And then she rang off."

"She was probably a bit tired, that's all."

"Yes, I suppose you're right. But you will look her
up when you go to New York, won't you?"

"I expect so. In fact I might even stay with her,"
and Kat didn't miss the twinkle in his eyes as he turned
to look at her.

When they reached Taplow, Kate directed him to
Cliveden. As they turned into the long drive, she sat
back to let the scenery and aura of the place flow over
her once again. And Nick had to admit that he felt it
too. There was something about Cliveden, almost the
minute you entered the grounds, that seemed to embrace you with a sense of warmth and welcome.

He turned to look at Kate, and thought how lovely
she looked, sitting there beside him, enchanted by everything around her.

They turned into the Main Avenue, and Nick
pulled the car to a stop. They sat a moment, marvelling
at the intricacy and romance of the Fountain of Love.

"And now look up," said Kate.

Nick turned to see the house resting proudly at the
end of the avenue of limes. Despite its austerity, it
seemed to be waiting, as if it had been waiting pa-
tiently, for a long time, just for them.

He started to drive slowly toward it.

"I know what you're thinking," said Kate. "Apparently everyone who cares feels the same way. It's

as if the house is yours, isn't it? As if it is there, just for you."

Nick looked at her in surprise, and she smiled.

"Over there," she said, as they entered the court-yard, "behind the wall, is a swimming pool, with the most beautiful little summer house you've ever seen at one end. Beside it is a croquet lawn. And the clock tower," she went on, "was built for the Duchess of Sutherland in 1861."

Nick nodded. "For some reason it reminds me of the old nursery rhyme. Who built it?"

"Henry Clutton."

He looked at her, impressed. "You've done your homework."

"Of course," she said. "Now pull up over there, in front of the west wing."

No sooner had he switched off the engine than a footman was standing beside Kate's door, ready to open it and show them into the house.

The butler was waiting for them inside the Grand Hall, and Kate greeted him like an old friend. Then, after she had introduced Nick, he asked if they would like to take tea.

Nick looked at Kate, and almost burst out laughing when she asked for it to be served in the Boudoir. But the butler seemed to be prepared for this, and led the way to a small, at least by Cliveden standards, blue room, at the corner of the house. Nick loved the room on sight; he felt as though he had been invited into someone's home, rather than a hotel drawing room. Kate's face was beaming, and she pointed him to the window.

What he saw as he looked out took his breath away. The parterre was quite staggering in its splen-dour, with the most intricate and immaculately mani-cured hedges he had ever seen running down each side. Kate came to stand beside him. "The balustrade in front comes from the Villa Borghese in Rome."

He slipped an arm round her shoulder. "It's all so, well, humbling."

"Isn't it?" she said. "After we've had tea, I'll take you back out into the Grand Hall, and show you the portraits. You'll love Nancy Astor, she's so beautiful. And I'll tell you the story of the second Duke of Buckingham, who eloped with the Countess of Shrewsbury and came here to live in 1668. Their portraits are hanging there too."

Nick lifted his hand, and stroked her hair. She was like a child in her enthusiasm for the place.

"Kate! You're here at last. I thought you'd got lost. How are you? It's so good to see you."

Kate turned round to see Jillian coming across the room toward them, looking taller and more striking than ever, arms open ready to embrace her. Kate hugged her and laughed when Jillian let her go and told her in a very proprietorial voice that the footman was on his way with tea. "He's a bit slow, dear, but you know how it is. So difficult to get the staff these days," and she sat down on the settee.

Kate covered her face with her hand and turned away as she saw the footman standing at the door with the tray.

"Will that be all, madam?" the footman asked Jillian as he put the tray on the table in front of her.

"For now," said Jillian, as cool as you like. "I'll ring if there's anything else."

"Thank you, madam. And next time, madam, I'll try to be a little quicker." He stopped at the door and looked back at Kate. "The *Sally Anne* will be leaving at four," he said.

"Oh, yes, yes, thank you," Kate stammered. "Thank you." And he went away. "Jillian!" she burst out when she was sure he had gone.

"Sorry," said Jillian. "I just couldn't resist it. You don't think he minded, do you?"

Kate laughed. "Probably not. No sugar for me."

Jillian handed her a cup and turned to Nick. "You haven't introduced us, Kate," she said, keeping her eyes fixed on Nick. She stood up, holding out her hand. "Jillian Jones," she said. "And you're Nicholas Gough, I recognized you immediately. Kate's told me all about you."

"She has?" said Nick. Kate turned away, fighting a sudden urge to strangle Jillian.

Nick took Jillian's hand and shook it. "No sugar for me either thanks." He wandered over to a small table beside the fireplace and picked up a silver framed picture of Nancy Astor.

Jillian caught Kate's eye. "He's divine!" she mouthed, and then sat down again to pour his tea. Kate didn't miss the dazzling smile she gave him as she handed it to him.

"Thanks." He turned to Kate. "The Sally Anne?"

"Oh yes. It's the small Edwardian boat that belongs to the house. It takes you up and down the river. For guests only, but I asked the butler if we could go, as a special treat."

"It seems you scored quite a hit last time you were here," Jillian remarked, sitting back and relaxing with her cup of tea.

"It was mutual, I can assure you," said Kate, walking round the settee. "Where would you like to start?"

But Jillian wasn't listening, she was still watching Nick, though he seemed to be unaware of it. "Weren't you in *Romeo and Juliet* at the Old Vic a little while ago?"

Nick looked surprised. "Yes, I was."

"Now don't tell me, you were," she put her hand to her head while she thought, "you were Benvolio."

Nick was impressed. "That's right. You saw it?"

"I certainly did. And before that you were in something else at the National, weren't you? Was it *The Shoemaker's Holiday?*"

Nick shook his head. "No. I was in Shaw's *Man and Superman.* And then *Lady Windermere's Fan.*"

"Of course, *Man and Superman.* You were Octavius Robinson. Do you know, I went to see it twice."

"You did? You actually sat through Don Juan in Hell more than once?"

Jillian giggled and Kate wished she wouldn't. "I have to confess, the second time round I skipped the Don Juan bit. Not that I didn't think it was good. In fact it was brilliant, but it's very heavy. I suppose I just wasn't feeling in a heavy mood that night."

"I had no idea," said Kate, going to sit beside Nick, "that you were such an avid theater-goer, Jillian."

"Are you kidding? I go at least three times a month. I love the theater." She turned back to Nick again. "What are you doing at the moment?"

"We've just finished *Twelfth Night.*"

"Oh yes, at the London? I missed it. Couldn't get tickets. I should have come to you, Kate. But why didn't you say something?"

"As I said," Kate answered a little more sourly than she intended, "I didn't know you were so interested."

"What's coming up?" said Jillian, seemingly unperturbed by Kate's tone. "More Shakespeare?"

Nick smiled. "Not for the moment."

"Then what?"

This time he chuckled. "Oh, you know what we actors are, never like to talk about things until they're signed and sealed."

"Then I'll have to squeeze it out of Kate when I next see her. Don't want to miss it, especially now that I've actually met you."

"You don't mean to tell me I've actually got a fan?"

"Devoted," Jillian laughed.

"Shall we be getting on with it?" said Kate, putting her cup back on the tray.

"If we must. Shall we start outside? It's such a lovely day, let's go for a walk. What do you say?" The question was clearly directed toward Nick.

"Sounds fine to me," he said.

"Oh good." Kate moved toward the door. "Then shall we go?"

"Lead on," said Jillian.

"Won't you be needing your camera?" Kate asked, looking pointedly to where Jillian had left it on the settee.

"I thought we were going for a walk."

"To take photographs."

Jillian shrugged. "OK. She's not always like this, you know," she said to Nick. "All work and no play. It's usually me trying to get her to do something. I think she's trying to impress you."

"Actually," said Kate, "it was you I was thinking of. I thought the quicker we got to work, the quicker you could be off."

Nick tried to hide his smile behind his hand, but Jillian didn't miss it.

The next hour or so passed pleasantly enough, though Kate couldn't help wishing that Jillian would be a little less attentive to Nick and more aware of why she was there, but she said nothing. She was too fond of Jillian, really, to be unkind.

Much later, while Jillian went inside to get shots of the staff at work, Nick and Kate strolled down to the river, where the *Sally Anne* was waiting for them. There was no one else around, so they had the boat to themselves. At last Kate felt she could relax. She had been afraid that Jillian might insist on coming with them on the boat; it was one part of the day that she had particularly wanted to spend alone with Nick.

The *Sally Anne's* skipper was discreet, and he realized there was no need to give his usual talk on the sights they were passing.

Nick was most interested when they passed Spring Cottage, tucked in among the trees on the riverbank.

"It was there," Kate told him, "that the Profumo affair took place."

"There? I had always assumed it had happened in the house itself."

"No," said Kate. "It all happened right there. And somewhere around here must be the lawn where they say the Prime Minister danced naked."

"What, Macmillan?" said Nick. "The mind boggles. Are you sure it was a prime minister?"

"Well, that's what they say. But who knows?"

"Interesting, isn't it?" he remarked. "The Tory party, the party of morality and Victorian values, is the party that has had the most scandal attached to it. Still, all I can say is, if the Conservative government were to face a downfall, where better to face it, and what better way to do it?"

Kate laughed. "I think Mrs. Thatcher might have something to say about that."

"Well, I don't suppose anyone will ever catch her dancing naked on the lawn," and from the front of the boat he heard the captain chuckle.

When they disembarked Nick wandered on up the hill while Kate stayed a moment to talk to the boatman. When she turned to follow, she saw that Nick was already halfway up the steep slope. She stayed where she was and watched him.

They had known one another for several months now, and still he had never made any advance, or any suggestion, that perhaps their relationship was more than mere friendship. She knew that without him she might never have got through that terrible time. He had understood, in a way that so many men would never understand, what she had been suffering then. Her longing for a child, her desperate guilt at having . . . She found it difficult to form the words even now. It had brought them close together, but now she wanted much more. She wanted him to love her, in the way a man loved a woman. She wanted him to hold her and tell her he would always be there for her. Hardly a day went by when they didn't speak to one another, or see one another, but their relationship had never gone beyond the affection known between friends.

It was because she was in love with him that she had brought him to Cliveden. When she had last been here, she had been struck more than anything else by the feeling of romance that pervaded the place. And if he couldn't feel it too, with her and in these surroundings, then maybe he never would. Damn Margaret Stanley for sending Jillian. If she hadn't, then maybe things would have worked out.

Nick looked back and waved to her. She waved back, and started to climb the hill. He waited for her, and took her hand as she caught up with him. Was this all there was ever to be between them? That sometimes he would hold her hand? Sometimes he would slip his arm round her shoulders? Once, when he was leaving her flat one night, he had brushed his lips against her cheek, but he had pulled away again before she could turn her face. No, it seemed that theirs was no more than a deep and lasting friendship. She wished she had the courage to ask for more. The day was coming to an end and her heart was heavy, and she was suddenly struggling with herself to hold back the tears. Cliveden, dear, precious Cliveden, where she had believed that if Nick would ever turn to her in love, it would be here. The entire place was filled with love, it had an air for lovers. But he was walking on, a little in front, leading her back toward the house.

"Nick."

He turned back to look at her, but seeing the question in his eyes, she couldn't go on.

She shook her head. "Nothing."

He laughed. "I think someone is getting a little misty-eyed over their history."

They walked on into the house. In the hall she turned to him. "I was wondering . . ."

"Ah, there you are. You've been gone ages."

Kate closed her eyes in exasperation. "Jillian," she said, forcing a smile. "You still here?"

"Been upstairs," she said. "I watched you two love-birds, hand in hand across the lawns. Don't worry, I've captured it on film. I'll send it to you."

"Thank you," said Kate, gritting her teeth and avoiding Nick's eyes.

"Tell you what," said Nick, taking Kate's hand, "why don't we have a cocktail before we get back on the road?"

"What an absolutely splendid idea," Jillian cried. Kate tried to catch her eye, but she was looking at Nick. "I'll just go and put these in the car. Champagne cocktail for me, be right back."

"And for you?" said the butler.

Kate looked at him, she hadn't seen him come in. "Uh, the same please."

"Make that three," said Nick.

"Would you like to have them served by the pool?" the butler suggested.

"Good idea," said Nick. "I'll go and tell Jillian where we'll be."

"We have to walk past her to get there," Kate pointed out.

"Then we can both go and tell her where we'll be."

"Thank you," said Kate, as the butler started to walk away.

She followed Nick outside. "Jillian!" he called. "We're going over to the pool."

"OK," she called back, poking her head out of the car.

Kate walked on. She knew she was sulking, but she was furious with Jillian for having stayed so long. She walked round the edge of the pool, and heard Nick behind her.

"You're very quiet all of a sudden," he said.

"Am I?"

"Yes. Something upset you?"

"I'm here!" Jillian cried, coming in through the door in the wall.

"Yes," Kate muttered, "I think you could say that."

Nick gave a knowing smile but Kate wasn't looking at him.

"Now, where shall we sit?" said Jillian, as she caught up with them. "I know, how about in that darling little summer house over there?"

"I think I'll sit here," said Kate, plonking herself down on a sun lounger.

"Right you are then, here it'll be." Jillian sat down beside her. Nick sat the other side of Jillian.

A footman arrived and placed their cocktails on a small table in front of them. "The butler asked me to inform you," he said to Kate, "that the Lady Astor and Buckingham suite has been vacated now, if you would like to take a look round."

"Oh, yes, thank you," said Kate, sitting up. "I'd almost forgotten."

"How wonderful!" said Jillian. "I've been wanting to see that suite all day, but they wouldn't let me in."

They sat in silence as they sipped their cocktails. Kate was fuming, and trying hard not to show it, and Nick was amused, and trying equally hard not to show it. Jillian lay back on her sun lounger, apparently completely oblivious.

"Isn't it the most glorious evening," she sighed. "You know, it's been so wonderful meeting you, Nick."

Kate flinched and felt her nails digging into the palms of her hands. It was no good, she simply couldn't stand it any longer. She jerked herself to her feet and started to walk away. Nick glanced at Jillian and winked before he got up.

"Where are you off to?" he asked Kate, as he caught her up.

"Two's company," she snapped through clenched teeth, and walked on.

Laughing, he caught her by the arm as she was going through the door in the wall. "What's up?"

"What do you think?"

"Jillian?"

"Ten out of ten."

"I rather like her, myself."

"So I'd noticed."

"Well, you guys," said Jillian, sauntering up to them, still clutching her cocktail, "I suppose it's time I was making tracks." She looked at Kate and couldn't resist adding: "Sorry I can't stay any longer." Nick turned away to hide his smile.

They walked Jillian to her car and stood in front of the house, waving her off, until she disappeared round the corner at the Fountain of Love.

"And not a moment too soon," said Kate, turning back to the house.

"Oh, don't be like that."

"I'll have a few words to say to her next time I see her."

"She was winding you up, you know, the whole time," said Nick. "Couldn't you see that?"

Kate turned her head very slowly to look at him. He nodded. "Now come on. The Lady Astor suite, please."

While Kate went off to get the key and return the champagne glasses, Nick strolled round the hall looking at the portraits again. He was struck by how almost everyone, with the exception of Nancy Astor, had bald eyes. Maybe artists didn't feel the need to paint eyelashes in those days. Shame though, they'd look much better with them. He walked to the end of the room, and stood before the portraits of the second Duke of Buckingham, and the Countess of Shrewsbury. He grinned at the Duke, and winked. And then he turned his eyes to the haughty Countess, and thought how dreadfully ugly she was. Kate would be horrified! But honestly, one had to admit, the Countess was a bit of a dragon. The Duke wasn't much to write home about either. He shrugged, and turned away. Probably thought to be great beauties in their day, he told himself, and wandered back toward the door.

Kate came back, holding the key, and waved to him to follow her. He was pleased to see that her enthusiasm for the place had returned, and followed her up over the staircase. A portrait of George III looked down at him with a knowing smile, and Nick smiled back. Yes, Your Majesty, he said silently, you might well be right, and he continued on to the top of the stairs. Kate led the way down the hall, and then stopped to unlock a door at the end.

Nick followed her inside. He almost gasped to see the splendor of the room. So this was the famous Lady Astor suite. Everything was so delicate and feminine that he felt as though he had stepped into a lady's bedchamber, and almost expected the lady herself to appear beside the magnificent fireplace. He walked over to the heavily draped windows, and looked down on the parterre below, trying to imagine what it would be like to wake up every morning, and look out on all this.

Kate was sitting on one of the blue sofas that flanked the hearth, watching him, waiting for him to say something. He walked over to the bed, and touched the drapes that flared round the headboard. Everything was so beautiful, almost too beautiful to touch. He crossed over to the fireplace and, putting his hands behind his back, stood with his legs apart, marveling at the room.

"You look quite the lord, standing there like that."

"I feel it."

After a little while she said, "I wasn't jealous, you know."

Nick gave a shout of laughter. "You were!"

"I was not."

"You were. And so you should have been. She fancied me rotten."

"I noticed. And I was *not* jealous."

He went to sit beside her on the sofa. Putting his hands behind his head, he stretched his long legs out in front of him. "Didn't she used to be a fashion model, Jillian? She's very beautiful, don't you think?"

Kate shrugged.

"Lovely figure she's got."

Kate was silent.

"I have to admit, I could hardly keep my eyes off her legs."

Kate started to stand up.

He reached out and pulled her back. "Of course," he said, sitting forward and turning her face toward him, "she couldn't hold a candle to you. But then in my eyes no one could." His eyes were still laughing, and despite herself Kate felt a smile creeping up on her.

"And," he went on, "I'm glad you were jealous."

She opened her mouth to protest, but before she could speak he leaned forward and kissed her. Gently he pushed her back against the cushions, and for a long time held her in his arms, just kissing her. When he let her go he looked down into her eyes, searching her face, waiting for her to speak. She looked away, embarrassed and not knowing what to say. He pulled her face back again and brushed his lips gently against hers.

"I think," he said, "that the romance of this place is beginning to get to me."

She smiled. "I confess, I hoped it would."

He brushed the hair away from her face and kissed the tip of her nose. He looked round the room again, and she followed his eyes.

"Only the very rich, or very fortunate, ever get to stay here."

"A pity we're not rich, you're thinking," he said, gazing at her.

She didn't look away.

"However, who knows, we could be fortunate." He raised his hand, and began to stroke her cheek. "Would you like to stay?"

She swallowed, and tried to speak, but nothing would come out. She nodded.

"Tonight?" His face had become serious.

Her heart was racing, and she tried to smile. He was teasing her, he must be. "Are you making improper suggestions, Mr. Gough?"

"I doubt that anyone could do anything improper in surroundings like these."

So he had been teasing her. She turned away, trying to hide her disappointment.

"But it wouldn't be improper," he said, "if you were to say you'd marry me."

Her heart did an exquisitely painful somersault, and she looked into his face, expecting to see him laughing at her. But his eyes were soft and serious, and she couldn't think of a thing to say.

"Well?"

"But we've never . . . we hardly . . . we haven't even . . ."

"Then where better to begin?" Taking her face between his hands, he bent his head to hers, and kissed her so tenderly she thought her heart would burst. "You still haven't given me an answer," he said, as he let her go.

Suddenly she felt her eyes fill with tears, and she nodded, "Yes."

He kissed her again, and she clung to him; she never wanted to let him go. He pulled away, and once again his eyes were laughing. "I think we had better go down and check in, don't you?"

"It's very expensive," she said, as she was closing the door behind them. "Are you sure you want to stay?"

"Yes, I'm sure." He ran his hand across the back of her neck.

The butler seemed to be delighted that they had decided to stay the night, and he smiled a King George III smile as he pushed the book toward Nick for him to sign. Nick picked up the pen, and it was all he could do not to gulp when he saw how much the room was going to cost. But he knew it was worth it.

"How about an early dinner?" said Nick, as he took the key from Kate.

Her eyes had a mischievous gleam. "If we must."

The butler came back. "A table's been set for you in the dining room. And breakfast? Will you be taking that in your room, or will you be joining us in the French dining room?"

"Dinner we will have in the dining room," said Nick, "but breakfast we won't."

The butler smiled. "If you'd like to follow me."

A table had been laid for them in a corner, beside the window. They sat in silence a while, looking out across the gardens to the lazy hills in the semi-distance, a sparkling triangle of river in its midst. The distant horizon was hazy, blending with the sky, giving the impression that it was joined with heaven. The sound of a lawn mower could be heard, but there was not a soul in sight.

Nick turned his eyes back to Kate's, and reached out for her hand. The footman brought the menu, and he let her go again.

They looked the menus over, Kate trying to decide what she would have, Nick trying not to look at the price.

The footman came back and took their order, and presented Nick with the wine list. There was nothing for it but to order champagne, so checking for the third time that he hadn't come without his wallet, he ordered a bottle of Louis Roederer Cristal '79.

Their food arrived. The terrine of broccoli and foie gras, first. Then the poached fillet of salmon with chive sauce. But neither of them ate much.

"Dessert?" said the footman, wheeling a trolley to their table.

Kate looked at Nick, and they both shook their heads.

"Coffee?"

"No thank you," said Nick, before Kate could answer, and the footman went away again.

Nick turned back to Kate, and took her hand. "Are you ready?" he said, and his eyes were dark. The breath caught in her throat and she nodded.

He led her from the dining room, and back up the stairs. He glanced at George III, and smiled. When they reached their suite, it was Nick who this time unlocked the door. He pushed it open, turned back to Kate, and took her in his arms.

"There's something I haven't told you."

She looked at him curiously.

He smiled. "I love you."

"Oh Nick," she cried, putting her arms round him. "And I love you. I love you."

"Come along," he said, and pulling her inside he closed the door.

THIRTY-THREE

THE TABLE WAS LAID, NOW ALL THAT WAS NEEDED WAS FOR the candles to be lit. Linda looked around for the matches, and found them on the sideboard. As she picked them up she stopped a moment, and looked down at the photograph sitting beside them. It was the one that had always been on the window sill in their bedroom. She had moved it this morning, and put it where it was now. Strange, she mused, how a photograph can sit, hardly noticed for so many years, and then suddenly it can come to life again, willing you to relive the memory of the day it has captured. She hoped that Bob would remember too.

She went back to the table, and leaned across to light the candles. Then she turned down the lights. It had been so long since they had used the dining room. So long, since the days when many people had come to stay.

She caught a glimpse of herself in the mirror, looked away quickly and went to walk on. Then she changed her mind and turned back to it again. She had had her hair done that day at the hairdresser's in the village. She studied it critically, then twisted the stray wisps that had fallen from the knot on top of her head and were now curling round her neck. In the warm, rosy hue of the candles her complexion looked good, and she knew, or at least hoped, that she looked younger than her thirty-eight years. She tidied the white collar of her black dress, and rearranged the diamond pin at her throat. It was the one Bob had given her on their wedding anniversary last year.

She turned away from the mirror and tried to stop her mind going back over the years, wondering where she had gone wrong, wondering what she might have done to make things different. She didn't want to think about that now. She must concentrate now on how she was going to keep him. On what she was going to say when he told her he was leaving. For there was no point in fooling herself any longer, she had sensed, in the last few weeks, that things were coming to a head, and she had known, ever since she had got out of bed this morning, that tonight he would tell her he was leaving her.

She shuddered inwardly, but fought to stay calm.

Whatever she did, she must remain calm. In her worst moments she had wondered if she could carry on, but her mother-in-law did everything she could to keep her going. Dear Violet. Dear, dear Violet. She had never broken her confidence and told her son that Linda knew there was someone else. She had agreed to let Linda work it out in her own way, and Linda wondered now, what she would ever have done without Violet to talk to in these last weeks.

But now, tonight, it was up to her. She felt that awful sickening feeling that had kept coming over her all day. It had been so many years since she had felt like that, it was almost like being a teenager again, except now the stakes were so much higher.

"I say," said Bob, making her jump, "what's going on here?" He was standing at the door, smiling, and she smiled too.

"Have I forgotten something?" he said, looking at the candlelit table and silver cutlery, only brought out for special occasions.

"No," she answered, going over to him. "No, I just thought that we could have a nice quiet dinner together. Just the two of us." She didn't add that she was afraid it would be the last. She put her arms round his neck, and kissed him lightly on the cheek. He returned her embrace, and then held her at arm's length.

"You look beautiful."

"Thank you," she said. He was behaving so naturally, she couldn't bear to think that it all meant nothing to him. She had no way of knowing that when he looked at her, he felt as though a knife had been thrust into his heart. "If you open some wine," she said, turning away, "I'll go and see how things are coming along in the kitchen."

When she had gone, Bob picked up the bottle of wine from the table and opened it. He filled the two glasses, but only picked up his own. He knew he should take one to her, but he couldn't.

Why, oh why, tonight of all nights, was she being like this? So warm, so affectionate, and looking lovelier than he had seen her for a long time. How in God's name was he to tell her?

He sat down and took a sip of his wine. He looked around the room, and thought of how many happy hours they had spent here. Whether together, just the two of them, or with other people around. His eye fell on the photograph she had left on the sideboard, and he looked at it, remembering the day they were married, how happy they had been. Even after being together for so long before the wedding, it had truly been the happiest day of their lives. And there, on that photograph, they looked so much in love.

He looked away. What had happened to them? Why had things come to this? It was all his own doing, but that made it no easier to bear. Why the hell did it have to be like this? Why the hell did he have to hurt anyone? And how could he stand to see her face when he told her?

He picked up a knife, and began playing with it. His nerves were so taut he felt they might snap any minute. And if anyone were to ask him now what he truly wanted, he knew in his heart that he would have to answer that he never wanted to leave her. He never wanted to leave all this. Their home, where they had lived together and shared such happiness together. The stables where she kept her horses, and the freshness of each morning, when they rode together, over their own land, and out into the countryside beyond. He could see her now, with the wind in her hair, laughing and teasing him because he couldn't keep up. And the nights they sat together, as man and wife do, relaxing and reading, or talking, content in each other's company. How could he give it all up? But he knew he must. He had promised Ellamarie, and he couldn't let her down, not now.

He heard Linda's footsteps outside, and quickly

pulled himself together. When she came in he was standing beside the table, holding out a glass to her.

She took it from him. "What shall we drink to?"

"To us of course," he answered, feeling so wretched, he wanted to die. But he smiled, and held his glass to hers.

"To us," she repeated, and they drank. "Everything's ready. I'll bring in the first course."

She came back carrying two bowls of soup on a tray. She put it down on the table, and placed one of the bowls in front of him.

"Gazpacho," he said, starting to look up, but he didn't. It was his favorite, and not for the first time today, he wondered if she knew what was to come.

"I hope you like it," she said, and wished that they could stop being polite with one another.

Bob almost had to force it down. His appetite had been stolen by guilt and self-hatred.

"Don't you like it?"

"Of course I do." He picked his spoon up again. Finally, with a sigh of relief, he pushed the empty bowl away. "More wine?"

"Mm, yes please."

He refilled the glasses, praying that she wouldn't notice how his hand shook.

"Are you ready for the next course?"

"Bring it on," he said, trying to sound lighthearted.

When she brought the poached salmon and put it before him, it was all he could do not to groan. Still, at least it wasn't Boeuf Wellington, another favorite of his. That he would never be able to manage.

She filled a plate with salad, and handed it to him, then sat down to serve herself. She felt as though she was in the middle of a farce, and that any minute now the audience would applaud and this whole grotesque charade would end. But there was no audience. She looked at his face, and saw the lines around his eyes that had seemed deeper of late, and her heart went out to him in his confusion. It must all be so difficult for him, and he looked so tired, and alone. She wanted to hold him, and tell him that everything would be all right; but maybe she wasn't the woman he wanted to be held by.

She fought back her tears, and picked up her knife and fork. "Violet rang today."

"Oh?"

"Yes, when you drove into the village."

"How is she?"

"She's well. She asked if she could come and stay for a while at the end of the month. She's got some decorators coming, and doesn't want to be around when they're around."

The end of the month. Dear God, he wouldn't be here at the end of the month. And in all this he had never thought of his mother. "Well, that's fine by me. What did you say?"

"I said of course she could. She's going to drive, she says, so neither of us have to pick her up in London."

"Drive? All this way?"

"That's what she says. I tried to persuade her not to, but she wouldn't hear of it."

"I'll speak to her," he said. "It's too far for her, at her age. She's nervous enough on the roads as it is. Maybe I could go and pick her up." What was he saying? How could he possibly pick her up, he wouldn't be here?

She looked at him. What was he saying? Did this mean that he wasn't going to leave? At least, not before the end of the month?

"I think she'd like that, though it'll still take some persuading, if I know Violet."

Bob smiled. Of course she knew Violet. Violet was her mother-in-law, and Linda loved her like her own mother. But they could still see one another, when he was gone. He closed his eyes. When he was gone. And the two of them would sit here, in this house that he loved so much, and talk about him, and try to console one another for what he had done to them.

"I think Moonlight's leg is on the mend. Maybe we could take a ride out in the morning. He could do with the exercise, and I daresay you could too." Her meagre attempt to inject a little intimacy into their conversation failed, and she looked back at her food. She had hardly touched it, and she noticed that neither had he. "Any news on the *Queen of Cornwall?*"

"Adrian's off to New York next week, we'll know more then."

"Will you be going with him?"

"Can't," he said. "At least, not straightaway. I said I'd speak at the Arts Conference and dinner. Adrian's a little put out about it, but I can't let them down. He wants me to fly out and join him after the conference."

"Are you going to?"

"I don't think I have any choice."

"That sounds as though you don't want to."

He shrugged. "I hate all this wheeling and dealing, and begging for money."

"I thought you liked New York."

"I do. It's just that right now I don't really feel like going."

She didn't ask why.

"Anyway," Bob went on, "Adrian will have Nicholas Gough to hold his hand until I get there."

"Nicholas Gough? Wasn't he Sebastian in *Twelfth Night?*"

Bob nodded. "We're casting him as Tristram in the *Famous Tragedy.*"

"Oh." She took a tiny mouthful of food and pushed it around with her tongue. "Have you found anyone to play the Queen yet?"

She saw the muscles in his face tense and noticed a warm flush creeping around his neck. "Uh, well, we haven't actually decided yet." And then she saw the look in his eyes as he turned back to his dinner.

So now she knew who the other woman was. All she needed to find out was her name. But it would make no difference whether she knew or not. In some ways she preferred not to, but something inside pushed her, until finally, despite the other voice that screamed out to her not to ask, she said: "Have you got anyone in mind?"

He put his fork down and picked up his wine. The tremble of his hand was almost indiscernible, but it did not escape her. So she had been right. Whoever the other woman was, she was to play the Queen of Cornwall. And whoever she was, she was going to be a part of his life for quite some time to come. Perhaps, for the rest of his life.

"Did you read about John Hart in the paper today?" she asked, suddenly.

Bob looked at her in surprise, and he knew by the look on her face that she knew.

He put his glass down. "No," he said wearily, shaking his head. He wondered how long this pretense could go on. And for God's sake, why did his plate never seem to get any emptier? "No," he repeated. "What did it say?"

"It seems that he's been rather a naughty boy. Something to do with the accounts at his firm, but there were no details."

"I didn't know John had hit upon hard times," said Bob.

"Neither did I. Still, we don't know if it's true yet."

"Perhaps I should give him a call. After all, he's done enough favors for me in the past. Maybe I could help him out."

"That would be nice," said Linda. "I'm sure he'd appreciate it. I tried to ring Janice, his wife, today, but there was no reply. I should think the scandal will hit her very hard. You know what a stickler she is for doing things right. And now to have her entire life spread across the pages of some rag, it must be awful for her."

"Yes," he said, "it must." And he looked at her and wondered how she would cope when her whole life was spread across the pages of some rag, which, there was no doubt, it would be. And that was another thing he had never really considered. That he and Ellamarie would hit the headlines he had never doubted, but he had never considered Linda, what it might do to her. Being pestered every day by lurking reporters, having photographers springing out of the bushes every time she took a ride. Her life would be plagued by a bunch of unscrupulous hacks.

Jesus Christ! It was no good. Everything they said had double meanings. They had known one another too long to go on pretending like this.

He pushed his plate away. "I can't eat any more."

"Me neither," she said, and put her knife and fork down.

"I think we should talk, Linda. Can we go and sit down?"

The panic rushed at her with such force that she couldn't speak. He was going to tell her now. He was going to say that he didn't love her any more, and that he was going to leave her. She must stop him from speaking. She must speak first.

She followed him into the sitting room, and went to sit in the big armchair beside the fire. He was sitting in the other chair, looking into the flames. She topped up his glass from the bottle she had brought with her, and then leaned back in the chair.

"Bob . . ."

"Linda . . ."

They had spoken at the same time.

"Sorry," he said.

"No," she said.

He knew she was looking at him but he couldn't

meet her eyes. "Linda, there's something I have to tell you. This won't be easy, but I have to say it."

"No, don't," she whispered, "please don't say it. Not yet. I don't think I can take it."

He shook his head sadly, and watched her as she twisted the strands of loose hair around her fingers.

"Can I say something first?" she said.

He nodded.

She gulped at her wine, and he heard her swallow. Again her fingers were tugging at the loose hair, as she fought to keep control. "I know what you're going to say, Bob. I've known for some time. I don't want you to think I blame you. As a matter of fact, I don't blame you at all. I could have tried harder. I know that now, but you always know those things when it's too late. But I want you to know that I still love you, and that if ever you change your mind, I will be here. And I will wait for you, Bob. I will pray each night that you will come back to me. But seeing the pain you're in, seeing your eyes each time you look at me, and knowing that you're seeing her, feeling your hands, whenever you touch me, and knowing that you are thinking of her, well, I know that it can't go on any longer. I know that I have lost you, and that it's not me that you love any more. I wish to God that I could turn back the clock, but it's too late now. And I wanted to make you happy, believe me, I so wanted to make you happy. But in the end I failed. And I don't blame you. I will never blame you. I only hope that she can make you happy, my darling."

Bob pressed his fingers to his eyes, and swallowed hard. "I'm sorry," he choked. "Oh God, I'm sorry." He reached out for her hand and looked into her face. "I don't want you to think that I wasn't happy, because I was. I don't want to leave you, believe me, I don't want to leave you. But I have to. Please don't ask me to explain, but I have to go. And I still love you. That's what hurts more than anything, I still love you. And to know that you still love me, despite everything I have done, well, I . . . God, if you only knew how much I shall miss you. But it doesn't help to say it, does it?"

She shook her head, and looked up to the ceiling. He heard her sob, but he couldn't look at her.

"Do you love her?"

"I won't lie to you," he said, "not any more . . ."

"No, don't say it. I don't think I could stand it."

"No."

For a long time they said nothing. She wanted to ask him when he would go, but she couldn't. There were so many things she wanted to ask him, but the words just wouldn't come. Any minute now he would get up from the chair, and he would never sit there again. For a long time to come, she would look at that chair, and think of him, and torture herself with what he might be doing now. Every Friday she would listen for his key in the door. And every time she left the house, she would come back praying that when she turned the corner, his car would be waiting outside. And at night she would think of them together, and wonder if he laughed at all, or if he thought of her at all.

Finally he took a deep breath, and she looked over at him. He looked so tired, and so unhappy, but she could offer him no comfort. He shook his head. "If only you knew. If only you knew how different all this might have been. If only you hadn't come to the theater the night you did."

"So many if onlys."

"Yes, so many. And now it's too late."

Her breath caught in her throat, and she put her hands to her face to stem the flow of tears. "I know I shouldn't do this to you, Bob, I know it won't change anything, and you won't stop loving her. But, please, say that you will never regret the night I came to the theater. Please."

He looked at her, the question in his eyes.

"Just say it, please."

"I can't," he said. "If you knew the truth, you would know that I can't."

"Oh Bob," she sobbed. "If you knew the truth, you would never have said that."

"The truth? What truth?"

She looked down into her lap, and fiddled with the stem of her glass. "Nothing. Please, forget I said it," and the pain and sadness in her voice hurt him more than anything throughout all this had hurt him. And he knew, now that it came right down to it, that he truly loved his wife. It was her whom he wanted to be with, for ever. But now it could never be.

He stood up. "I'll sleep in the guest room tonight."

She looked up at him, and he thought if she asked him to go to her, he wouldn't be able to stop himself. But she didn't speak.

He walked across to the door. "Linda," he said, not turning to look at her. "I'm sorry. You'll never know how sorry I am," and pulling the door open, he left.

The following morning, just before six, Linda went upstairs to change. She had sat in the chair all night, unable to face their bed alone, knowing that he was in the next room. She had slept fitfully, but that was almost worse than not sleeping at all. Each time she woke, and found herself fully clothed, sitting in the chair, she would remember, and wave after wave of despair would come over her, until finally she could not bear to sit there any longer.

She pulled her jodhpurs and riding boots from the cupboard and, slipping out of her dress, she put them on. She knew it would be painful for her, to go out riding this morning, across the fields that they had ridden together, but she had to get out. She had to be with her horse, feel him nuzzle her neck, and put her arms round him.

When she got outside, she almost turned back again. The sun was so bright, it was going to be a lovely day. Nature did not share her grief. But she walked on; Barry had already saddled her beloved Petruchio. She took the reins from him, and led the horse out of the yard.

As she jumped onto his back, she didn't turn round. If she had she might have seen Bob, standing at the window, watching her. But she would not have seen the sorrow in his eyes, nor the tears on his cheeks. He watched her until she was out of sight, then turned away. He went into their bedroom and opened the drawers that contained his clothes. He stared at them for a long time, unable to bring himself to touch them.

Finally he sat down heavily on the bed and tried to think. But he was so confused that one thought ran into another, until his mind was spinning so relentlessly he lay down, and closed his eyes.

He must have fallen asleep; it was almost eight o'clock when he looked up again. He walked over to the window. No one was in sight. She was probably giving him time to go, and didn't want to be here when he did.

He picked up the phone and dialed. It rang several times at the other end, and then he heard his mother's voice saying hello.

"Mother, it's Bob."

"How are you, dear?"

"Fine. No, that's a lie. I'm not fine."

"Oh, I see," she said, and the way she said it surprised him.

"There's something I have to tell you, Mother."

"Yes."

"Maybe I should come and see you."

"Maybe," she said. "But I'd rather you told me now."

There was a silence on the line, but she knew he was still there, so she waited.

"It's about Linda," he said. "Linda and me."

He heard his mother give a long and drawn-out sigh. "So, you've told her."

So his mother had known too. He wondered how long she had known.

"How did she take it?" Violet asked, when it seemed that he wasn't going to answer.

"Not very well."

"Where is she now?"

"Riding."

"I see. Are you sure you're doing the right thing?"

"No, but I have to do it."

"Why?"

"I don't want to explain, Mother, just believe me, I have to."

"Do you love this other woman?"

He hesitated. "Yes. Yes, I do."

"And what about Linda? Do you love her?"

"Yes. Probably more than I realised. But there's nothing I can do about it now."

"That sounds as though you've been trapped."

"It's not quite like that."

"Well, I don't want to know the details, but would I be right in thinking that, given the choice, you wouldn't leave Linda?"

There was a long silence.

"Are you still there?"

"Yes," he said, "I'm still here."

"You haven't answered my question."

"I can't answer it. It's too late now. It's gone too far."

He heard his mother sigh again. "Sit down, Bob, if you're not already. I think it's time that you and I had a long chat."

THIRTY-FOUR

HEATHER GAVE A DELIGHTED SQUEAL AND DISAPPEARED BE-
hind a tree. Jenneen went running after her, and the
child screamed as Jenneen popped her head round, and
whispered "Boo!"

"Your turn to find me now," said Jenneen. "Cover
your eyes, and this time count right up to ten."

The little girl covered her face with her hands.
"One, two, three . . ." The chubby fingers parted.

"You're cheating again!" Jenneen cried. "You're
not allowed to look."

Heather giggled, and pressed her face up against
the tree. "One, two, three," she began again.

Jenneen ran behind the summer house, and crept
in under the hedge.

". . . nine, ten. Coming, ready or not!" Heather
shouted, and ran in pursuit.

Vicky stood at the door of her parents' old farmhouse, smiling as she watched Jenneen playing with her
young cousin in the garden. They had arrived on Friday
evening. Jenneen had been so tired, it had been an effort for her to drag herself up to bed. And now, here
she was, two days later, full of life, and ready to face
the world again. Well, perhaps not the whole world,
but certainly Vicky's family.

Her cousin Paul and his wife had arrived unexpectedly that morning, declaring that they were staying

for three days, en route to Cornwall. His aunt had been delighted to see them. Vicky had sensed an atmosphere when Jenneen first saw Paul, and guessed that he had probably been one of Jenneen's conquests in the past. Most likely the night of Robert Blackwell's party. Vicky set about trying to put them both at their ease, and Paul's wife was such a vague woman, she probably wouldn't have noticed if Jenneen had tried to repeat the performance in front of her. But she was a friendly woman, and talked to Jenneen, asking her all about herself and her family, and wanting to know everything about her life in television. Jenneen warmed to her immediately. Who wouldn't when she was such an ardent fan?

After lunch Vicky's parents took their customary afternoon nap, and Paul and his wife went for a walk. Heather, their four-year-old daughter, had pleaded with them to let her stay behind with Jenneen and play. Vicky had some accounts she wanted to go over, and the afternoon passed peacefully.

When her work was finished Vicky thought she might go and join Jenneen and Heather, but they were having such fun together, she felt she might be intruding, so she remained at the door, watching them playing in the sunshine.

"Penny for them."

"Paul," she said, turning round. "I didn't hear you come in."

"You were miles away. Where's Aunt Grace?"

"Still up in bed. I'm afraid the Sunday afternoon naps are getting longer and longer these days. Where's Susan?"

"Gone to have a bath."

"Where on earth does that daughter of yours get all her energy?"

"Her father, of course."

Vicky lifted an eyebrow. "Silly question. Like some tea?"

"I'll put the kettle on."

Vicky sat down at the table, looking out through the open door at Jenneen and Heather. After a while she looked up and smiled to see Paul standing behind her, looking out into the garden too. He put his hand on her shoulder, and squeezed it.

"Have you told her yet?"

She turned to look at him. "Who?"

"Jenneen."

"What about?"

He looked at her, but said nothing.

She turned away. "No, I haven't."

"Are you going to?"

"I don't know. I don't know if I should."

He strolled over to the door, and put his hands in his pockets. "I think you should."

"You do?"

"Mmm," he nodded.

"How do you think she will take it?"

"You know her better."

Vicky shrugged. "Sometimes I do. But then there are other times . . . ."

"But isn't that the same with everyone?"

"It's just, well, I don't know how to tell her."

"It can't be easy."

"Kettle's boiling," said Vicky. "You going to make it, or shall I?"

"You can. I think I'll go and rescue Jenneen. Heather can go and romp in the bath with Susan."

"Ah! You've got the kettle boiling," said Mrs. Deane, as she came into the kitchen. "Heard us moving around, did you?"

"Heard you moving around?" said Paul. "We were beginning to wonder what you and the old man were up to, up there."

Mrs. Deane giggled. "You'd be surprised," she said, to Vicky's surprise.

"Dad coming down too?"

"Yes. He's getting dressed. Goodness, those two still out in the garden?" Mrs. Deane remarked, as she strolled outside.

"They've been out there all afternoon."

"And I'm about to go and relieve Jenneen of her charge," said Paul, walking down the few steps to the garden.

"Thanks, dear," said her mother, as Vicky handed her a cup of tea. She took a sip. "Do you think your friend has enjoyed herself?"

"I'm sure she has," said Vicky. "You've all been so kind to her."

"Well, I won't ask what was wrong, but she definitely looks better now than she did when she arrived."

"I think she feels it."

"You leaving tonight?"

"Well, we were going to leave tomorrow, if that's all right with you."

"Course it's all right with me. You can stay as long as you like, you know that."

"Yes," Vicky smiled, going to sit beside her mother.

Mrs. Deane stared down at her cup. "Is Jenneen . . .? Do you . . .?"

Vicky laughed uneasily. "No," she said.

"I just wondered."

Paul came back, carrying Heather under his arm, Jenneen following behind.

"There's tea in the pot," said Vicky, "help yourselves."

"Can I have some lemonade, Grandma?"

"Yes, darling, I'll get it for you."

"Don't worry," said Jenneen. "I'll get it," and she went to the fridge to pour some for herself as well. "I'm shattered," she said, collapsing into a chair. "Children always amaze me, where they get their energy from. Or am I getting old?"

"You're getting old," said Vicky, and Jenneen picked up Heather's sponge ball and threw it at her.

"Bath time," said Paul, taking the glass from Heather.

"I don't want a bath, I had one yesterday."

"And you can have one today. Come on, Mummy's up there. Perhaps we can all three get in," and he turned to the table and winked at the others.

"Just mind you clear up all that water when you've finished," Mrs. Deane called after them.

"I don't know about the rest of you," Vicky said, getting to her feet, "but I'm going for a walk."

"I don't think I've got the strength," Jenneen yawned, then laughed as she saw Vicky's look. "All right, all right, I'm coming."

"How about you, mum?" said Vicky.

"No. No thanks, dear."

"You're so lucky, you know," said Jenneen, as they strolled into the tiny copse that marked the border between the Deanes' land and that of the farm beyond.

"Lucky? Why?"

"I don't know. Having all this, I suppose," said Jenneen, waving her arms toward the trees. "And your family. They're such wonderful people. I wish my family were like them. And now, of course, I feel guilty for even thinking it."

Vicky smiled.

"It's not that I don't love my family, I do. But my life is so different from theirs now. And that makes me sad. It's like living in two separate worlds. I know theirs, of course, but they don't know mine, and it's almost as if they're afraid of it."

"I'd like to meet your family one day."

Jenneen turned to look at her, and smiled. "It would be nice, but I'm afraid it would never work. They'd be so uncomfortable, and it would embarrass you, and me. But thank you for saying it."

"I meant it."

"I know you did."

They walked on in silence for a while, pulling the early autumn leaves from the trees, and picking up fallen branches, using them as sticks. There was no one else around, and Jenneen felt as though they were in a small part of heaven, where everything was perfect. She smiled at her thought.

"What are you smiling at?"

"Just thinking. It's so beautiful here. It makes you feel you never want to leave."

"I know," said Vicky. "But you can always come again."

They came to the edge of the wood. Jenneen climbed the stile, and sat on top of it. Vicky leaned against it, beside her.

"Vicky," said Jenneen, after a while.

"Yes."

"Can I ask you a question?"

"What kind of question?"

"A personal one, I suppose."

Vicky shrugged. "Try me."

"Have you ever been in love?"

Vicky looked at her, surprised at the question. "Yes, I have. What makes you ask?"

"I don't know," said Jenneen. "Probably because you've never talked about it."

"There's not much to tell, really. What about you? Have you ever been in love?"

Jenneen pondered the question a while, and then shook her head. "No, I don't think I have."

Vicky smiled.

"Of course, there have been times when I've thought I was in love," Jenneen went on, "but when I talk to Ashley or Ellamarie, well, then I know, I've never felt the way they do, about anyone."

"You will."

"That's what everyone says. Mr. Right is just

round the corner. He'll be here any day, sweep you off your feet."

"Tedious, isn't it?"

"Very."

Jenneen got down from the stile, and began walking back toward the woods. "Do you think he is, though? Just round the corner, I mean."

"Maybe it depends on whether you want him to be. Do you?"

"Yes and no. I don't know if I'd know it, even if he was there, not any more."

They reached a small clearing in the woods and Vicky stopped and leaned against the old gnarled oak tree where she and Paul had so often played as children. Jenneen stooped to pick the daisies; sitting on the ground, she started to make a chain.

Vicky watched her and smiled at how childlike she seemed. "Jenn," she said after a while, her voice quiet, "you're going to have to face it sometime, you know."

Jenneen stopped what she was doing, but she didn't look up. "I know."

"Have you ever thought about why you do it? What it is that makes you do it?"

Jenneen shook her head.

"There must be a reason," Vicky continued. "Somewhere there must be a reason. I can't understand why you want to hurt yourself like you do."

"I don't understand it either."

"Does Matthew know?"

"About Mrs. Green?"

"Yes."

"Yes, he knows everything."

"What are you going to do?"

Jenneen turned to face her. "Maybe you should ask Matthew that question. What is he going to do?"

"But I'm asking you."

Jenneen got up and walked over to a tree close to

the one Vicky was leaning against. She began to pick at the bark. "I think I'm going to kill him."

Vicky watched her but said nothing.

"I've got a gun." Jenneen turned round and leaned her back against the tree.

"And you really intend to use it?"

"I don't know."

"If you kill him, he will win."

"I know."

They stood in silence.

"That's not the answer, Jenn, is it?"

"No, maybe not. Why do you think he hates me so much?"

"Who knows the workings of a mind like his?"

Jenneen gave a dry laugh. "Or a mind like mine?"

Vicky smiled. "Yes, or yours."

There was a scuffle nearby in the undergrowth, and they watched a squirrel run up the trunk of a tree and disappear.

"I don't like doing it, you know. I hate myself afterwards. But I just don't seem to be able to stop myself. Perhaps it's the same with Matthew, who knows?"

"No," said Vicky. "Matthew is sick. Really sick. He's an alcoholic, remember. His brain is tortured by whiskey."

"Not always."

"And that is why he is truly sick. He's a sadist. There's little point in trying to analyze why he does what he does, we neither of us could come up with an answer."

"My mother always used to tell me that there is some good in everyone, even the very worst people."

Vicky laughed. "Mine too. But people like Matthew, well, I suppose there are exceptions to every rule."

"Do you think he gets pleasure out of what he does to me?"

"Who knows?" Vicky shrugged. "In a perverse

way, yes, he probably does. And you, do you get any
pleasure from Mrs. Green?''

Jenneen stared at her, horrified. "I hate Mrs. Green.
I loathe her, I thought you knew that.''

"Then why do you do it?''

"I told you," Jenneen snapped, "I don't know. I
can't help myself. I just do it. It just happens.''

"And the men you choose?''

"What about them? Do they get any pleasure out
of it?'' Jenneen's smile was bitter. "How do I know?
Why don't you ask them?''

Vicky ignored the subtle reference to Paul. "Do
you mind that they might get pleasure from you, or
Mrs. Green?''

Jenneen looked away and watched a rabbit scurry
into a hole at the base of a tree. A bird screeched above
her head and she looked up. Vicky was still waiting.
"Well?''

Jenneen's eyes blazed. Her sudden anger surprised
Vicky. "Yes," she said. "If you must know. Yes, I fucking well mind. But Mrs. Green doesn't. Mrs. Green
wants them to do it. But I hate them. Every last one
of them. I hate them for being them, for their weakness,
and most of all I hate them for touching me. Yes, I
mind. I mind so much I feel like killing them after. Hah!
That's a joke, isn't it? After! Notice I say after. Not before. No, before I beg them. Do you know that? Sometimes I actually beg them to fuck me. Can you believe
it? And then, when they do I just want to kill them,
or castrate them, because I hate them. But most of all
I hate myself." She pushed herself away from the tree
and went to walk on. When she reached the edge of
the clearing she stopped.

Neither of them spoke. Vicky watched her, and
thought that perhaps she was crying. But when she
turned round her eyes were dry, and now her expression was softer. "You see, I'm every bit as sick as Matthew. And who knows, maybe even worse.''

"No, you're not sick. Only confused."

"Confused!" Jenneen cried, throwing her hands in the air. "Confused, she says! I'm more than confused, I'm twisted. I'm a schizophrenic. I'm two people, Vicky, can't you see that? It's like being possessed, having an evil spirit inside, that you can't control. And you never know what it will make you do next. What depths of depravity it will take you to next. It hides, it goes away, but then it comes back, more evil, more determined than ever. It takes my whole body, it takes my brain, my limbs, my senses, it takes my whole fucking soul, and dear God I don't know what I'm going to do any more."

Vicky walked over to her and took her in her arms. Jenneen turned and buried her face against Vicky's shoulder. "What am I going to do?" she sobbed. "Please, tell me what I can do."

"It might not be as difficult as you think, you know."

"It won't change. Believe me, it won't change."

"It will, if you want it to."

Jenneen pulled herself away. "Of course I want it to. Didn't you hear me? I hate myself. I hate Matthew. I hate it all."

"Tell me, Jenn, deep down, right deep down inside, do you love Matthew?"

Jenneen looked into Vicky's face. Her eyes were bright. "Deep down I despise him. I loathe him." Her voice was calm, and Vicky knew that she spoke the truth. "I despise them all," Jenneen added. "Every single last one of them. I want to be rid of them, all of them. But I don't know how."

Taking Jenneen by the arm, Vicky started to walk her back toward the house. "I know," was all she said.

When they got back to the house, Jenneen excused herself and went up to her room. She was feeling calmer now, but she didn't feel up to idle chat.

An hour or more later there was a knock at the

door and Vicky let herself in, carrying two glasses of wine. "Thought you might like to try some of Dad's home brew."

"Thanks," said Jenneen, taking a glass from her.

"How do you feel now?"

Jenneen went to stand by the window. "I don't know. I don't feel anything really."

Vicky stood beside her.

"Look at the sunset," Jenneen said, in a quiet voice, gazing out over the countryside.

"Beautiful, isn't it?"

" 'Tis the sunset of life gives me mystical lore, And coming events cast their shadows before."

Vicky turned to look at her.

"Thomas Campbell," Jenneen said.

Together they stood at the window, watching the blaze of changing colors until the sun had disappeared over the horizon.

"Vicky," Jenneen whispered, when it was quite dark outside.

"Yes?"

"Just, thank you. Thank you for making me think, and thank you for listening, and being there. I don't know if it's helped, but thank you anyway."

"It's important for someone to be there. Paul was there for me once. It seems like another life now, but that's why we're so close. He knows everything about me."

Jenneen looked at her. "And you know everything about me."

"Almost."

Jenneen sighed. "It's been such a lovely weekend. I'm glad you brought me here," and she put her arms round Vicky and held her close.

Vicky hugged her back. "I'm glad you've enjoyed it. I know I have."

Jenneen pulled away, and stood looking into Vicky's face. "You're so kind," she whispered. Vicky leaned forward and brushed her lips very gently against Jenneen's. It was a gentle kiss, of friendship, and love, and Jenneen thought how right it felt. She lifted her hand to touch Vicky's face. "Thank you."

Vicky covered her hand with her own. She pulled it round to her lips, and gently kissed her palm. Jenneen watched her eyes, as they watched her. Then she took Vicky's hand, and pulled it to her mouth; softly she kissed it. Vicky stroked Jenneen's hair, and then leaned toward her, and kissed her again. Jenneen felt her lips begin to tremble in response.

Abruptly, Vicky pulled away. "I'm sorry," she said, and started to turn away.

"No, please, don't be sorry."

Vicky smiled at her sadly. "You're so lovely."

"So are you."

Vicky's eyes became soft again, and she took Jenneen's face between her hands. Jenneen leaned toward her and pressed her mouth gently against hers. She slipped her arms about her waist, and held her closely. Then she laid her head on her shoulder.

"Are you sure this is what you want?" said Vicky, a tremor in her voice.

"I don't know." Jenneen kept her head on Vicky's shoulder. "All I know is that I want you to go on holding me."

Finally she pulled away. "I'm going to get into bed now."

Vicky's face clouded over. "I'll go."

"No, please don't."

"But Jenn . . ."

"Sssh. I'm not afraid. Not if you're not."

Vicky smiled and pushed Jenneen's hair back behind her ears. "Is this Mrs. Green talking, or is it Jenneen?"

"It's me, Jenneen."

"Then I'm not afraid."

They undressed in silence, neither of them looking

at the other. Still in silence, they got into bed. Vicky reached up and turned out the light, and they lay there, side by side in the darkness, still saying nothing.

"Jenn."

"Yes?"

"Did you know? About me, I mean?"

"No," said Jenneen. "No, I never knew."

"I should have told you."

"It doesn't matter."

"Do you mind?"

Jenneen turned over toward her. "No."

"Honestly?"

"Honestly. Give me your hand."

Vicky pulled her arms from beneath the covers, and laid one hand in Jenneen's. Jenneen took it, and held it to her heart. Then she lifted the hand to her lips, and kissed it.

"I'd like to hold you again, Jenn," Vicky whispered, "very much."

Jenneen moved over, and laid her body against Vicky's and Vicky wound her arms round her. "You feel so good. So soft."

They kissed again, and this time there was the hint of passion in the kiss. Jenneen pushed her body closer. She heard Vicky gasp, and then she felt her hands, gently caressing her, and she too lifted a hand, and laid it on Vicky's breast.

The lovemaking that followed was like nothing Jenneen had ever experienced before. New and hidden sensations stirred inside her and she marveled at the warmth and softness of the skin beneath her fingers, and the tenderness of the lips that touched hers. And as they stroked and caressed one another in the darkness, Jenneen could feel herself changing and moving, and knew that Vicky was with her, and would never leave her. She fell back against the pillows, and pushed away the covers, until Vicky's hands and lips had taken her through the journey to its end, a journey she had never taken before, in love. It didn't end with an earth-shattering explosion inside, but with a sensation so warm, so deep, that it transcended any other. She smiled.

Vicky was looking down into her face.

"No regrets?"

"None. This is the first time, for I don't care to think how long, that I have made love with someone, and not hated them after. Do you know what you've done?"

Vicky shook her head.

"You've just shown me that Jenneen Grey is capable of making love with someone, without becoming Mrs. Green."

"I'm glad. That's what I wanted to hear."

Jenneen lay back on the bed. "I suppose that I should feel that I've got myself into yet another situation. But I don't. Did you know this was going to happen?"

"Not at first."

"And you're not sorry now that it has?"

Vicky smiled and took Jenneen's hand. "How could I be sorry?"

"But you sound so sad. What's the matter?"

"Nothing," said Vicky, turning her head away.

Jenneen took her face, and pulled it back. Gently she kissed her on the mouth. "Please. Tell me, what is it?"

"This might seem like the answer, Jenn, but it's not. At least not all of it. It might be that this is what you have been fighting all along, that this is why you do what you do, to deny what is really there. Maybe you have been afraid of yourself. But I don't know, neither of us can know that. You will have to have help, you know, more than I can give."

Jenneen was silent.

"Will you?"

"If you'll stay with me."

Vicky took Jenneen in her arms and kissed her tenderly. "Yes, I'll stay with you."

THIRTY-FIVE

PUTTING THE PHONE DOWN, ASHLEY GAZED UP AT THE painting on the wall. It had been a gift from Ellamarie, Kate and Jenneen, "just a little something to hang in your smart new apartment," Ellamarie had said. Ashley had cried when she opened it and found a reproduction of Claude Monet's "A Corner of an Apartment," featuring his wife Camille and son Jean. She wished her friends were here with her now, she so badly needed to talk to them. Turning back to Keith, she sighed as she saw that his face was still taut with anger.

"That was Conrad," she said, needlessly waving her hand toward the telephone. "I have to meet him in his office at eight in the morning before we go to see David Burgess."

"So the big man has spoken, and Ashley goes running."

"He's my boss." She wished Keith would go back to his hotel. It was late, and she had had a long day.

"And is that all he is, Ashley? Your boss?"

"I'm not even going to bother to answer that."

"And is that how it's always going to be?" Keith went on. "Conrad speaks and Ashley runs? Because if it is, you're making a big mistake as far as my son is concerned. You're making a big mistake full stop. But

I'm not going to let you ruin Alex's life as well. I'm warning you, now. I will not allow you to take him out of the school he's already got to know, and bring him here to New York."

"I have custody of him," Ashley pointed out, wishing she could find a way to end this conversation.

"Not for much longer, if I have anything to do with it. Which I will."

Ashley paled slightly. "Look, if everything goes according to plan, I'm likely to be here for at least another five years. Maybe longer. I don't want him to grow up without me."

"Selfish to the end. You'll let him grow up without me!"

"You can always visit him, you know you can."

"New York is not exactly round the corner."

"But we'll be coming back often, to visit Mum and Dad."

"For God's sake, Ashley, just where do you get off patronizing me?"

"Keith, don't shout. You'll only wake Alex."

"And you don't want him to know that his mother is planning to take him away from his father, is that it?"

"That is not the motive for bringing him here, and you know it."

"Ashley, don't you care about the fact that he's English? That he was born there, that he has grown up there? Doesn't any of that matter to you?"

"Of course it matters to me, but I don't see that it's so important. I think he would be better here, with me."

"With you! You're so damned wrapped up in yourself and that bloody agency, when will you ever find time for him?"

"I will."

"When? For an hour after work once or twice a week, when you don't have to stay late at the office?

And what about the nights you go swanning off with Conrad Frazier? What about Alex then?"

"I don't, as you put it, go swanning off with Conrad Frazier. We had one night out together last Thursday. It was an official function, nothing more."

"You want it all, don't you? You want the career, you want the social life, you want the money, you want the bloody Chairman. And it would seem any bloody chairman will do."

"You're being ridiculous," said Ashley, turning away so that he wouldn't see the heat in her face. "There is nothing between me and Conrad, you're imagining things."

"Imagining him taking my son to a baseball game? Imagining him take my wife to a ball?"

"I am not your wife!"

"Then why do you still wear my ring?"

Ashley looked at her left hand. She had never known quite why she continued to wear it. Perhaps it was for Alex's sake. Now she realized how stupid it was, that it made no difference whether she wore it or not. She twisted it off her finger and handed it to him.

"Thank you, but you can keep it. No doubt the only reason you've taken it off now is to make room for the one you're hoping Conrad Frazier will put there."

"Keith, shut up, for God's sake, shut up."

"A harder nut to crack than you thought, is he?" he jeered. "I must say, you really have moved in to the big time. Chairman of his own advertising agency, and in New York. Makes poor Julian look positively parochial over there in London."

"How many times do I have to tell you, there is nothing between me and Conrad and never will be. For one thing, he doesn't even like me."

"So it was just chance that he happened to turn up at the weekend, and take Alex riding? Because, of course, he'd do that for the son of someone he doesn't like."

"Maybe he likes Alex? Have you thought of that?"

"Don't be so naive. Bit of a shock, though, when Alex came back and told you about the 'fantastic lady' he had met at Conrad's. The one who'd gone riding with them. Wouldn't you like to know who she was?"

"As a matter of fact, I do know who she was. It was Candida Rayne. She and Conrad have been seeing one another for some time. Now does that satisfy you?"

"It might satisfy me, but it obviously does nothing for you."

"Precisely. It does nothing for me because it is none of my business." She got up and walked across the room. She didn't want to continue this conversation. They had to discuss Alex's future, and his coming to New York, but she didn't want to discuss Conrad Frazier. Not with Keith, or with anyone else, come to that.

"Well, whatever happens to you, Alex is not coming to live here, and that's my final word."

Ashley turned and looked at him. "It might be yours, Keith, but I can assure you, it's not mine."

"I'm going to fight you for custody," he said.

"Don't be stupid."

"I just thought I would give you fair warning. I will put it in motion the minute I get back to England. He is not coming to America. And if you want to see him, then you will have to cross the Atlantic, not me."

Ashley's face had turned white. She knew, from the look on his face, that Keith wasn't bluffing, and the thought of a custody battle for her son was terrifying—and not only for what it would do to Alex. "You'll never win," she said. "With your past you'll never win. No judge in his right mind will ever give you custody. You're not stable, and you know it."

"And you call yourself stable? Running off to New

York the minute you couldn't make a decision. Where will you run to next, Ashley, when Conrad leaves you high and dry? At least if Alex was with me he could continue his schooling in England, where it began, and where he is familiar with his surroundings. And his grandparents will be there, the grandparents who have brought him up. What kind of a mother have you been, Ashley? What kind of a mother do you call yourself?"

"He's my son," she spat. "And no one on God's earth is going to take him away from me. So get that into your head now."

"And he's my son. And no one, least of all you, is going to take him away from me. So you think on that, Ashley darling."

"Do you actually mean to tell me that you want the whole sordid story of the break up of our marriage to go back into court? The drunken father, the womanizing father, the one who abandoned his wife and son and went off screwing someone else the night the child was born. The father who all but threatened to kill him rather than see him stay with me. Do you want all that brought up again? Alex is eight now, Keith, he will understand. Do you want him to know what you're really like?"

"You bitch!" he snarled. "You'll do anything, won't you, to get what you want."

"I don't want him growing up with you, and if you must know, I never did. You're no good, Keith. You're a failure."

He lifted his hand to strike her. She didn't flinch. "Go on, hit me. Show us all what you're really like. You haven't changed, Keith, and you never will. And that's why you will never win custody of your own son. I will see to it that you don't."

"You're going to regret this, Ashley. I'm warning you, you will regret this."

"There's nothing you can do, and you know it."

"Alex will stay in England with me. I'll do everything I can to discredit you. You and your advertising lover. The man who won't marry you. The man who will only use you, and then leave you, just like his partner did. You're out of your league, Ashley, I'm going to take Alex away from you. I gave you your chance, but no, you chose yourself and your career instead. Well, now you'll see just how dearly you're going to have to pay for that."

"If you do anything to hurt him, or to take him away from me, so help me, Keith, I'll kill you. I swear it, I'll kill you."

"Then you'd better change your mind about keeping him here in New York. Because he's never coming here to live. Never!"

Ellamarie wandered through the deserted theater, dragging her feet and running her hands along the back of the chairs. She hadn't seen Bob since Friday morning, and she hadn't heard from him. Before he went he had thought that he might have been back again on Saturday night, after he'd told his wife. Or Sunday morning at the very latest. But now it was Monday morning, and there was still no sign of him.

She had rung and rung the mews house, but there was no answer. She was tempted almost beyond endurance to call his home, but managed to stop herself. And now, because she had to get out, she had come to the theater. She hadn't really expected him to be here, but her heart had sunk when his secretary said she hadn't seen him.

Every minute that passed increased the fear that he had changed his mind. She fought hard against even thinking about it, but she had to face the fact that as she hadn't heard from him, it could only mean one thing. But perhaps Linda had taken it harder than either of them realized she would. Perhaps he was having to comfort her. What if she had threatened to kill herself? He would have to stay then. It was the not knowing that tore at Ellamarie.

She looked up at the stage and pictured him standing there, his back to her, talking with the actors and making them laugh. The way he would run his fingers through his beard, his eyes belying the stern expression.

It was all over now. In her heart she knew it, and in her heart she knew that no matter what, she would always love him. Maybe it would never have worked between them, knowing what had happened that terrible night over four months ago now. But if only she could see him just one last time. To say goodbye to him and tell him that she didn't blame him, that she understood that he could never leave his wife to take on the bastard of a rapist. She understood, and would never reproach him.

This was the meeting Nick had not been looking forward to. In fact, he had been dreading it. Now, standing face to face with Kate's father in the library of their home in Surrey, the meeting had all the promise of failure.

Calloway's face was stern, yet there was something close to a sneer around his mouth as he scrutinized Nick's face. Kate had tactfully disappeared to somewhere else in the house, and there was no sign of Mrs. Calloway.

"Sit down," Calloway said, waving Nick to a chair.

"Thank you," Nick answered, and walked across to one of the pair of neo-rococo armchairs that flanked the hearth. Calloway sat in the one opposite.

"I guess you probably know why I'm here."

Calloway put his head to one side and continued to stare at him.

"It's about Kate."

"Yes."

"We'd like to get married." Not for the first time,

it struck Nick as absurd that in this day and age he should be asking Kate's father for permission to marry her. But it was what she had wanted.

"Yes," said Calloway.

Nick moved slightly in his chair. It was obvious the older man was going to do nothing to help him. He cleared his throat. "It was Kate's idea, that you and I should have this talk."

Calloway nodded.

Nick looked around the room, along the rows of old books that Kate's father had collected over the years. The desk beneath the window where he sometimes worked was piled high with papers, and the slightly threadbare carpet reached comfortably across the floor as if trying to eke itself out to the walls. "Well," he said, looking back at the older man, "I expect you would like to know the date we have set."

Calloway paused before he answered. "No, not really."

Nick watched his face, trying to see if it would tell him anything, but it remained inscrutable. "Does that mean you won't be coming?"

Calloway seemed to ponder the question. Finally he said: "I think you would be right in that assumption."

"But surely you must know how much it would mean to Kate, to have you there?"

Again Calloway seemed to think about this. "It might," he answered. "Tell me, Mr. Gough, are you actually asking for my permission to marry my daughter?"

"Well, yes, I suppose I am."

"And if I refuse?"

"Kate is past the age where she needs parental consent."

"Yes." Calloway stood up and walked slowly over to a small cabinet in the corner. "Would you like a drink? Scotch?"

If it hadn't been so important to Kat that they do things right, as she had put it, Nick would have refused and said that he was leaving. But as it was . . . "Just a small one, thank you."

Calloway poured the drinks and handed one to Nick. "Kate has accepted you, I take it."

"Of course," Nick answered.

"Yes, of course, she would." Calloway sat down again.

"We're very much in love." Nick felt foolish even as he said it.

"I don't doubt that you are."

"Are you going to refuse?" Nick asked him.

Calloway lifted his glass to his mouth and took a large mouthful of whiskey. "I have to."

"Can I ask why?"

"You can ask."

Nick could have sworn with exasperation. Instead he stayed silent. Two can play at this game, he thought.

Calloway stood up again. He walked to the window and looked out across the sloping garden. He stayed there for a long time. Nick waited.

"Mr. Gough . . ."

"Maybe you should call me Nick."

Calloway ignored the interruption. "There is a great deal in this family, Mr. Gough, of which you know nothing."

It was perhaps more the tone of Calloway's voice than the actual words that made Nick uneasy. He waited for him to go on.

"I don't know," Calloway eventually continued, "Whether it would be right to tell you."

"Whatever it is," said Nick, "I can assure you that nothing you say will change the fact that I am going to marry Kate."

Calloway walked back to his chair and sat down. He gazed into the empty hearth. "You think you know

Kate, don't you?" he said. "You think you know everything there is to know about her."

"Not everything, no."

"Good. Because you don't."

"I know what I feel to be important."

"And what, may I ask, is that?"

"I know that I love her, isn't that enough?"

"No. No, it is not enough."

Nick's patience snapped. "For God's sake, you're
behaving like somebody who hasn't seen their way out
of Victorian times. I don't have to sit here and listen
to your mysterious meanderings, I'm only here because
Kate wanted me to come. If it had been up to me we
would have just got married and been done with it."

"It's as well for you that you didn't." Calloway
didn't appear to be in the slightest put out by Nick's
outburst. "Did you not wonder why Kate asked you
to speak to me first?"

"Because of how close you are. There's nothing to
wonder about in that."

"But you must admit that it was, shall we say, a
little odd for her to have insisted that you come."

"Not odd, no. And she didn't insist. She asked, and
I agreed."

"But you'd rather not have come?"

"I won't deny it. Especially now."

"But you would have had to come sooner or later,"
said Calloway, "of that you can be certain."

"Whatever you say, nothing is going to change my
mind about marrying Kate. Now if there is something
you want to tell me, then by all means do. But as I said,
whatever it is, Kate and I are getting married at the beginning of next month, and nothing you say or do will
alter that fact."

Calloway looked surprised, and a little ruffled.
"The beginning of next month," he repeated. "So
soon?"

"No, she is not pregnant," Nick snapped. He stood

up and put his glass on the mantelpiece. "Now, if you've quite finished . . ."

"Sit down," said Calloway.

Nick glared at him.

"I said, sit down."

Nick sat down.

"Another drink?"

"No thank you."

Calloway took the glass from the mantelpiece and went to refill it. He handed it to Nick. "Take it," he said. Not knowing what else to do, Nick took it.

"I mentioned earlier," Calloway said, as he sat down, "that there were things in this family of which you know nothing. Because I am forced to, I'm going to tell you what they are. But before I do I want you to remember something. I say this, not as a threat, but as a statement of fact which you will do well to heed for your own good, and indeed my daughter's. I am a very powerful man, Mr. Gough. Probably a great deal more powerful than you realize. Joel Martin found that out to his cost. I have no wish to illustrate it again to you, but I will if you force me to."

Nick watched his face closely, but there seemed to be no violence in it.

"I want you to remember that, and remember it for a long time after what I have told you." He waited to see if Nick was going to speak, but when it was evident that he had nothing to say, Calloway continued. "Mr. Gough, you cannot marry my daughter."

Nick sat forward. "And I tell you, I will marry her."

"Will and can have two entirely separate meanings," said Calloway. "You say you will, and I say you cannot. And I will explain why indeed she *can* marry you, but why you *cannot* marry her. She can marry you because she knows. You cannot marry her because you don't know."

"Mr. Calloway," said Nick, trying to hold back his

anger, "I am getting a little tired of your riddles. Please, come to the point."

"Yes, the point." Calloway looked down into his glass. "You cannot marry Kate, because Kate is in love with me."

The color drained from Nick's face. He stared at the man sitting opposite him. "You're insane!"

"No," said Calloway, "I am in full possession of my faculties, and what I tell you, unfortunate as it might be, is the truth."

"You're a liar," Nick said, the full force of his disgust sounding in his voice. "She's not in love with you, it's you who are in love with her. Your own daughter. Your own bloody daughter. I knew it, but I didn't want to believe it. I didn't want to believe that anyone was that . . . that, depraved! It *was* you who was phoning, wasn't it?"

Calloway looked perplexed for a moment. "Phoning?"

"Ringing Kate and whispering your foul lust down the telephone. Terrifying the hell out of her."

"Is that what she told you? Yes, I suppose she would have to."

"For God's sake, she didn't even know it was you." Nick couldn't stop himself from shouting.

"Please, keep your voice down. Of course she knew it was me. But obviously if I called whilst any of her friends were present, she had to pretend."

"That was no pretense," Nick cried. "I was there, I saw her face. She was terrified, I tell you. Terrified."

"Terrified that any of you would find out, yes."

Nick sprang up from his chair and began to pace the room. "Dear God, you're sick, Calloway. Kate knows nothing about this, does she? She doesn't know the way her own father lusts after her. The way his mind warps around what he would like to do to her. Good God, I've got to get her away from you."

Calloway smiled. "That wouldn't be wise. Besides,

she wouldn't go. Perhaps if I tell you why she agreed to marry you, it will help you to accept what I am telling you. Having a husband would give her the respectability she needs, and the cover that perhaps both of us need. However, I have no wish for her to take those measures.'

"This is a nightmare," Nick cried. "It's all a bloody nightmare."

"I'm sorry, you must accept it. You cannot marry Kate, can you see that now? You cannot marry her for your own sake."

Nick stared at him, for the moment speechless.

"Ask yourself, can you really live with a woman whom you know to be making love with someone else? Can you marry a woman who is already in love with someone else? Can you accept a woman whom you know is doing what Kate is doing, with her own father? Of course you can't. No one could."

"You're a liar, a filthy stinking liar." Nick was panting with rage. "She's a normal, decent human being."

"Mr. Gough, Kate is already mine. Kate has been mine for a long time now. We have shared . . . shall we say, experiences? We share a love that no one, not even you, can come between. If you must put her to the test, well, then you must. But it will be a bitter and hard lesson for you to learn. Why not spare her the agony of having to admit it? It is hard enough for her as it is. But everything she does, you know, is for me. I daresay, if you think about it, you will already have realized that. Even that silly mistake with Joel Martin. Yes, even that was for me. She wanted us to have a child, you see. But of course, for us, there can never be any children, not of our own. But she needed Martin to say that it was his, can you see that? She needed him to say that it was his, in order to avoid any suspicion falling on us. And then she even went out and stole a baby." His face was sad as he spoke, and he looked into the empty fireplace again. "I told her, after what had happened with Martin, that one day we would have a child that we could call our own, and so she went out and stole one, even though she knew it was wrong." He stopped and looked up. "And now she has agreed to marry you. She has agreed to marry you, so that she can have that child. And when she does, your marriage will be over. She will leave you, and bring the baby to me."

"I don't believe anything you're saying," said Nick, but the conviction had gone from his voice. There was something in what the man was saying that had started alarm bells in his head. An odd comment here, a look there, so many little things that seemed to give some insane truth to what he was saying.

"Would you like me to call her? I was hoping that you wouldn't need her to confirm any of this, but if that's what you want, well . . ."

Nick looked at him. "You could go to prison for what you're telling me now."

"Perhaps I should remind you of how this conversation began," Calloway answered.

Nick turned away. "It's not true," he said, "it's not true. It can't be true." He was speaking more to himself than to Calloway.

Nick found himself at the window. Kate was at the end of the garden, sitting on the bank and looking down into the stream. She looked so innocent, so lovely.

"I'm sorry," Calloway said. "I understand how you must be feeling. You see, I love her too."

"Shut up! Shut up!" Nick yelled. "I don't want to hear any more. I don't believe you. I'll never believe you. OK, call her in. Let's get her in here. Let her tell me. If she tells me it's true, then I'll go. I'll go and I'll never come back. But until I hear it from Kate herself, I'll never believe it."

"If you're sure that's what you want," said Calloway, getting to his feet.

Nick was far from being sure, but he nodded.

"Wait here."

Nick stayed beside the window, and watched as Calloway walked across the length of the neat lawn to where his daughter was sitting. His heart was beating so hard he thought it might burst from his body. He saw Kate throw her hands up in the air, and turn away. He watched her as she turned back to her father, and she seemed to be shouting at him. And then she beat her fists against him, and he tried to take her in his arms. She pushed him away, and walked back toward the house. Her father came after her, and now Nick could see that she was crying.

"Why!" he heard her scream. "Why?"

He couldn't hear anything else that was being said, they were still too far away. Her father was speaking; Kate clearly didn't want to listen. Then she fell to her knees, and began to pound the ground with her fists.

Calloway knelt beside her, and tried to lift her into his arms, but she pushed him away. He managed to keep hold of her hand, and he was still speaking. Now she was listening, and then she was looking at him. She fell back on the grass, and Calloway sat in front of her, so that Nick could no longer see her.

Then he saw her arms go round her father's neck and Nick watched in morbid fascination as he realized that Calloway was kissing his daughter, and his daughter was kissing him back.

He couldn't stand to see any more. He ran from the house, leapt into his car and drove away. His mouth was coated with a bitter bile, and his gut twisted in protest at what he had witnessed. He felt sick to his very soul.

In the garden, her face buried in her father's neck, Kate begged him to tell her why Nick no longer wanted to marry her.

THIRTY-SIX

ELLAMARIE STOOD IN THE DOORWAY, LOOKING AT BOB. HE was sitting in a chair, the odd one that matched nothing else in the room, and now, for the first time, she thought he looked just as out of place. His face was weary, the laughter lines round his eyes drawn as if they were trying to shape his face into that of an old man. Outside, the wind was humming the tune of approaching autumn, and she looked up as a steady beat of rain began to drum against the windows.

Bob buried his head in his hands. Her heart ached and she wanted to go to him. Instead she asked, "Would you like a drink? Some coffee? Something stronger?"

He shook his head, "No, nothing."

She walked into the room, and sat down on the sofa. As the silence lengthened the feeling of nausea in the pit of her stomach grew. Finally, he lifted his head from his hands and looked at her, but when he didn't speak she said: "I was worried. I thought you might have called. It doesn't matter," she added, hurriedly, "you're here now, and I can see that you're all right."

He got up from his chair. "Look, Ellamarie, we both know why I'm here, so let's not pretend any more."

Ellamarie didn't answer. The cold hand that had

been hovering around her heart for days was now beginning to close.

"The truth is, I can't go on like this. I've got to get away. I need some time to think. Some time on my own."

"I see."

"For God's sake, don't sound like that. Don't you know how difficult this is already?"

"What am I supposed to say?" she said, knowing that she was speaking to a stranger.

"I don't know," he answered. "And that's the trouble. I don't know anything any more."

She had to ask him. "Does that mean that you don't love me any more?"

"Look, I've just said I don't know. All I know is that I can't make a decision right now."

"Have you told your wife?"

"Yes."

"How did she take it?"

"How do you think she took it?"

Ellamarie turned away. So now she knew what it was like at the end. So often she had wondered, thought about the things he might say, but she had never dreamt that he would hurt her like this. She looked at him, barely hearing his words as they came across the room at her like knives achieving an easy target. His face was anguished as he told her that probably he did still love her, but he loved his wife too. OK, he knew he had lied, but he hadn't meant to. He didn't know how any of this had happened, but it had, and now he was sorry he was hurting her. He'd do anything he could to make it up to her. She could still play the part of the Queen in the *Famous Tragedy,* they'd shoot round her pregnancy if it showed. And then she'd have the baby, and he'd give her money to help her look after it. But the way things were right now, he just had to get away.

Ellamarie stood up, swallowing hard against the

pain that was threatening to engulf her. She moved around the room, not knowing where she was going or why, she just knew she had to move. Her fingers were trembling, clutching her throat.

"Your things," she said finally. "Shall I help you to pack? I've got most of it ready." She smiled at him, and the barrier he'd carefully tried to hold in place fell completely.

"Stop it!" he yelled. "Stop behaving like this. Why don't you cry? Stamp, shout, say something, but stop being so bloody noble."

"I don't know what to say," she answered, her voice barely audible. "You see, I love you, Bob."

"For Christ's sake," he shouted, grabbing her by the shoulders. "I'm only going to spend some time on my own. The way you're behaving anyone would think I was running out and deserting you."

"Aren't you?"

The blow to her cheek stunned them both. After a long moment she looked up into his eyes and saw that he was crying. She reached out for him, trying to take him in her arms, but he turned away. "Please, I don't want you to touch me." He walked away from her and stood in front of the fireplace, his hands pressed against the shelf, looking down into the ashes.

"You don't have to hurt me like this," she said, her voice shaking.

His face was stricken as he turned to her, but the phone rang at that moment preventing him from speaking. Ellamarie went to answer it. It was Kate.

As she listened while Kate told her that it was all over between her and Nick, Ellamarie watched Bob pace the room. It didn't occur to her to end the telephone call, she had been too long a source of support and strength to her friends when they needed it. Once or twice Bob glanced up, as if he were waiting for her to finish. She looked back at him, barely listening to what Kate was saying. Her cheek still stung from the blow and unconsciously she was stroking it with her fingers. Suddenly he stopped pacing and turned to look at her. His face was a mask, and the eyes that had always looked at her with laughter and love were steely. He bent to pick up his coat. He didn't look at her again, but walked past her and out through the door.

By the time Kate rang off the pain had become so intense it was threatening to choke her. She didn't know what she had said to Kate. She looked across the room to the door. In the end, he had walked away. Quietly, with no backward glance, he had detached himself from her life. He hadn't even said goodbye.

Normally Ashley walked to work, the brief half-hour alone in the mornings gave her time to think without interruption. But this morning, overwhelmed by lack of sleep, she flagged a passing taxi and collapsed into the back seat.

Her eyes were sore, and she rubbed her fingers against them. Her mind started to spin again. She had returned home in the early hours of the morning, after sitting up half the night with Nick in his room at the Waldorf. She couldn't think about that now, she didn't want to think about it ever. A bitter clench of nausea gripped at her stomach. She tried to shake it off, but it persisted.

She knew it wasn't just the conversation that she had had with Nick, though God, that was bad enough.

Alex had been irritable when she'd left that morning, and Keith's mood had only got worse since the scene they had had on Monday evening. She was tempted to go back home again, but looking at her watch she knew that she didn't have time. They would be leaving for Boston about now, where they were spending the night with some distant relatives of Keith. Besides, Conrad had asked to see her at eleven-thirty; he would know the results of yesterday's meeting with David Burgess.

It was eleven o'clock when she walked into the IBM building. She knew she must try to reach Kate. She closed her eyes as she thought of her friend, and wondered what the hell she was going to do. But it couldn't be true, no matter what Nick thought he had seen, it just simply couldn't be true. She had to speak to Kate. She had no idea what she was going to say, but she had to find out the truth for herself.

As she walked into her office she told Jan that she was not to be disturbed and, closing the door behind her, she went straight to the telephone.

There was no reply from Kat's flat. She let it ring and ring, willing Kate to answer, but it was no use. She didn't want to ring her at her parents' home, but there seemed no other way.

Kate's mother answered the phone and Ashley apologized for ringing so early in the morning, but Kate wasn't there either.

Replacing the receiver, Ashley buried her face in her hands. She must think. There must be something she could do. Did she dare tell Jenneen or Ellamarie? Nick had told her in confidence. But, Jesus Christ, they had to trust one another; if they didn't, then it would be the end.

She picked up the phone again. She was aware that her voice was shaking as she told Jenneen all she knew. Jenneen was every bit as horrified as Ashley had been. "But it's not true, Ash," she said, when Ashley had finished, "you know it's not true."

"I hope you're right, Jenn."

"Jesus Christ, it can't be. I must see her."

"She's not at home. I've tried."

"Leave it with me," Jenneen said. "I'll find her."

Ashley heaved a sigh of relief as she hung up. There was nothing more she could do, except pray that Jenneen was right, and that it wasn't true.

She buzzed through to Jan to bring her some coffee, wishing that the feeling of impending disaster would go away. She rang her apartment. There was no reply; she hadn't really expected one.

Jan came in with her coffee. "You've been summoned."

"Already?" said Ashley, looking at her watch. "Christ, it's twenty to twelve. Why didn't you remind me?"

"You asked not to be disturbed." And then, looking a little sheepish, Jan said, "Sorry, I forgot."

"Don't worry," Ashley smiled. She took several mouthfuls of coffee. "Oh well, here goes," she said, "Mohammed to the Mountain again. Wish me luck, otherwise you might have a new boss before the week's out."

"Good luck," said Jan. "And I don't think so somehow."

"He's waiting for you," said Candice, as Ashley walked into the outer office of the Chairman's suite.

"What kind of mood is he in?"

Candice pulled a face.

"Oh God," Ashley groaned. She knocked on Conrad's door and let herself in, closing the door behind her.

Conrad looked up from his desk. "Come and sit down," he said, waving her to the chair at the other side of his desk, and then turned his attention back to what he had been doing before she'd come in.

She sat down in the chair, and gazed out of the window. It was several minutes before she realized that he was watching her. "You're looking a bit pale," he said.

"I had a bad night, I'm afraid."

"Worrying over the account?"

"Partly."

Conrad smiled, and looking into his face Ashley felt her heart turn over. He was so strong, always in control, and she wondered what it would be like if she could turn to him at times like this, when she was feeling so bloody vulnerable and confused. His hands were resting on the desk in front of him, strong, capable hands, that had held her only once. If only she could reach out and touch them now, and draw some of their strength into her bones. She pushed the thought away quickly. It was because she was tired, she told herself. Conrad was watching her, and for one uneasy moment she thought he might have read her mind.

"So," he said, leaning back in his chair and stretching his legs out in front of him, "to Mercer Burgess."

Ashley felt her stomach begin to churn. She smiled. "To Mercer Burgess," she repeated, in a quiet but steady voice.

"I spoke with David Burgess early this morning, and he's given me his decision."

Ashley looked into his face, but as ever, it was inscrutable.

"I'm afraid," said Conrad, "that your pitch was not successful. They have turned it down."

"What!" Ashley gasped.

"The decision was made late last night, as far as I'm aware."

Ashley couldn't speak. Her eyes began to dart about the room. This was impossible, she had been so sure they were going to accept. David Burgess had more or less told her so when they'd shown him the video at their meeting yesterday morning. They couldn't have turned it down. But Conrad wouldn't lie about something like that. Jesus Christ, it was as important to him as it was to her.

She looked back at him. "I see," she said.

"I'm sorry."

Her jaw was tight as she said: "Yes, I'm sure you are."

He got up and started to walk round the desk.

She leapt to her feet. "Well, let's make this quick, shall we? I'll go and collect my things together now. I can be out of my office by the end of the day, although

I can't promise to be out of New York quite so quickly. Would the end of the week be acceptable to you?" She was already walking toward the door.

"Ashley, come and sit down."

She turned back to face him, her eyes blazing. "Conrad, really, I'd rather not go over this. You made it perfectly clear when all this started, that if the presentation did not win through then you wanted me on the next plane back to London. Well, you've got your wish. I'm sorry that Mercer Burgess did not take us on, but I rather think that in the end that had nothing to do with whether or not I stayed. Now, if you will excuse me . . ."

"Sit down!" He barked rather than spoke the words.

She stopped with her hand resting on the door handle.

"Please," he said. He leaned across the desk and buzzed through to Candice. "We'll have coffee now, Candice."

Ashley took a few steps away from the door. For the moment she was too angry to realize how hurt and disappointed she was. Or to admit how it was going to wrench at her heart to leave him, knowing that that was all he had wanted, almost from the very start. That she should go.

"I think I owe you an explanation," he said, turning away from the desk. "I'd like you to stay and listen. Better still, it might help me a little if you were sitting down and not standing there looking like a bull getting ready to charge."

Candice came in with the coffee and put the tray on Conrad's desk. Ashley waited, tapping her foot, as Candice poured the coffee. She didn't even manage to muster a smile when Candice handed her a cup as she left the office.

"Well," said Ashley, "Let's get it over with."

"Ah, where to begin?" Conrad perched himself on

the edge of his desk and sipped his coffee. Ashley watched him, but made no attempt to drink hers.

"I suppose," he began, "that it all starts with Candida really." He noticed how Ashley's face darkened at the mention of Candida's name and he couldn't resist allowing himself a quick smile. "Unfortunately, when Candy discovered that you were coming to New York, she flew into what you English might call a fit of the pique."

"Why on earth should she do that?"

Conrad shrugged. "What Candy does, Candy does for reasons best known to herself. But take it from me, she was not at all impressed by the idea of your coming here. In fact, I think I can go as far as to say, she was furious. And when Candida Rayne is furious, the whole of New York has to know about it. In this case, the victim of her fury was you. But not only you. She was furious with me too. And there is something you should know about Candy. There are very few people in this town who can afford to get on the wrong side of her, me included. So, I had to think of something, that, shall we say, would get us, and by us I mean Frazier, Nelmes, out of a situation where she might want to exercise her power over us." And watching him sitting there, that arrogant smile on his face that she had hated and then loved, and now hated again, she felt the beginnings of a volcanic rage. She hated him for telling her about Candida. She hated him for wanting her to return to London. She hated him for smiling at her that way. And she hated him most of all for not knowing how much she loved him.

She took a deep breath, and with her head on one side, and her teeth clenched against her rising anger, she said: "So she is the reason, I suppose, that come what may, win or lose with Mercer Burgess, I had to be sent back to London. Candida, Candy," she almost spat the name, "did not want me here."

Conrad lifted an eyebrow, and began to smile.

Ashley wanted either to cry, or to throw her coffee at him.

"You don't see at all," he said. "Did you know that Candy is the granddaughter of David Burgess?"

"Yes," said Ashley, wishing that he would stop referring to Candida as Candy.

"There are three main accounts that keep this agency afloat," Conrad continued. "David Burgess happens to be on the board of all three of those companies. Does that help to explain the situation?"

"I don't think that explains anything," said Ashley, deliberately being obtuse.

"All right, I'll spell it out. David Burgess is extremely fond of his granddaughter. If Candy wants, then Candy gets, and David is almost always the one to deliver. If Candy had been so minded, she could have put this entire company in jeopardy. And with you around, she was very nearly so minded."

Ashley shrugged. "So you're sending me back to London to save the agency. Thanks for telling me, it helps," and she turned toward the door.

"I'm not sending you anywhere," said Conrad. "If you want to go back to London, then I'll do everything I can to stop you, but in the end it's your decision."

Ashley's hand froze on the door handle. "I beg your pardon?"

"David Burgess has offered you a job with any one of his companies you might choose. I turned the offer down on your behalf, I might add."

"You did what?" she gasped.

"I said I thought you might wish to stay with Frazier, Nelmes. I hope I was right."

Ashley was completely at a loss for words.

"You see," Conrad went on, "the whole thing paid off in the end, as I hoped it would. After you had got such an impressive package together, which I was counting on your doing, I knew that David Burgess would want to meet you. It was the only way of keeping his business, and keeping you in New York too."

"I'm still not with you," Ashley said.

"The bottom line is, you impressed the hell out of the old man, and now even though he can't give us the account this quarter, they are seriously considering it for next quarter, and he wants you to run it. Better still, he wants you to go and work for him, but as I told him, that was out of the question. So now, no matter what Candy has to say about it, you and Frazier, Nelmes are safe. The old man loves you, you've got him practically eating out of your hand."

Ashley's frown was puzzled. "So, who did get the account?"

"J.S. & A."

"J.S. & A? But you saw what they were offering."

"Yes," said Conrad. "And by the way, it was you who took their file, I've since discovered. No, no," he said, raising his hand as she made to interrupt him, "you didn't know it. You picked it up with your own things the day you went to see Arthur Fellowman. He wasn't in the least put out by it, in fact I think he looked on it more as a favour to me that I should see it. Probably trying to stop me from spending any more money than you already had."

"So are you telling me that I don't have to go back to London?"

"Not unless you want to."

She shook her head.

"Good," he said, sliding a hand into his pocket. "That's what I hoped you'd say."

"Tell me," she said, "did you actually mean it when you . . . well, you implied that you actually wanted me to stay?"

"Naturally."

"Even though we didn't win the account?"

"It was never that important," he said. "What was important was that you should be able to stay, and that

Candy wouldn't be in a position to make the agency, or me, suffer for it."

Ashley swallowed hard. "This is all a little too much for me to take in."

"Maybe you would like to sit down now?" he suggested.

"No," she shook her head. "No thank you." She walked over to his desk and put her cup back on the tray. "One other thing," she said, after all, she might just as well have it all out in the open now. "I'm curious, but was it Candida who Alex met when you took him riding at the weekend?"

Conrad seemed uncomfortable with the question. "Ah, yes, it was Candy. She arrived unannounced, and with the results of your pitch still not decided I wasn't in a position to ask her to leave."

"I see," was all she said.

He put his cup beside hers on the tray, and then, to her utter confusion, took her hand in his. "You don't, but I'm not going to explain." Reaching out for her other hand he added, "I'm glad you want to stay."

She looked up into his face, and her heart suddenly tightened as she saw the serious look in his dark eyes. He grinned and then, putting his hand behind her head, he pulled her toward him and kissed her full on the mouth.

"Oh," she said, as he let her go.

"Is that all you're going to say?"

She realized that once again she was impersonating a goldfish. She gulped and tried to regain control of her mouth. "I can't think of anything else."

He laughed. "Did you know that I've been in love with you since the very first time I saw you?"

"Oh Conrad, that's not true, and you know it."

"If it's not," he said, "then it should be," and pulling himself to his feet he took her face between his hands and looked into her eyes. She looked back at him, not daring to speak for fear that one word would shatter this moment and bring them tumbling back to reality. That any moment she would wake up and find herself back in London. He lowered his head very slowly toward her, his lips parting as he pulled her to him. He pressed his mouth against hers, and as she reached up to put her arms round him he pulled her hard against him.

She clung to him, feeling her body melt against his, wanting to be even closer to him, forgetting everything, knowing only that this was what she wanted, more than anything else in the world, to be here with him like this.

The buzzer on his desk brought them abruptly back to reality. Not letting her go, Conrad leaned over and flicked the switch. "Your car's out front," said Candice, and the line went dead.

He turned back to Ashley, and smiled to see the question in her eyes, and the disappointment too. He couldn't be going out, not now.

"Come along," he said.

"Where are we going?"

He stopped at the door and turned back to take her in his arms. "Do you seriously think I can wait a moment longer?"

She felt herself begin to shake, and he caught her to him. "Say you'll come."

They said very little as they drove. The air between them was charged with a desire that had been suppressed for too long. Occasionally he turned to look at her, but she didn't dare to look back. She knew if he touched her she might lose control all together. She wanted him so badly, her body ached.

When they pulled up outside his apartment block he tossed the keys to the doorman and ushered her inside.

By the time the elevator reached the ninth floor every inch of her body was on fire for him. He closed his apartment door behind them, and pulled her into the bedroom.

With desperation they tore at one another's clothes. Naked, she stepped into his arms. He lowered his head to kiss her, moulding her body against his so she could feel the hardness of his thighs against hers, the strength of his arms as they circled her waist, and the thrill of his hands pressing against her buttocks. Then pushing her back onto the bed, for a moment he stood looking down at her. His eyes were like a caress on her skin, and she moaned softly as she felt her body responding. He stepped toward her and her eyes dropped to his penis, pushing up against his belly, achingly swollen, ready to take her. Her eyes flew back to his and she began to tremble as, taking her legs in his hands, he lifted them apart and dropped to his knees in front of her. His tongue was hard and manipulative, making her cry out as she snaked her fingers through his hair. Cupping her breasts roughly in his hands he took her nipples, squeezing and pulling them until they rose like hard beads from her body. And then his mouth was there, kissing them and soothing them with his tongue. She reached down and took his penis in her hand. He gasped then groaned as he felt his control slipping away. And then he was beside her and his fingers were pushing into her, and she thrust her hips toward him. He opened his mouth wide and took hers in a bruising embrace. Catching her savagely about the waist, with one swift move he was inside her. She cried out with a voice she barely recognized as her own as she felt the full depth of his penetration. His passion was violent, and his tongue demanding as he pushed it deep into her mouth. She clutched at his hair, and dug her nails into his back as he ground into her, faster and faster. And beneath him she drove her body to his, meeting him with unleashed urgency. Briefly he raised his head and looked down into her eyes, and then as the seed began to rush from his body he called out her name, and as if from a long way away she heard her own voice, crying out for him, as their bodies burst into waves of the most intense and exquisite pleasure they had ever known.

It was several minutes before either of them had gained enough breath to speak. When she looked into his face she saw that his eyes were tender and he was concerned that he had been too violent, but she only smiled and pulled his face down to hers and kissed him. He laughed then, saying perhaps it was her who had been too violent with him. She sank her teeth into his fingers, making him laugh again, and he rolled over onto his back, pulling her into his arms. Idly he ran his fingers over her skin, pausing at her breasts and teasing her nipples back into the achingly erect buds they had been before. She groaned and turned in his arms, taking the laughter from his face as he saw the dark look in her eyes.

"Jesus Christ," he breathed, as he felt himself begin to respond. And this time they were tender and patient, holding one another close, allowing their bodies to speak in a way that words never could.

Later, lying contentedly in his arms and idly running her fingers over his thighs, Ashley sighed and turned to kiss his shoulder. She felt a warm glow ripple softly around her heart as his arms tightened about her, and feeling him looking down at her, she turned to gaze into his face, his lopsided grin appearing more precious to her than she could ever have imagined. "I love you," she whispered.

"Sure you do," he said.

She opened her mouth to deliver a hasty retort, but he caught her face in his hands and kissed her. "And I love you," he said, as he let her go. And then his eyes were teasing again. "Hell, I ought to, you're the best roll in the hay a man's ever had."

She choked.

"Yes?" he said, and she fell against him laughing.

"You know there's one thing for sure here," he said, after a few minutes.

"And what would that be?"

"This afternoon beats the pants off the first time we made love. And I didn't think that was possible."

She lifted her head from his chest and looked into his face. "What do you mean, the first time?" she asked, finally.

He cupped her face in his hand and ran his thumb along her cheek. "Remember the swimming pool?"

Ashley pushed herself away from him, but before she could speak he had caught her in his arms and planted his mouth very firmly on hers. At that moment the phone started to ring. Swearing under his breath, Conrad reached out and picked it up.

"I'm sorry," Candice's voice came over, "but this is important."

"Can't it wait?"

" 'Fraid not," she said.

Conrad sighed and pulled himself up from the bed. "OK, go ahead."

"Ashley's maid is here."

"What does she want?" Conrad turned to look at Ashley, who smiled at him and began to trace tiny patterns across his back.

"She's brought a note with her, that she found in Ashley's apartment."

"What do you mean, a note? What sort of note?"

"Well, it's from her husband, uh, ex-husband. It says that he has gone back to England, and taken her little boy with him."

"What!" Conrad almost shouted.

Ashley's hand stopped on his back. A sixth sense seemed to tell her that this might be something to do with her.

"Does it say anything else?"

"I'm afraid so," Candice answered. "It says that if she tries to get him back, then, hell look, I'll read it to you. He says, 'I told you, Ashley, that you would never have Alex in New York. Now perhaps you will believe me. I have taken him back to England, and if you do anything, and I mean anything, to get him back again, then I will not hesitate, I will kill him, and kill myself too. This time it is not a threat. I told you you would never win. Now perhaps you will believe me.' He signed himself, your husband, Keith.''

Ashley was watching Conrad's face, and he was only too aware of her eyes on him. He turned away. "Get on to the airport," he said to Candice, "book two tickets on the next Concorde out. Or the next flight, whichever gets there first. Send someone round to her apartment," he glanced at Ashley, "and collect the necessary and have it sent straight over to Kennedy."

"Right on it," said Candice, but Conrad had already put the phone down.

"What is it?" said Ashley, her face ashen. The uneasy feeling she had started the day with suddenly hammered against her head.

He put his arms round her, but her body was tense. "Just put your clothes on."

"No," she said, "no. What's happened, Conrad? Tell me. Alex, it's something to do with Alex, isn't it? Tell me, please!"

"Sssh," he tried to soothe her. "Come along now. I'll tell you on the way to the airport."

"But where are we going?"

"To London."

THIRTY-SEVEN

"**P**HONE FOR YOU, JENN!"

Jenneen turned back, looking at her watch. "I'm already late for editing," she said, as she took the phone from the secretary. "Who is it?"

"Didn't say," the secretary answered, and walked off to her own desk.

"Hello, Jenneen Grey."

"It's Matthew."

Jenneen froze. It was the first time she'd heard from him since the day he had beaten her up.

"I want to see you tonight, Jenn. Seven-thirty, your place."

Jenneen was surprised, it wasn't like Matthew to make an appointment. "Well," she said, "I'm glad you do, because it so happens that I want to see you too."

"Good," said Matthew. "I won't be staying long so you don't have to cancel any engagements."

"How considerate of you," Jenneen remarked, and hung up.

She wandered on up to VTR on the fifth floor, her mind only half on what she was doing or where she was going.

But it wasn't Matthew she was thinking about. She was still in the hold of the strange and alien feeling that had been with her ever since the weekend. At first she had been unable to identify it. It wasn't a bad feeling, in fact it was quite the reverse. She liked the way it seeped into her bones when she woke in the mornings, the way it followed her through the day and sometimes into her dreams. And as the days went by and she and Vicky spent more and more time together, she finally began to understand that the feeling was one of completeness. Completeness, and honesty. Finally she was facing up to the things she felt inside. There was nothing to run away from any more, because she had found what she always needed, had she but known it.

It was still a little difficult to grasp sometimes, that she and Vicky had become lovers. It seemed incredible. And even now as she remembered the softness of Vicky's skin, the beauty of her eyes, and the way she kissed her, a part of her still burned with shame. But the shame was becoming less and less as each day passed, and Jenneen was growing to accept that other part of her that almost rejoiced in the feelings. It was right. So right. For some reason it didn't seem sordid, not like she might have expected it to. And not like all the other times, the times when she had been with a man. It was clean and gentle and good.

She had talked to no one about what had happened, not even Dr. Bryant, the psychiatrist she had seen the day before; that would have to come later. One step at a time, Vicky had told her, there was no hurry. Jenneen could see her face now, looking at her, her eyes shining, her voice gentle.

"You're not the first person in the world this has happened to," Vicky had smiled, "and you won't be the last. For some it is easier. All the prejudices that have been implanted in you by your family over the years won't go away quickly. You must give it time. But you will see, there is nothing to be ashamed of."

Jenneen smiled. Dear Vicky. Of the two of them she had always been the strong one, the one who would never let life get her down. But this morning she had seemed vulnerable, and almost afraid. Jenneen wondered if Vicky was already in love with her, and surprisingly the thought didn't frighten her. She had to admit to a certain sense of foreboding, and there was no doubt the whole thing would be complicated, but Jenneen knew that in her heart she wanted Vicky to be in love with her.

She wanted to call her now, or go round to the shop and see her. She wanted to hold her in her arms again. It was a strange sensation, holding another woman, in a way she had only ever held a man before. There was something so exhilarating about it, as if she could become drunk on the mere aroma of another woman's skin.

Jenneen laughed out loud. To think that she was fantasising about something she had never even dared to think about before. And now it was already beyond fantasy. The touch of Vicky's lips, moving so gently against hers, sent waves of emotion through her that she had never experienced before. The feel of her breasts against her own, and her small hands running lightly across her neck and down over her shoulders. Less than a week ago it would have been something that Jenneen thought she might have found repulsive, and unthinkable. Yet now all she wanted was to feel her close again.

She walked into the VTR booth where an insert was being edited for the following day's program. Greg, the editor, looked up as she came in. "I carried on without you," he said. "Do you want to see what I've done so far?"

"If you like," said Jenneen. "But I'm sure it'll be just fine."

Greg's fingers hovered over the buttons. "Shall I spin back, or not?"

"Go on then, let's have a look."

Moving his fingers like a clumsy pianist he pressed the appropriate buttons and sent the machine outside spinning back to the beginning of the tape. Jenneen wandered over to the door and looked out into the main area that housed the large video tape machines.

"How many machines have we got?"

"Two."

"Silly question," she said. "When do we ever get more than two? But I thought we were getting three today?"

"We were," he answered, "but the news have taken one for an hour to transmit some interview on the six o'clock."

She looked over at the machines again as she heard the tape wind off the end.

"Damn!" Greg muttered. He got up from his chair. "Hang on, I'll just go and lace up again."

Jenneen followed him over and watched him as he threaded the tape back into the machine. Suddenly she thought she heard a voice she recognized. She looked around, trying to see where the voice was coming from. "Hey," she cried, looking at the little monitor on the machine adjacent to theirs, "isn't that Bob McElfrey?"

Greg looked up. "Know him, do you?" He sounded impressed.

"Yes. What's he doing here? Which program is that?"

"The news."

"I'll be right back," said Jenneen, and she disappeared into the booth next to theirs. "Mind if I watch?" she asked the engineer who was transmitting the interview.

He cleared his briefcase from the chair beside him. "Be my guest."

The interview was already half through. She had been battling with her guilt for days now that she had not been in touch with Ellamarie, but she had been so busy since she had returned from Vicky's. Still, if she watched the interview, she'd ring Ellamarie after and tell her how wonderful she thought Bob was.

Bob was talking about the Arts Conference that he was attending later that evening, and Jenneen remembered that she too had been invited. She was rather regretting not accepting now that she knew Bob was going to be there, when the camera pulled back to a two shot, to reveal the woman sitting beside Bob.

Jenneen sat forward as the woman began to speak. "... yes," she was saying, "yes, I still do some eventing myself on occasions, but not often. And Bob used to, in his younger days, didn't you?" she said, turning to look at him.

Bob laughed, and it was then that Jenneen noticed that they were holding hands.

"Have you ever found it to be a strain on your marriage, with you being so busy with your horses and Bob being away such a lot?" the interviewer asked.

"Not a strain exactly," was the reply, "but I have to admit I do miss him when he's not at home."

The interviewer turned back to Bob. "I believe that you are flying to New York on Friday."

Bob nodded.

"Would that be anything to do with the rumors that you are to make a film of the *Queen of Cornwall?*"

Bob laughed.

"We've heard rumors that you might have found someone to play the part of the Queen. Can I ask who it's to be?"

"Only rumors," Bob answered. "We did have someone in mind, but that has fallen through now."

"And you, Mrs. McElfrey. Will you be going to New York with your husband?"

"As a matter of fact," she said, "I am. I don't usually go with him, but we thought that perhaps we would make this trip into a holiday. It might be the last one we have for a little while," and she turned to look at her husband again.

Dumbfounded as she was, Jenneen didn't miss the

sudden flash of discomfort that flitted across Bob's face before he smiled.

"I suppose your husband's heavy workload prevents too many holidays?" said the interviewer.

"Sometimes," Linda smiled, and she looked at Bob again before she leaned forward, her face more than a little flushed. "Actually, I'll let you into a little secret. The real reason that Bob and I won't be taking too many holidays, at least in the next year or two, is that we are expecting our first baby in February."

Jenneen turned her head toward the engineer, dimly aware of the interviewer gushing his congratulations. "Oh my God!" she muttered. "Oh my God!" She jumped to her feet. "Where's the phone?"

The engineer pointed her to the main office outside. Thankfully there was no one in it. Quickly she dialed. It was a long time before Ellamarie answered.

"Ellamarie!" Jenneen cried.

"It's all right, Jenn, I've seen it."

"Oh my God!" Jenneen gasped. "Ellamarie, I don't know what to say. Did you know?"

Ignoring the question, Ellamarie said: "Can you come over, Jenn? I don't think I could stand to be on my own tonight."

Jenneen looked out to the edit booth where she should be right now. If she walked out she knew she would be putting her new program in jeopardy. Oh hell, what could she do? Thinking fast, she said: "Look, I'll come as soon as I can. But meanwhile, call Kate and get her to come round right away. Oh Ellamarie, I'm sorry."

"I know," Ellamarie said, and she hung up.

Ellamarie looked at the phone for a long time before she dialed Kate's number. What could any of them do? She had lost him for good now, she knew that. And in case she had ever doubted it, he had allowed Linda to announce it to the world. But her friends would help her through this, they had to.

Kate sounded rushed when she answered the phone. "I'm dashing to the airport," she explained. "Nick's waiting for me in New York. Didn't Jenneen tell you? No, I didn't see the news tonight, did something happen? Nothing? Oh, you are funny at times, Ellamarie. Look, tell you what, I'll call over on my way to the airport, how does that suit? No, no of course it won't be any trouble; my flight's not until much later. Oh, what a lovely thing to say, of course you can drive me to the airport. Must rush now, see you later," and she rang off.

Calloway used his own key to let himself into Kate's flat. As he turned to close the door behind him she rushed past, carrying a pile of clothes, and disappeared into the bedroom.

He hung up his coat and followed her in. "What are you doing?" he asked, seeing the open suitcase laid out on her bed.

For a second she tensed, then abruptly carried on with what she was doing. "I'm going to New York."

"New York?" he said, starting to walk toward the bed. "Are you being sent on an assignment? You never mentioned it."

She dragged a bundle of underwear out of a drawer and flung it into the suitcase. "No, I'm going to New York because Nick's there."

Her father stopped in his tracks, and stared at her. "Nick!"

"Yes, Nick."

"But I thought . . ." He stopped, and Kate carried on with her packing, trying to stop her hands shaking. Her father watched her, as determinedly she moved between the bed and the wardrobe. "You mean to tell me," he finally managed to splutter, "that you're actually going running to him, after what he did to you?"

Kate's fingers tightened round the dress she was holding. She hadn't reckoned on her father coming here tonight, and the effort of keeping her mind empty of the things Jenneen had told her was becoming too great. Slowly she turned to face him. "And what did he do to me, Daddy? Just what did Nick do to me?"

"Kate, for God's sake, you can't have forgotten already."

Kate was looking into the face she had known and loved all her life. Even now that she knew what he had told Nick, she still didn't want to believe it. But she had spoken to Nick, and he had told her himself. He had told her that she must come to New York right away. "Don't see your father first," he had said, "just get on the next flight." And that was what she had intended to do. But now he was here, and despite her anger and confusion, she knew she didn't want to leave him like this. She loved him, and no matter what he had done he was still her father.

He started to walk toward her, and despite her turmoil, she felt herself beginning to slip into his arms.

"Daddy, oh Daddy," she cried, "what is happening? Why did they say all those things? Tell me they aren't true. Please say you never said any of it."

"Sssh," he whispered, holding her and stroking her hair.

"Please," she begged him, "please say it's not true."

"What have they been saying? Who have you been talking to?"

She looked down as she felt him take her hand in his, and a sudden wave of disgust twisted her gut. She leapt away. "No!" she gasped. "No, you can't touch me. You mustn't. Not after . . ." her voice trailed away.

"Darling, what is it?" Her father tried to take her in his arms again.

"No!" she shrieked. "They said . . . Jenneen, Nick, they said . . . No, don't come near me. You can't. You shouldn't be here. Oh my God, what's happening? I've got to go to Nick."

She looked around the room in desperation. She wanted to get away from him, but at the same time she wanted him to take her in his arms and tell her it was all just a nightmare. If she faced what in her heart she knew to be the truth then she would have to accept that this was the end for her and her father. That they could never see one another again.

"Kate," he said.

She looked at him and saw the love in his eyes. It was the love she had always seen in his eyes—ever since she was a child.

Seeing her weaken again he held his hand out to her. Very slowly she lifted her own and placed it in his. "There, there," he soothed, "let's just gather up your things and go home, shall we? I've got the car waiting downstairs."

She buried her face in his shoulder. "Oh Daddy," she sobbed. "Everything's going so horribly wrong."

"Shush, my darling. Everything's going to be all right. You're very tired, that's all. You need a nice long rest. Come along now."

He lifted her face and looked into her eyes. She tried to blink away the tears, tried to think of what she should be doing, but her mind had ceased to function. Her father had run her life for so long that the only thing she could do was listen to him now. He was the only one she could trust. Her friends had lied to her. They must have. Hadn't they lied to her before about Joel? And now they were lying to her again. Her father could never be capable of what they were suggesting. It was horrible and disgusting.

Gazing into her eyes, as she looked up at him so helplessly, he felt an overpowering surge of love flood through his body. And with it went his last vestige of control. Slowly he bent his head and placed his lips over hers.

She didn't resist. Paralyzed by the sheer horror of what was happening, she felt her father's mouth moving gently against her own. His arm circled her shoulder, holding her in the way he had when she was a child. But she was no longer a child, and something a long way inside her started to scream that this was wrong. That what he was doing to her was evil. This man was her father, and he was holding her and kissing her like a lover.

"No!" She flung herself away from him. "It can't be true. Why are you doing this?" He made to grab her but she backed away. "I've got to get away from you," she cried. "No, don't touch me. Oh my God, Nick! Yes, Nick. I must go to him."

"Kate, you can't," her father's voice was pleading. "Stop it! Please, just stop."

Calloway tried to pull the suitcase from the bed. "I won't let you."

"Let go," she cried, trying to pull it back again. "Let go, let go."

"Kate," he begged, "listen to me. You can't go to him. You're making a terrible mistake. He doesn't love you, you've got to believe me. He doesn't love you."

"He does!" she yelled. "He loves me, and he wants me. Oh, let go." She tugged at the suitcase again.

Her father tore the case away from her and threw it across the floor. "You're not going anywhere. You're staying here, with me."

"No," she screamed.

He looked at her with eyes so determined, she felt herself begin to give way again.

"Oh Daddy, don't, don't," she wailed. "Don't you see? I love him," and she ran from the room.

He found her in the kitchen, rummaging frenziedly through a drawer, searching for her passport.

"Kate," he said, swallowing hard. "You've got to listen to me."

"No. I don't want to listen to you any more. Leave

me alone. Just go away and leave me alone. Haven't you done enough damage?"

"Please. Just listen. You can't go to New York. You can't go to Nick. He doesn't want you, Kate. He doesn't need you. It's me who needs you. Can't you see that? I need you here, with me. I need you. Don't leave me, Kate. I'm begging you, don't leave me."

She tried to push past him. He caught hold of her by the shoulders, and forced her to look into his face. "You can't do this to me, Kate. You can't leave me. He'll never be able to do all the things for you that I can. Don't go, my darling, please say you won't leave me. I love you, Kate. Don't you understand that? I love you."

Kate stared at him in horror.

"Kate," his voice was a little calmer now, and feeling no resistance from her he pulled her toward him and pushed his mouth against hers.

"Noooooo!" she screamed, and with every fiber of strength in her body she pushed him away. He fell back against the wall.

She watched him as he pulled himself up again, and started to come toward her. She stepped back, holding her hands out in front of her, and shaking her head. She was sobbing, and whimpering, begging him to stay away, but he kept on coming.

"Kate, don't look at me like that. Don't look at me with your eyes like that. It'll be all right, don't you see? Everything will be all right."

"Don't touch me."

He took her hands, and pushed her back against the cupboard.

She closed her eyes. "This isn't happening," she whispered. "Please God, this isn't happening."

"Don't say that." His face was very close to hers. "You love me too, Kate, you know you do. In your heart, you know you do."

"No, please. Oh God help me. Help me, someone please, help me!"

She tried to pull her hands away, but his grip was too tight. And then he had her hands pinned behind her back, and he was pushing himself against her. He pressed his mouth to hers again, and she wrenched her head away, choking on the bile in her throat. His hands were fumbling with her shirt, and she could feel them hard against her skin.

She screamed, and managed to break free. She fled to the other side of the kitchen, trying to catch her breath. He turned to face her.

"Don't come near me," she sobbed, as he started to walk toward her again, but he didn't stop. She fumbled with the drawer behind her, and dug her hand inside.

"Kate," he said again.

"No, stay where you are. Please, stay where you are. Don't come any closer."

He kept coming.

Her fingers curled round the handle of the knife. As he sobbed on her name she thrust the knife between them, but it was too late, he was already throwing himself against her.

Their eyes locked in disbelief. She watched her father's face as slowly it began to contort in agony. Then silently he fell away from her, leaving her clutching the knife, her face wide with horror.

Seconds later she spun round as a knock on the door echoed through the silent flat.

Two hours later, Ellamarie was still waiting for Kate. But Jenneen would be here soon, there was no need to panic. Don't think about Bob, don't think about him being at the Arts Conference with his wife. Don't think about all the cruel things he said. Close your eyes, don't look round the room, it will only remind you. How

many times had she said all these things to herself, but
still she thought, and still she looked.

Where was Jenneen? Why didn't she come now?
Kate had said she'd come . . .

The minutes slipped past and still there was no
knock on the door. She stood at the window, looking
out on the empty street. The night was so silent, if only
something would happen. If only someone would
come. She pressed her face against the windowpane.
Bob! Oh Bob! She could see him walking round the corner now. There he was, taking his keys out of his
pocket. He was coming in. He had come back to her.

She blinked, and the street was empty again.

Finally she had to accept that no one was going to
come. Alone, in a place she had come to think of as
home, she was now a stranger.

She picked up the phone and dialed.

"Mom?"

"Oh Ellamarie, it's you. How are you, dear?"

"I want to come home, Mom."

"But we're going away, dear. Didn't I tell you? No?
Oh well, we are. Three weeks. We're going down to
Florida. Sure, I'll give your love to Daddy. Did you call
for anything else? No. Speak to you soon then, dear.
Goodbye."

Ellamarie could feel the precipice drawing closer.

With a relaxed, almost nonchalant air, his hands
stuffed into his trouser pockets, Matthew strolled along
the hallway of Jenneen's flat. He looked around, as if
he were seeing it for the first time. Once or twice he
stopped to look at the photographs in their clip frames
hanging on the wall. No paintings, only photographs.
There were some of Jenneen on location, some of her
with guests in the studio, and others, weird sort of ab-
stract ones, taken by professionals. He walked on.

Jenneen followed him, her arms folded, and

stopped whenever he stopped, as if she was showing someone round a gallery.

He had arrived earlier than she had expected him; she was wearing her bathrobe, a towel wrapped round her hair. She looked at her watch, praying that this wouldn't take long. She was worried about Ellamarie and wanted to get over there as quick as she could.

Eventually Matthew pushed open the door of the lounge, went over to the dining table at the other end of the room and sat down. Jenneen was surprised by this. Normally he made straight for the whiskey.

She followed him toward the table but stopped halfway across the room. He was sitting with his legs stretched out in front of him, his hands still in his pockets. His chin was almost resting on his chest, but she could see that he had a smile on his lips, a pleasant enough one, and he was only half watching her.

She kept her arms folded, and shifted her weight onto one leg. "So, Matthew, here we are again. Things don't change much, do they?"

He looked at her for a second or two, then taking a hand out of his pocket he put his elbow on the table and rested his head on his hand.

"Well, at least you're not drunk tonight," she said. "So perhaps some things do change." When he didn't say anything she turned to a pile of books she had left lying on the small table under the window. She took them across to the bookshelves and began to slot them into place. He sat watching her, but still didn't speak.

"Matthew, do you think we could get on with this," she said, as she slid the last one in. "I'm in a bit of a hurry." She turned back to face him.

"Suits me," he answered. "Exactly what is it you'd like to be getting on with?"

"Oh, cut the crap, Matthew," she said. "You called me, remember? How much do you want? Fifty, a hundred, hundred and fifty?"

"Very generous of you," he drawled.

"It'll be the last you get," she said. "After tonight there will be no more."

"Oh? You've made up your mind about that, have you?"

"I have."

"Good."

She didn't like the way he was behaving. This easy, relaxed attitude was not like him. "Well?"

He looked up at the ceiling, chewing his bottom lip and thinking. "I'm glad you've arrived at that decision," he said after a minute or two. "It fits in rather nicely with my own decision. By the way, what news on the new program?"

"It's going into the spring schedules. But you probably know that already."

He laughed. "You're right, I do."

She looked at her watch.

"And the roving reporter's job?"

"Is gone. Bill appointed someone last week. It was his decision, I had no say in it."

"Fine by me," he said.

She eyed him warily. That was not the reaction she had expected at all. She folded her arms again. "Just what is this all about, Matthew?"

He lifted his arm from the table, and stuffed his hand back in his pocket. He looked down at his legs as he crossed one over the other, then lifted his head again. "How's Vicky?"

Jenneen froze.

"Sorry," he said, "I should have asked earlier. Very remiss of me, I know."

Jenneen turned to face him, her eyes blazing with hatred. "You filthy, scheming, blackmailing little toad. Get out of here."

"Sorry," he said. "Obviously I've upset you. Let's forget I mentioned Vicky, shall we? Let's pretend I never said a word about her. After all, I didn't mention anything about her being a lesbian, did I? And I didn't say a thing about what you two dykes get up to in bed at night. So let's forget I ever said anything."

She glared at him, with loathing. "God, you really hate me, don't you?"

"Hate you? No, I don't hate you, Jenn. Not me. Now Maggie, yes, remember little Maggie? She hates you. Don't ask me why, but she does. And I keep telling her, don't worry, Maggie, I say, you're not Jenneen's type. But it makes no difference, she just carries on hating you. Still, I wouldn't let it bother you, she'll probably get over it."

"OK," said Jenneen. "OK. You're right. Vicky and I are lovers. Yes, you're right. We sleep together, and we make love together. Are you happy now? I've admitted it. Does that satisfy you?"

"Does it satisfy you, Jenneen?"

"You're disgusting."

"And you're not?" He shrugged. "Anyway, I haven't come here to discuss your perverted life with Vicky. No, I've come to say goodbye." He walked across to the settee and sat down. "I've got a little something for you, actually," he said. Delving into his jacket he pulled out a brown envelope, and handed it to her.

She didn't take it, so he put it on the table. "No rush," he said.

She looked at the envelope. Her curiosity got the better of her reluctance and she walked over to the table and picked it up.

Her voice escaped in a strangled cry as she saw the photographs inside, and for one horrifying moment she thought she was going to pass out.

"Nice town, Brighton, isn't it?" he said.

Her face was ashen.

As he laughed she felt a white-hot furnace of hatred begin to rage inside her. He looked so ugly sitting there. His face unshaven, and angry red spots on his neck. His hair was greasy and uncombed. He looked like a tramp.

He reached out and took the envelope from her, turning it over in his hand as if he were making a study of it. "You know, it's just occurred to me, do you think Vicky would like to see them? Jenneen on a day trip to Brighton? Well, I've got another set, I'll let you have them, you can look at them together. Tell me, just out of interest, does the sight of two men fucking one woman turn you lesbians on?"

Her throat was dry and her voice croaked as she spoke. "There's nothing you can do with those photographs, Matthew, and you know it. No newspaper in the land would print them. They wouldn't be able to."

"Oh, but they can. Not in their entirety, I grant you, but there are ways. And magazines of course. But they don't get a wide enough circulation. And you want to be famous, don't you, Jenneen? Sorry, I can't help there. Well, I could, but I'm not going to. No, I'm not going to send these photographs to a newspaper or a pornographic magazine. No, I'm sending them somewhere quite different. The envelope is already addressed. Look, you can read it." He pushed it toward her.

The thumping of her heart pounded through her ears and all she could do was look back at him.

"It doesn't matter," he said. "I'll read it to you if you like," and he turned the envelope over. "Number 23, Hallsinger Street, Oak . . ."

"Noooo!" she screamed. She rushed for the envelope and tore it out of his hand. And with unnatural strength, she ripped it into tiny pieces.

Matthew took another envelope from his pocket, identical to the last.

"You bastard! You fucking bastard! What have they ever done to you?"

"Your parents? Nothing. Leastways, nothing I can remember. No, I merely thought that they might be interested to know what their precious Jenneen gets up to, down here in little old London town. Or in this case, Brighton town."

Jenneen felt her blood run cold. "How did you find their address?"

"Oh come on, Jenneen, it doesn't take Sherlock Holmes to work that one out. Maggie. Remember, dear little Maggie. She's got a set too. I think she wants to send them to her mother. Lives quite close to yours, doesn't she?"

Jenneen's mouth twisted in disgust. "Vicky was right about you. You're evil. Sick, evil, sadistic and callous."

"Back to Vicky, are we? Course, Mumsy doesn't know about Vicky either, does she? Wonder if I should drop her a line and tell her about that too." He got up from the chair and tucked the envelope back inside his jacket. "Still, didn't you say something earlier about being in a hurry? So I'll be off. Just thought I'd drop in and give you the news. Goodbye, Jenneen. Good luck," and he walked toward the door.

"Stop, Matthew!" she hissed. "Just stop right where you are."

He was smiling as he turned. "Did you want to say some . . ."

"Give me the envelope, Matthew. Give it to me, now." Her hand shook very slightly as she tightened her grip on the barrel of the gun.

Matthew's smile faded.

"Give it to me, Matthew."

"You haven't got the guts," he sneered. "It's probably not even loaded."

"There's only one way to find out. Now give me the envelope."

"Jenneen, darling," he said, poking his head forward, "go fuck yourself."

"I mean it, Matthew. Give me the envelope, and

then you can go. But you are not walking through that door until you do."

"You're mad! You can't kill me, and you know it. What would that do to your precious image? Nympho, lesbian, and murderer. Oh yes, it'll all come out if you kill me. Have you stopped to think about that?"

She stayed rooted, pointing the gun.

"I said put it down, dyke! Go on, put it down. You're not going to use it. You might be a pervert, but you're not stupid. Look at yourself, you're pathetic. Go on then, shoot me. Look, I'll even hold up my arms for . . ."

"Shut up!" she screamed.

"Shoot me, you bitch, and I'll come back and haunt you. Go on, shoot me!"

"JENNEEN, NO!" Vicky screamed from the door. And the blast was deafening.

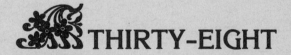

THIRTY-EIGHT

Conrad and Ashley rushed through Customs at Heathrow Airport, and Conrad silently swore a vow to increase Candice's salary as he saw a board being held up with his name on it. It was something he had completely forgotten, how he and Ashley were to get into London when they reached Heathrow. Obviously Candice hadn't.

Ashley gave the driver her address in Onslow Square, and sensing their urgency, the driver sped

along the M4 and arrived in South Kensington in a record seventeen minutes.

As they got out the driver handed the keys of the
black Mercedes to Conrad. "Mr. Arbrey-Nelmes
thought you might have need of the car," he said, and
turned and walked off down the street.

Ashley rushed inside. Thank God Conrad had
threatened to send her back to London, otherwise she
might already have left her flat. It was empty, cold and
rather cheerless, but she didn't notice any of that. As
she ran to the phone it started to ring. She snatched it
up, but her fingers were shaking so badly she dropped
it. Coming in behind her, Conrad picked it up and
handed it to her.

"Hello!" she gasped.

"Ash! It's me."

"Ellamarie!"

"I called your office, they told me what
happened . . ."

"Oh Ellamarie!"

"Ash, is there anything I can do? Please, let me
help."

"Yes, no . . ."

"Shall I come over?"

"Conrad's here. I'm sorry, Ellamarie, I've got to
ring off," and banging her fingers against the connec-
tors she cut the line. Quickly she dialed again.

"I'll make some coffee," said Conrad.

"I need something stronger than that," she said as
she waited for the connection. "Over there," she waved
her hand toward the drinks cabinet.

"Coffee," said Conrad. "You'll need a clear head,"
and he walked into the kitchen.

She waited as the steady ringing tone came across
the line. She counted how many times it rang. She must
stay calm. Whatever she did, she must stay calm.
Twenty, twenty-one, twenty-two, twenty-three.

Conrad came back into the room.

"He's not at home," said Ashley, and her face began to crumple.

Conrad took the receiver from her hand and placed it back on the telephone. Then, taking her in his arms, he whispered: "It's all right. Don't worry, we'll find him."

"But where is he? Why isn't he answering?"

"Is there anywhere else he might have gone?"

"I don't know, I just don't know. I can't think. His mother, maybe he's gone to his mother."

"Have you got her number?"

"In my diary."

Conrad walked across the room and picked up her handbag which she had thrown on the floor as she had run into the flat.

But no, Keith wasn't at his mother's and no, Mrs. Mayne didn't know where he was. She thought he was still in New York. Ashley didn't explain why she was calling, she just asked Mrs. Mayne to have Keith call her at her flat in London, should he get in touch.

Conrad handed her a cup of coffee, and taking her by the arm he led her over to a chair.

"What do we do now?" she said, looking up into his face.

"Is there anyone else you can call? Anyone else who might know where he is? What about your friends?"

Ashley shook her head. "Oh my God! Kate!" she said, suddenly remembering. She covered her face with her hands. "Dear God, what's happening? Why is everything going so horribly wrong?"

"Hey, hey there," he said, putting his arms round her. "We'll find him. Don't worry, I promise you we'll find him. But for the time being we're just going to have to wait."

"But where is Alex? What if . . ." Her voice trailed off as she began to cry again.

"What about your folks?" Conrad suggested. "Do you think he might have taken him there?"

"No. But maybe I should ring them, just in case." She went back to the phone. She was half through dialing when Conrad took it away from her.

"No," he said. "No. We don't want to worry them yet. If he's not there, then they'll want to know why you're in London. There's got to be a better way of contacting them." He took her back to the chair again. Then walking back to the phone he picked it up and dialed a number. "Julian?"

"Conrad," said Julian. "At last. Any news? Candice told me everything. Was the car waiting for you at the airport? How's Ashley? Where is she?"

"She's here. We're at her apartment in Kensington."

"Is she all right?"

"Yes, at least she will be. Look . . ."

"Is there anything I can do?"

"That's just what I was going to ask you. Get on the phone to Ashley's folks. Don't tell them anything about what has happened. Just ask if Alex is back from New York yet because you've got a birthday present for him, and then ring me back here. I take it you've got the number."

Julian allowed himself a quick grin at the irony in Conrad's voice. "Yes, I've got the number. I'll call you as soon as I know anything."

Conrad walked back across the room to Ashley, and pulling her up into his arms he led her across to the settee, where he sat down with her for what was going to be a long night.

It turned out to be the longest night of all of their lives. Ashley, Jenneen, Ellamarie, and Kate.

Ellamarie sat on the floor, clutching the telephone to her breasts and moaning quietly. In her worst nightmares she had never known anything like this. She had to speak to someone, please God there had to be someone out there who would listen. Where were Kate and Jenneen? Why didn't they come? But in her heart she knew that there was only one person left now to whom she could turn.

Wiping her hand across her eyes she dialed the number. When the voice at the other end answered, in a halting voice she explained that she must speak with Bob McElfrey. It was very important.

It was a long wait, but she didn't hang up. And eventually he was there.

"Bob," she whispered.

There was a pause before he answered. "Ellamarie."

She fought to keep her voice steady. "Bob, I must see you." The tears were streaming silently down her face now. "I have to see you."

"Ellamarie, I thought we'd said all there was to say."

The tears threatened to drown her voice. "We said so little," she stammered. And when he didn't answer she cried: "Oh Bob, why did you walk away like that?"

He sounded impatient. "Look, I can't talk now."

Ellamarie looked down at the letter that was lying on the floor beside her. She picked it up and turned it over in her hand. "I saw the interview," she said. "Why didn't you tell me? Why did you let me find out like that?"

Bob glanced over his shoulder and saw that Linda was coming toward him. He thought quickly. "Look, meet me at the mews house," he said, thinking that if he said the mews house he could arrange for Linda to ring him there, which meant he could get away quickly.

"What time?"

He looked at his watch. "In an hour," he said. "It won't take long will it?" He shook his head to show his exasperation, then smiled as he slipped an arm around Linda.

"No," said Ellamarie, "it won't ta . . ." but he had already rung off.

The time was passing slowly. At regular intervals Ashley rang Keith's number in Surrey, but there was no reply. Once her phone had rung, but it had only been Julian reporting back after his telephone call to Ashley's parents. Her mother had told him that Alex wasn't going to be home until late the following week.

Ashley was much calmer now, though her face was white, and haggard with worry. Whenever she looked at Conrad it made his heart wrench to see the look in her eyes. It was as if she were asking him, almost begging him, to make it all right. He went to sit beside her and took her hand.

"I had a feeling," she said, after a minute or two. "I knew something was going to happen. And then I thought, when you told me about Mercer Burgess, that that was what it had been—the feeling. That that was what was going to go wrong. But now . . . Oh Conrad, where do you think he's taken him? Where are they?"

"I wish I could answer that," he said. "But we'll find them, I promise you, we'll find them."

"You don't really think . . . Keith wouldn't . . ." and she started to cry again.

He wiped the tears from her cheeks, and kissed her. "No," he said, "no, he wouldn't. He loves Alex."

Ashley felt so tired, but she mustn't sleep. What if Alex needed her? She must be there, she must stay awake. But Conrad's hands were so soothing, and his voice so calm. She listened to him breathing, and tried to breathe in time with him.

Conrad looked down at her and saw her eyelids flickering as she fell into a doze. He bent his head and brushed his lips against her hair, then laid his head back against the cushions. He stared up at the ceiling knowing that there would be no sleep for him. This was a position he had never found himself in before, where something was beyond his control, and he didn't like it. The feeling made him uneasy, and the frustration made him angry. He couldn't understand a man who could do this to his own son.

Suddenly the telephone crashed into the silence. Ashley sat up with a start and looked at Conrad. He was watching her face, and he could see that she was afraid.

"Would you like me to answer?"

She shook her head. "No. If Keith knows that you're here, then . . . no, I'll go."

She got up and walked to the phone. Her hand was shaking as she reached out to pick it up.

"Hello."

"Ashley."

"Keith, where are you?"

"I told you not to come."

"Where's Alex? What have you done to him? Where is he? Is he all right?"

"Yes, he's all right. He's here, with me."

"Where are you?"

"Not far," he said. "I have to give you credit for getting to London so quickly, Ashley. My mother told me you'd phoned."

"Your mother? Is that where you are?"

"No."

"Then where are you, Keith? Please, tell me where you are."

"Did you read my letter?"

"Yes, I read it. You don't mean those things, Keith, you know you don't. You can't hurt him, he's only a baby. You can't use him like this. Please, tell me where you are. Let me come and get him."

"I told you, Ashley, you're not having him back. You're not taking him to New York."

"All right," she said. "All right. Anything. If that's what you want, I won't take him to New York. He can stay here, only don't hurt him. Please, promise me you won't hurt him."

"He's my son, Ashley, something I seem to have to keep reminding you of."

"Then you didn't mean all those things you said in the letter?"

"I meant them. If you try to take him back with you, then I'll do it."

"But I've already said, I won't take him away. I'll do anything, Keith, anything, only say you won't hurt him. Where is he? Can I speak to him?"

"He's asleep right now."

"Has he asked for me? Oh Keith, how could you do this? How could you do it?"

"I've done it because I love him. Because I care about him and what happens to him. Because he's my son, and I want him here with me."

"I understand how you're feeling, Keith, believe me I do. I know you love him, and he loves you. But he's my son too, I wouldn't do anything to harm him, you know I wouldn't. I only want what's best for him."

"And I think it's best for him to stay here in England, with me. You've got a career now, Ashley. You chose that career. No one asked you to go to New York. No one asked you to give up your son and go to New York. It was your decision, and now you're going to have to pay the price. I told you, I want my son, and I'm going to have him."

"But Keith . . ."

"You're no good as a mother, Ashley. You failed, a long time ago."

"Oh Keith," she cried. "Please don't do this to me. Please stop. Just let me see him. Just let me see that he is all right. I won't try to take him away, I promise. I just need to see him. Tell me where you are, please. I'll come right away."

"I told you, he's sleeping."

"I won't wake him. I won't even touch him, I just

want to see him. Please, Keith. I'm begging you, please, please let me see him."

"Who knows about this? Who have you told?"

"No one, I promise you, no one."

"Are you alone now?"

"Yes. Please, please say that I can see him. Give me the address, I'll come straight over."

"No."

"Keith!" she called. "Keith, please. I am begging you. Please! I just want to see that he's all right. Nothing else, nothing more. I just want to see him. Please, Keith, please . . ." She began to sob.

"I'm at my brother's flat in Fulham," he said at last. "Make sure you come on your own. You haven't told the police, have you? It will only be the worse for you if you have."

"No, I haven't told the police. I'll come alone. I promise. What's the address?" Conrad was beside her with pen and paper.

"Are you sure there's no one there with you?"

"Yes, I'm sure," she answered, looking at Conrad.

"This doesn't mean that you are taking him away with you tonight, you understand that, don't you?"

"Yes, I understand. I told you, I only want to see him. To see for myself that he's all right."

"Tomorrow I will get a court order that says he remains in this country, at least until the whole thing is settled. So there's no point in trying anything fancy."

Her heart lurched, and she fought hard not to cry again. "The address, Keith. Give me the address."

As he spoke she wrote quickly. "I'll be over right away. And Keith."

"Yes?"

"You will be there, won't you?"

"We'll be here," and he hung up.

She put down the receiver and pressed her hands to her cheeks. "The car," she said, not looking at Conrad. "Can I use the car?"

"I'll drive you."

"No. He said I must go alone."

"I am not letting you go alone. Here, put your coat on."

"No. Conrad, please. I promised him. I said I would go alone. Wait here for me. Please."

"You can go in alone. I'll wait in the car, somewhere along the street if necessary, but you're not going alone, Ashley. Now put your coat on."

She didn't argue further, she would only be wasting valuable time.

It was a clear night, and the roads were practically empty. It took them no time at all to get to Fulham, though to Ashley it felt like a lifetime.

Keith's brother's flat was at the top of an old Victorian building, with no intercom system. Ashley pushed the bell and waited. Finally she heard Keith's footsteps coming along the hall, and then he was opening the door. Pushing past him she flew up the stairs. Keith turned and ran after her, only managing to overtake her as she was going into the flat.

"Where is he?" she cried. "Let me see him. Let me go to him."

"Mummy!" Alex called.

Ashley turned round and saw her son standing in the hall. "Alex!" she gasped, and ran to him. "Oh Alex! My darling. My baby. Are you all right?"

"Sure I'm all right, Mum," he said, bewildered and rubbing the sleep from his eyes. "I'm glad you're here."

"Oh darling, so am I." So am I. She looked up at Keith. He was still standing in the doorway, watching them. "You know none of this was necessary," she said. "You didn't have to do this to him."

Keith turned away and walked into the sitting room. Ashley took Alex's hand and they followed him inside.

Outside Conrad got out of the car and began to walk up and down the street. He glanced up at the window from time to time, but the curtains were pulled and there was no sign of life.

Keith was standing with his back to the window, his arms folded. Ashley kept her arm round Alex and looked at him.

"So it's all over, Ash," he said, very quietly. "At last, it's all over."

She shook her head. "What do you mean? What's over?"

"You, me, Alex. It's over."

"You mean you're going to let me take him?"

"I mean that you lied. I mean that Conrad Frazier is down there in the street. Conrad Frazier, all the way from New York. You lied to me, Ashley. Did you really think I was such a fool? I saw you pull up outside. You think you're going to take him with you, don't you? You think you're going to take him away and back to New York."

"No," she cried. "No. I told you, I just wanted to see him."

"You're a liar, Ashley." His voice was still calm. "I might have believed you, but Conrad, here in England, only confirms what you intend to do. What you think you intend to do. It might have been all right, Ashley. It might all have worked out. But you cheated on me. You said you were alone, when all the time you were with him." He began to shake his head. "Why did you have to lie?"

"You would never have let me see him if I'd told you the truth. Please try and understand, Keith. All I was thinking about was Alex."

"All you were thinking about was yourself." He looked down at Alex, and then lifted his eyes back to Ashley. "You're not going to have him, Ashley, so whatever you're thinking you can get it out of your head now. You'll never take him away from me again, that I promise you. You have sealed his fate, and mine, and yours. You should never have come here with Conrad. It was your biggest mistake yet."

Ashley felt Alex press his little body against her, and she held him closer. "Keith, stop talking like that. Can't you see what it's doing to Alex? Don't you care what it's doing to him?"

Keith turned to his son. "Alex, go into the bedroom."

Alex's small face was round with fear, and he clutched at Ashley.

"No," said Ashley. "No. Can't you see he's frightened?"

"Alex," Keith said again. "Go into the bedroom. Nothing's going to happen to you. Just go into the bedroom. I want to talk to your mother alone."

Alex looked up at Ashley. "Do I have to, Mummy?"

Ashley looked down into his face and her heart turned over. She looked back at Keith, and then again at Alex. "Do as Daddy says, darling. I'll come in to you in a minute."

Very reluctantly Alex let go of his mother's hand, and walked out of the room. Ashley watched him go, and Keith watched Ashley.

When he had gone Ashley turned to face Keith. He unfolded his arms and started to walk across the room toward the fire. His voice was quiet as he spoke and she had to strain her ears to hear him. "You're wondering just what it is that I'm going to do, to prove to you how much my son means to me." He stopped walking, but he didn't turn round. "I would have done it anyway, if I'd had to. But I'm glad you're here. It'll make more sense with you here."

Ashley watched him, afraid to speak.

He reached up to a shelf above the fire and took down a small parcel. He unwrapped it slowly, his hands quite steady, and as the wrapping fell to the floor, he turned to face her.

Her eyes rounded with horror as she saw what he was holding. "No!" she whispered. "No, Keith."

He looked down at the gun and turned it over in his hands.

"What, what are you going to . . . to do?"

"What I said I'd do if you tried to take him away."

She shook her head, feeling a wave of panic rising in her, so strong it was blinding her. Her heart thumped against her ribs, pounding, irregular and unnatural. And as she tried to speak her voice felt strangled by her own throat. "No! You can't do it. He's only a child, he's got his whole life in front of him. Keith, he's your son, for God's sake, I thought you loved him."

Conrad was still pacing up and down outside. He rubbed his fingers against his eyes and looked at his watch. Somebody came out of a nearby house and started to walk down the street toward him. The man gave him a suspicious look. Conrad nodded to him, and then looked up at the window.

Still there was nothing to see so he turned to walk on. It was cold and the sky was alight with stars and a near full moon. He pulled his coat tighter round him as the wind started to pick up. It was then that he heard the scream. He froze, and as he started to turn his head back to the window, he heard the gunshot.

"Ashley," he breathed, and started to run. There was a second shot. "Ashley!" he yelled as he ran in through the door.

Several seconds later another shot was fired, and then there was silence.

Bob ran his fingers through his hair in exasperation. "Look, Ellamarie, I haven't got long, please, come to the point."

Ellamarie didn't answer.

He turned away and went to stand beside his desk. Any minute now the phone would ring and he could get away. He closed his eyes and willed Linda not to

wait any longer. Finally he said: "Look, I've said I'm
sorry about the interview, I didn't mean for you to find
out like that, but it's done now, and you would have
found out in the end anyway."

"Does that mean you weren't going to tell me
yourself?" Ellamarie looked up at him, her face red and
swollen, still wet with tears.

He looked away.

"Does that mean you weren't going to tell me
yourself?" she repeated.

A siren blasted into the night and Bob pulled back
the curtain to look outside.

Ellamarie yelled: "Does that mean you . . ."

"Yes!" He swung round to face her. "If that's what
you want me to say, then yes. That is what it means."

Ellamarie eyed him, pain darkening her eyes.
"How could you? How could you?"

"What else could I do?" he shouted. "For Christ's
sake, I didn't know it was going to happen like that.
Anyway, I told you, it's over. For me and you, it's over,
Ellamarie. Stop hurting yourself like this, stop making
me say it."

"To make it easier for you? Is that what you
want?"

"Yes. And for you too."

"Does your wife know I'm pregnant, Bob? Did
you tell her, or shall we wait for that to hit the news
too?"

"You wouldn't!" he gasped.

"Wouldn't what? Tell the world that you made me
pregnant at the same time as you made your wife pregnant, then ran out on me? Wouldn't I do it, Bob?
Wouldn't I?"

"You couldn't! And for all I know, that child
you're carrying isn't even . . ."

"You bastard!" she screamed. "Say it! Go on, say
it! Isn't even yours, that's what you were going to say,
isn't it? No, it's the bastard of a rapist, it couldn't possi-

bly be the child of the great Bob McElfrey. And that's just what you'd do, isn't it, Bob? You'd tell the whole world that I was raped, and that I got pregnant straight after. That's what you'd do, isn't it?"

His eyes were cold. "If you force me to."

She threw herself at him, screaming and beating her fists against his chest. He caught her by the arms and pushed her back onto the settee. "Stop this, Ellamarie. You're making a fool of yourself."

"Making a fool of myself?" she screamed. "Well, that's nothing to what you've made of me, Bob McElfrey. Do you know where I went before I came here? Do you? I went to the theater, and they were throwing the scripts for *Twelfth Night* into the garbage, just like you're trying to do with me."

"Shut up, Ellamarie. Do you have to dramatise everything? I thought you got me here because you wanted to talk . . ."

"I got you here for one thing, and one thing only."

Looking at her now, Bob wondered how he could do this to someone he loved.

"I'm going to kill you, you bastard. I'm going to kill you for what you've done to me."

As he saw her snatch the gun from her bag he leapt across the room toward her. But he was too late. The sound reverberated around the room and he clutched his hands to his chest as his knees started to buckle beneath him. He rolled over, groaning in agony. "Ellamarie!" he gasped. "Ellamarie."

Ellamarie gazed down at him in horror. The gun slipped through her fingers and landed with a thud on the floor. She began moving her head from side to side. "Oh Bob," she whispered. "Oh my God, Bob! Bob!"

Sobbing, she threw herself down beside him. She could hear the air bubbling in his lungs. She was so afraid, she could only cling to him. After a minute she felt his hand, weak and trembling, running over her hair. She lifted her head to look into his face. He was watching her. "I loved you. Didn't you know that?" he murmured.

"No," she moaned. "No, you can't tell me that now." He gasped as she pulled him to her again. "Why? Oh Bob, why?"

"I didn't know any other way." He closed his eyes and his head fell back against the floor.

"Bob!" she screamed. "Bob! Don't die. You can't die now. We can work this out. If you still love me, then we can work it out. *Bob!*"

His eyelids flickered, and it was with great effort that he managed to take a breath. His lips were moving, and she lowered her ear to listen, but the sound of the telephone shrilling into the room drowned his words.

". . . and earlier today a police spokesman confirmed that a full scale-hunt for the killer is now underway. So far there has been no evidence to suggest a motive for the killing, and police are asking anyone who was in the vicinity who might have seen or heard anything suspicious to come forward . . ." The sound of the newsreader's voice was coming through an open door in the block.

She squeezed her eyes shut tightly in an effort not to listen. She didn't want to think about the murder. Not now.

Using the bannister as a steadying guide she continued up the stairs, trying to ignore the fear that had crept its way into her heart.

Finally she reached the door at the top. She hesitated a moment not knowing what to do. She looked around the empty hallway—it offered no encouragement. The telephone began to ring inside the flat, making her jump. She listened as it continued to ring, but no one answered. The door downstairs slammed and as abruptly the ringing stopped.

Silence.

Slowly, she lifted her hand and knocked. The dull sound echoed along the hallway.

She looked around again. She was quite alone. Fumbling in her bag, she pulled out a key. As she slid it into the lock, her heart began to pound. All she wanted to do was run away.

The door clicked open and she stepped through. The flat was in darkness despite the bright sunlight outside. All the curtains were pulled.

She called out, loudly, but there was no reply.

Edging her way down the hall she came to a halt outside the bedroom door. She pushed her hand against it, then realizing that her deliberate movements were making her more nervous, she pushed it sharply and stepped inside. The room was empty.

She swallowed hard, and looked around. The curtains were closed in here too.

She turned back into the hall. A few more steps and she was in the kitchen. She called out again, but still there was no reply.

The window was open and a cat suddenly leapt from the sill and landed on the floor in front of her.

Catching her breath and trying to ignore the violent beating of her heart, she stooped to stroke it.

Suddenly the phone began to ring again, and putting the cat onto a chair, she walked to the sitting room to answer it. Unafraid now, the telephone giving her the sense of another presence in the flat, she pushed open the door.

And then she screamed—and screamed and screamed. And the phone rang—and rang and rang.

She fell against the wall, sobbing and retching, covering her face with her hands, unable to look. The phone continued to ring. She could barely manage to lift it, her hands were shaking so violently.

"Hello? Hello?" said an urgent voice at the other end. "Ellamarie, are you there?"

"Ashley! Oh God, Ashley!"

"Jenneen? Is that you?"

"Yes, it's me," Jenneen sobbed. "Ashley! Oh my God, Ashley!"

"Jenneen, what is it? What's happened? I heard the news, I've been trying to get in touch. What's happened?"

"It's Ellamarie."

Ashley's voice was shrill. "What's happened, Jenneen? Tell me, what's happened?"

"Oh God," Jenneen sobbed. "She's dead. Ashley, she's dead."

THIRTY-NINE

J AN LOOKED UP AS CONRAD STROLLED INTO THE OFFICE. HE nodded toward Ashley's door. "She in there?"

"On the phone," Jan answered, glancing over at the switch lights on the desk.

Conrad pushed open the door. Ashley looked up and smiled as she saw that it was him. She beckoned for him to come right in.

"Sure," she was saying into the phone, "yes, yes, we'll be there. Around seven. OK, will do. Yes, yes. See you then," and she hung up. "Candice," she explained, "telling me that London is the most exciting place in the whole wide world, and she might never come back."

Conrad gave a wry smile and nodded. "Yes, I can see Candice in London. If I know her she'll have taken the whole town by storm." He walked across the room and helped himself to a Scotch. "Did she see Alex?"

"Yesterday. Said he was wonderful and she's driving down again to pick him up from school tomorrow. I said we'd be at the flat around seven."

Seeing her face cloud over Conrad went to put an arm round her. "Still miss him?"

Ashley sighed. "Like crazy. It seems that no sooner do his holidays begin than they're over and he's flying back to London again. I can hardly believe that it was only six weeks since Christmas. It feels more like six months.''

Conrad hugged her to him. "You'll be seeing him tomorrow," he said, gently.

Ashley turned and smiled up into his face. "And I can't wait." Then teasing his collar with her fingers she said: "But how about now? Don't I get a kiss?"

Putting his glass on the desk Conrad folded her into his arms. Several minutes later he pushed her away gently. "Don't want a repeat of what happened last night," he grinned, referring to their urgency of the night before, when, unable to wait until they got home, they had locked the door of his office and made love.

"Who doesn't?" Ashley pouted, and he dropped a kiss on the tip of her nose.

"Pardon me for interrupting," Jan said from the door. They turned round and Jan's smile widened as she received a rather dour look from Conrad. "Your tickets just arrived," she said, coming further into the room, "and I'm about to go."

"Leave them on my desk," said Ashley, going to pour herself a drink.

Jan dropped them beside the blotter, then making no attempt to go, she beamed at Conrad. Realizing what she was about, he waited for Ashley to turn round.

Ashley looked from one to the other, and sensing that Jan was waiting to say something she gave her an encouraging smile.

"Hell, I just wanted to say," Jan began, "that, well, everyone here will be thinking of you. We'll miss you."

"We'll only be gone a month," Conrad pointed out.

"Sure, but we'll still miss you. You have a great time, both of you."

"Oh, we will," said Ashley, slipping her arm through Conrad's.

"Now, is there anything you want me to do before I go?"

"I think you've done everything," said Ashley, looking around the office: "Did you get in touch with Mr. Halworth, by the way?"

"Spoke to his secretary. She's fixed everything. They fly out the day after tomorrow."

"Halworth?" said Conrad, looking at Ashley.

Ashley winked at Jan. "See you in a month then," and to Jan's absolute delight both Ashley and Conrad gave her a tremendous hug before she went off.

"Halworth?" Conrad asked again, as the door closed behind Jan.

"He once expressed a desire to be informed when we decided to name the day," Ashley explained. "Therefore, I have informed him. And he's coming to the wedding."

"Halworth!"

"That's the third time you've said his name. Yes, Dick Halworth. He seems to think that he was the cupid that shot the arrow for us."

Conrad gave a shout of laughter. "You never cease to surprise me." He took her in his arms. "Now, where were we before Jan interrupted us?"

"Oh, I think about here," said Ashley, raising her mouth to his.

"And if I remember rightly, I had just turned you down."

"I'd hoped you'd forgotten that."

Conrad picked the tickets up from the desk. "Here, put these in your purse," he said, handing them to her. "As you've insisted we fly Concorde we don't want any last-minute hiccups. What time is the flight?"

"Nine o'clock." She turned to look at him. "Darling, you don't really mind about getting married in England, do you?"

"Well, as the best part of my family, and indeed

my company, are over there right now," he remarked dryly, "I suppose it makes sense."

"They're only there for the wedding."

He grunted. "Like hell. Any excuse for a vacation. Hadn't you noticed how they're all there before us?"

"Preparing things."

"Like what?"

"Don't ask silly questions. There's an awful lot to do, and Candice, together with Jenneen and Vicky, have been fixing it all up. And if my mother didn't have them to nag at them she'd only be on the phone to us the whole time. And your mother too. Did you speak to her?"

"No. She spoke to me. I couldn't get a word in."

Ashley laughed and put her arms round him. "I do love you, you know."

"Yes, I know," he grinned, then winced as she trod on his foot.

"That's a bad habit of yours."

"Tell me you love me," she said.

He looked into her eyes and felt his heart skip a beat. His face was serious as he told her how very much he did love her.

"What about Keith?" he said, later.

Ashley sighed and looked away. "It won't be easy, I can't deny it," she said, "but I'm glad he's agreed to come to the wedding."

"I've been thinking about that," Conrad said. "It'll be the first time you've seen him since that night, maybe we should arrange to see him before the wedding."

"You mean take him to dinner or something?"

"Him and Alex."

"I think it's a wonderful idea," Ashley answered. She sat down behind her desk. "You know, in a way I'm glad Alex decided he wanted to stay at Caldicott. Oh, I miss him dreadfully, but I think he's happier there, he knows the school, and it means so much to

Keith." She looked up. "You know, Conrad, you've never told me what it was you said to him that night. After . . . When you drove him back home."

"I didn't say anything to him. He did most of the talking." He looked into her face and saw the nightmare begin to pass through her eyes. "You must try to forget it, darling. It's all in the past now. He never intended to hurt anyone, he just lost his grip for a while, that's all."

"But I thought he was going to kill us all."

"By firing blanks into a wall?"

Ashley gave a grim smile. "I didn't know that at the time. Still, as you say, it's all in the past now."

Conrad went to stand beside her. Not for the first time she wondered how she would have got through the last six months without him. He was there when she woke in the night, her body drenched in cold sweat as she relived the horrifying events that had taken place that summer's night in a quiet street in Fulham. And he was there to soothe her when her imagination contorted into a profusion of cruel images that left her son lying in a pool of blood and Keith still facing her with the gun. And he held her close when the fear and horror were stripped away by the pain she felt at Ellamarie's death. She knew she would never understand the fate that had lashed out to tear their lives apart that night.

She rested her face in the palm of Conrad's hand. What right had she to be so happy when she had deserted her friend in a time of unbearable distress? If she had listened, if she had agreed to let Ellamarie help as she had tried to, then she might still be alive today. But she had slammed the phone down on her, leaving her alone to face the bitter agony of what was to follow. What had she been thinking, in those final hours? What kind of hell had she known?

"Ashley, darling," Conrad's voice was gentle, and Ashley raised her eyes to look at him. He smiled as he saw the tears about to spill over. "Stop it. Stop torturing yourself."

She swallowed hard, and tried to force a smile. "I'm sorry," she said, and caught his face between her hands as he stopped to kiss her.

"Now," he said, pulling her to her feet. His face suddenly darkened and he was frowning.

"What is it?"

He shrugged. "Hell, with Jan gone, I don't suppose I've got any excuse for turning you down now."

Ashley burst out laughing and felt the cloud lift from her. "Not so fast, mister," she said, as he walked across the room to lock the door. "I'm taking you home, where we can celebrate in style."

"Celebrate?"

Ashley's face had turned pink. "I was going to wait until later, but I think I'll burst if I don't tell you now." Suddenly she was embarrassed, and lowered her eyes.

Conrad watched her, waiting for her to go on. "Well, I don't see any explosion."

Ashley took a deep breath. "I don't suppose there's any other way of saying this," she said, "so here goes. We're going to have a baby."

The smile fell from Conrad's face as he looked at her in awe. "Say that again."

Ashley smiled at his expression and began to walk round the desk toward him. "I said we're going to have a . . ."

"I heard you the first time," he interrupted, and suddenly he was beside her, taking her in his arms. "Oh God, Ashley, I love you," he murmured. "When did you find out? Why didn't you say something before?"

"I wanted it to be a surprise. Are you pleased?"

"Jesus Christ, you have to ask? When?"

"Another seven months. September."

He lowered his hand and placed it over her tummy. She laughed. "You won't be able to feel anything yet."

"No, but it's enough to know that you are carrying my child," and Ashley felt her heart contract as she saw the tears welling in his eyes. She threw her arms round his neck, and realized that she was crying too.

Much later, when they were leaving the office, Ashley said: "You know, I thought that maybe, if it's a girl, we might call her Anna." Conrad stopped at the door and turned to face her. Under his steady gaze she felt her voice trailing away as she went on to tell him what he already knew. That if Ellamarie had had a little girl then Anna was the name she would have chosen.

He took her face in his hands. "The answer is no," he said, very gently. "This baby is ours, yours and mine. I know how much Ellamarie meant to you, darling, but she wouldn't want this either. You can't have the baby for her, Ashley."

Ashley's face crumpled and he caught her to his shoulder. "I know it sounds hard, but you're going to have to come to terms with what happened. You've got to stop blaming yourself."

"I know you're right, but I can't help . . ."

"She would understand," Conrad interrupted. "She loved you too much to want you to spend the rest of your life castigating yourself for something that was out of your control. Her baby was hers, Ashley, and the one you are carrying is ours."

"Maybe . . ."

"Maybe if you talk to Jenneen and Kate when we get to London. It's time the three of you tried to face what happened and accept it. Perhaps then you can get on with your own lives. And if Ellamarie was only half the friend you said she was, then you must know that she would want you to put it all behind you. Cherish her memory, darling, but don't try to live her life."

"What time did you say they were getting in?" Vicky asked, flicking the indicator and swerving dangerously to avoid a truck passing on the inside.

Jenneen winced. "Five. Providing it's not been delayed. God, I'm so nervous," she added, after her heart had settled down again.

Vicky glanced at her and smiled. "It'll be all right. You'll see."

"But it'll be the first time I've seen her since . . ." her voice trailed away.

"Ellamarie. I know."

Jenneen turned to look out of the window. The pain she felt on hearing Ellamarie's name had not lessened in the six months since she had died. The strange, macabre coincidences of that cold summer night was something that none of them had been able to speak of since. Ashley had flown back to New York almost immediately, and with Matthew in the hospital and not knowing what her own fate was to be, Jenneen had been left to face Ellamarie's parents. But Vicky had been with her throughout everything. If only they could have done something for Kate. She closed her eyes. How was she going to tell Ashley about Kate?

"Ah, you're awake," said Vicky, looking in the mirror.

Jenneen turned to the back seat. "I'm surprised you can sleep," she smiled. "How do you feel?"

"Terrific. And I wasn't sleeping, I was just resting my eyes," Matthew answered, making them laugh.

"Got your ticket?"

Matthew dug it out of his breast pocket.

"Passport?"

"We went all through this before we left."

"Just make sure it's to hand," said Jenneen.

"Nag, nag, nag. I don't know how you put up with it, Vicky."

"With difficulty," Vicky grinned.

"Now, there'll be a car waiting for you at da Vinci airport to take you to the Excelsior in Rome. You don't have to worry about paying for it, the film company will settle up. Then tomorrow you've got a day free before you start filming. Someone will be in touch with you to tell you . . ."

"All right, all right," Matthew laughed, holding up his hand. "You've been over this a thousand times, Jenn. I can manage, honest."

Jenneen smiled. "Sure you can. It's going to be a great success, I just know it."

Matthew caught Vicky's eye in the mirror and they exchanged exasperated smiles. Jenneen turned to look out of the window again.

It still seemed a miracle to her that Matthew had lived, and every night she thanked God for it. It had been touch and go for so long that she had very nearly given up hope. And the constant guilt that had plagued her, not only for the elaborate cover-up she, Vicky and Vicky's cousin Paul had concocted for the police but for not being there for Ellamarie too. It had almost driven her out of her mind. And she had lived in perpetual terror that today would be the day that Matthew would tell someone what had really happened that night, and smash the intricate web of lies they had all told. But he hadn't. And finally, two long months after she had fired the gun, the tubes had been removed from Matthew's arms and face, and he had sat up in his bed for the first time. She had been there when he'd done it, and had wept all over him. A month later he had been discharged from the hospital and Jenneen had taken him home to her flat where together she and Vicky had nursed him back to health.

And now, with her new program under way, and the many contacts she was making in the film world, she had managed to secure a part in a movie for him. It wasn't a big part, but it was enough to get him started again. They had never discussed exactly why it was that he had never pressed charges against her, and she wondered now if maybe he had been telling the truth when he had said that he loved her. Would he or Maggie ever have posted those photographs? She would never know now, and never wanted to know either. Just thank God that he was alive and that the torture of the last two years was over for both of them.

"Well, here we are," said Vicky, pulling up outside Terminal 2. "I'll drop you here then circle for a bit. Pick you up in ten minutes, Jenn."

Jenneen got out of the car with Matthew and walked to the Alitalia check-in desk with him. She would have carried his case if he'd let her, but he managed to grab it before she could take it.

"I wish you'd stop worrying, Jenn," he said, after they had checked his luggage through. "I'm going to be all right. I'm a big boy now."

She linked her arm through his. "I know, but that doesn't stop me wishing I was coming with you."

"When you've got so much going on here? I can't believe that. But if it'll make you feel any better I'll call you every day."

"Promise?"

"Promise."

"And by the time you come back I'll see if I can't have fixed you up with something else."

Matthew smiled. "You've got to stop this guilt, Jenn. I think we're about quits now, don't you?"

"We'll never be that, Matthew. I'll never be able to forgive myself for what I nearly did to you. And every time I think of Ellamarie and Bob, I . . ."

"Sssh, don't think about it," he said, knowing how upset she got every time she mentioned Ellamarie and Bob. "We've got to look to the future now. It's what Ellamarie would have wanted too. Maybe we've all learned something from that night."

Jenneen's eyes were swimming in tears as she looked into his face, and he took her in his arms. "Be happy, Jenn. Please, be happy."

She held him tightly, and tried to swallow the lump in her throat. "Come back safely."

"You can bet on it."

*　　　*　　　*

An hour later Jenneen was waving madly as she caught a glimpse of Conrad and Ashley coming through Customs. Seeing her, Ashley almost cried out with joy, and ran on ahead.

"Jenn, oh Jenn!" she cried, as Jenneen caught her in her arms. "You look so wonderful. Oh, you don't know how good it is to see you. Let me look at you."

Laughing and crying, Jenneen did an overstated twirl then fell back into Ashley's arms. "There's so much to tell you, everything's been organized. Oh Ash, this is going to be the best wedding anyone ever had."

Conrad stood behind them, watching with amusement as Ashley turned to Vicky and embraced her. "It's so good to meet you at long last," Ashley said. "I've heard so much about you. And I'm just dying to see your new house." She turned round and took Jenneen by the hand.

"There's so much needs doing to it," Vicky laughed, "and Jenneen is not the world's greatest painter. No staying power."

Jenneen nudged her. "Take no notice of her, I'm simply brilliant." She looked around. "Where's Conrad got to? Ah, Blanche's cousin!" she cried, and taking Conrad quite by surprise she threw her arms round him. "Did you know that you're the luckiest man in the world to be getting her?"

"Sure I know it."

Ashley's face was glowing. "Oh Jenn, I've missed you so terribly." And Conrad looked bored as they began hugging all over again. "Where's Kate?" Ashley wanted to know when she finally let Jenneen go again. "Isn't she here too?"

"I've got the car waiting outside," Vicky jumped in. "We'd better hurry or someone will tow it away."

With Heathrow behind them, and the familiar lights of London spreading out on the horizon, Ashley sat forward on the back seat. "You didn't say," she said, resting her hand on Jenneen's shoulder, "where Kate was."

She saw Jenneen and Vicky exchange a quick look, and sensing that there was something Jenneen was hiding from her, Ashley reached out for Conrad's hand. "Nothing's wrong, is there? You said in your letter that she was coming home yesterday. I thought she might have come with you to the airport."

Jenneen looked at Vicky again, and Vicky nodded. Jenneen turned in her seat to face Ashley. "You're right, she was coming home yesterday, and yes, she was coming to the airport, but she's disappeared, Ash. No one knows where she is."

The blood drained from Ashley's face. "Disappeared? What do you mean? I thought you said she was coming home?"

"She was, but she never arrived. I checked and she was released from prison as planned yesterday, but it seems she told her probation officer that I was collecting her, and she told me her probation officer was collecting her. And now she's disappeared."

"What about Nick? Have you tried him? She'll be with him."

Jenneen shook her head. "He hasn't heard a word from her since she went in."

The bitterness in Ashley's voice was thinly disguised as she said: "You don't think she's gone back to her father?"

"No. I spoke to him this morning. She's not there."

"Thank God for that. But where could she have gone? Didn't she give you any idea at all?"

"None. I haven't seen her, Ash. She would never agree to see anyone."

Their eyes locked in shared anguish. What had been a nightmare for them had turned out to be so much worse for Kate. If only that stupid, nosy old woman from upstairs who had knocked on Kate's door that night hadn't panicked and called the police. If only her father had had the decency to speak up and tell the police what had really happened then she would surely never have gone to prison. And if only Kate had told the truth herself. So many if onlys. But thank God Nick had managed to get one of London's top solicitors. If he hadn't then it was almost certain that Kate would have been charged with grievous bodily harm, and gone to prison for a very long time. As it was, she had been sentenced to nine months for assault, and was now out after six. But even after everything Nick had done for her, Kate had still refused to see him.

Two months after it had happened Jenneen had visited Kate's father in Surrey. She had noticed, and had felt sure that she was meant to notice, the difficulty he had in moving his left arm. Jenneen had deliberately not mentioned the wound, but had pleaded with him to do something about getting Kate released. Throughout their short encounter he had remained impervious to her pleas.

"She'll only go back to him," was the only answer Jenneen had been able to get.

Now Calloway was sitting at home, firm in the belief that his daughter would return to him when she was released. And despite the anger Jenneen felt toward him, she felt pity too for his dying sanity.

"Haven't you heard anything from her? Nothing at all?" Ashley pleaded.

"Just one letter. I received it last week. You can read it when we get back, but you'd better steel yourself first, it's not the Kate we know."

"What does it say?"

"That she feels no remorse for what she did to her father. Reading between the lines, I think she almost wishes she had . . . Well, it doesn't matter now. There is no doubt, though, that she believes she's been doing penance for Ellamarie."

Ashley felt Conrad's hand tighten round hers and

realized that what he had said to her the night before, that the three of them must sit down and talk everything through, was more crucial than ever.

But first they must find Kate.

FORTY

Mrs. Duff looked up from the battered old typewriter she was using, allowing her half-lensed spectacles to slip to the tip of her nose. Her eyes followed the young woman from the bottom of the stairs to the front door, and as she disappeared outside into the rain, Mrs. Duff got up and went to the window.

The concern on the old lady's face was less this morning—the young woman was looking better now. There had been a healthier hue to her cheeks, and a spring to her step that hadn't been there before. Whatever it was, it was a change from when she had arrived, just over a week ago. Her face had been gaunt, and her eyes had seemed to sink back into their sockets if anyone peered too closely. It was because of that that Mrs. Duff hadn't recognised her immediately, but the name had struck a chord on her memory, and looking over her register she had found it.

"How is she today?"

Mrs. Duff turned away from the window to find her husband standing in the doorway of the small sitting room-cum-office. She smiled, rather sadly. "Better, I think."

"Did you tell her about the telephone call?"

His wife shook her head. "He asked me not to, so I won't."

Mr. Duff smiled and picked up the newspaper that was lying on the desk. "You've taken a fondness for the lassie, Mary."

Mrs. Duff didn't deny it. She had no idea what it was that Kate had suffered these past months, but her air of loneliness and confusion had stirred something in the old woman.

She watched her husband as he packed his pipe and settled down in his favorite armchair to read the paper. As he turned the pages, Mrs. Duff stood over him, glancing down at the occasional headline. She wondered if she was doing the right thing in not telling Kate about the telephone call she had received the night before.

Suddenly she reached out to stop her husband from turning the next page. "Isn't that that director's wife?" she said, looking at the picture of a woman holding a baby.

"Who?"

"You remember, Bob McElfrey. He stayed here once." She stooped to get a closer look at the photograph. "So that's his wife. I thought the young lassie he was with was his wife, but it seems not. Do you remember her? She was American. Organized us all into chaos and still managed to make us laugh."

Mr. Duff chuckled. "How could I forget her? She took the place over." He frowned. "She came back again, didn't she? After that."

"Aye," his wife answered. "She came back with the wee lassie who's with us now."

Mr. Duff turned in his chair to look up at his wife. "You know, I thought I'd seen her before." He paused. "So the other one, the American, do you suppose she was the mistress? The one who killed him?"

Mrs. Duff nodded very slowly. "Aye, 'twas her all right. She killed herself after. Such a tragedy all that.

They say she was pregnant too, you know." She sighed. "I wonder what really happened there?"

Together they read the story beneath the photograph, announcing the birth of Bob McElfrey's son. "So she's going to call the laddie Robert," Mrs. Duff remarked. "Och dear, it fair makes your heart bleed."

"It says here," her husband read on, "that 'Linda McElfrey is working closely with Adrian Cowley and Nicholas Gough, on trying to set up the *Famous Tragedy of the Queen of Cornwall* once again. The film will be dedicated to her husband, who died before it could be made.' "

He sucked silently on his pipe. It had gone out so he leaned forward to pick up a match. His wife was there before him. "The young lassie with us now," he said, accepting the light from his wife, "why do you suppose she's come back?"

"I don't know," Mrs. Duff answered, shaking out the match, "but she's here for a reason, you can be sure of that."

She said no more, and mumbling to himself her husband went back to the paper. Mrs. Duff stooped to kiss the top of his head before she went off to prepare rooms for the guests arriving later in the day.

The rain was less heavy now, but it was still cold. Kate pulled the collar of her coat higher around her face and pressed on.

There was no one else around and from time to time she stopped on the rocky path to watch the river, far below, gushing its way toward the distant loch. Sometimes the trees grew thicker, curling their twisted limbs across the pathway; and boulders that had long since fallen from the mountain interrupted the easy climb.

Finally, with the rain still streaming into her face, she reached the suspended valley. As it rolled out in front of her she felt her heart swell and wanted to cry

out at the stark and unexpected beauty. She tilted her
face to the sky, inhaling deeply, and willed the rain to
come faster. In the distance, coming from far above, she
could hear the wind as it whipped around the mountain
tops. It was a gentle, almost comforting sough by the
time it reached her ears.

She stretched out her arms and turned slowly,
looking up at the peaks, shrouded secretly in a gently
smoking mist. The rugged challenge of the mountains,
the aura of victory and defiance that emanated from
every gully made her skin prickle. And the gentle swell
of the breeze that was suddenly whipped into gale
seemed to speak straight to her heart. At last she was
free.

She climbed down onto a small ledge that jutted
from the pathway. Leaning against the tree that over-
hung the strath far below, she watched the quickening
water as it splashed and roared across the rocks.

The feeling of euphoria that had gripped her body
was slowly locking itself into her heart. She had waited
so long for this and wanted to savor every moment.

It was some time later that she pulled the newspaper cutting from her pocket and looked down at the
photograph of Linda McElfrey and her baby. Then she
smiled sadly as once again she read the story that ran
alongside the picture. When she came across Nick's
name she stopped and looked up to the mountains. Her
heart was beating a little faster. She so badly wanted
to be with him now.

Time slipped by and the rain stopped. The gray
clouds became ringed with irregular circles of bright
light as the sun forced its way through and coated the
mountains with dark shadows.

It had been many years since Kate had prayed, but
now, surrounded by the awe-inspiring beauty of nature, she found herself whispering to God.

When she had finished she raised her eyes to the
sky. Her heart was full and she had to swallow against

the rush of emotion that forced tears to her eyes. Not only had she gained her freedom, but by coming here she had found Ellamarie and Bob. Their presence was so strong that she felt if she reached out she might touch them. She had found them, but it was time now to leave them in peace. She knew she would never come here again.

Kate turned back to the path and took the hand that reached out to her. She looked up and as she saw his face her breath caught in her throat.

His face broke into a grin and he pulled her up beside him. She looked searchingly into his eyes, hardly able to believe her own. For a long time neither of them spoke, until Nick suddenly laughed and pulled her into his arms. And then she was laughing too, as tears streamed down over her cheeks. "You got my card?" she said, finally.

"I did."

"But how did you know where I was? I never said."

Nick pushed the damp hair from her face. "It didn't take much working out," he answered, "once I knew you were in Scotland."

She turned away, and quietly he watched her face, as for the very last time her eyes slipped from mountain to valley.

"They came here, you know. Ellamarie and Bob."

He slipped an arm about her shoulder. "I know."

"It's over now. I came to say goodbye."

Nick smiled and ran his fingers across her cheek. "Come along, I'm taking you home."

As she followed him down the mountain she watched him move from rock to rock. She had missed him, even more than she had allowed herself to admit. And now, looking at his dark hair soaked by the rain and curling over his collar and his broad back tilting toward the rockface as he reached out to steady himself, she was overcome by the strength of her love for him.

"Nick," she called.

He turned his head, his eyebrows raised in question, but as he saw the look in her eyes he stopped.

The rain grew heavier, but neither of them moved. The wind caught her hair and blew it about her face. Then, with droplets of rain running down her face and curling into her mouth, she whispered, "I love you, Nick. I love you so very much."

His eyes held hers as he moved toward her, and taking her in his arms he pressed his mouth to her hair. "Don't go away again, Kate," he murmured.

"Oh Nick!" she cried, and clung to him fiercely.

He took her face between his hands and covered it with tiny kisses, tasting the salt of her tears through the rain. When he lifted his head to look at her she looked back, letting her eyes speak the words she was suddenly too shy to utter. His arms closed behind her, almost lifting her from the ground, and this time it was with a growing desperation that they kissed, molding their bodies together and pushing their desire to the point where it could no longer be denied.

Taking her by the hand he led her into the trees.

Making love in the rain on the side of a mountain, waterfalls gushing downward to join the river below, was something that neither of them would ever forget. And in the years to come they would look back and know that it was then that their daughter was conceived.

As Nick pulled the car to a stop outside the old stone-built hotel, Mrs. Duff was waiting at the door.

"Och, there you are," she said. "Come along in . . . Oh dear! And just look at you, what have you been doing to yourself?"

Kate looked at Nick and saw that he was laughing. "Mud," he explained. "It's all over your face."

"Oh, you might have told me," Kate cried, wiping at her cheeks but only succeeding in spreading the mud down over her chin.

Mrs. Duff caught Nick's eye and broke into a beaming smile as he shrugged his innocence. Then, standing back, she ushered Kate in through the door. As Kate looked across the dimly lit room her expression suddenly changed and her voice escaped in a cry of pure joy.

"Jenneen!" she cried. "What are you . . . ?" But she didn't have a chance to finish the question. Jenneen leapt up and threw her arms about her friend.

Nick laughed as he came in and found them both crying. He took out a crumpled handkerchief, but as he didn't know which one of them to give it to he stuffed it back into his pocket again.

Mrs. Duff came bustling in behind them, carrying a tray of tea which she set out on the table.

"Think I'll go up and change," said Nick.

"Oh, but there's a cup of tea for you here," Kate protested.

"Not for me," Nick answered, and he turned away as he heard footsteps on the stairs.

Kate followed his eyes, then gasped as she saw Ashley coming toward her.

Later, after Nick had sat on the side of the bath sponging the mud from Kate's face and legs, he lay back on the bed and watched her as she dressed for dinner.

"You'll be late," she said, catching his eye in the mirror as she combed out her hair.

"I intend to be," he answered. "You've got a lot to catch up on, you three. Besides, I think they've got something they want to show you."

"Oh?"

Nick was prevented from answering by a knock on the door.

Kate followed Ashley and Jenneen down to the

small bar. They were the only ones staying at the hotel so had as much privacy as they could have wanted. Jenneen ordered the drinks, which Mr. Duff brought to the table and then disappeared.

Catching Jenneen's eye, Ashley nodded. Kate watched them and waited while Jenneen took something from her handbag.

It was a letter. Jenneen handed it to Kate. "From Ellamarie," she said quietly. "She wrote it the night she died. I think it's time you read it."

The blood had drained from Kate's face and her hand was shaking as she took the letter from the envelope.

During all the long months she had spent in prison, Kate had struggled to come to terms with everything that had happened. Jenneen had guessed rightly that Kate had believed herself to be doing penance for Ellamarie's death as well as for what had happened between her and her father. Watching her closely, both Jenneen and Ashley were afraid that she might not be able to take it. But a long time had passed since that night. And now, as Kate read Ellamarie's final letter, she could almost hear her speaking the words and felt her friend's strength and courage reaching out to her in the way it always had. She realized the love and happiness Ellamarie had known before despair and heartbreak had claimed her. And she knew too what Ellamarie was asking. She was asking their forgiveness.

When Kate had read the last word she put the letter on the table and looked up. Her eyes were filled with tears, and with relief Jenneen and Ashley saw that they were tears of real grief, no longer remorse.

"So he did still love her?" Kate whispered.

Jenneen nodded.

"You see, it had nothing to do with us letting her down the night she . . ." Ashley's voice trailed away. "She believed that by doing what she did, she could be with Bob for ever."

Kate looked away and out through the uncurtained window. The clouds were passing overhead, billowing in the wind. In the distance the mountains pushed their way manfully through the misty dusk; they had brought her close to Ellamarie that day. Jenneen and Ashley followed her gaze.

"And she is," Kate whispered. "Oh she is."

There was a long silence. As they looked into one another's faces they realized that it had been Ellamarie who had brought them all here tonight, not Kate.

Jenneen reached out for Kate's hand. Kate swallowed hard, and lifted her other hand to take Ashley's. She smiled, and her voice came in a broken whisper. "Sometimes it takes tragedy to make one appreciate life—and what would life be without friendship?"

SUSAN LEWIS has worked in television production for the last fifteen years, and is the author of DANCE WHILE YOU CAN and STOLEN BEGINNINGS. She lives in London.